Progeny of the Cursed Egg

DRAGONIS ACADEMY YEAR THREE

SERENITY RAYNE

Aurelian Conservatory
Northen Dorms
Southern Dorms
Instructors Hou
Ialivore Conservatory
Sea of Whispers

SHADOWCARVE CAMPUS
NORTH SEA
RANATHOR KEEP
ARCANUM CAMPUS
VELORIAN HALL
BAHAMUT TEMPLE

His crimson flecked amber eyes flick over the ruins before settling on me with a quiet intensity. "Where is your nest, mate?" he asks, his voice a low rumble that seems to resonate in my bones.

I move closer, the rough gravel grinding beneath my sandals, and point to the tall peaks looming above us. The night air is chilly against my face, carrying the faint scent of decay from the rubble. "Up there. For now, there's only enough room for a dragon my size to land." My breath hitches in a sardonic laugh as I glimpse the curiosity in his gaze. "You're too big to manage it on your own. I'll have to carry you. Your massive drake won't fit."

Klauth's gaze slides from me to the narrow gap between the crags, then back to my face. A breeze ruffles his russet hair, carrying the faint smell of sulfur from our earlier flight. "You chose a brilliant place for your nest. Show it to me." He steps back and gestures for me to go ahead, as if I'm some kind of tour guide.

I inhale the cool mountain air, laced with the metallic tang of stone on stone, and shift again. My bones realign, the stretch of tendons and sinew accompanied by an electric hum beneath my skin. Once in my dragonic form, I lower myself to the ground, my scales scraping over rubble. Klauth's hands are warm against my hide as he climbs onto my back. His weight is a steady pressure, and I can feel each subtle shift of his body through the sensitive ridges of my spine.

The moment he settles, I unfurl my wings and push off into the night. The rush of air fills my ears, drowning out any thoughts that have been plaguing me. Even through the freezing gusts, I sense the faint heat radiating from Klauth. As we circle the future courtyard—little more than a wide, stony ledge that juts out from the mountainside—our shadows graze the cracked stone below like wraiths. The echo of my wingbeats resonates among the jagged cliffs until I finally angle downward and land with a controlled thump.

I crouch to let Klauth slide off my back, each of his steps against the rocky ground sending small echoes into the yawning darkness. I shift back once more, my limbs tingling from the quick change. The courtyard is empty but for a few large boulders and the partial walls we've carved out, leaving the space open to the star-streaked sky above.

To light our way, I manifest a small ball of crackling lightning in my palm—its glow a sudden, fierce white that spills across the carved stone. The air instantly tastes of charged ozone, and the hair on my arms prickles. I use its flicker to ignite a few torches mounted along the walls; the flames sputtering to life with the pungent smell of smoke and old oil. A faint warmth seeps into the chamber, pushing back the mountain chill.

"This is what we have so far," I say quietly, voice echoing off half-finished corridors. Tiny motes of dust swirl in the torchlight, dancing through the air like fireflies. My heart thuds in my chest, uncertain if Klauth approves of what I've built here. Despite the shadows still clinging to the corners, there's a hushed sense of possibility in this place—my future nest, where an entirely new chapter of my life awaits. And for now, I can only hope Klauth keeps his promise—and lets Abraxis stay in charge where it truly matters.

I watch him study the jagged opening of the tunnel we partially glassed to narrow the entrance. The air here is cool and faintly damp, carrying a lingering scent of scorched stone from when Abraxis melted the rock. My gaze follows Klauth's as he runs his hand along the curved patches of glass—it shimmers in the torchlight, reflecting the distorted shapes of his massive form.

"Whose fire made the glass?" he asks, arching his scarred eyebrow at me. His voice resonates low, each word echoing softly off the tunnel walls.

"Abraxis did," I reply, my voice quiet in the stillness. The faint crackle of a distant torch punctuates my words. "We didn't feel it was safe for me to sleep through my yearly with the entrance so wide open." There's a subtle chill creeping into my bones down here, and I rub my forearm, fingertips brushing over the smooth glass of the implant nestled beneath my skin.

Klauth moves closer, the heat radiating from his body chasing away the damp chill. He takes hold of my arm and sniffs the skin just above the implant, nostrils flaring. His warm breath ghosts over my flesh, making the hair at the back of my neck prickle. "Why is there a strange smell in your skin here?" His thumb glides over the implant, the ridges of his scarred hand catching the dim torchlight.

"I have the implant in my arm to prevent me from bearing eggs," I say, my heartbeat thrumming in my ears as I meet his gaze. "I'm too young to do it safely. The odds of me laying duds or becoming egg bound are too great." My voice drops, unsteady. Memories rush in, thick in the back of my throat like smoke I can't cough out. "Abraxis's sister is only a week younger than me, and she became egg bound. I had to help her deliver her egg." My stomach twists at the recollection, the bitter taste of fear spreading across my tongue. My scales ripple uneasily beneath my skin.

Klauth closes the distance further, cupping my cheeks in his hands. I feel the calluses of his palms, rough like stone, but his touch is surprisingly gentle. He searches my eyes, his breath warm on my face. "She became egg bound as her dragon?" He nuzzles me, his enormous frame blocking out the faint glow of the torches, trying to soothe the anxious tension that's all but rolling off me.

"No, as her human form," I whisper, leaning against him. The fabric of his shirt brushes softly against my nose, and I draw in his earthy scent, finding a momentary solace in it. I rest the bridge of my nose under his jaw and close my eyes, letting my breath slow.

"Why did she try to birth the egg as a human? That's unnatural for us." His dragon rumbles softly in his chest, a sound that vibrates through my own ribs, reminding me of my own primal side just beneath the surface.

"Because that's how it's always been done," I murmur, lifting my head to meet his gaze. My voice echoes faintly against the tunnel walls. "Well, my mom laid my egg as her dragon." The memory makes me sigh, and I wrap my arms around his waist. My grip is tight, born of old fears and new hopes all tangling inside me.

"We never allowed our females to lay their eggs in their human form. It's far too dangerous for the female," Klauth explains, pressing a soothing kiss to my hair. His voice is deep, reverberating through me. "You can conceive the eggs as a human—that way is more fun and safer for both parties. But when it's time to lay the eggs, the dragoness must do it. As soon as the heat ends, the female shifts to her dragoness and remains in that form until the eggs are laid." His lips brush my temple, and I catch the faintest taste of ash in the air, a reminder of fires we both can breathe.

He pulls my arm free, our movements echoing in the hollow space. We stare down at the implant together, the light of a distant lantern glinting off the metal beneath my skin. "Take it out," I whisper, pulse thrumming.

"Are you sure, mate?" His question is a rumble that trembles through my body. "You will go into heat again in several months once all the toxins are out of your system." He nuzzles my cheek and then kisses it. The warmth of him, the spice of his breath, kindles something deep inside me.

"I have enemies hunting me—my father, the green dragon you drove off, and a large nest of fire and ambush drakes, plus wyverns," I say, pulling my gaze from the implant to meet his eyes. They glimmer in the low light, crimson flecks catching each flicker of flame. "I can't risk them finding me vulnerable."

He rests his hand over the implant and gives my arm a gentle squeeze. The faint scent of smoke clings to his skin, a promise of protection. "We will wait until it is safe. I will not risk my mate or our clutch over it." He leans down and nibbles my neck, pausing when he meets the layer of scales. I shiver at the rasp of his teeth over my flesh.

He draws back, spinning me so my back faces him. A small crackle fills the air as he summons a ball of fire in his hand — to see better in the dark corridor. The flames illuminate the emerald and iron scales that fan out over my shoulder blades like butterfly wings. Klauth runs his fingers over them slowly, and the sensation sends sparks of awareness down my spine. He tugs gently at the back of my sundress, peering down to see how far the scales extend. "Only the strongest females bear this many scales. You honor me, mate." He kisses my shoulder, and I feel the press of his lips against the cool ridges.

Without another word, he leads me out of the chamber. My heart thuds, and the damp chill of the corridor finally gives way to the open air. We step outside into a breeze that carries the faint scents of night-blooming flowers and wet grass.

"Introduce me to your other mates. I wish to court you before we bond," Klauth says, his voice gaining that smoky, sultry quality that sends a pulse of heat deep in my core.

"Of course," I manage, my voice shaky. The night sky stretches over-head, on the brink of dawn. I step away, letting my dragoness push forward. My bones realign and my flesh warms as I shift, scales rippling over my arms and torso until I stand on all fours. I lay down, allowing Klauth to climb onto my back.

"I will not shift," he says, moving up to place one hand firmly on my horn. "No sense scaring the entire academy with my presence." His weight is comforting, and I feel his warmth through my scales. "The world has changed so much since I was last free."

I rumble softly in agreement, letting him know I understand. I promise him, wordlessly, that we will help each other find justice for the pains of our pasts. His acceptance hums through the bond that connects us, an unspoken vow.

"I know you will, and I will help you with yours," Klauth says as we fly back toward the academy. As we break the horizon, the sun rises in a flourish of gold, painting the academy grounds in warm, russet tones. I feel the cool morning air rush over my face, and beneath it all, the faint smell of dew-damp grass. "I was but a hatchling when the first stone was set in the foundation for the dragon dorms. It was my father's dream to make a place for all shifters to go to school safely." His voice holds a melancholy that tugs at my heart, a reminder of how much time has passed—and how much has been lost.

We approach Malivore and I circle the building twice, scanning for any hint of threat. My vision is sharper in my dragon form, each silhouette, and subtle movement catching my attention. Satisfied, I land and carefully fold my wings, lowering my body. Klauth slides off my back, eyes alert as he scours the surroundings for any hidden danger. We share a look of mutual understanding before I shift back and take his hand in mine.

This moment—leading him into my nest—is either going to solidify my standing or shatter it entirely. The academy grounds smell of fresh earth and the faint tang of metal from the gates. My heart pounds in my chest, a mixture of fear and hope crowding my senses.

I squeeze Klauth's hand, drawing strength from his presence. Together, we walk toward the entrance, the golden light of dawn spilling across the corridors, guiding us to whatever awaits.

pulse. He urges me forward with a gentle push. After we step inside, I hear the lock click behind us, metal sliding into place. The finality of that sound rattles through me, and my eyes dart around the suite, my gaze flitting from one mate to another. My heart thunders so violently, I swear they can see it pulsing beneath my skin.

"Everyone, I'd like to introduce you to Klauth." My voice quivers with adrenaline as I tilt my head back, looking up at Klauth upside down. He bends to kiss my forehead, a brief brush of warmth that steadies me before I shift my attention back to the others.

By custom, Abraxis is the first bonded drake, so he's the one to formally introduce Klauth to the nest. He reaches for another mug on the counter, the scent of strong coffee rising between us, and offers it to me. I tip my neck to the side, exposing my throat as a gesture of submission to my dragon mate. The air crackles with an undercurrent of tension.

"Abraxis Havock, I hail from the Blackhaven nest." Abraxis's voice rumbles through the space, and he lifts his fist over his heart in greeting before extending his hand to Klauth. The weight of their individual strength makes the tiny hairs on my arms stand on end.

"Blackhaven, you say?" Klauth replies, his tone gruff but carrying a note of respect. "That is the same nesting grounds Thauglor comes from. Good strong stock come out of Blackhaven." He clasps Abraxis's hand firmly, and a wave of relief washes through me—like my veins flush with cool water. "I accept our mate's choice to let you lead this nest. Unless," he adds with the ghost of a smirk, "my influence better protects it."

With that, I feel a million pounds of tension lift from my shoulders. My entire body sags with gratitude, even though my heart still hammers away.

Klauth slips his fingers into my hair, gently brushing it aside. I sense his breath against my neck, warm and steady. He gestures to the faint purple bruises and faint tooth impressions left by Abraxis. "Typical black dragon—biting their mate constantly," he teases in a low rumble. He then tilts my chin, displaying Abraxis's mark on the front of my throat and his on the right side.. "If I know my old friend, he'll leave his mark on the opposite side, giving our mate here a full collar of bites." There's a note of dark amusement in his voice as he lifts my hair again, his gaze landing on the crescent-shaped imprint Leander left at the back of my neck. "Who did this one?" he growls softly, amber eyes flecked with crimson sweep the room.

Leander, usually so silent and watchful, steps forward. The heat of his presence mingles with the earthy scent of coffee, and his voice is quiet. "I did."

Klauth arches a brow, tilting his head as though analyzing Leander from every angle. "Tactically brilliant to bring a nightmare cross into the nest. I smell a displacer beast, a basilisk, and a gryphon..." His attention drifts to Vaughn's gargoyle form. The flickering overhead light skims the stone texture of Vaughn's skin, making him appear carved from living rock. "Did someone steal his amulet?" Klauth's brow furrows as he scans the space.

"During the attack—right before you saved me," I explain, turning so that my back now presses to Abraxis's chest. His warmth anchors me, and I lean into him, tilting my gaze up at Klauth.

"Where's Thauglor?" Klauth's voice rumbles through the silence, a soft inquiry weighted with concern.

I answer with a small smile, slipping out onto the balcony, where a chill wind cuts across my cheeks. I return moments later, cradling Thauglor's ebony egg in my arms. Its glossy surface gleams under the harsh overhead light, and I can feel the slow, rhythmic pulse that matches my heartbeat. "Klauth, hatched in time to keep me safe," I whisper to the egg, which vibrates with a restless urgency. A soft complaint thrums in my mind. "Shhh," I murmur, pressing a gentle kiss to its smooth shell. "Your time will come, I swear it."

I glance between Abraxis and Klauth, noticing the way the tension in the room seems to recede at the sight of me holding this precious piece of our family. I point a finger at Abraxis. "You, of all people, know how much I talk to my eggs. Don't act like this is new."

The corner of Klauth's lips curves faintly as he watches me with the egg. A rare softness lights his gaze. "Your voice is what gave me hope I'd be free," he says, voice hushed. "I heard every word, felt every kiss, and understood how fiercely you fought to keep me with you always. We are lucky to have such a strong dragoness."

The ambient light flickers, and I catch sight of Klauth's reflection in the window, tall and confident as he brushes a hand gently over Thauglor's shell. "Rest easy, old friend," he murmurs to the egg, his tone dipped in respect. "A descendant of your line stands in our nest. We are safe."

Klauth meets Abraxis's eyes then, a silent exchange passing between them. I hold my breath, feeling the tension coil between all of us like a living thing, yet tempered by relief and acceptance. The hush in the suite is electric as the rest of my mates come forward, ready to greet the new drake, each footstep echoing softly on the tiled floor. The scent of coffee, the warmth of my dragon nest, and the steady pulse of Thauglor's egg promise a tenuous but powerful bond—one I must protect at any cost.

I turn my attention to my other mates and take Klauth by the hand, guiding him over to the kitchen island. The polished stone surface gleams in the morning light, cool against my fingertips. He settles onto one of the tall stools, and I am pulled onto his lap. Apparently, Abraxis isn't the only dragon who believes I'm incapable of sitting by myself. Though I can't deny the warmth of Klauth's arms around me is comforting.

"Balor, what's for breakfast?" I ask, trying to keep my tone light. The sizzling snap of bacon crackles in the background, and the rich smell of melting butter drifts through the kitchen, making my mouth water.

"Bacon, eggs, and ham steak with a side of potatoes," Balor answers. Klauth's stomach rumbles against my back, a low, hungry sound that makes me smile.

"Two plates, please. Apparently, I'm not the only one starving this morning." I turn and place a soft kiss on the tip of Klauth's nose. His skin is warm under my lips, and I catch the faint scent of embers lingering from his dragon form. Then I reach out, fingertips brushing each of my mates—an unspoken greeting, a reminder that I need them all here.

Balor slides two plates in front of us. The aromas of crispy bacon and fluffy scrambled eggs fill the air, and the savory ham steak, glossy with its own juices, makes my stomach twist with anticipation. Klauth wastes no time digging in, cutting through the ham with quick, efficient motions. I pick at my breakfast, letting the flavors of salted meat and starchy potatoes coat my tongue, but my attention drifts elsewhere.

My gaze settles on the last painting I had hung on the far wall, the canvas catching a stray ray of morning sunlight. It's a portrait—an image of four hatchlings gathered around my dragoness. Callan notices my gaze and quietly takes the painting down, bringing it over for me to see up close. The brushstrokes are slightly raised under my fingertips, the paint still faintly smelling of turpentine if I lean in close enough.

"I can't wait until we're safe and this becomes a reality," I sigh, fingers tracing over the little shapes of wings and scales. A melancholy tug in my chest reminds me that safety is a luxury we don't have yet.

Ziggy approaches with the single egg carrier cradled in his hands. The soft lining rustles as he opens it, the faint scent of fresh linen mixing with the familiar musk of dragon egg. Carefully, I slide Thauglor inside, and the egg's warmth pulses through the fabric as I secure the carrier around me. I wrap my arms around it in a gentle hug, heart clenching at the prospect of what's growing inside.

"Mind telling me whose hatchlings are in the image?" Klauth's voice hums against my ear as he nuzzles my cheek, the shadow of his stubble brushing my skin.

"This one is yours," I say, pointing to the reddish hatchling with greenish silver edges marking its scales. The paint glistens like real dragon hide in the morning light. "The one over here is Balor's." He raises his hand in acknowledgement as I point to the pitch-black hatchling with vivid green edges. The contrast is sharp, and the brush-strokes add depth to the darkness of its scales.

"This little one is Vaughn's." Abraxis tilts his head toward the gargoyle statue when I point to a slate-gray and green hatchling, almost camou-flaged against its surroundings. "And this one is Abraxis's hatchling," I finish, my finger trailing to the final dragon. Its scales match mine—a greenish silver that catches every ray of light—framed by a thick band of black around each edge. I can practically feel my dragoness stir at the sight, a reminder of the bond we share.

A deep purr rumbles in Klauth's chest, vibrating against my side as he keeps one muscled arm around me while he eats. The savory aroma of sausage and fresh coffee hangs in the air. Warmth radiates from Klauth's body, a comforting contrast to the cool stone floor beneath the stools.

"I educated our mate on how females used to birth their young," Klauth says. His voice is low and measured as he takes a long sip of coffee, the mug clinking softly against his teeth before he looks at the others again. The steam rises in gentle curls.

"What do you mean, used to?" Abraxis asks, leaning on the counter. His posture is relaxed, but I see tension thrumming in his shoulders, the same undercurrent I sense whenever something challenges our world's norms.

"Apparently females used to lay their eggs as their dragons. Like my mom did with me." My voice softens by several octaves, my tone hushed, as my hand caresses the carrier holding Thauglor. The shell is smooth beneath my fingertips, the faint warmth it gives off calming my nerves. Thauglor sends a soft vibration through the egg that pulses into my hand—like a gentle hum singing straight to my heart.

Klauth chooses that moment to lean forward and press a hot, lingering kiss just under my ear. His breath tickles my skin, smelling of coffee and something smoky. "To watch you seek comfort from his egg makes me understand what you were doing when I was trapped," he murmurs. "I felt every caress, heard every word, and clung to it. Your strength became mine, and mine yours." He presses his lips to my temple, and I inhale his woodsy scent, letting it ground me. When he looks back at the others, his voice hardens a notch. "We never allowed our females to lay their eggs as humans. It's far too dangerous for them. Why it's allowed now is beyond me." He grumbles before stabbing a piece of sausage, the tines scraping against the plate with a sharp clang.

Callan pulls a thick, leather-bound tome off a nearby shelf. Dust swirls in the overhead light as he places it on the counter and flips through pages that crackle with age. Finding what he's looking for, he smooths a page and points. "Apparently, a thousand years ago, to prevent what happened to Syrax from happening again, dragonesses were banned from laying eggs. Their human form would have to bear the duty."

"Who's Syrax?" I ask, turning to look at Klauth. My voice echoes slightly off the vaulted ceiling.

"My betrothed," Klauth says after a measured pause. "I destroyed several dens, half the countryside, and wiped out two nests in my rampage. We had four viable eggs." He closes his eyes, drawing in a long, slow breath.

I can feel the ripple of tension in him, can practically taste the metallic tang of his suppressed fury in the air. His dragon moves under his skin, coiling and restless. Heart fluttering, I motion for the others to back up. Slowly, I turn in his lap and press my nose under his jaw, showing submissiveness. His skin is warm against the tip of my nose, and the scrape of his slight stubble grounds me.

"Help me dig a better nest for me to be safe in," I whisper, letting my dragoness's purr rumble up through my throat. "I will shift and remain as my dragoness when it's time for me to bear eggs. History will not repeat itself." My gaze flicks to Abraxis, silently pleading for him to hold back. The tension in the room crackles like a brewing storm. Even the overhead lights seem to hum with heightened energy. The last thing we need is for their drakes to fight. That is one fight Abraxis will not win.

"We will dig it as a nest," Klauth says, voice still rough around the edges. "Unfortunately, some of what you have already done will be destroyed in the process. It is my duty and honor to dig you a nest worthy of the hatchlings you one day will bear." He lifts my chin, his fingers calloused yet gentle, until our eyes meet. I nod, agreeing.

"Looks like I need to rearrange the date nights." Callan sets the tome aside and strides over to a small dry-erase board on the wall. The marker squeaks as he flips the cap.

"Date nights?" Klauth tilts his head, curiosity replacing some of the tension.

"Each of us gets a night in the rotation to have Mina all to ourselves," Leander explains, gesturing to the schedule scrawled across the board. I can smell the faint chemical scent of the erasable marker.

"By the looks of it, we have another pressing issue that needs to be handled after that," Klauth says, his gaze landing on Vaughn's stone form in the corner. Even through the low lighting, it's impossible to ignore that statue-like pose.

"It's on the list," Balor replies, his attention shifting between the dry-erase board and Vaughn, whose stony silhouette looms ominously.

"What are we going to do about sleeping arrangements?" Ziggy pipes up, flexing his slender fingers. The black nail polish he sports gleams in the harsh overhead lighting. "We have one spare room, but when Thauglor hatches, Mina will be displaced."

"I rarely sleep in my room anymore," I admit, sliding off Klauth's lap and moving to snuggle against Ziggy. The familiar scent of his leather jacket and spicy cologne eases some of my remaining tension. "Klauth can take my room. That gives us time to get the spare room in order for Thauglor." My gaze shifts between Abraxis and Klauth. "You two are close in size. Maybe find something more modern for Klauth to wear, and I'll go shopping for him later today. I'll take measurements so I can get suitable clothing for him."

"You don't need to go through so much trouble for me, mate," Klauth protests, his tone laced with genuine surprise. But I close the distance and place a finger to his lips, feeling the whisper of his exhaled breath.

"Allow me to do my duty of taking care of my mate. This is my nest. My mates..." I gesture broadly to all the males in the room, feeling their eyes on me. The overhead lights flicker slightly, as though acknowledging the gravity of my words. "It would please me greatly to do this for you." I can almost sense his pride bristle, so I soften my voice.

"If it pleases you, then it pleases me as well," he finally says, lowering his head in acceptance. A proud, powerful great wyrm bowing to me ... The weight of that gesture hums in my veins.

"I have the bath drawn and fresh linens in the bathroom for you," Ziggy says from the doorway, the warm glow of the bathroom light spilling out behind him. Steam drifts into the hall, carrying the clean scent of soap and crisp towels.

"Go get cleaned up. I have knives and other things to prepare for the gauntlets," I say, pressing a quick kiss to Klauth's cheek. His skin is hot to the touch, a reminder of just how capable he is of unleashing destruction if threatened.

"Gauntlets? There's only supposed to be one. The entry to what will be Shadowcarve," Klauth murmurs, sliding off the stool. He takes my hands in his. I feel the slight tremor still coursing through him, the echo of his dragon's agitation.

"The academy is a war college. There's a yearly gauntlet to weed out the weak. Then there's the one specifically for Shadowcarve. I have two gauntlets to run over the next two days." I flash him a grin, trying to mask my excitement. I watch the color drain from his face, his nostrils flaring.

"Our mate is the first female in the history of Shadowcarve to be strong enough and smart enough to attend. She's lethal," Abraxis cuts in, his feral grin exposing slightly elongated canines.

Klauth turns to look at me with a newfound respect in his eyes and exhales a slow breath. "Oh, this is going to be fun … I will assist you however you desire, my mate." He brings his fist to his chest, the impact making a dull thud, and bows. Abraxis's jaw slacks; the shock in his gaze is clear. A great wyrm just honored me by raising his fist to his heart, swearing his life eternal to me.

As Klauth heads to the bathroom, the faint trickle of running water and the rich smell of soap drift through the open doorway. I glance around at the others, heart thudding in my chest. The memory of Klauth's vow lingers in my mind. Outside, a sudden gust rattles the tall windows of the apartment, adding a final note of tension to the moment.

I let my fingertips run gently over Thauglor's carrier, feeling the humming warmth of the egg beneath the shell. Within this ancient fortress, with its cold corridors and whispering shadows, we forge bonds that could reshape our future—or tear us apart.

Mina sits on a low stone wall beneath the drooping boughs of a gnarled old tree, the same spot she's claimed the last two years for watching and waiting. The bark above her is twisted, rough with age, and I can almost smell the damp moss clinging to the branches. Klauth stands at her right side, arms crossed over his chest, muscles tense as if ready to pounce. Balor is on her left, gaze sweeping the crowd in silent vigilance. Ziggy perches high in the tree, his silhouette barely visible through the leaves, always watching with that uncanny stillness of his.

Callan and Leander are off helping with the main gauntlet, leaving me here with Mina. After last night's shopping experience, Klauth is sporting a modernized look—pressed trousers, a crisp shirt that accentuates his broad shoulders, and a dark, stylish jacket. He looks like he's stepped straight out of one of those high-fashion magazines Cora is fond of. Standing next to him makes me feel like the ugly duckling. I resist the urge to straighten my jacket, swallowing the small knot of self-consciousness.

A member of the senior staff approaches, footsteps crunching on the gravel before he halts in front of Mina. The wind carries a faint hint of cologne—sharp and citrusy.

"Willamina Havock?" he asks. The use of my surname jolts me, and I see Klauth's red-flecked gaze flick toward the staff member.

"Yes?" Mina's voice is cool as she steps forward, the gravel shifting softly under her feet.

"General," he says, bowing to me. There's a wary glance cast at Klauth, and I sense the tension in the air, like a cord stretched too tight.

"Your number," he says, offering Mina a small card in a white envelope. His hand trembles slightly. There's a reverence in his posture that I haven't witnessed in nearly a decade of teaching here—certainly not toward any dragoness.

Mina's eyes flick down to the envelope, but Balor takes it in her stead. "She doesn't like being handed things by beings outside her nest,"

Balor states, his voice ice-cold. The staff member stiffens, then quickly turns and leaves, boots scuffing away on the gravel.

Klauth lifts one thick eyebrow at me, and I can feel the silent question prickling between us. "She chose to use my surname instead of her father's after what he did to her," I explain quietly, shifting my weight as a breeze stirs the leaves overhead. My mind drifts for a moment to the nightmares Mina shared—dark corridors, betrayal, pain.

Mina steps aside with Balor. He's already opened the envelope, and I catch a glimpse of the card's black lettering. She nods, expression guarded.

"She showed us those memories," Klauth murmurs. He stares at the ground, the flesh between his eyebrows pinching. "I'd like to offer her my surname as well—if that's acceptable to you." His tone is deep, resonant, carrying the weight of the beast that dwells inside him.

I meet those amber eyes flecked with crimson, the vertical slits narrowing ever so slightly. That ancient predator lurks just beneath his calm façade. "Of course," I say. "As the great wyrm of our nest, you have every right to offer or request that she use your surname." I bow and lower my gaze, the gesture automatic. If it came down to dragon versus dragon, I wouldn't stand a chance.

When I lift my head, I see Klauth striding toward Mina. She tips her face up, slightly puzzled, and listens intently as he speaks in a low voice. I catch fragments of her expression—surprise, then a small, thoughtful smile. She says something about 'considering it' and returns his bow. Klauth steps back, reclaiming his place beneath the tree, the damp grass brushing the hem of his trousers.

Another number is called over the loudspeakers, the metallic buzz reverberating across the courtyard. Mina pulls up her hood and slides down her black face mask, concealing the lethal elegance of her features. She thrusts both hands down, and with a soft rasp, her silver

talons extend. My breath hitches at the change that comes over her—
it's like watching a predator uncoil.

She strides toward the gauntlet, each footfall so silent it's unnerving,
especially on gravel. The hush is as deadly as it is impressive. The
wooden stairs leading up to the gauntlet creak for everyone else, but
for her, there's not a single groan. She moves like a wraith—one foot in
front of the other, body balanced and poised.

Shadowblade ... That's what they call her. She's trained her entire life
for this lethal grace. The hair on my arms stands on end as I recall
whispered rumors about her past. Ziggy and Balor mutter to Klauth
about what she was made to be, how she was honed into this weapon.

And me? I stand here, my heart thudding heavily against my ribs,
tension twisting in my stomach like a coiled spring. I have to worry
about Mina facing the gauntlet—there's a real chance she might push
too far. And then there's the ancient wyrm at our side, a war machine
in human skin, who might snap if he thinks Mina's in danger. The idea
of Klauth laying waste to the gauntlet with a single shift flickers across
my mind like a dark omen.

A faint rustle draws my attention back to Mina. She pauses at the top
of the stairs; the wind teasing the edges of her hood. Then she disappears into the shadows of the gauntlet. My pulse pounds, and the
world narrows to the pounding of blood in my ears. Whatever happens
next, I need to be ready—to protect her, to keep Klauth in check, to
ensure we don't reduce this entire academy to smoldering wreckage.

I GRIT my teeth and scan the courtyard under the afternoon sun. The
stone walls radiate lingering warmth, and my boots scuff against the
cracked tiles, sending small puffs of dust into the air. A clammy breeze

drifts past, carrying the faint metallic tang of gears grinding somewhere within the gauntlet's guts. I can practically taste the tension—bitter as old copper on my tongue.

From what Ziggy tells us—after phasing in and out of the gauntlet several times, spying on our mate—it's worse than last year. More moving parts, more poisons, more living threats lurking in the corridors. The mere thought of Mina in that pit of death sets my muscles quivering with protective fury.

Klauth stands nearby, leaning against the sun-baked wall with uncanny stillness. He's a vision of composure, his eyelids lowered as if meditating, while I watch a few of his red scales ripple up and down the corded muscles of his neck. The late-day light catches each crimson ridge, revealing the raw power just beneath his skin.

"Abraxis, who is your guest?" Lysander's voice comes from my right, as soft and sly as a serpent's hiss. Just the sound of the headmaster's words makes Klauth tense, lifting his head from the wall to glare Lysander down. My ears pick up the faint scrape of Klauth's talons on the stone, his tension palpable.

Ziggy suddenly drops down from a nearby tree with an almost inaudible thud, leaves rustling above him. He's sporting a double egg carrier—odd, considering Thauglor's egg is back in Mina's poison garden. Lysander briefly glances at Ziggy before turning his scrutiny on Klauth.

That ancient aura I felt from Klauth earlier is now masked, though I sense it churning beneath his calm, like distant thunder before a storm. "Oh, friend of the family on my mother's side," I say, a pinprick of tension needling my temples.

"Ragnar..." Klauth rumbles as he steps forward, looming over Lysander by a full head. The air feels charged with the faint pulse of that ancient power, and my adrenaline spikes. His presence is suffocating, laced with a smoldering intensity that raises the fine hairs on my arms.

"Lysander, headmaster of the academy," the man says stiffly, stepping away but never breaking eye contact with Klauth's towering form. He keeps his hands close, clearly wary. "Where is your young mate, Abraxis?"

I pivot so I can keep an eye on both Lysander and the gauntlet. Bolts and hinges glint beneath the sunlight, and wisps of steam or smoke seep from hidden vents. "She's about eighty percent through," I say, nodding toward a series of colored indicators climbing the gauntlet's side. My gaze follows the pulsing lights as they near the last obstacle.

"I wonder if she will pass this year's like the last two years?" Lysander's voice takes on a venomous edge toward the end, sending a chill crawling across my skin. I don't miss the slight sneer tugging at his lips.

"What did you do?" My hand shoots out to seize his collar, the fabric rasping under my fingertips. I slam him against a nearby pillar with a dull crack, the sound echoing across the courtyard. He dangles in my grip, feet scrabbling in the empty air.

"There are watch spiders at the end of the gauntlet," he says, maddeningly calm. "I'm allowed one live threat inside, and I chose them this year." He smirks, flicking his gaze to the monstrous contraption behind me. "She's almost there, going by the lights."

Fury boils in my chest, hotter than a dragon's flame. I flick my eyes to Ziggy, who's clutching a thick, worn rulebook with trembling hands. Pages rustle as he finds the relevant section. "It's all in accordance with the rules," he manages, voice unsteady. "One live threat in the gaunt-let, limited to six entities of that species."

A snarl tears from my throat as I drop Lysander. He coughs and stumbles, nearly losing his footing on the sunbaked tiles, but my attention is on the gauntlet's mechanical roars and hissing vents.

"You better pray Tiamat and Bahamut favor my mate," I growl. The oppressive afternoon heat bakes my shoulders, and my anger simmers just beneath my skin. "Because if she dies..." My laugh is a razor's edge. "Neither you nor this academy will survive the terrors I will unleash. Fire will rain from the sky and reduce everything here to glass. Night-mares will stalk anyone who dared lift a talon against my mate."

I lean in close, the pungent stench of Lysander's fear wafting toward me—sharp, sour, and impossible to miss. I let a thin curl of acid breath escape, spraying a few sizzling drops onto his tie. It melts away, leaving a hideous burn mark. Lysander pales and scrambles off, foot-steps pounding across the courtyard.

A large hand falls on my shoulder, and I whirl to find Klauth wearing a malicious grin, rows of razor-sharp teeth bared. The heat radiating from him is like a furnace, and I catch the acrid smell of scorching embers on the breeze. Sunlight sparkles off his red scales, as though an inner fire glows beneath them. "Good job," he snarls, voice underlaid with his dragon's growl. "I want his head on a pike next to her father's."

The very air around Klauth shimmers with the threat of his dragon form taking over. My pulse hammers in my veins, the tension so thick it's suffocating. I can only hope Mina finishes the gauntlet soon—otherwise, we'll be dealing with a great wyrm's wrath.

Again.

to see what the other sees and sense exact locations.' His words end with a low rumble that vibrates through my nerves.

I feel my lips twitch in a humorless smile. *'A thousand years of bottled-up urges,'* I think more to myself than to him, dodging a sudden volley of arrows. The sharp hiss of their flight reminds me how narrow this passage is.

'I wasn't awake the entire time. So not a thousand ... just two years...' Klauth's tone trails off, and the realization dawns on me—two years is exactly how long I carried his egg.

Below me, the floor is stained with streaks of blood. I follow the splatters, picking out which mechanisms must have caused them and avoiding each trigger. Rolling logs, shifting floors, and overhead nozzles that spray oil across angled platforms leading down to a spike-filled pit—it all reeks of old wood, rancid grease, and decaying gore. My talons ache from the constant grip they maintain against wet planks and jagged stone.

Mid-second level, I come across a severed foot. Dark, drying blood crusts its edges. I clench my jaw, tasting bile at the back of my throat. The foot is followed by a severed lower leg, then a gruesome drag mark leading around a corner. My stomach twists at the coppery stench lingering in the stagnant air. Pausing, I leap up, narrowly missing a series of blades swinging from the walls below. They slice the air with a harsh metallic clang, spraying sparks against the stone. I keep moving, claws biting into the beam, so I don't have to set foot on the treacherous floor. At times like this, I wish I had Abraxis's wings instead of testing every plank and beam with my weight.

'You are beautiful just how you are, mate,' Klauth murmurs in my mind, his voice silky with affection.

I snort softly. *'I'm the first female you've seen in a thousand years. There are others more beautiful than me,'* I counter, forcing my attention back to the tasks at hand. My gear—a mix of battered leather, ace wraps, and a sports bra—always reminds me how little I've indulged in anything remotely "girly." Abraxis tried, but I've rarely felt safe enough to care.

'Why do you bind yourself, mate? Are females not treasured these days?' Klauth's question makes me pause, hanging upside down from a rafter. My hood and face mask clinging to my face, carrying the faint scent of sweat and dust.

I grit my teeth, the dark memories returning. *'No. Females are bought and traded between families for alliances and political gain. The drake who sired me stole my mother to create the ultimate weapon.'* Anger flares hot in my chest, matching the sting of fresh sweat on my brow. *'I am the weapon he intended my betrothed to wield. Once married, females are collared and have no choice.'* My mental snarl reverberates through our bond, and I share jagged flashes of what my life was like before Abraxis. The sickening taste of fear clings to the back of my tongue as I recall that *"family"* dinner in my father's nest.

'He will die at my talons, mate. I promise you this.' Klauth's voice is laced with reverence, and I feel the first true strands of love weaving through our bond. It's as warm as Abraxis's presence—a steady, unwavering pillar of steel at my back.

I climb toward the third level, and a chill sluices through me. The atmosphere is different here—stifling and thick, as if something is watching from the shadows. Instead of climbing the rest of the way, I fish out a small mirrored dagger to peek around the lip of the floor. Torchlight glints off of dozens of trip wires crisscrossing at ankle, knee, and even ceiling level. The air is stale but tinged with a faint chemical odor. I grimace, testing each vantage point until I get a clear view.

'Hmmm...' I dangle from the beam, my heart pounding in my chest. *'This level feels different from the last two. The layout is ... too thorough.'*

'What has you puzzled, mate?' Klauth asks, the same gentle curiosity he showed when he was just an egg reaching me through the bond.

'Trip wires on the floor, the walls, and up by the rafters. Let's see what they do,' I whisper mentally. Gripping one of Abraxis's daggers, I fling it downward, slicing through several wires at once. A series of black spikes hurtle out from hidden slots in the walls and slam into the opposite side, leaving deep gouges.

My pupils narrow as I examine the spike tips. *'They're oozing some kind of orange fluid...'*

'Likely a nerve toxin. Most are orange or yellow-orange, if I recall correctly,' Klauth informs me. There's a proud edge to his tone, and I can't help the soft purr that escapes my lips.

'I feel like I just pleased my mate. You're not the only poison master here,' he adds, amusement lacing his words.

I blow out a breath, refocusing on the mission. The black spikes appear to fire at hip-level, so I climb higher, letting my hardened scales shift beneath my leather armor. My chest, abdomen, and throat are well protected, but I make sure my arms and legs gain a defensive layer of scales, just in case. Tensing my muscles, I spring across the room with as much force as I can muster. My boots skid against the dusty floor, and I drop into a roll. The cacophony of spikes firing from all directions slams into the walls, the thunderous echo drumming in my ears like a raging storm.

I come to a stop, lying flat on my back, panting in quick gasps. The odor of burnt oil and cracked stone is overwhelming. Dozens of those black spike balls embed themselves in the stone, forming a wicked pattern behind me. I stare at them for a long, tense moment, listening for any more traps. By some twisted stroke of luck, none of them struck me. My muscles quiver from the close call, and I blow out a shaky breath.

I'm still alive. *For now.*

ONE MORE LEVEL and I can call it a day. The gritty feel of the cold stone wall at my back reminds me there's no margin for error. A stale draft drifts down the staircase, carrying the faint scent of damp earth and rotting fabric—decaying banners, maybe. Every breath tastes like dust. Tension rises through all of my mates, and I can't afford to be distracted, so I stop moving entirely, holding my breath until the tightness in the air settles. Instead, Abraxis is nearly in a rage. I can sense his heated pulse thrumming through our bond—while Klauth is stone cold. That calm aura of his pressing in around me like a glacier. Both species of drakes usually have a hot temper, so it's unexpected that the one most prone to going on a rampage is the calmer of the two.

Just as I climb the last few steps, Klauth yells through the bond, his voice crashing into my head like thunder. '*Stop, mate. There are watch spiders on the top floor.*'

A static prickle zips down my spine at the panic in Klauth's tone. It doesn't match the measured concern I feel from him through the bond, which only sharpens my awareness of the danger above.

'*If I remember, they were bred to have a paralyzing venom; the effect sets in after one to two minutes. Victims can see and hear but can't move or speak, and eventually they die.*' I recite the page in my mind from the guide we received in Callan's art of war class. My heart thunders at the memory. It's one thing to read about them, but another thing entirely to face them.

'*Correct. There are six of them on that upper floor. Their webs are super sensitive. Can you manifest enough lightning to destroy the webs?*' Klauth asks, his words tinged with caution. Usually, it's considered rude to ask about the strength of another dragon's breath weapon. You can ask the type, but never the potency.

'It's harder and more exhausting without Iris. But I can do it.' I inhale the stale, cobweb-laden air as I climb up and stop a foot from the opening, spotting the silken threads shimmering in the dim light. *'The webs are by the entrance to the fourth floor. I'm going to burn them.'*

'Be careful, my treasure.' That single word—**treasure**—makes my chest tighten, sending a rush of heat through my veins. For a dragon to call someone their treasure means they hold them above even their own life. A tear slides down my cheek before I can stop it, warm and salty on my lips. Not even Abraxis has called me his treasure yet.

'I'm sorry I upset you. I feel conflicting emotions,' Klauth offers quickly, his concern wrapping around me like a gentle cloak.

'Tears of joy. I will bring you a fang from my kill.' Determination sharpens my senses. My dragoness roars in approval inside me, that raw power sizzling through my bloodstream.

I push my body as close as I can to a partial shift without breaking any rules. My bones vibrate under the strain, scales pricking at the tops of my forearms. Cupping my right hand, I let sparks of lightning jump between the tips of my talons. The faint crackle hums in my ears; the surrounding air thickens with the sharp tang of ozone, like the moment before a thunderstorm breaks. Lightning arcs wildly as I widen the space between my talons.

With a snap and a hiss, I reach out and set the webs on fire. The acrid smell of burning silk and tiny fibers hits my nostrils. Wisps of smoke coil upward, stinging my eyes.

I watch the fire race across the sticky strands, spreading through the entire room with a hungry crackle. High-pitched shrieks slice the silence, echoing from somewhere on the far side of the room and the adjoining hallway. My pulse pounds in my ears. As the flames clear near the opening, I strike again, unleashing another spark to burn any remaining webbing.

Cautiously, I climb out onto the floor, drawing the two short swords from my back. My scales fuse across my hands and forearms, creating rough gauntlets that shift and clack softly with my every movement. Dust motes swirl in the smoky air. Silent as a wraith, I prowl forward, my eyes shifting to my dragon's vision—everything in sharper focus, the corners of the room bathed in faintly pulsating shadows.

Six of those spiders are in here somewhere. The air seems thicker with their presence, each breath tinged with a mix of stale cobwebs and fear-sweat. I have two options: slip away unseen or wipe them out. A third option floats in my mind—kill only what I need to—more practical, less risky.

A tapping sound echoes around me, nails or legs scratching across the stone. My heart beats like a war drum. The glint of a cluster of eyes draws my attention. Without hesitation, I tuck one sword under my arm and pull a throwing knife. The cool metal in my fingers steadies me as I take aim. I let the blade fly, catching a spider dead in its glistening eye. A shriek reverberates, followed by the heavy thud of its body hitting the floor. The smell of spider ichor, a mix of brine and decaying leaves, wafts over as it spasms once, then goes still.

Its carcass lies in a corner thick with soot-stained webbing. I crouch beside it, blackened blades at the ready. Another spider scuttles into view, tapping its shorter front legs. Perhaps they rely on vibrations more than sight. My heart hammers as I draw another throwing knife and send it straight into the creature's jaw. No scream this time—only a fleshy thunk and a final twitch.

I'm sorry, but I need these. I whisper inwardly, feeling a pang of guilt as I use my short sword to hack free both fangs of the spider I'm crouched behind. Its exoskeleton cracks under the blade, and the damp sound makes my stomach churn. I slip the fangs into the pouch on the lower back of my leathers, ignoring the dark fluid that seeps across my hands.

'How are you, mate? Abraxis is losing his mind out here,' Klauth says calmly, his words a soothing counterpoint to the brutal scene around me.

'Two spiders down, four to go. I'm going to sneak out.' I feel a swell of pride through the bond, warming me like a gentle ember in the cold.

'Solid plan, mate. I'll let the hatchling know, so he settles down.' Klauth's voice carries a hint of teasing, and I almost choke on a laugh. If I didn't need to be silent, I'd be giggling at Abraxis's expense.

'That makes me a hatchling, too. This is my twenty-third summer coming up.' My mind's voice is a near whisper, as if the spiders could sense the tremor of sound.

'Wait, why can I only talk to you like this?' A flicker of curiosity darts through me. I can't communicate with Abraxis in this way.

'Great wyrm status grants us gifts. In time, you will have access to more because you're my mate and Thauglor's.' Klauth's tone puffs up with that faintly arrogant warmth I'm starting to associate with older dragons. I roll my eyes, uncertain if I find it charming or irritating. Possibly both.

I press my back against the rough-hewn wall, inhaling slowly as I weigh my next step. The taste of adrenaline lingers, coppery and bitter on my tongue. Smoke curls in the corners, and the echo of distant tapping keeps my nerves on edge. I have to stay focused—four more spiders, or a clean escape. One misstep, one whisper too loud, and that paralyzing venom will be the last thing I ever taste.

EVERY FEW MOMENTS, a cool draft filters in from the hallway behind me. The rest of this place smells like damp stone and old rot, so the clean edge of fresh air is an unsettling contrast. I'm guessing the remaining spiders are out there. My gaze flicks around the cramped room, trailing over the cracked walls and the silvery webs glistening in the faint light. I need to be absolutely sure nothing's waiting to pounce on me from behind before I move on.

Once I'm convinced the room is clear, I push forward. I grimace at the tacky spider ichor clinging to my fingers and the scales covering my hands and forearms—it's thick, warm, and has a faintly sour odor that sets my teeth on edge.

I climb the wall, pressing my booted feet carefully against the chipped paint and splintered wood until I reach the beam suspended near the ceiling. The slight groan of the timber beneath me sends a shiver up my spine. Two more spiders lurk beneath the exit, their spindly legs shifting in the corridor's dim glow. That's only four in total. *'Are you sure there's six? I count four.'*

A tense silence follows, broken only by the blood pounding in my ears. *'Zigmander just checked the roof—it's clear. If you only see four down there, I believe that,'* Klauth's voice comes through, low and calm. I resume moving, my breath shallow with anticipation.

I inch forward, methodical and quiet, ensuring my talons sink into the wood without a sound. Dust swirls around me with every shift, and a faint mustiness invades my nostrils. Below, the two spiders scuttle down the hallway. Maybe they're searching for the ones I already dealt with. Whatever they're doing, I don't have time to wonder.

The moment I'm in position, I punch through the flimsy hatch over-head. Brittle wood cracks under my fist, raining splinters across my shoulders. Dragging myself onto the roof, I suck in a lungful of cool night air, tasting relief on my tongue as I rise to my feet. I head toward the edge and ring the bell. Its metallic clang reverberates in my bones, echoing across the academy grounds.

A shrill screech slices through the night behind me, and my muscles coil with raw adrenaline. The spider launches itself in my direction, claws scraping against the roof's uneven tiles. I can feel its hot, fetid breath even before I see the gleam of its too-many eyes. Instinct takes over—I draw both swords, metal shrieking as it slides free. My first strike shears off four legs on its left side, ichor spurting in a sticky spray that spatters against my armor and scales.

I pivot and drop into a low crouch, chest heaving. The spider shrieks again, trying to pivot toward me despite its severed limbs. Not giving it a chance to recover, I spring forward, lifting my blades overhead. When they come down, I drive them through the hardened area behind its eyes. The impact jarring up my arms as steel meets chitin and the roof beneath.

My heart thrashes in my chest as I back up, watching the spider's body convulse in its death throes. Blackish ichor seeps from the ragged stumps of its legs and pools around my embedded blades. The acrid stench curls in my nostrils, and rage burns in my gut. I tilt my head back and roar my fury into the swirling wind, a primal sound that carries every ounce of my hatred for these cursed creatures.

"Mina?" Ziggy's voice cuts through the haze, soft yet urgent. I turn, still keyed up with battle-lust, but relief flickers through me at the sight of him manifesting by my side.

"I lost the swords you gave me," I say, gesturing to where they remain lodged in the spider's skull.

Ziggy's gaze follows mine, and he nods grimly. "I'll get them back later. Let's get you back to the guys. We've been worried sick."

He opens his arms, and I allow myself to sink into his warmth. My pulse drums in my ears as the world blurs, the scent of spider ichor and the ringing of the bell fading into nothingness.

My ears pick up a shifting sound as Ziggy phases into the gauntlet again to spy on Mina for Abraxis. The scrape of his boots against gravel grates at my nerves—I know he's capable of stealth, but the tension has me on edge, amplifying every noise.

"Are you going to tell him?" I jerk my chin in Abraxis's direction, and watch Klauth lean his head back like a cat stretching in a sunbeam—though there's no actual sun to bask in anymore, only the weak orange glow from the distant torches.

"After our unwanted guest leaves." Klauth's words are as calm as the evening breeze. I follow his gaze and notice Lysander approaching, the heavy thunk of his steps muffled by the soft ground.

The whole thing feels surreal, as if I'm watching a carefully crafted play unfold under the eerie half-light. Klauth uses his surname as his first name. The headmaster leaves shortly after, but not before Abraxis wrests a live threat from him: giant, deadly spiders. My stomach clenches at the mental image of swollen abdomens and skittering legs.

"What are we going to do?" Abraxis demands, nostrils flaring as he prepares to storm the gauntlet. He reeks of adrenaline, a sharp, tangy scent that stings my nose.

"Settle down, hatchling. Mina is fine and now aware of the threat." Klauth's voice carries a deeper resonance, and I see the dragonic slits eclipse his eyes, reminding me of molten embers. It's the same look he had earlier—another sign he's in direct contact with Mina.

"How?" Abraxis growls, ignoring or missing the slight at being called a hatchling.

Klauth closes the distance between them, looming mere inches away. The tense crackle in the air raises the hairs on the back of my neck. "When you reach great wyrm status, you are afforded certain gifts. Speaking to our mate is one of them. Be grateful for the boon—I warned her about the spiders. She will be victorious."

Abraxis's eyes flicker, and then he wisely dips his chin, baring his throat to the older drake. The gesture makes my spine tingle. I've never seen Abraxis submit to anyone besides Mina, and that was purely for... recreation.

Klauth goes still then, lips curving into a secretive smile. "She's on the roof." His gaze snaps over to Ziggy. In a blink, Ziggy's gone—vanishing into the gauntlet with a barely audible pop of air rushing back into the spot he occupied.

A moment later, a high-pitched screech splits the night—unlike anything I've ever heard. It sends a chill skittering down my arms. Klauth's eyes go an even brighter crimson, glowing in the half-dark as if lit from within. He stares at a point in the distance, nothing directly in front of him but empty air.

"One of the missing spiders is on the roof," he murmurs. "Correction— was on the roof. Mina just killed it." I stare at Klauth, my mouth agape. He must be seeing through her eyes. Rumors have long whispered how powerful a great wyrm can become, but everyone said none ever made it to that age. Well, it seems we have a living mythic in our midst.

Ziggy reappears moments later, cradling Mina in his arms. My nose wrinkles at the assaulting odor that clings to her—mold and dust from the ancient structure, mixed with an acidic tang I can't place. It makes my mouth water and my stomach churn at the same time.

Mina can't even speak before Abraxis snatches her away, pressing her to his chest. She peels off her face mask and hood, her lips curving into a triumphant grin. "Five-time champion, baby!"

Abraxis finally lets her go, and she steps slowly toward Klauth. Her head tilts from side to side, and I can see the reptilian sheen take over her eyes—that brilliant golden hue that marks her dragon's presence. Klauth's shift giving away that they're conversing mind to mind. The courtyard feels impossibly silent, as though everyone holds their breath to avoid disturbing whatever intangible link they share.

Mina reaches into a pouch at the small of her back and pulls out a giant spider's fang, the nasty toxin gland still attached. My stomach lurches at the sight, but I can't look away. "I promised you a trophy," she says, lifting it in offering as she bows her head to Klauth.

With deliberate care, Klauth hooks the side of his index finger beneath her chin and lifts her gaze. "You lower your eyes to no one ever again," he rumbles, the timbre of his voice reverberating in my chest. A slow smirk plays on his lips. "That is, unless you want to. You are my equal, my **treasure**, my queen."

Then, in a dazzling gesture of complete surrender, Klauth drops to his knees and bares his throat—revealing the place she marked him. Mina leans in, pressing a tender kiss over the bite mark. A shiver of awe ripples through the onlookers, me included. A great wyrm submits to no one but their mate.

When Klauth stands, he sweeps Mina into his arms, kissing her gently before setting her back onto her feet. She giggles, a light sound in the heavy night air, and moves to Abraxis, who stands like a shadow against the courtyard's gloom.

"I brought you a trophy, too." She retrieves another spider fang from the pouch, handing it to Abraxis. He cups her cheek, returns her smile with a soft kiss, then tips his head, baring his throat to her. The general cannot kneel before a female in public; his rank won't allow it, yet the display of submission in his own way isn't lost on anyone. I notice how Mina's lips part in a quick, silent understanding of the different ways these two drakes show their devotion.

Then she steps toward me, weaving between the shifting bodies of her other mates. My nostrils flare at the faint hint of her shampoo beneath the metallic tang and dust. The cool night wind tugs at the edges of her jacket, and she leans into me.

"I'm tired, B…" she murmurs, resting her head on my chest. Her yawn is a soft gust of warm air against my collarbone.

"It's been a long day," I agree quietly, nuzzling my chin against her hair. The sun set an hour ago, painting the sky in deep purples and blues, and I can practically feel Vaughn stirring awake somewhere in the tower behind us.

"Let's go see mate number seven," I say, rolling my shoulders to ease the lingering tension. The gauntlet is conveniently close to Malivore's main building, which means a short trek back home if we choose to walk.

"Do you want me to take you home the fast way?" Ziggy asks, wiggling his fingers at Mina in a playful gesture. The faint scent of cedar clings to him—whatever power he uses to phase in and out leaves the air charged.

"Yes, please." Mina slips from my hold into Ziggy's waiting arms. She flashes me a small smile, a secret just between us. "I'll sleep with you tonight, Balor." Her gaze flicks to the two drakes, who watch from the sidelines, and then returns to me. The next second, she vanishes from sight with a hush of displaced air.

I exhale, the tension in my chest easing. The courtyard is still, the only sound the soft crackle of distant torches and the quiet pulse of my heartbeat, heavy with anticipation of what's yet to come.

By the time we finally catch up, I notice immediately that Mina is missing. The kitchen's overhead lights flicker, casting sharp shadows on the scuffed tile floor. The air is thick with the lingering scent of something spicy—maybe the remains of this evening's takeout—mixed with a tang of beer. Vaughn stands near the island counter, one hip braced against the cool granite. I can hear the fridge hum behind me as I approach, the low sound intensifying the stillness.

"Hey, Vaughn." I slap him on the back, feeling the slight dampness of his shirt—he's probably been sweating from nerves or pacing around.

"Hey, Balor ... Hey everyone..." Vaughn greets the others as they trickle in behind me. His tone is calm at first, but the moment Klauth enters, Vaughn's eyes widen. He stiffens like a startled deer, and I swear I can almost taste his anxiety in the air. "Oh shit. Is that? Are you?" His gaze darts from me to Abraxis and back again. "That's King Klauth Ragnar, the high king of the Marzana Empire." Vaughn's hand shakes as he points at the redhead in question, like he can't quite believe what he's seeing.

Klauth slowly lifts his hand in a gesture of peace and straightens his powerful frame. The overhead light gleams on his hair. "I haven't been a king in over a thousand years. Consider me one of your friends—a bond brother." His voice is polite, but there's something regal in every syllable, an undercurrent of old-world formality that feels impossible to shake.

"Of course..." Vaughn swallows hard and then motions toward the bathroom at the far end of the hall. "Mina is taking her bath. She'll be right out."

A sudden squeal echoes off the tiled walls, followed by a ripple of girlish giggles and splashing water. The bathroom door muffles most of it, but you can still catch the playful, almost feral undercurrent in Mina's laugh.

"Sneaky bastard..." I mutter under my breath, shaking my head in amusement as I stride to the fridge. The cool air hits my face when I open the door, and the faint scent of leftover pizza mingles with the cold metallic tang inside. I grab two beers and pop their caps against the edge of the counter, offering one to Klauth.

He takes the bottle, lifts it to his nose, and inhales deeply before taking a swig. The hush in the room is broken by the faint hiss of carbonation and the low rumble in his chest. "I missed beer ... This is better than I remember it." Another high-pitched squeal comes from the bathroom, followed by a splash. Klauth chuckles, the rich sound vibrating through the living area. "The displacer beast is with her?" He settles onto the arm of the couch as if he's perched on a throne.

"Yeah, Mina gets a little worked up after a fight." I tip my bottle toward Abraxis. My pulse quickens at the memory of her roaring in the training ring. "When we've sparred most of the day, he's the only one she'll seek because she's borderline feral. He can use his scales to protect himself."

Klauth's gaze shifts to Abraxis, curiosity lighting up his eyes. "Feral? Like aggressive?" He levels him with a piercing look. "Please tell me you have made her submit during her yearly."

Abraxis tilts his head. His voice hushed, as though reluctant to recount the memory. "The first year, yes—we expected it. She was still smaller than me then. This past cycle it took me, my dad, and Balor coiling around her neck just to get her to pass out so we could give her the tonic." Vaughn hands him a cold beer, the bottle already sweating from the room's warmth. Abraxis takes a sip, and then a moment of realization flares across his face. "Oh shit, I wasn't strong enough to get her to submit." His gaze snaps anxiously around the room.

Klauth just exhales through his nose, disapproval darkening his features. "We're going to have our work cut out for us this year." He shakes his head again. "By my calculations, in the next few months— after we complete our bond—she will cycle again. It won't be yearly anymore; it'll become bi-yearly because there are two viable drakes." The subtle scrape of his fingers against the couch makes my skin prickle. "The stronger she becomes, the less likely the tonic or implant will work." He fixes us all with a stern stare, the unspoken command to listen echoing in the hush. "If it's timed right, she'll lay eggs over the break according to your calendar over there." He gestures at the wall where a monthly planner hangs, pages curling at the corners.

"So ... what happens after she lays her eggs?" I step closer, the laminate floor squeaking beneath my boots, trying to absorb every word. My heartbeat thrums in my ears at the thought of Mina and eggs—how it all might change our future.

"She will entrust her mate to guard them when she's not present." Klauth's voice is soft yet resolute. "The best part is, she won't cycle again unless she wants to, after the first clutch. Her body becomes her own to control."

A soft click draws our attention. The bathroom door opens, and Mina steps out, wrapped in a towel, steam rolling out behind her. She briefly meets our gaze; I notice her wet hair clinging to her shoulders and the faint flush on her cheeks. Water droplets glisten on her collarbone under the overhead lights. She simply nods and then disappears into her bedroom, presumably to get dressed.

Ziggy shuffles into view next. His hair is a tangled mess, plastered awkwardly on his forehead. He's got multiple bite marks lining both shoulders, and when he turns his back, I see fresh sets of talon marks clawed into his skin. The metallic scent of blood mixes with the warm air, and I resist the urge to cringe.

Klauth arches a brow at the sight. "I see what you mean—she gets aggressive. That's what happens when a young dragoness isn't settled into her nest like she should be. The urge to mark repeatedly means she's anxious about something." He shifts his gaze to Abraxis.

Abraxis sighs, rubbing the back of his neck as though remembering similar marks of his own. "Her biggest fear is having the eggs stolen. Well, egg. I mean Thauglor," he clarifies with a small shrug.

"There's something else," Klauth begins, but his words are cut short. Mina reenters, and when she looks at us, her eyes are glowing. It's the same eerie luminescence I've seen before, a sign she's tapped into her deeper instincts.

I close the distance and guide her into the nearest chair, resting a hand on her shoulder. My skin prickles from the electric charge of her aura. "Lysander is coming with the elders to see the eggs," she relays quietly.

Mina's eyes shift back to normal as she blinks. She glances swiftly between Vaughn and Ziggy. "Get Klauth's shell as fast as you can." Her voice trembles with urgency, and Ziggy disappears down the hall in a flash. Meanwhile, Mina darts into her small poison garden—a cramped alcove near the patio door where the pungent scent of spiky vines and poisonous blossoms is almost overwhelming.

She returns with Thauglor's egg cradled to her chest, eyes glowing once more as she cradles it like a precious gem. Only a heartbeat passes before Ziggy appears, holding the pieces of Klauth's old shell. Mina's movements are swift and sure as she glues them together, then nestles the reassembled shell alongside Thauglor on top of the pillow she uses. The heavy atmosphere presses down on us all—tension, concern, and a fierce protectiveness swirling in the air.

I can feel my pulse racing, blood pounding in my ears at the sight of that egg. Though there's no magic here, the primal sense of danger and uncertainty is as thick as the shadows that cling to the corners of the dorm's walls. If Lysander and the elders are coming, we have precious little time to ensure Mina's precious cargo remains safe.

the shell appear even more lifeless. My gaze lingers. "Mate?" Klauth's voice rumbles softly behind me, low and full of concern.

"I need him to believe you went dormant," I murmur, voice wavering just enough to play the part. "Step into my room and wait. He'll take the egg back to the chamber and be happy I have one less egg for him to worry about." I glance up at Klauth, forcing a small smile. His skin is warm to the touch as he bends down, his hand slipping around my throat in a gentle squeeze that sends a dark thrill through me. He kisses me—brief, possessive—before disappearing into my room.

Silence settles like dust motes in the lamplit air until the knock I've been expecting raps against the wooden door. The hollow echo disrupts my breath; I let my eyes burn with tears. My mind flicks to the memory of my father killing me. That cold, helpless feeling makes the tears spill faster. Reaching out, I brush my fingertips over the egg's rough shell, letting my despair radiate.

'Mate, are you okay? Do you need me?' Klauth's voice resonates gently in my head, a calming pressure against the panic.

'It's an act,' I answer, working to keep the grief in my expression. *'They need to believe you went dormant. I'm forcing myself to cry over a failure.'*

My throat tightens around a fresh sob right as Lysander steps inside. There's a subtle, almost reptilian hiss in the way he breathes, and I catch a whiff of something metallic—like old coins—on the air. "Miss Mina? Is something wrong with the red egg?" His feral smile stretches across his thin lips. He's enjoying this far too much.

"He went dormant while I ran the gauntlet..." I sniffle, thinking about my mother's rejection of me because of my scale color. The heartbreak of that memory fuels my tears. They slip hot and fast down my cheeks.

"Then I shall return him to the chamber." Lysander tilts his head, and his basilisk eyes flash as they lock onto mine. "I told you not to pick him. He never chooses anyone."

He flicks his gaze down, tries his stone gaze. It fails, just as I knew it would. "You do realize your stone gaze doesn't work on me." My words come out rough, heavy with the residual ache of crying. He blinks twice, a twitch of surprise, then reaches for the pillow.

"Why not give me the black egg as well? I'll take them back to their resting place." He shoves the pillow nearer, the red egg perched precariously atop. Iris—the small, ever-watchful creature that she is—alights on my shoulder with a brief rustle of scales. There's a crackle in the air around her, a faint scent of ozone that prickles the back of my throat. Iris's tail coils tightly around my neck as I stare at the headmaster.

My grip tightens around Thauglor's egg, hugging it protectively against my chest. "He's mine until he decides I am unworthy." The timber of my dragoness resonates through my vocal cords, making my words thrash with warning. Tension thickens, a palpable weight pressing against everyone in the room. Even some of my bonded mates shrink back, pressing themselves to the walls. My heartbeat pulses through my veins, feeding that savage edge in my voice. "I suggest you leave, Headmaster. I am hungry and agitated. We wouldn't want an accident ... like with the spiders in the gauntlet." I finish on a low growl, shifting my gaze between him and the elders clustered behind him.

They blanch at my not-so-subtle threat, faces losing color under the sickly glow of the overhead lamps. Without further protest, Lysander, and the elders exit, the dead egg resting on the pillow. I exhale shakily, trying to steady the adrenaline coursing through me. My eyes slide closed, and I coax my dragoness back, feeling her curl into the recesses of my mind. When I open my eyes again, the tension in the room has lessened. I give my mates a puzzled look, raising a brow. "Did I miss something?"

Klauth emerges from my room and settles beside me, the heat of his body comforting in the sudden hush. "You passed my empty egg off as my real egg," he says. "That was tactically brilliant, my treasure." When he presses his lips to my temple, I feel an uncanny wave of peace settle over my nerves. It's a welcome balm. My gaze drifts to his eyes—darkening, shifting, reflecting the power beneath his calm exterior.

"Let's eat dinner. I'm tired, and I still have the Shadowcarve gauntlet," I say, sliding my thumb gently over his cheek before stepping away. My footsteps echo dully against the polished floor as I cross over to the kitchen island, where Leander mans the stove with a focused intensity.

"Steak, pasta, and fried zucchini with a side salad," he announces. The air is fragrant with sizzling butter and garlic, making my stomach clench in anticipation. Leander, being the only vegetarian, usually finds it easier to cook for all of us, and a small flush colors his cheeks as I approach.

"Sounds amazing. Can I have my steak seasoned and warmed? I'm starving." A teasing smile plays on my lips. I lean forward, resting on my forearms, gazing up at him. It's a stance he loves—reminiscent of the times he's taken me right here, bent over the counter. The memory tangles with the savory scent of our meal, and I hear his breath hitch. His chest lifts in a subtle show of pride.

Tension still lingers in the air like a low-hanging storm cloud, but the promise of food and the thrill of our small victory offer a shred of normalcy. I let myself savor it, if only for a moment, before the darkness of this academy closes in again.

A soft chuckle escapes Klauth's lips as he pulls up a stool at the island, the wooden legs scraping against the tiled floor with a sharp squeal. Overhead, a single light flickers, casting long shadows across the chipped countertop and illuminating the steam rising from the untouched plates of food. "You submit to the nightmare," he says, his low voice reverberating in the cramped space, "but not your dragon mate."

My throat feels tight as I catch a faint, bitter taste in the back of my mouth—fear, perhaps, or regret. I bite my bottom lip, wincing at the sharp sting of my canines against the tender flesh. Then I glance over at Callan, noting the tension in his broad shoulders and the flicker of concern behind his eyes. "The gryphon too?" Klauth muses. "Interesting turn of events."

"They are smaller, softer than I am. Leander is prey, and in a sense, so is Callan." Even as the words leave my mouth, there's a deep rumble in my chest. The tight press of my heart quickens with shame. I hate talking about my mates like this. My gaze flickers to the floor, focusing on the faint pattern of scuffed linoleum. I turn my face away, not wanting to speak about it anymore; even the air feels charged, dense with unspoken truths.

"Your nest is unbalanced, mate. We need to figure out what's wrong." Klauth's voice vibrates through the quiet kitchen, echoing off the walls in a low growl. It's the same discussion Abraxis tried having with me before, the one that made me bristle and snarl. My lip curls, and the growl rumbles through me without warning—until Klauth slams me against the wall. The sudden impact sends a dull ache through my shoulders.

He presses his taloned hand around my throat, the cold bite of his claws sending prickles of alarm through my skin. His hot breath fans across my cheek. "This is serious. Dragonesses go mad when their nests are in disarray." He snaps his teeth at me, the sound echoing in my ears. The overhead light casts flickering shadows across his features, making him look even more predatory.

I clench my jaw and turn my face away, letting out a warning snarl through bared teeth. Nearby, the soft flutter of Iris's wings tugs at the edges of my hearing. She's trying to land on my shoulder, but Klauth won't let her close. "Mina..." His voice shifts when he uses my name, taking on a note of concern. Against my better judgment, I fix him with a glare.

"What is wrong?" he demands, his words coming out in a deep growl. "We can't fix it if we don't know what it is." I see Balor and the others edge closer, the ring of bodies around me radiating tense heat. A faint click of nails against tile draws my attention back to Klauth. "Balor, do it…"

"Do what?" I rasp, my breath catching in my throat. My gaze darts to Balor. His dark eyes gleam in the half-light, and for a moment, sadness softens his expression.

"I'm sorry, Mina. I love you," he murmurs, and I feel a strange pulsing sensation behind my eyes. Like a heavy blanket settling over my mind, it presses me into obedience. All the fight drains out of my muscles.

"Abraxis, you are her first mate. It would be best coming from you," Klauth says, and Abraxis steps forward. I can feel the warmth of his body as he moves closer, filling the tight space between us with his musky scent.

"What is wrong with your nest? What can we fix to make you feel safer?" Abraxis asks. There's a soothing purr in his voice that washes over me, but I can still taste the metallic tang of panic in my mouth.

My words spill out in disjointed fragments. "I don't feel safe here. Buildings burn. It's not able to be defended. We're too low." My lungs feel tight, and the closeness of everyone presses on me like a vise. "I will be hunted for what I am. It's not safe here. No stone. I can't shift in here." My dragoness roars under my skin, bone plates shifting beneath the surface in a sickening ripple. I see Klauth's eyes flash in warning.

"You will quiet and let your human half speak," Klauth commands, his voice booming through the cramped apartment. I gasp, feeling my dragoness recoil, her presence diminishing, though I can still feel her coiled tension in the back of my mind.

"Do you want your nest or to go to Abraxis's chalet?" Balor asks, carefully enunciating each word. His gaze, reflecting in the dim overhead light, holds a sympathetic sadness.

"My nest. My place, my home ... It's not done; it's not safe yet. Nowhere's safe." The moment Balor's hold on me releases, I slump with exhaustion. A single tear drips down my cheek, burning hot as it slides over my skin. My deepest fears have been laid bare, and the vulnerability is suffocating.

"I will go in the morning to work on your nest site," Klauth says, pressing his lips to my temple in a surprisingly gentle gesture. His breath warms my skin. "I agree this place isn't able to be defended well. We will make a safe place for you, mate." With that, he strides out of the apartment. His heavy footsteps echo down the hallway, and the chill draft from the open door sends a shiver through me.

"Where's he going?" Abraxis asks, gathering me into his arms. The steady beat of his heart thumps against my ear, strangely comforting in the stillness.

"He's starting on my nest." My voice hitches. I close my eyes, inhaling Abraxis's scent—smoke and steel—and the lingering aroma of the half-eaten meal on the countertop. I'm always a problem for everyone around me. Nothing but a huge burden to everyone I care about.

"Hey..." Balor's voice softens as he appears in front of me. He cups my cheek, his palm rough with calluses yet warm against my skin. "Don't do that to yourself. You are worth everything we go through as a nest. A large, functional nest doesn't happen overnight." He glances at Abraxis, who reluctantly loosens his hold so Balor can draw me nearer. "As much as you want Abraxis to stay in charge, your dragoness needs someone bigger and stronger than she is."

Abraxis's eyes flash with protest, but Callan steps closer, resting a hand on Abraxis's shoulder. "We've been in denial for months," Callan says, his voice subdued. "She's stronger and more lethal than any of us when she shifts. If Klauth can keep her from going on a rampage, let him bear that burden."

The thick tension in the room is broken only by the hum of the refrigerator and the muted thud of the pipes in the wall. I follow Balor to my favorite chair, the worn leather creaking as I sink into it. Leander hands me a plate of food—some steak and a few sides. The savory aroma once made my mouth water, but now it's tinged with a bitterness that sours my appetite. The dull glow from the nearby floor lamp shows the sadness in his fiery gaze; it's an unspoken empathy that cuts me to the bone.

I know, deep down, that Balor and Callan are right. I need a stronger drake in charge. Maybe tonight I'll sleep on it and make changes after the gauntlet tomorrow. My stomach clenches, and I force the steak down despite its loss of flavor. Every bite feels like lead in my mouth.

Once I'm finished, I push the plate aside, ignoring the greasy residue that clings to my fingers. Balor guides me gently toward his room, the warmth of his hand on my back steadying my swirling thoughts. Vaughn will be nothing but stone tomorrow—he can't run with me. The sudden distance between all of us weighs heavily in my chest. My world feels smaller, darker ... lonelier.

As I settle onto Balor's bed, the sheets cool against my tired body, my senses remain on high alert. I can still smell the leftover food in the apartment, hear the soft drip of a leaky faucet in the sink, and feel the press of my dragoness just beneath my skin. Even so, exhaustion wins out. I close my eyes, praying for sleep to overtake me and for a safer tomorrow to arrive.

steam rising with a hiss when it touches cooler rock. Its surface glints in the faint pre-dawn light, reflecting sparks of fiery orange from within. There are only a few hours until daybreak, and I need to return before the final gauntlet. My skin prickles with the chill that creeps in as night wanes, but I work quickly, determined to complete three out of four glass walls.

I'm nearly done when I sense movement behind me. The displacer beast, Ziggy, arrives. His faintly musky scent hits me first, followed by the soft padding of his footsteps on the rocky ground.

"Wow, this looks like Mina's painting," he says, studying the still-hot glass walls. Warm wind from the magma flow ruffles his hair, and I see the reflection of glowing cracks dancing across his features.

Shifting back to my human form, I walk over to him. The cooling rock presses uncomfortably against my bare feet, reminding me how far underground we are. "Painting?" I echo. Ziggy holds up his phone—strange technology I haven't fully grasped yet—and I peer at the glowing image. My gaze drifts between the digital painting and the shining glass structure I've built.

"Are there more?" I ask, curiosity prickling at the back of my mind.

"She has a room of paintings at Shadowcarve. We have time; I can take you there now," Ziggy says, stretching out his hand. A faint, electrifying sense of displacement stirs in the surrounding air.

I clamp my mouth shut on any protest and nod. "Let's go."

The instant our hands connect, I feel weightless. My stomach flips as if I'm falling from a great height. Then the sensation slams to a stop, and my feet find solid ground beneath them. The sudden shift makes my head spin. I blink away the vertigo, trying to steady my breathing. The air in this new room is warmer, comforting—wrapped in a subtle, familiar scent that reminds me of Mina. It sets my instincts at ease.

"Over here..." Ziggy calls out, leading me into the next room. The space is dimly lit, the walls lined with dozens of canvases. My footsteps sound hollow against the polished floor, and the faint smell of turpentine mingles with the lingering hint of paint. It's a shrine of images—my entire life, it seems, strewn across these walls.

I feel the shift in air as Ziggy leaves, then reappears a moment later, but my focus stays on a painting of me—half human, half dragon. The brushstrokes are bold, capturing the primal ferocity in my eyes, the tension in my posture. My mate is truly a veil walker, and her very existence is in danger. "When did she paint this?" I murmur, brushing my fingertips across the canvas, marveling at the fine ridges of dried paint.

"A few weeks before you hatched to save me." Mina's voice is soft, hesitant. The faint tap of her boots on the floor announces her approach. She loops her arm with mine and rests her head against the curve of my shoulder. Her body's warmth cutting through the chill of the converted living space. "The visions started shortly after you began talking to me. I don't know if it's part of the mate bond or a gift because of you being a great wyrm." She shrugs, her eyes drawn to the painting again.

One painting shows me flying over Shadowcarve's wall to save her. I can almost taste the adrenaline I felt that day—spiced fear and raw determination. The detail on her father's face, twisted in terror, makes me chuckle. My dragon form in the painting snarls with palpable rage, and the reflection of her father's green dragon in my eye in the next painting is phenomenal. "You are an incredible artist," I say, pressing my lips to her temple. Just then, I notice she's clad in her fighting leathers, the faint squeak of well-worn leather accompanying her every movement.

"Walk me to the gauntlet?" She draws a deep breath, forcing a smile that doesn't quite reach her eyes.

"Of course. You realize once you have your first clutch, they can't force the gauntlets on you anymore?" I press my lips to her temple again.

Her skin smells faintly of smoky incense, the same kind used in Shadowcarve's training halls.

"I know. Sadly, I live for moments like this—the thrill of the hunt and the chase. It makes me feel alive." Her gaze meets mine, a spark of fierce determination. "I don't want to run a flight. I think I'd rather fight beside my mate than rot in an egg chamber."

Her words strike me, and I still, taking both her hands in mine. Her fingers feel cold against my warmer skin. "Why would you be trapped in an egg chamber? Historically, a dragoness with a nest or clutch is more dangerous than any drake." My brows knit, a surge of protective anger stirring in my chest.

"It's the way it's done now." She sighs, turning to face the looming structure of the gauntlet. The surrounding air crackles with tension, and I can make out the faint metallic tang of hidden traps waiting inside. "They open and close sections and levels; no two runs are ever the same. But it's relatively similar year after year," she says in a detached tone that makes my gut clench with worry.

"When did they start making females run the gauntlets? That was never my intention; it was to weed out weak males." I drag a hand down my face, frustration pounding like a war drum in my head. The intention has clearly been twisted.

Mina bursts into laughter as she spots Balor on the platform. "I need to check in. I usually climb the wall over there and wait my turn if you want to meet me there." Her voice echoes slightly in the chamber, vibrant with excitement despite the gloom. She gestures toward a section of the wall across from the main entrance of the gauntlet.

"I'll meet you there." I give her forehead a quick kiss before she strides off to check in. I scale the wall in a few swift movements, the rough stone scraping my palms. I settle at the top, the vantage point allowing me a clear view of the sprawling gauntlet, lit by smoldering torches and faint lantern light. Callan and Abraxis join me, leaning on the wall below.

"How is she? She usually gets amped up before the run," Abraxis says, glancing up at me with a mix of curiosity and concern.

"She's calm," I answer, though I can sense the coiled tension in her that's ready to explode. "She showed me her paintings, so I think she's got her head in the right place." Deep inside, I know it's because I put her dragoness in its place last night, taming that feral edge just enough.

Mina doesn't even bother coming to us; instead, she waves a golden ticket in the air and approaches the gauntlet head-on. Balor tries to talk her down—his voice carries a note of caution I can't quite make out. Mina brushes him off, pulling her hood low and lifting her mask. Then she leaps into the gauntlet like a child diving into a pile of autumn leaves. My heart thunders in my chest, the sound roaring in my ears. Even from this distance, I can taste the tang of anticipation on my tongue, stoking the embers of a primal need to protect my mate ... or join her in the fight.

I watch the younger males in the nest, their pupils wide as they track every flicker of light sparking to life along the gauntlet's walls. The air here is thick with tension, laced with the stale smell of sweat and old timber. The wooden structure groans under the strain of footsteps racing within it. In the distance, I can make out the tang of something burning—likely a torch sputtering somewhere in this labyrinth of trials. Unlike the main gauntlet, they tell me multiple students are allowed to run at once, heightening the chaos.

Abraxis's laugh cuts through the hushed dread. I see him leaning forward, eyes narrowed with amusement, and the faintest whiff of acid trails off his breath—an echo of his own power. "That male is in Arista's flight. If Mina finds out, she's going to hunt him and kill him," Abraxis says offhandedly. Then he stiffens, glancing up at me with sudden unease.

A sick, twisted grin curls the corner of my lip as I relay his words to Mina through our bond. The moment she hears, her roar reverberates through the gauntlet walls, making the torch flames shudder. I sense the primal fury in her voice resonate through my chest. On the gauntlet's glowing map, I watch her dot abruptly stop, then backtrack. My heart beats faster, a low, thunderous rhythm in my ears.

Her dot is close to that male's, but she's on a level above him. Wood splinters and wails under her assault — **Crack ... Crack... Crack...** The snapping echoes across the cavernous space as dust drifts from the structure. Everything falls silent for a moment, the taste of adrenaline thick in the back of my throat.

"Oh, shit ... I think she's found him," Callan mutters, pacing. The scrape of his boots on the rough stone floor sets my nerves on edge.

"Who found who?" Ziggy asks, sauntering up with a drink in hand, the smell of ale mingling with the smoky air.

"This one," Abraxis grunts, jerking his thumb at me. "Told Mina that Taylor from Arista's flight is in the gauntlet with her."

Another loud **crack** draws all eyes to the gauntlet's map. Taylor's dot is moving erratically now, as if fleeing for his life.

"Oh, shit..." Ziggy mutters. "I wonder if he remembers he's a fire drake and can burn her, or if he'll just run scared." The acrid scent of singed wood curls through the air, and I see flames suddenly blooming on the gauntlet's far side.

Callan smacks Ziggy's head. "Not helping."

No sooner do the words leave Ziggy's mouth than part of the gauntlet fully ignites. Thick black smoke rolls out, stinging my eyes and throat. "Bloody hell," I snarl, leaping off the low stone wall where I had perched, ready to tear Mina out of there. Abraxis grabs my arm, his fingers digging in.

"She'll be disqualified if you interfere—kicked out. That would piss her off worse than anything I can think of." His voice is grim, and the sparks of ember dancing in the smoky air reflect in his eyes.

A rumble like thunder shakes the arena, and a bolt of lightning tears through the gauntlet. The sharp tang of ozone invades my nostrils. I watch, breath bated, as the fire drake tries to climb out of the jagged, two-foot hole left behind. My gut twists when I see Mina's silver talons sink into his flesh, dragging him back in. Wood creaks and moans around them, and the drake's pained roar slices through the haze.

"Oh, shit..." Ziggy says again, voice trembling. We see Balor moving along the outer edges, monitoring their progress, but there's no mistaking the fear in his eyes.

A shrieking roar sounds, followed by another thunderous crack that shakes my bones. Then—**Silence.** An eerie quiet blankets the gauntlet. The flickering lights on the board go dark. Half the structure is aflame, while the other half is drenched in the harsh smell of ozone. My fellow bond mates all turn to me. I focus on my bond with Mina, letting her sight flood my mind. The warmth of her rage seeps into my every sense. Then I catch a glimpse of the aftermath: two bodies, torn and smoking.

"He wasn't the only fire drake in there," I rasp, pulling out of her vision with a violent jolt. The gritty taste of ash coats my tongue. "There was a female lying in wait, too. She says her name was Ardent..." Blinking, I find Abraxis pale as a corpse. His nostrils flared from the shock.

"Our mate unshifted ... killed two fire drakes alone?" His voice quakes, as if seeking to deny the truth.

I give him a curt nod. "I told you she was worthy of being my queen. My stubborn ass would only hatch for an equal—a female who can hold her own and isn't afraid to do what's necessary. Thauglor feels the same way." I stare down at Abraxis, the metallic scent of his sweat cutting through the smoky air, then glance back at the gauntlet's flames licking the sky. "Our mate is proving herself to be a powerful dragoness."

The structure shudders, and out from the smoke, Mina emerges at the top of the gauntlet. The heat shimmers around her, and in her fists are the severed heads of the two fire drakes. She hurls them down in front of the remaining onlookers and rips off her hood and mask, tossing them aside. The stench of blood wafts up, making my stomach clench. With a furious roar, she dives off the gauntlet, shifting into her dragon form mid-leap, emerald, and silver scales glinting in the roaring flames. Instinct surges through me, demanding I join her in flight, but I can't risk revealing that I've hatched.

"Zigmander," I growl softly, turning to Ziggy at my side, "take me to Mina's nest in the mountains. I'll track her from there."

With a nod, Ziggy closes the distance and grips my shoulder. I look at Abraxis and Balor, feeling the heat from the blazing gauntlet at my back. "Get her trophies home. She'll be even more pissed if they aren't prepared for her."

Ziggy blinks us out of sight, and the world tilts. We land in the apartment, the abrupt silence disorienting after the phasing. The familiar smell of old furniture and the faint hint of soap linger here.

"We should gather food and clothes for her, plus some blankets," Ziggy suggests, darting into what used to be her room. My heart still hammers, adrenaline stoking my every nerve, reminding me how violent the night has become.

It hits me then how amped up she'll be after this gauntlet. Last time, she tore up Ziggy and bit the hell out of him. This time, she killed two drakes. My stomach clenches at the thought of her bloodlust—and my own. I collect an assortment of meats, bread, and water, stuffing it all in a basket I find in the pantry. By the time I'm done, Ziggy returns with a sack of clothes and blankets.

He eyes my basket, nods once in approval, and grabs my arm again. We blink away, reappearing deep in Mina's nest site. The sudden drop in temperature is bracing. I smell damp stone and the crisp air of high altitudes. Deeper in, near the egg chamber, we arrange everything on the smooth rock floor.

"Good luck..." Ziggy says, his voice echoing off the cavern walls before he vanishes.

I walk back to the surface, my steps echoing on the stone, and shift into my dragon form. The scrape of my scales against the cool rock sends a tremor through me. Lifting my head to the moonlit sky, I let my call rumble from deep in my chest, summoning my mate. The night air vibrates with my roar, and distant peaks send it back in haunting echoes. Eventually, her call resonates in reply, pure and fierce, and my heart skips a beat. It's been more than a thousand years since I last felt the pleasure of a female's presence—my wings tremble at the prospect.

I only hope I don't embarrass myself.

As I ponder my life choices, I hear Klauth's drake calling for me—its low, resonant timbre echoes through the open skies, setting my veins aflame with recognition. It's rare for a drake to sing for its mate, especially one as ancient and powerful as he is. I adjust my wings, banking on the next updraft, and head toward his song. The crisp air brushes against my face, and I inhale the fleeting scent of pine and distant smoke. The song that escapes my lips in answer to his speaks of the promise of forever vibrating from deep in my chest. I am his queen, his treasure, as his song continues, speaking of his love eternal.

His voice leads me to my nest in the mountains, and I spot the start of dragon glass walls glinting dully in the waning sunlight. The sharp tang of heated stone reaches my nose, reminding me of molten rock cooling rapidly. *He remembered* ... When he sees my silhouette on the horizon, Klauth shifts back to his human form, giving me enough space to land. I circle what will one day be the courtyard several times, scanning the fresh ridges of rock and inhaling the earthy smell of newly unearthed soil. On the third pass, I come in for a landing, my talons scraping against the rough ground, and then shift back to my human form.

Thankfully, the enchantments on the fighting leathers keep them snug around my body, leaving only the taste of ozone on my tongue from the residual energy. Slowly, I turn in a circle, marveling at how much he's dug out for me. The courtyard is now twice its original size, and the entrance—already half-covered in dragon glass—yawns large enough to fit his drake.

"Do you like it? I hope I didn't overstep." Klauth's voice is low and tentative as he steps closer, the gentle warmth of his presence enveloping me before he even touches me. Then he pulls me into his arms. The earlier rage that burned in my chest fizzles out, replaced by deep gratitude.

"It's amazing, thank you." My voice wavers as I struggle to keep my emotions in check. The faint mineral scent of dragon glass and stone dust lingers in the air. But all I really sense is the warmth of Klauth's body against mine. He didn't have to dig my nest for me, but he did.

"I want to show you what I did." He presses his lips to my temple with reverence, and we walk slowly into what will be our family's home.

My eyes move from wall to wall, taking in his deep gouges, evidence of his drake's powerful talons. The acrid smell of freshly cut rock mixed with the slight sulfuric tang still hanging in the corridors from his breath weapon. I pause several times, reaching out to feel the smooth planes where he has melted the stone into glass. It's almost warm to the touch, like it's holding on to the lingering heat of his flame. The original small chamber I dug remains in place, its entrance jagged from where I first carved out the rock.

"I'm too big to expand that room. I left it as a possible sitting room." We step inside, and I take in the pile of furs spread across the floor. The dim light reveals the worn edges of the pelts, each telling the story of hunts past.

"It's where I slept for my yearly." A wave of distaste washes over me as I recall those nights—forced sleep, trapped in my mind with no choice in the matter.

"You know how I feel about that," he rumbles softly next to my ear before guiding me out of the room, the warmth of his breath ghosting over my skin.

"I do, and I'm seeing the wisdom in it." I sigh a little, the faint echo bouncing off the cavern walls. "I've been conditioned to believe that I'm only good for two things: a weapon or a breeder." I let out a mirthless laugh as I stop walking. "I don't want to be either. Yes, I want hatchlings of my own. But I don't want to wage war anymore." The quiet dripping of condensation from somewhere deeper in the cave punctuates my words. I look down at our joined hands, feeling the rough calluses of his palms, as we enter a larger area he's carved out.

Here, the walls gleam with glassy patches, reflecting the flicker of torchlight. The smell of heated stone intensifies. "Do I smell limestone?"

Klauth nods and leads me into a heated limestone room that makes my skin prickle. The temperature is perfect—balmy, soothing. I release his hand and run my fingertips over the grooves left by his talons, feeling the cool ridges and lingering dampness.

"I didn't know if you wanted a structure in the middle, like most drag-onesses, or if you wanted the gryphon to make a nest." He stands behind me, the heat of his chest pressed gently against my back. "Over in that corner would be best—the temperature is milder, so you'd have an equal chance at both genders." He rests his cheek atop my head, and I close my eyes, letting the rumbling of his voice resonate through me.

"I remember. Cooler for females, warmer for males." I spin in his arms, looking up into his crimson-flecked amber eyes. My heart thrums with a mixture of excitement and apprehension. "Please tell me we don't have to betroth our children. It's cruel and barbaric."

"I took a chosen bride at the age of two hundred and twenty-seven," he says, his voice resonating with regret. "I paid the dowry price, and when the female reached maturity, we met. She wasn't you." He forces a smile. "A drake can go mad without a female to temper his rage. She was a means to an end. Then my clutch was burned, and I went on a rampage. Not to avenge her, but for my lost children." His face tightens with sadness, and the flickering torchlight casts shadows across his features.

"I'm sorry for your loss." I stand on my tiptoes, and he bends to meet me halfway. Klauth is nearly a foot taller than me, so our kiss is a careful dance. My senses fill with the musk of his skin, and I taste the tang of ash on his lips, born from days of shifting and building. When we break apart, he leads me through the winding corridors. The walls are uneven but majestic, each raw edge carved by his drake's brutal strength. Klauth has accomplished more in one night than we did in a month.

"Thank you for digging my nest." I rest my head against his broad chest, listening to the steady rhythm of his heart, letting it ground me.

"You're welcome, my treasure." His hand cups the back of my head, pressing me closer, while his other arm wraps around my waist in a firm embrace. "Come, I have food and drink for us in the next chamber." He takes my hand and guides me into a room lined with candles, their flames dancing against the glossy walls. Ziggy's scent lingers here —an inviting aroma of cedar and the faint sweetness of honeyed cakes —reminding me I'm never truly alone in this new home.

A low, comforting warmth radiates through the smooth stone beneath me, pulsing upward like the heartbeat of the mountain itself. We're deep inside a hidden cavern high in the peaks, where the heat from natural underground vents seeps through cracks in the rock, banishing the alpine chill. The cavern's walls curve around us in dark, sinuous shapes, flecked with faint veins of minerals that glimmer dully in the muted glow of the candlelight. Outside, a fierce wind whistles across the mountainside, but in here, we're cocooned in silence and warmth.

Klauth has gone to great lengths for our comfort—he's brought a blanket to cover the rough stone, some food in leather pouches, and a skin of cool water. He settles next to me, describing how he painstakingly dug out this new nest for me here in the mountain. His voice is a soothing bass, but I'm too captivated by the way his neck and jaw flex with every word. The faint scratch of stubble catching the cavern's candle light. My gaze drifts to his eyes, where crimson flecks catch the glow each time he shifts his attention around the shadowy space.

A deep, satisfied purr ripples in my chest as I watch him—my ancient drake who saved me from certain death and gave me this sanctuary. He hasn't demanded his rightful claim, though everything in my blood screams I should give in. Still, I have my own designs on him. Slowly, I rise to all fours, the blanket's coarse weave rubbing against my palms and knees. A soft purr vibrates in my throat as I prowl toward him. I'm coiled with tension and desire—after all, we are alone in a cavern beyond the academy's reach. I feel strangely safe with Klauth. But that doesn't dampen my hunger. I want him to be mine.

"Mina?" he murmurs, leaning back a fraction when I draw closer.

I press my nose against his abdomen, inhaling the warm, masculine scent clinging to his skin—a tang of sweat, a strong drake musk made richer by the cavern's heat. A throaty purr escapes me, and my pulse quickens as I pick up the subtle undertone of his desire. Klauth leans back without a word, granting me free access to his throat. I sweep my tongue from his collarbone to just beneath his ear. My taste buds tingle with the salt of his skin.

"Mate, my mate..." I purr, teasing my teeth along the spot near my first bite on his neck. A wave of heat burns through me, tightening my core. I could devour him if I let myself go.

"Mina..." he breathes, husky and reverent, while his strong fingers move to the buckles on my leather jacket. The metallic snap of each fastening echoes through the cavern, mingling with the distant drip of water seeping somewhere behind us.

I recline onto my haunches, popping the final buckle free, and let the jacket fall away. The sudden rush of warm air against my skin makes me shiver. Beneath, I wear an ace wrap over my sports bra, binding my chest flat.

"Why?" Klauth's tone is curious, laced with concern. His eyes hold mine steadily as he carefully slips one talon under the bandage, slicing it open.

"Boobs get in the way of archery and swordplay," I mutter, feeling a stab of insecurity. The real reason is more complicated. I never wanted the unwanted attention. Even the leathers can't entirely hide my curves. My breath stutters at the intensity of Klauth's stare as the wrap unwinds, revealing the simple sports bra that barely contains me.

I force a casual shrug. "I take after my father's mother—big breasts, short stature." My hands move to the zippers on my boots, the scrape of metal surprisingly loud in the hush of the cavern. I peel off my leather pants, kneeling in just my sports bra and thong, goosebumps rising on my skin despite the heat from the stone floor. I eye him pointedly. "Your turn. You're overdressed."

He blinks as though coming out of a trance, a flush darkening the scars on his cheeks. Without another word, he strips off his shirt, tossing it aside. In the dim, golden lamplight, every scar on his torso stands in relief, a crisscross map of battles waged over centuries. Abraxis is marred too, but he can't compare to Klauth's unyielding history etched into his flesh.

My sports bra hits the ground next, followed by my thong. The moist air of the cavern caresses my bare skin, drawing out a sharp intake of breath. Klauth glances my way, and when he fully turns, I see his length throb in time with his heartbeat. Heat flares in my belly. Before he can take another breath, I launch myself at him, hoping to pin him like I would Abraxis. But Klauth has centuries of experience on me. He catches me mid-leap, swinging me around so my back lands against the blanket in a surprisingly gentle collision. A husky growl escapes him, reverberating in my chest as his strong arms cage me.

His dragonic eyes blaze like molten blood. The human side of me twists with indignation at being overpowered. But my dragoness side is gleefully purring, thrilled at his display of dominance.

"If you love me..." His voice is gravelly, fluttering over the sensitive spots along my neck. He peppers kisses along my jaw, tracing a path to his original mark. "If you are mine ... You will submit to me here and now. Forever." His breath washes hot across my pulse.

Inside my mind, my dragoness rolls onto her back, baring her throat to his drake in a gesture of acceptance. I tilt my head, exposing the scar he left on me recently. "I am yours, and you are mine. Eternally."

He thrusts forward in a single fluid motion, making me gasp as his length fills me completely. I hear my heartbeat pounding in my ears. He bites down over the old mark on my throat, and a jolt of pleasure and pain surges through me, stoking the fire in my core. Each roll of his hips sends sparks igniting through my body. The heated stone beneath me amplifying the sensation of being trapped in the arms of a red dragon.

Then I feel him shift, his length growing more textured, ridged in a way that has me crying out with each thrust. I dig my nails into the stone, half expecting to gouge it, as wave after wave of pleasure rips through me. My climax slams into me, molten and overwhelming, while Klauth's canines stay locked in my throat. Suddenly, he rears up and throws his head back. His roar fills the cavern as he finds his own release, his dragonic ridges flaring and holding me fast. Another surge of ecstasy crashes over me at the feel of him locking inside me.

He finally lowers his head to my neck, lapping gently at the sensitive wound. The metallic tang of blood mingles with the humid air, while sweat slicks our bodies. My breaths come in panting gasps as I meet his gaze—there's awe there, quickly replaced by a flicker of alarm.

"I've never ... It's never..." He glances down at our still-joined bodies, and I see understanding dawn in his eyes. "Apparently, my drake used his knot and flare. It's usually just for ... breeding. I've never done it before."

I rest my hand on his chest, feeling the pounding of his heart under my palm. "Then we shared a first." A breathless laugh escapes me, though

I feel a shiver of adrenaline at the idea of being stuck like this. The heated floor seems to amplify every subtle movement, intensifying the press of our bodies.

Klauth settles more of his weight on me, careful not to hurt me. The stifling cavern air wraps around us like a second skin. I slide my hands along his jaw, drawing him into a slow, tender kiss. My frantic need to bite and claim him fully has faded, replaced by a deep sense of belonging.

After a moment, I catch a glimpse of the small rod implanted in my forearm. "Take it out," I whisper, voice trembling with conviction. "I'm done living by everyone else's decisions. I want to live on my terms now."

His gaze drifts to the tiny outline on my arm. "What changed your mind?" He presses a soft kiss to my cheek, and I feel the grit of the cavern floor shifting beneath us.

"Everything I've done until now—enrolling in the academy, training for war—it was all because my father demanded it. I was supposed to be a weapon. I don't want to be one. I want to be me, whoever she may be." My voice tightens, a tear slipping down my cheek. Gently, Klauth kisses it away, his breath warm on my skin.

"If this is your wish, I will grant it." With a deft flick of his talon, he cuts a small line on my arm. We work together to push the implant free until it clatters onto the stone. It splinters on impact, a quiet echo in the steamy darkness. Klauth kisses the fresh wound, his saliva sealing it with the faintest tingle of heat.

I purr low in my throat, wrapping my arms around his neck once more. The distant rush of wind through the mountain pass and the constant hush of the magma flow make the world feel strangely alive around us. But in this moment, all that matters is him and the choice I just made.

I run my fingers through his hair, my gaze fixed on the scarred planes of his face. For nearly twenty-three years, I've moved through life on rails set down by someone else. Now, for the first time, I'm free to choose. And it's all because of this beautiful, war-torn drake I saved from an egg—who saved me right back, and gives me the strength to finally live.

ably from the old pipes or the fridge humming in the corner. He looks like his legs have given out.

"Are you alright?" My voice comes out scratchy as I rush over. I pull out a rickety chair for him to collapse into, then grab a water bottle from the fridge. The cold condensation slicks my palm.

"It's done … They bonded." Abraxis's words hang in the silent apartment, his tone hollow. It sets my nerves on edge.

"That's a good thing, right?" I crack the bottle open and hand it to him, trying to focus on the cool plastic against my fingertips, anything to ground me. "I mean, we have a great wyrm on our side permanently."

Abraxis stares at the bottle for a moment before taking a swig. "His bond with her is stronger than mine. The stronger drake will always have the stronger bond and the female's attention." He runs a trembling hand through his hair; the motion ruffles the strands, and he looks away.

"Mina loves you. You're her first mate. She's your first love." My anxiety flutters in my stomach as I say it, the echo of that bond's pulse still rattling my senses.

"It's the way of dragons, Ziggy." Abraxis exhales heavily, pushing a sealed envelope toward me. I catch a faint whiff of parchment as I pick it up. "Cora's egg hatched. We've been invited to the anointing ceremony." He motions toward a box off to the side and shakes his head. "Mom sent a dress for Mina. She's going to be asked to be the hatchling's guardian."

"That should make you happy and proud." My eyes flick to the box. The cardboard is damp in one corner, like it's been sitting against a drafty window.

Abraxis avoids my gaze. "Her mate's brother is the guardian for his family. I wasn't asked because I'm a general." He stands abruptly, the sound of the chair scraping on the worn floor making my teeth clench.

Without another word, he heads into the bathroom. The distant rush of water echoes in the silent apartment.

I linger, staring at the closed door, then make my way back to my bedroom. The hallway is dim, the single light overhead flickering. Before I can so much as slide under the blanket, a familiar caress along the bond makes me shiver. Mina's summoning me; her desire to come home feels like a gentle tug at my ribcage.

I phase again, that swift moment of disorientation hitting me, and land just inside the cavern she shares with Klauth. The space smells of warm skin and lingering passion—an intangible mix of musk that makes my throat tighten. They're getting dressed, and I manage a wide grin.

"Ta-da! I have arrived." My voice wobbles slightly as I take in Klauth. There's not a single scratch on him, not even a bruise. "You're not torn to shreds?" I circle him, eyes narrowed. "Not a single bite."

Klauth's gaze follows me. "Is there something wrong, Zigmander?" He sounds genuinely puzzled, but his posture is casual, maybe even smug.

Mina's cheeks flush. She turns her head away, her hair spilling over her shoulder. His mark on her neck stands out—freshly bitten multiple times, each layer of scar tissue raised. "I asked to have the implant taken out, Ziggy," she says softly. "I want my first clutch ... so we don't have to keep forcing me to sleep when I go feral from my yearly."

A tightness grips my chest. "Is that true?" I search her face. "Will she be able to control when she's fertile after she has her first clutch?" My voice lowers, mind racing. The memory of Mina's feral side, wild and untamed, still sends shivers along my arms.

Klauth adjusts the collar of his shirt. "The older bloodlines—ancient, powerful dragonesses—can control their cycles after laying eggs as their dragons. Many females lost that ability by giving birth in human form."

Mina steps into the sundress I packed for her, the light fabric draping over her scales. When she moves, the plates over her shoulder blades and spine catch the overhead light, reflecting a pearly sheen. They spread out at her hips and backside in what almost looks like butterfly wings, mesmerizing in their shifting pattern.

"The reason I'm here," I say, regaining my composure, "is we have to go to Blackhaven. Cora's egg hatched, and the anointing is today."

Mina's eyes light up as she squeals, bouncing on the balls of her feet. The rocks crunch under her shoes. "I can't wait to see the little one," she exclaims, darting over to Klauth. "I helped deliver her egg. Cora was egg-bound and tore some. I stitched her back up and saved both her and the egg." Her smile is so radiant it makes the corners of my own lips twitch upward.

"Are you feeling okay, Mina?" I ask, taking the bag she hands me. The weight of it drags down my arm, but I hold steady.

She bites her bottom lip, then meets my gaze. "I don't want to be a weapon anymore," she admits, voice hushed like she's sharing a secret. "I enjoy being a tactician. I just don't want to fight if I don't have to."

Her words hang in the charged air before she freezes, glancing between me and Klauth. "Abraxis will not be happy. I was bred to be the weapon my betrothed would wield." Her eyes dart around the cavern, searching for threats where there are none.

"Mate." Klauth's tone is firm, each syllable resonating with a deep rumble. "If he loves you as much as you say he does, it won't be an issue." A wicked grin stretches across his face, revealing his teeth. The heat in his gaze feels like the sudden flare of a furnace. "If it is an issue, the hatchling and I will have a very long, very painful conversation." He cracks his knuckles, the sound loud in the quiet.

I swallow hard, the tension thick enough to taste in the back of my throat. His threat is clear, and I can only hope Abraxis knows how to

bite his tongue. If he doesn't, this day could take an even darker turn—
one we might not recover from.

I watch Mina sweep past us, the soft rustle of her gown and the tap of
her heels on the cold marble floor echoing in the hallway. She clutches
the box from the counter, her knuckles tight around it as she slips into
her room. A faint click of the latch follows, and I release a slow breath,
the tension in my chest loosening just a little. The air here always
seems tinged with a metallic chill, a constant reminder that this
academy is more fortress than school.

I shift my gaze to Abraxis, who's standing under the dim glow of a
single overhead light. Shadows cling to the angles of his face. "Mina
doesn't want to fight anymore," I whisper. My words feel heavy, like
the weight of old tomes in the academy's ancient library. "It was her
father's goal for her to be a fighter, but she'd rather be a tactician." The
smell of fresh coffee wafts by—dark and bitter—reminding me that
the taste of conflict still lingers in the air.

Abraxis's eyes flick from Mina's door back to me. The tension in his
shoulders ebbs as he exhales, almost as if he's been holding his breath
for days. "I was so worried about her joining the battles," he murmurs.
"She's powerful, especially with that breath weapon of hers." His voice
resonates through the quiet room, and I can't help but notice how his
hand curls around the edge of the counter, fingertips tapping a restless
rhythm.

Klauth and Balor draw closer, their footsteps resonating against the
tile. The faint clink of cups meeting saucers cuts through the hush as
Balor slides a steaming mug of coffee toward Klauth. "If it makes her

happy to be in the planning room with Callan, then that's what will happen," Abraxis says, a small smile playing across his lips.

"I'm glad you're putting our young mate's desires before your needs, hatchling," Klauth adds, taking a careful sip of his drink. I catch a whiff of the coffee's strong aroma, which mingles with Klauth's lingering smoky scent—a telltale sign of his dragon close to the surface.

Abraxis bristles at the word "hatchling," color flooding his cheeks. "Why do you keep calling me hatchling? I am a grown man." His voice reverberates in the kitchen, the faint hum of fluorescent lights overhead doing little to soften the edge in his tone.

Klauth, unruffled, lifts his chin. "Fine, I will call you youngling. Which is accurate since you are not yet over a century old." His stare bores into Abraxis, cool and condescending.

With a sharp huff, Abraxis turns and strides out, his heels striking against the floor in a staccato beat that gradually fades down the corridor. The air feels a little clearer once he's gone, as if he took some of the tension with him.

Moments later, Callan enters. The subtle scent of starched fabric reaches my nose before I fully register his pewter suit, a touch of green in the pocket square honoring Mina's scales. "I left a suit for you on Mina's bed, Klauth," he says politely, giving a small bow. "Based on the measurements our mate took for your clothing."

"Thank you," Klauth replies, inclining his head. "I appreciate your forethought, Callan." Then he crosses the room, disappearing through the door that leads to Mina's quarters.

A hush settles over the space again. The overhead light flickers once, casting quick shadows over the counters. My heart thuds a little faster with anticipation. Whatever Mina's planning to wear, she always has a way of commanding attention without trying.

And then she appears. The door opens, and she steps out in a shimmering silver strapless gown that moves like liquid mercury around her body. The satin ties in the back catch the light, revealing glimpses of the iridescent scales trailing down her spine and across her shoulder blades. A faint metallic scent rises from her, reminding me of the strength coiled beneath her delicate exterior. She looks regal and dangerous, a perfect reflection of what lurks behind these academy walls—and in the hearts of those who live within them.

"Ziggy, you didn't have to." I kiss him softly, savoring the gentle warmth of his lips against mine, and pull away slowly.

"I hope you'll wear it. It was my mother's." His tone is gentle, and there's a quiet reverence in his eyes. Whatever is in this box means a lot to him, and I handle it with care as I move to the marble counter. The ancient stone feels chilled beneath my hand, a stark contrast to the warmth buzzing through my veins. I set the box down and loosen the ribbons.

Inside is a diadem—a simple circlet of titanium and moonstone. At its front, a cat's-eye-shaped stone dangles from a delicate peak. I run my fingers over the pale metal, which feels as light as a feather, yet somehow sturdier, as if it's both real and unreal at once. "Are you sure? It's so delicate."

He smiles and lifts it from the box, placing it on my head. The cool moonstone settles against my forehead, and the dangling gem sways slightly just above the space between my eyebrows.

"I'm sure," Ziggy says, voice hushed with affection. "I may not be able to give you a title or a nest or even cubs, but I can give you this." He presses a tender kiss to the stone, and then to me. "My mom was the leader of our den. This was her crown, for lack of a better term."

"You're a prince?" I arch a brow, shocked. A faint draft skitters along my neck, sending a chill down my spine.

"No, not a prince. Males don't rule in our society. Females do, just like dragonesses did once upon a time." He chuckles and offers me his arm. "Shall we join the others? Before Klauth kills Abraxis or Abraxis says something stupid to piss the old man off." His laugh, low and warm, vibrates through my chest, lightening the tension I've been carrying.

I laugh with him, letting the sound echo around us. "I get to see and hold my first niece or nephew—no one is dying today." I lean up and kiss him, the taste of his breath reminding me of smoky juniper, and in that moment, we're gone. The world shifts, and there's a muffled whoosh in my ears as he transports us to the rest of our group.

Both drakes say "Mate" and their twin growls draw a snicker from me. "Either you two play nice or I'll pick someone else's arm to hang on tonight." The flickering torchlight reveals Abraxis and Klauth exchanging sulky looks; it's almost comical the way they resemble reprimanded children.

"Mina!" Cerce's voice rings out, bright and melodic, over the hush of the room. The faint aroma of incense hangs in the air, and the soft glow of wall sconces dances across my mother-in-law's dress as I practically sprint over to hug her. We rub our jaws together, purring softly, a deep vibration resonating in my chest.

"Where's the little one?" My excitement crackles through me, and I feel like I'm about to bounce right out of my skin.

"With Cora." Cerce's gaze flickers to Klauth before returning to me. "Who is the new male?"

Heat flushes my cheeks as I gently draw Thauglor's egg from its silken pouch. The egg's surface is warm to the touch, a smooth black shell that gleams ominously under the firelight. Cerce's eyes lock on it, then dart to Klauth. Her posture changes instantly; she lowers her head in deference. "Your majesty, welcome back."

I raise an eyebrow, looking between Klauth and my mother-in-law, confusion gnawing at me. A slow realization dawns—he wasn't joking. Klauth really is ancient dragonic royalty, and Cerce knows who he is. My brow arches higher as I turn to him. He just smiles—smug asshole. I thought it was a joke, calling him that because of his age. No, they were serious.

"Breathe, Mina," Abraxis murmurs, resting his hand against my elbow. The warmth of his skin is calming, but the roaring in my ears doesn't quite subside.

I turn my gaze to Abraxis, meeting his calm stare. "Now is the time you choose not to be a wiseass ... I am mated to a dragon royal." My heart thunders in my chest, each beat echoing in my ears. The next thing I know, Klauth's crimson-flecked amber eyes are inches from mine.

He touches the tip of his nose to mine. The faint musk of old leather and embers envelops me, stirring my dragoness just beneath my skin. "My treasure. I am no more a royal anymore than you are. I could be if you wish it." He brushes his cheek against mine in soft arcs, and a soothing warmth floods my body. "Let's go meet the hatchling like you wanted." He presses a gentle kiss to my forehead before placing my hand on Abraxis's. "This is the nest of your family. I will defer the honor of walking with our mate to you."

Klauth steps back, and there's a lazy confidence in his movements—every tilt of his head seems perfectly controlled. I'm half-tempted to roll my eyes, but I can't deny how flawlessly he says and does exactly what will calm me.

"Shall we?" Abraxis offers softly, resting my hand on his forearm. The taut muscles beneath his sleeve remind me he's coiled for action if anything goes wrong.

"Yes, please." My voice trembles slightly with the remnants of adrenaline. I glance back over my shoulder at Klauth, my dragoness stirring for his approval. He gives me a subtle nod, and the tension in my shoulders eases. Turning back to Abraxis, I feel my pulse quicken again with anticipation—soon, I'll be meeting the hatchling. The air crackles with the promise of what's coming, and I can't wait.

It's a flurry of movement the minute we enter the main hall. The space smells faintly of old parchment and polished wood, an undercurrent of incense lingering in the air. Rows of chairs line both sides of the aisle like we've stumbled upon a grand elvish wedding. The echo of hurried footsteps and hushed voices surrounds us, every sound bouncing off the vaulted ceiling.

"Mina, you're needed up front." Cerce's voice cuts through the commotion. She takes my arm and guides me away from Abraxis, our steps quick as we rush down the aisle. The floor beneath us is cool, smooth stone, and my heels tap a brisk beat as we hurry. At the bottom, we head up a short flight of stairs and disappear behind a heavy curtain. The thick material rustles against my shoulders, carrying with it a faint musty scent of old stage dust.

A soft chirping noise makes my scales prickle along my shoulders. The sound is thin and reedy—urgent, almost like a plea. My dragoness stirs at the pit of my stomach, longing to soothe the tiny creature in distress. I push forward quickly, my heart thudding against my rib cage with each step.

Cora stands with her hatchling cradled to her chest, the little one squirming and protesting in her hold. "Mina, you came." Cora's voice is warm, though edged with relief, as she leans in to hug me carefully, mindful of the hatchling's delicate body.

"Of course I did." My gaze settles on the mostly black hatchling. Its scales catch the overhead lights, reflecting a faint iridescent sheen. My dragoness croons in the back of my mind, a subtle vibration that trembles through my bones. The little one turns its head, fixing tiny golden eyes on mine. I feel an odd shift in the surrounding air, a moment of stillness as if the entire hall is holding its breath.

"He never makes eye contact that long," Cora remarks, shifting the hatchling's weight. With a gentle but deliberate motion, she extends her arms and passes me her son.

I cradle the hatchling against my breasts, resting it over my heart. Its small claws graze my skin, and I sense the hatchling's rapid heartbeat thudding in time with my own. I keep up that gentle croon, letting the low hum resonate in my chest. The hatchling blinks and slowly stills, its eyelids drooping until it drifts into slumber.

"He was just overtired and way too excited about all the new people," I say, my voice soft, almost lost beneath the distant murmurs of onlookers shuffling nearby. The comforting weight and warmth of the baby in my arms tugs at some primal part of me.

"Do you want to carry him out since you are one of his guardians?" Cora asks, sliding in beside me. She rests her head lightly on my shoulder, gazing at her son with such tenderness it makes my chest ache.

"Of course. It would be my honor." I lean down and press a gentle kiss to the crown of Cora's head. A faint trace of floral soap and worry-tinged sweat fills my nostrils as I breathe her in. My attention flickers to her mate, whose eyes linger on me. "You've been behaving, I assume?" A low, warning growl rumbles in my throat as I stare at Warwick.

"Um, yes..." Warwick ducks his head quickly, avoiding my gaze.

"Let's get going." Cerce's smile lights up her face as she steps out from behind the curtain, guiding us onto the stage. Vox follows her, his firm hand at her elbow. I walk behind them, acutely aware of the hush that falls over the crowd as they catch sight of the hatchling sleeping against me. Warwick's brother matches my pace, his curious eyes roving over the bite marks and scaling on my shoulders. My skin prickles under his scrutiny; it feels like I'm being dissected under a microscope.

I want to strike him with lightning, I think, my jaw tensing. The overhead lights cast heavy shadows on the stage floor, adding to the tension coiling in my stomach.

'Mate? Why are you uneasy?' Klauth's voice slips into my mind just as we reach our designated positions at the front.

'*Warwick's brother has a staring problem. It makes my scales crawl.*' I can almost feel Klauth's protective instincts stir. '*Make Abraxis move closer. Maybe the male will get the hint. If not, you can give it to him personally.*' My gaze leaves the sleeping hatchling and shifts to meet Klauth's, then slides over to Abraxis. I see the moment he receives Klauth's message; his posture changes, and he prowls closer.

The ceremony begins, and an elder's voice drones on about the significance of a first son: ancient rites, lineage, and tradition swirl in the stale air. My attention drifts until I feel Cora motion to take back her hatchling. The minute she lifts him from my arms, he rouses with a jolt —chirping and flailing in panic. The flutter of his small wings against her chest sets my nerves on edge.

"The little one needs to take its human form," the elder announces, the timbre of his voice echoing through the hall. One by one, the grandparents try to coax the shift, but the hatchling thrashes in protest, high-pitched squeals echoing off the stage floor.

Cora passes the hatchling to Warwick; he too fails, frustration etched in the tight lines of his jaw. The little one remains stubborn, its black scales quivering with either fear or discomfort.

'*It will shift for you, mate. You are the dominant dragoness in the room.*' Klauth's certainty resonates through our bond.

I swallow, drawing in a deep breath of the incense-scented air. My heart pounds with anticipation as I step forward. "May I?" I ask, extending my arms. Cerce hands me the hatchling, who immediately stills against my palms. The gathered witnesses look on in silence, tension practically crackling like static.

I shift my eyes to the tiny dragon in my hold. There's a spreading warmth coursing through me, guided by my dragoness's instincts. Gently, I roll the hatchling onto its back and stare down at it, lowering my voice to a low, resonant tone. "Shift, little one. You are safe. I will burn the world to ash to protect you."

There's a palpable energy in the air, a subtle vibration that makes the hair on the back of my neck stand on end. Then, in the blink of an eye, the hatchling dissolves into a chunky baby boy. The smell of newborn skin—sweet and slightly milky—washes over me as I hold him.

His hair is black as midnight, and the eyes peering up at me have the same golden hue as Abraxis and Cora. "Welcome to the world, little one," I whisper, pressing a tender kiss to his forehead and placing him gently back into his mother's arms. Cora's tears glisten in the stage lights, relief radiating from every shaky breath she takes.

The elder resumes talking, droning on about ancient bloodlines and the power in their lineage. His words seem distant as I look over at the audience to spot Klauth. He's holding the silk purse that contains Thauglor—an ancestor set to hatch soon, though no one else here is aware.

I shift my gaze to my nephew as the elder dabs anointing oil on his tiny forehead. Cora beams down at her son, and I can't help the small smile that tugs at my lips. Twice now, I've done what the others couldn't— first saving Cora and her egg, and now guiding her son's shift. The tension in the hall lifts, replaced by an undercurrent of awe.

Today, I decide, is a good day indeed.

past the dryness in my mouth. My palms feel clammy, and I rub them against my thighs. "She doesn't like being spoken about."

"She is being recognized as the strongest dragoness in the room. How is this not a good thing?" Klauth tilts his head, confusion etched across his features. The ambient hum of the crowd crescendos behind us, and I catch the faint smell of spiced wine on someone's breath nearby.

"They are looking at her as breeding stock," I explain. My voice comes out more bitter than I intend. "Abraxis is a feared general, Mina a powerful dragoness in her own right." The weight of these facts sits like a stone in my gut, and I notice how the color drains from Klauth's face.

Abraxis returns, his formidable silhouette cutting through the torch lit haze. There's a tension in the set of his shoulders, and when he looks at the crowd, his eyes blaze with unadulterated rage. I swear I can feel the heat of his fury radiating across the distance. He hears the whispers too, and he roars at the gathering, the sound vibrating through my ribcage. Some onlookers flinch, and a wave of murmurs follows.

"My mate is not breeding stock," he bellows, voice echoing off the high-arched ceiling. I see the color drain from Mina's face, but there's a spark of defiance in her eyes as well.

Vox wisely ushers Mina off the stage and out of sight. Her retreating form, with those shimmering scales glinting under the torchlight, burns into my vision. I grab Klauth's hand and drag him along, weaving through the press of bodies. The rest of the nest follows close behind, leaving Abraxis to deal with the masses. The crowd parts for us, some stepping back warily, as though afraid to brush against the tension clinging to us.

When we finally catch up, Mina paces in a dim corridor, her growls echoing off the stone walls. The sharp click of her talons sends a shiver down my spine. The smell of her agitation—a mix of adrenaline and something distinctly dragonic—hangs in the air.

"I will not be trapped in an egg chamber," she yells, voice reverberating. Bits of dust sift from the ceiling, and the pitch of her fury raises gooseflesh on my arms.

She whips around to face us, eyes wild, and I see the truth there—*she's scared*. My heart clenches. Carefully, I step forward, both hands raised. My pulse pounds so loudly I wonder if she can hear it. "Mina, no one is going to put you in an egg chamber. We will not allow that to ever happen. Worst case, I'll sit on my nest in the chamber on the eggs," I joke, trying to chase the darkness from her eyes.

Mina stops pacing. A shaky laugh slips from her lips, and I feel the tension in the corridor ease just a fraction. The sweet sound of her laughter—unexpected and raw—sparks relief in my chest. The soft rumbling purr of her dragon follows, an undercurrent that makes my nerves settle. She moves fast, closing the distance and diving into my arms. I hold her tight, inhaling the warm, musky scent of her hair and the faint tang of dragon essence that clings to her.

"Will you build me a big nest?" she asks, pressing a playful kiss to the underside of my jaw. The dryness in my mouth from earlier disappears, replaced by a sudden rush of warmth. I catch Klauth raising an eyebrow, clearly surprised by Mina's submissive gesture toward me.

"Whatever size you desire. What size are dragon eggs?" I try to keep my voice steady as I stare into Mina's eyes. She just shrugs.

"Cora's was this big." She holds her hands apart, roughly the size of a grapefruit.

"That's small. It's because she did it as a human," Klauth chimes in, stepping closer. He gently pulls Mina's hands farther apart, demonstrating the correct size—closer to a watermelon. My stomach tightens as I see Mina's eyes dart between her hands, her expression dropping.

Her gaze flicks up to me, silently begging for reassurance. I place a calming hand on her shoulder. "Mina, your dragoness can easily pass an egg that size. Considering it's your first clutch and you're young, you may have slightly smaller eggs." I do my best to sound matter-of-fact, and when I glare at Klauth, he clamps his mouth shut.

"The one-eye glare thing is creepy," Klauth mutters, turning away to pour Mina a glass of wine. The rich aroma of fermented grapes fills the air as he hands it to her. I press a light kiss to Mina's temple, noting the tension in her posture melt as she sips the wine.

My attention snaps to the door when Abraxis strides in. The look on his face is grim—he's fuming, nostrils flared, his clawed fingers twitching at his sides. I swallow hard and glance down at Mina. "Why don't you go with Ziggy and take a nice hot bath? When I get home, we can figure out what kind of nest you want."

"Sounds good." She bounces up and kisses my lips, then moves between all the other mates with quick, soft touches of affection. Leander grabs her arm, and together with Ziggy, they whisk away through the heavy oak door. Once they're gone, the stillness in the room seems to amplify the scent of tension and leftover adrenaline.

I round on Abraxis, crossing my arms over my chest. "What happened?"

He exhales roughly, the breath hissing through his teeth. "I was made no less than twelve offers for betrothals when everyone saw what Mina did—and her scales." He shakes his head, walking over to the minibar. The distinct clink of glass on glass echoes as he pours himself a drink. The sharp aroma of whiskey wafts through the space.

"Mina will be furious," Klauth says, leaning against the bar with his bourbon in hand. His tone is flat, but his eyes gleam with seriousness. "You can tell her, since it's your family's den it happened in."

I rub the back of my neck, still standing by the wall. "Wait until they figure out who you are, Klauth, and how many offers are made after that. This is just the tip of the iceberg."

"Mina doesn't wish to betroth her hatchlings. She will torch the world, and I will help her do it," Klauth murmurs. The slow, dangerous conviction in his voice sends a slight chill through me.

"The betrothal system has been in place for hundreds of years," Abraxis retorts, downing his drink. His eyes dart around the room as though expecting someone else to jump in.

Klauth's lips curl into something that's almost a snarl. "It didn't exist in my day. You asked for a bride's hand after she was of age. We didn't betroth our hatchlings to older drakes." He arches a brow, daring Abraxis to challenge him. The tension crackles in the air, and I shift my stance, uneasy.

"Do you think you can change it?" Abraxis steps closer. The flickering torchlight plays across his tensed arms, emphasizing his clenched fists.

"When Mina is ready, we will announce my resurrection, so to speak," Klauth replies, slamming back the last of his bourbon. The force of it makes the glass clink loudly against his teeth. "The temple of Bahamut will verify who I am for those that need proof."

Before I can comment, Ziggy reappears to take the rest of us away. The rush of air that follows his arrival stirs the lingering smoke and whiskey fumes, making my eyes water. I shove my unease down, gripping Klauth's forearm as we ready ourselves to leave. Mina is waiting, and I can almost feel her anxious energy from here. One way or another, we'll do whatever it takes to protect her—and any future hatchlings—from a system that threatens her freedom.

When we finally arrive back at our suite in Malivore, the entire house feels like it's holding its breath. My footsteps echo on the polished floors, and a subtle draft tugs at the hem of my jacket, sending a faint chill up my spine. Despite the oppressive stillness, there's a lingering hint of damp air—like someone just ran the shower and left the steam to seep into every corner. Sure enough, the bathroom door stands wide open, and wet footprints trail across the tiles and down the hall, each print glistening under the dim light.

What really catches my attention, though, is the sheet of paper sitting on the cool marble of the kitchen island. The stone's smooth surface is cold against my fingertips as I pick up the sketch. Mina has drawn a sandstone room with a gryphon nest tucked in one corner. The nest looks rugged, lined with iridescent feathers that I can practically imagine rustling in a soft breeze. In the center, four dragon eggs rest among tufts of down, each egg rendered with a delicate, almost reverent touch. A subtle pang of longing grips my chest—this is far more than a simple drawing.

"I guess I know what kind of nest Mina wants," I say, my voice echoing in the hush. I hold out the sketch, and Klauth takes it from me. The paper rustles with a slight crackle, the only sound in the otherwise silent space.

"Ah, it's in the new egg chamber I dug for her," Klauth explains in a wistful tone, his gaze drifting across the drawing. "That corner is the most even temperature. There will be an equal chance for male and female hatchlings." The warmth in his voice contrasts with the chill of the room.

"What am I missing?" Abraxis asks, his eyes flicking between us. I can sense his unease in the tense line of his jaw. It seems our mate hasn't been filled in on what she did.

"That's Mina's story to tell," I murmur, the weight of impending conflict sending a prickle of electricity through my limbs.

"What's my story to tell?" Mina's voice cuts in, and I turn. She emerges from my bedroom wearing my sweats and a T-shirt that's a little too large for her, the fabric brushing her thighs. Her hair is still slightly damp, and the faint scent of her shampoo—something floral and earthy—reaches me.

I step closer, wrapping one arm around her shoulders. Under my palm, I can feel the place where her implant once sat. The skin is still tender, and she stiffens for a split second when I press there. Her eyebrows shoot up, accusation clear in her eyes, and I can hear her sharp intake of breath.

"Oh," she finally says, looking between Klauth and Ziggy. She backs up until she meets Ziggy's chest, reaching for his arms so he can enfold her from behind. The room smells faintly of stone and damp cloth, but now there's also the spike of tension—like charged air before a storm.

"I took out my implant," she announces. Her voice is steady, though I hear the tiniest edge of apprehension. "I want my first clutch and to have control over my body instead of almost killing you and your father again."

The words hit like a thunderclap. Balor sputters into his drink, coughing violently. Leander, who's just stepped into the kitchen, catches the mood immediately and pivots on his heel, slipping away before all hell breaks loose. Vaughn shifts to his gargoyle form with a low growl, stone scraping against bone in a way that sets my teeth on edge.

Abraxis stands there, mouth working silently as if he's tasting the air for the right response. Klauth squares his shoulders, turning to face Abraxis fully. "Anything less than *I support your decision* will result in us stepping outside to discuss this like drakes do," Klauth warns, his voice as cold as the marble beneath my hand.

Abraxis's eyes widen. He nods, his posture stiff and uncertain. "Is this truly what you want?" he finally manages, sounding as though someone just drained every last ounce of certainty from him.

"I do," Mina says, letting out a breath that seems to have been locked in her lungs. "The chemicals aren't good for me, and almost killing

people just because it's safer for me to sleep isn't the best game plan."
She snorts a laugh, pushing away from Ziggy's chest. "If a great wyrm
can't contain me, the world is in deep shit."

A small shiver courses down my spine at her casual prophecy of chaos.
Then she crosses the kitchen, taking my hand in hers—her grip is
warm, pulsing with life. She leads me into my room without another
word, leaving the others behind in the charged silence. The faint echo
of her footsteps mingles with my own, and I can't help but wonder
how the night will unfold.

I guess I know who she's sleeping with tonight.

When I roll out of bed, my feet sink into the thick rug, and the chill of the morning air coasts over my bare thighs. Callan stands on the other side, pulling on a fresh shirt. I slip my uniform dress over my head, feeling the crisp fabric slide along my skin.

"Who's walking you to class today?" he asks, buttoning his pants.

"I'm going to take Klauth with me. Ziggy is available until the end of second period, but I'd rather use him as an escape option," I say softly, snapping the dark green Shadowcarve ribbon around my waist. The faint rustle of the ribbon reminds me of a coiled serpent, making me feel both dangerous and protected.

"Are you considering his offer?" Callan steps close, the warmth of his body radiating across my shoulder.

I lower my eyes to my backpack and the empty egg carrier peeking from it. "I am. But it's something I feel I need to discuss with Abraxis alone." The thought weighs heavily on my heart. Part of me doesn't want to abandon the surname I chose. The other, Klauth's name— savage and ancient—holds more weight and could afford the nest more respect.

"Makes sense, Mina. I mean, you could take one of your other mates' names. Willamina Whitlocke sounds rather esteemed." He smiles at me, and I can almost taste his amusement on the air.

"Hmm ... If I wish to sound like an aristocrat, I will consider your surname first." I lean in, pressing a playful kiss to his lips, before padding out into the main sitting room. My bare feet make a light tapping noise on the polished floor.

A rich, roasted scent of coffee greets me as I pass the kitchen island, where the guys gather with steaming mugs in hand. There's a subtle undercurrent of tension in the air. Maybe I'm imagining it, or maybe it's just the usual buzz of morning energy in a place like this. I cross the room and step outside onto the balcony.

A cool gust of wind lifts my hair as I enter my miniature poison garden. The thick, earthy fragrance of damp soil mingles with the heady perfume of belladonna blooms. My breath catches at the sight of those glossy black berries hidden beneath the dusky leaves. They look like little glistening drops of night. I crouch beneath the low-hanging branches of the bush, retrieving Thauglor's egg with careful hands.

"Good morning, Thauglor." The shell is smooth and unexpectedly warm against my palms. I press my lips to it and smile when I feel a faint pulse—like a tiny heartbeat under my fingers.

"I imagined what you looked like when you spoke to us a hundred times," Klauth says, leaning on the doorframe. Behind him, the shadowed interior of our living quarters stands in stark contrast to the sunlight here. "My imagination pales compared to what you really do."

"I loved you from the moment I felt you respond to me." I gently run my fingertips over the egg's shifting patterns. A soft hum vibrates my palm, and I chuckle. "He's happy he's the center of attention now."

The belladonna leaves brush against my dress as I move past them to check the rest of my poison garden. A bitter, almost metallic tang lingers in the air—the promise of toxic power in each leaf, petal, and root. The watering can in my hand gurgles softly as I give a few plants a light drink.

"You realize most of the things in here can kill you, right?" Klauth says, motioning for me to step out. His gaze flicks from me to the menacing plants.

"They can kill you, not me. I apparently have the immunity of both my parents' species of dragons." I kiss Klauth's lips as I pass. The warmth of him is a stark contrast to the cool morning air, and the faint hint of coffee on his breath makes me smile.

Back inside, the warmth is instant and comforting. My nose picks up the scents of toast and lingering bacon grease from breakfast. Abraxis stands at the counter with a printout of my classes in hand, eyebrows raised.

"Mina, did you change your schedule?" he asks.

My stomach knots. "Yes. I felt with how I want to live my life, some classes are needed more than others." Reaching into my backpack, I pull out several folded sheets of paper, smoothing their edges on the counter. "Tactically, I want to rebuild what's left of my father's home at the base of the mountain."

"But you hate that place," Balor says, handing me a mug of coffee. The steam rises in delicate curls, and the first sip is a welcome burst of bitterness on my tongue.

"I do, and I will never live there. But we need a place to hold functions and house others that wish to join my flight. Like Cora and her dipshit mate." Ziggy unfolds my rough drawings on the table. Pencil marks outline the broken walls and potential expansions. "They need a place to live, and it's not with me in my home."

"Cora and her mate will never be able to defend themselves. At least in my territory, they can feel safe. Selfishly, I'll have my nephew close." I lift my chin, challenging anyone to argue.

"Do you think she'll accept?" Abraxis arches a brow.

I slide a piece of correspondence between me and his sister across the table. "She and Warwick accept, and his family offers to help with construction." Finishing my coffee, I savor the last bitter dregs. "Warwick's people are already on site, starting renovations in the lower living spaces. It's the tithe I require for them to be under our protection."

Setting my mug down, I catch the faint aroma of spiced coffee rising from its contents—earthy and a little bitter, though it does nothing to soothe me. My fingers tremble with pent-up energy as I stare at my hand, watching my nails lengthen into razor-edged talons. The dim light in the kitchen casts flickering shadows on the worn wooden table, and a low, involuntary growl rumbles from deep in my chest, reverberating through my ribs.

"They wish to discuss a betrothal." The words taste foul on my tongue. My lips peel back in a silent snarl, and I'm acutely aware of how the skin around my mouth stretches taut. "I told them they can petition for the hand of one of my children when they are old enough to make their own decisions." My gaze locks with Klauth's. His eyes flick with silent acknowledgment, and he gives me a terse nod of approval. The slight shift in his stance and the faint heat radiating from him help quell the prickling tension beneath my skin.

"But that's not how it's done," Abraxis says as he steps closer, gently enclosing my taloned hands in his. His touch is warm and firm, the calluses on his palms rasping against my skin.

"That's how it will be done," I snarl, voice rough, "or they will deal with my rage." A spike of pressure ripples across my cheeks and brow, and I feel the bone plates shift in my face. My snarl intensifies. "I will not risk binding one of my daughters with a male who is unworthy."

The protest in my throat rises again until I feel Klauth's mouth clamp down on his mate mark on my neck. His growl resonates against my skin, sending a shiver across my shoulders. The faint coppery tang of blood fills my nostrils as my scales brush against his teeth—his way of grounding me.

'Settle, mate. I agree with you. The youngling will have to deal with your decisions, or you simply don't let him have a hatchling.' Klauth's presence in my mind soothes me like a gentle hum. I exhale slowly, letting the tension slip from my muscles. I retract my talons and force the growl to fade. The moment he feels me tilt my head in submission, he finally releases his grip. I can still feel the warmth of his breath against my neck.

"You and Mina were lucky you were mates," Leander says, stepping forward with a steaming veggie omelet that smells of peppers and fresh herbs. There's a wistful undertone to his voice. "I can't imagine allowing my daughter to enter a contract with a male she doesn't love." He offers me the plate, and my stomach rumbles in response—my appetite returning now that my anger has slightly cooled.

"You were ready to hide your sister from Attor," Balor reminds Abraxis, his voice low as he moves between the two of us like a living barrier. "You wanted her to have the same experience you did—finding your mate."

Abraxis sighs, dipping his head. "Traditions are hard to break when it's all you've known." His words are almost lost beneath the distant clatter of dishes and hushed whispers in the corridor beyond.

Klauth shifts behind me and places a reassuring hand on Abraxis's shoulder, giving it a firm squeeze. "Change only happens when you fight for it. Otherwise, history is doomed to repeat itself."

The room is still, the air thick with the aftertaste of our heated discussion. I breathe in slowly, letting the tension drain, and allow the comforting scents of spiced coffee and warm food to settle over me like a tentative peace.

I FINISH MY BREAKFAST, savoring the last bite of warm toast slathered with rich butter, the salty sweetness lingering on my tongue. The faint scent of eggs and bacon still hangs in the air, mingling with the crisp morning chill that seeps in from the open window. Rising from the table, I move to kiss all of my mates goodbye, enjoying the mix of scents—warm fur, cool scales, rough stone—each one a distinct reminder of whom I'm leaving behind.

"Come on, Klauth. Let's get me to class." My voice echoes softly in the living room. Daylight spills in through tall windows, catching the swirling dust motes, and casts long shadows across Vaughn's stony form in the corner.

"He's taking you?" Abraxis asks, stepping closer. I catch the faint, musky scent of his skin—dark and alluring.

"You, Callan, and Balor all have classes all day," I say with a resigned sigh, running a hand over my notebooks. "Leander has midday classes to teach, Ziggy too. Vaughn can't be in my class because…" I gesture at his rigid silhouette. "He's a giant paperweight right now."

"Do you have a clue where his amulet is?" Ziggy's voice carries a note of worry, and I arch a brow.

"I haven't been able to see it. I've tried," I admit, tucking my notebooks —edges still sharp and pages smelling of fresh ink—into my backpack. My new pens and pencils clatter softly as I slide them into the side pocket. "I'll find it eventually," I add, determination prickling my skin.

From the kitchen counter, I pluck two apples, their cool skins glossy beneath my fingertips, and drop them into the outer pouch of my bag. My gaze lingers on the egg carrier; I slip it on and buckle it snugly, feeling a reassuring warmth where the egg rests close to my body. A soft rustle of fabric greets me as I pull my jacket over both me and the egg and zip it up.

"See everyone later." With a wave, I head for the door, Klauth's presence solid and comforting at my side. His warmth contrasts with the chill of the hallway beyond.

"Where to, my treasure?" He takes my hand, the roughness of his scales against my palm sending a pleasant shiver up my arm.

"Arcanum campus for the science class." I pull my schedule from my pocket, the paper crackling as I unfold it. "Apparently, it's the science of mate selection and pheromones." I can't help the wry smirk curling my lips. "Yet another pointless class for me. I have my mates and one on the way." My hand drifts to the egg carrier, and I smile down at my jacket, feeling the reassuring weight.

"They have to teach about mates and pheromones? Whatever happened to dragon instincts?" Klauth shakes his head, amusement rumbling in his chest before he leans down and brushes his lips over my forehead. A spark of his warmth lingers on my skin. "Let's see what this institution offers."

We leave Malivore and walk by the lake shore, the air cool and carrying the briny scent of the Sea of Whispers. Gulls circle overhead, their distant cries echoing across the water. The shoreline is smooth, pebbled, with black stones that crunch under our feet as we head toward the southern dorms. Cutting past the cove, we take a turn northeast. The breeze picks up, rustling the leaves in nearby trees—a gentle hush that brushes my hair away from my cheeks.

"It's a beautiful campus," Klauth says, nodding at the towering spires of Arcanum in the distance. "I remember watching its construction from my balcony."

"What was it like back then?" I step closer to him, relishing the warmth he radiates against the brisk wind.

"Wilder," he replies, eyes flicking toward the horizon. "Threats everywhere. Battles for territory, battles to keep territory. Yearly displays for when the females migrated, searching for males worth giving them offspring." He gestures toward the skyline, where ancient battlements and new buildings clash in a strange architectural dance.

"Females approached the males?" I ask, glancing up at him in surprise.

"It's why we would make grand displays when we were willing to take a mate." His smile is tinged with nostalgia, and he kisses my temple. "I dug you a nest instead of making a public spectacle. Better use of my time and energy."

"I agree. Abraxis made one within Shadowcarve," I say, remembering the crisp scent of fresh wood and the warmth of newly turned earth. "He nailed his to the tall wooden walls."

"That was his display?" Klauth arches a brow, looking genuinely intrigued.

"Yeah," I answer with a shrug as we reach the entrance to Arcanum. The grand stone steps are worn smooth by countless students over the years, and the building's tall doors creak as Klauth holds one open for me. A faint smell of chalk dust and old books washes over me when I step inside. "I guess it worked for him, too."

We climb the stairs to the lecture hall, our footsteps muffled by the threadbare carpet. My skin tingles in the stuffy warmth of the corridor, and I scan the white walls lined with old portraits and dusty fixtures before finding the correct door. Klauth follows me in, and we settle at the far back near an exit, the seats squeaking in protest under our weight.

"Today's class is going to be on the science of mate selection," Kai announces from the front of the room, marker squeaking against the whiteboard. The fluorescent lights overhead flicker softly, their hum joining the scattered whispers of other students. I note each point he writes, though my mind drifts as I watch Klauth gazing at the vaulted ceiling, curiosity flickering in his crimson flecked amber eyes.

Kai calls on the females in the room, one by one. My heartbeat quickens, a prickle of nerves threading through me as I think of what to say. Arista answers first, mentioning her three mates. Anxiety twists in my stomach—when Kai's gaze finally lands on me, my pulse throbs in my ears.

"Miss Mina, mind sharing with the class?" His tone is polite but firm.

I stand, feeling Klauth's hand at the small of my back—a solid reminder of his support. "I have seven mates," I say with a steady voice. "A black dragon, a red dragon, a basilisk, a gryphon, a displacer beast, a nightmare, and a gargoyle." Arista's eyes widen, her jaw practically hitting the desk. The corner of my mouth lifts in a triumphant smile, and I give her a playful wink before Klauth tugs me back down onto his lap.

He brushes his lips over the mark on my neck and rumbles softly, a reassuring vibration against my spine. Despite being the strongest dragon on the continent, he's a snuggler—and I can't help but melt into him. The steady rhythm of his breathing grounding me in this strange, crowded classroom.

tory, a sharp reminder that while most students are winding down, I'm just starting my day. I feel like such a burden to the nest, it's not even funny. They moved my night with Mina to Saturday, so classwork doesn't cut into my time with her.

"Hey Vaughn." Her voice, warm and lilting, greets me as she comes through the front door after her training. She smells like the night breeze and faint sweat—tangible proof of her hard work.

I close the distance and hug her tightly before kissing her. My senses flood with the sweet scent of her skin and the warmth of her body against mine. The soft rumble of her dragoness warms my soul. There is so much love in her heart, and I'm honestly shocked considering how she was raised. "What class did you have tonight?"

"Archery and weapons." She smiles and motions to Klauth as he comes through the door behind her. A slight gust of cool air follows him in. "Someone's a little rusty." Mina winks before heading to her room to grab clothes.

"You try being cursed and trapped in a dreamless sleep for a thousand years and see what happens." Klauth's voice is low and gravelly, carrying a faint undertone of centuries spent in silence. He shakes his head and looks at me, extending his hand. I can smell a hint of dust and old parchment on him, like he's been rummaging through the academy's long-forgotten corners. "Are you well?" he asks.

I grasp his hand. "I feel much better knowing you're able to be with Mina all day, keeping her safe," I say, smiling as relief settles over me. Even though I can't be by her side constantly, at least someone I trust is.

"Now, if we can get the youngling to be as sensible, it would be help-ful." Klauth grumbles a little before heading toward the kitchen counter, his footsteps echoing on the polished floor.

"Don't be late for your training." Mina's voice drifts from the bathroom door. She brushes past me, the faint smell of her soap trailing in the air as she presses a quick kiss to my cheek.

"I'll see you later," I call over my shoulder before leaving the suite. The corridor is dimly lit by old wall sconces, casting flickering shadows that make everything look slightly ominous. I walk until I am out of the building and into the open night. The sky is clear, spattered with stars, and the moon hangs low like a curious eye. The fresh air, tinged with the scent of damp grass, fills my lungs as I shift to my gargoyle form. My skin hardens, my senses sharpen, and with a powerful leap, I'm airborne.

Flying to Shadowcarve is always a rush—wind whipping past my stone-like wings, the academy grounds below me silent and sprawling. I spot the large courtyard, lit by torches lining the perimeter. When I land, my claws scraping the stone with a metallic screech, I find Abraxis and Balor training with dual-wielding swords. The ring is a circle of packed dirt, ringed by tall stands. The air here smells of sweat, iron, and the faint tang of tension.

I duck into the locker room, the overhead fluorescent lights flickering with a dull hum. I can almost taste the stale odor of well-worn leather and disinfectant. I slip into my own leathers, the material snug and smelling faintly of me—an odd blend of stone dust and night air. Stepping back out to the ring, the chill of the evening air pinches my exposed skin, and adrenaline tingles in my fingertips.

"I'm ready when you are." I stand by the weapons rack, waiting to be told what we're working with today. My eyes flick over the array of blades, noting how the torchlight gleams off their sharp edges.

"Grab a matched set of short swords. Mina kicked my ass today with them and made me look bad in front of Klauth." Abraxis's voice is rough, and he rubs at a bruise forming along his forearm. His eyes flick with simmering annoyance.

"Mina beat you? How is that even possible?" I ask, looking between Abraxis and Balor. The crunch of gravel underfoot reminds me to keep my stance loose, ready for anything.

"As a dragoness takes mates, she becomes stronger. The strength of the mate directly affects her strength." Balor's voice is steady, and he crosses his arms over his chest. I almost drop my swords, my grip momentarily going slack.

"So that means..." I turn, gaze drifting toward the distant outline of the Malivore Conservatory, where Mina should be settling in for her shower.

"Yes, she has the strength of a great wyrm and all our shifts." Balor answers as Abraxis grumbles under his breath. A faint breeze stirs the torch flames, throwing flickering shadows across Abraxis's scowling features.

"Remind me not to piss her off." I take a fighting stance, both swords held at the ready, the worn leather hilt fitting perfectly against my palms. My heart beats faster at the thought of Mina's growing power.

"Are you aware Mina wants her first clutch of eggs?" Abraxis asks, lunging forward with both swords. The clang of steel against steel echoes in the night air. I block and parry before his words register.

"How? Why?" I strike back, sending one sword high and the other slicing low. The friction of metal jars my arms, and I grit my teeth against the impact.

"She took out her implant apparently after her bonding with Klauth. Females of stronger lines can control when they reproduce. She doesn't want to hurt us when it's time to sedate her." Balor answers, his voice measured, as Abraxis rains down blows. The sound is thunderous, each strike sharper and angrier than the last.

"If I remember right, she overpowered everyone until Balor made her pass out." I throw Abraxis off his game by mentioning that. It's his greatest perceived failure to date, and a flicker of irritation crosses his face. He presses his lips into a hard line, stepping back just enough to glare at me through the dim torchlight.

I steady my breathing, my focus split between Abraxis's next strike and the tumult of emotions roiling within me. Mina's getting stronger. She wants a clutch of eggs, and I'm barely keeping up in class and in training. Yet somehow, despite all the chaos, I feel more alive than I have in a long time.

Training went about as well as expected. My muscles still tingle from exertion, and the faint tang of sweat lingers on my skin. Abraxis seems uneasy—like the raw scent of discomfort that hangs around him, sharp and acrid. He's feeling inadequate compared to Klauth. I can understand that feeling. It's how I feel most of the time when I look at his's imposing form.

When we get back to the apartment, the air is warm, smelling faintly of buttered popcorn and the distinctive musk of our nest. The low hum of a movie's soundtrack filters through the small living room. The glow from the TV bathes Mina in the flickering light as she snuggles in Klauth's arms, her feet perched in Leander's lap. Callan sits on the floor between Klauth's feet, and Mina idly runs her fingers through his hair. Ziggy is perched on the arm of the chair, popping kernels of popcorn into Mina's mouth at intervals. The atmosphere is surprisingly peaceful, despite the tension I sense humming beneath the surface.

"We're back," I announce. My voice feels a little scratchy, the dryness of my throat a reminder of the dust and heat from training. Mina looks over Klauth's shoulder and smiles, warmth radiating from her in waves.

"The movie just started. Get cleaned up and join us," she says, wrapping her arms around Klauth's neck. There's something about the way she looks at us, over the back of the couch, that momentarily steals the tension from my muscles.

"Maybe I'll skip it," Abraxis mutters, his voice tinged with a low resonance of bitterness. He heads into his room, the slight slam of his door betraying his frustration.

The joy on Mina's face falters, and she sighs before turning back to watch the movie. Shaking my head, I follow Abraxis and knock on his door. There's a slight echo in the narrow hallway, and I can hear the muffled drone of the movie through the walls. After several moments, he answers the door in just a towel, steam from a recent shower swirling around him, carrying the faint scent of soap and something spicy—his usual body wash.

"What?" he growls. I notice his shoulders are tense, and the water droplets running down his arms catch the overhead light, making him look even more on edge.

"Before you drive a wedge, you cannot repair in yours and Mina's relationship, you better get out there and talk to her," I say, tilting my head. I catch the faint flicker of pain in his eyes.

"What do you know?" Abraxis's tone is wary—he feels unworthy, and it spills out in each syllable. I catch the subtle clench of his jaw, the tension rolling off him.

"I know that what you're feeling is how most of us felt every day when you were the center of Mina's world." My voice is steady, but I can't keep all the exasperation out. "I, for one, will be present for our mate while I'm awake." I turn my back on him, the soft swish of his towel moving across the carpet the only sign he hasn't already slammed the door.

It isn't easy to walk away, but I refuse to miss out on time with Mina. When I get back to the living room, the buttery scent of popcorn is even stronger, and the TV's glow flickers across Mina's face. I grab Mina's favorite juice from the fridge—apple, spiced with a hint of cinnamon—and some extra popcorn for Ziggy to feed her.

"Here, baby." I offer her the drink, brushing my fingers lightly against hers. She beams at me, and I swear my chest tightens with a familiar warmth.

"Thanks, Vaughn." Her smile is bright, and it melts away some of the tension swirling in the room.

"What are we watching?" Abraxis's voice makes me turn my head. He's hovering in the doorway now, shoulders still set, but I detect an attempt at calm.

Before anyone can move, Mina jumps up. The couch cushions squeak as she pushes off, launching herself at Abraxis. The impact knocks him on his rear, pinning him to the floor. I can almost feel the vibration in the floorboards at their collision.

Abraxis laughs—a deep, throaty sound—and strokes Mina's sides as she sits on his chest. My heartbeat quickens because I see the moment her dragonic instincts flare: she goes for his throat. Before she can complete the motion, Klauth's presence rushes across the room. He grips her tightly, muscles rippling under his shirt as he pulls her off Abraxis and rips her upward. The shock of it makes the hair on the back of my neck prickle.

"I'm starting to see where the issue is." Klauth's voice rumbles as he holds Mina suspended, looking down at Abraxis. "You let your female dominate you. She pinned you, and you didn't even fight back. It's why her dragoness almost tore you and your father apart last season." Klauth sets Mina down and offers Abraxis a hand up, but his gaze is stern. "You need to get her dragoness to respect you; otherwise, the next fertile period she is going to rip more than scales off you." Klauth turns away, going to sit on the couch. The leather groans softly under his weight.

My thoughts flash to that violent memory. I know Balor and Abraxis still bear scars from the last cycle. The crisp smell of ozone floods my memory—and the tang of blood that seemed to cling to the air for days. If Balor hadn't gotten Mina to pass out, Abraxis or his father might have died.

Mina's eyes dart between Abraxis and Klauth, her posture rigid, before she crawls onto Leander's lap, pressing her nose under his chin. There's a softness to her surrender when she's with him. An acceptance of his nature that's vastly different from how she treats the rest of us. Klauth shakes his head, watching her submit to the nightmare of the group—the prey animal, in theory, of all creatures. Yet she's so gentle with Leander.

"Mina?" I call softly, trying to keep my voice soothing. Her gaze flicks to me, and I give her a small, understanding smile. "Can I ask you a question?"

She sits up a bit, wrapping her arm around Leander's neck. "Of course."

I move and sit on the floor in front of her, the fibers of the carpet rough beneath my palms. "Why do you submit to Leander and Callan? Balor and I, you press your cheek to ours. Ziggy, you alternate between pressing your nose under his jaw or his cheek. I'm just curious." I keep my hands up, nonthreatening, feeling the tension in the room gather like storm clouds.

Mina stands and starts pacing. The worn apartment floor creaks under her shifting weight. "Leander and Callan need to know I'm not going to hurt them," she says, her eyes lowering. When she looks up, I see the slitted pupils—her dragon side is near the surface. "They're precious and soft-skinned like Ziggy, but Ziggy's shift can use its poison barbs on me." She bites her bottom lip, looking momentarily haunted. "We tested it in a controlled setting. Ziggy's neurotoxin works on me. Generalized paralysis for almost three hours."

"You poisoned Mina?" Abraxis roars, the timbre of his voice vibrating through the floor. Mina immediately moves between them, letting out a warning growl. I catch a bitter tang in the air—adrenaline.

"No, we harvested a little of the toxin and stuck a needle in it. Then inserted it in the tip of my pinky," Mina explains, staring at that pinky as though it betrayed her. "It was numb for almost three hours. Ziggy and I wanted to test it in case the nest needed a way to stop me."

"What about me and Balor? Why touch our cheeks?" I ask, trying to maintain composure for Klauth's sake, but curiosity gnaws at me.

Mina looks away, a soft growl rumbling in her throat. "Balor's shift proved its point. It can knock me out. Gargoyles are practically indestructible."

"Do you perceive them as a threat or prey?" Klauth's question cuts through the tension, his tone clinical.

"Potential threat," she admits, eyes cast down.

"What about me? What am I?" Klauth presses, voice low but insistent.

"Eminent threat. Even though I know you would never hurt me on purpose," Mina whispers, and I watch the subtle shift of bone plates under her skin, the sign of her dragon features threatening to emerge.

"What about me, Mina?" Abraxis asks, stepping closer and using the side of his index finger to tilt her chin up. His voice resonates with something like regret.

A deep rumble grows in her chest as she shuts her eyes. "I don't want to answer."

"You need to answer, even if it's just to me, my treasure," Klauth urges, stepping closer. Abraxis stands rigidly beside him, the tension radiating from every line of his body. Klauth's eyes dart between them. "I see..." He sighs. "This changes things. Abraxis, a word, please." Klauth jerks his head toward the balcony, and the chilly night air rushes in when he opens the door.

As soon as they step out, Mina collapses into my arms. I feel the wetness of her tears soaking into my shirt, and I stroke her back, inhaling the subtle floral scent of her hair mixed with the salt of tears. Outside, Klauth, and Abraxis stand on the balcony, their silhouettes framed by the moonlight. Klauth leans casually on the rail, but the tension in Abraxis's stance is clear—his wings flicker in the night breeze.

"What did you tell Klauth?" I ask softly as Balor edges closer.

"I don't see Abraxis as a threat," Mina murmurs, burying her face in my chest. "I'm bigger than him now, and I can overpower him easily."

"Lee, you're the feelings guy," I say, glancing at Leander, whose empathy is palpable even in the dim light. "Mind taking Mina and helping her relax?"

I press a gentle kiss to Mina's lips, feeling her warmth. "I love you, Mina."

"I love you too, Vaughn," she whispers. She follows Leander into his room, and I hear the door click softly behind them. Her laughter floats through the air not long after, the sound fragile yet comforting.

"I had a feeling that was the problem," Balor murmurs, leaning against the back of the couch. I can still feel a subtle tension thrumming in the apartment, a storm brewing behind closed doors.

"But why does she still see us as a threat? I don't get that part," I admit, raking my fingers through my hair. The dryness in my throat intensifies, and I think about grabbing another drink.

"I think I can answer that," Callan offers, stepping closer and glancing at the balcony. "You two don't allow her to pin you—ever. Leander and I roll onto our backs immediately for her because we're prey. It's safer for us that way."

"Oh, shit, that's right," I say. "She enjoys being enclosed in my wings, so I have to pin her to the bed."

"Abraxis always has wings," Balor points out, folding his arms. "I can't see him letting her kneel on the leather of his wings."

"His wings don't attach like mine. She can get her leg between him and the leather," I mutter, keeping an eye on Klauth and Abraxis through the glass doors. It looks like their conversation isn't going well; Abraxis suddenly spreads his wings and takes off into the night sky, his silhouette disappearing against the darkness.

Klauth steps back into the suite, the night air swirling in with him for a moment before he closes the balcony door. There's a chill lingering in the air as he rakes a hand down his face. "Stubborn youngling."

"What happened?" Callan asks, voice tense.

"Abraxis has been letting Mina be in control most of the time during sex. He didn't think it was important to be the dominant." Klauth's voice is low, resonating with frustration. "We're going to be in deep shit if he doesn't change his ways. Someone could get hurt." His gaze drifts to Callan, then flicks toward Leander's door, where we can still hear Mina's soft laughter. A faint smile touches his lips before he heads to Mina's room to retire, the door clicking shut behind him.

"We'll try to talk some sense into Abraxis. We have about a month before Mina's next fertile cycle hits," Balor says, shaking his head before he heads to his own room.

"It's going to be a group effort. We have to correct him when he screws up," Callan mutters, rubbing the back of his neck. The hush of the apartment feels heavier now, thick with unspoken concerns.

"Good luck with that," I reply, crossing my arms and staring at the balcony doors, my reflection faint in the glass. "Abraxis doesn't listen to anyone except Mina."

We exchange uneasy looks, and the tension wraps around us like a suffocating blanket. We all share the same sinking feeling—Mina is going to be a handful when her dragoness is fertile again, and none of us truly knows how to handle it yet. The thought makes my stomach twist with a mixture of anticipation and dread, the air thick with the promise of storms to come.

side, and slowing my hurried attempts. The faint musk of leather from his jacket mingles with the damp ink as he places a hand over mine.

"This is going to be important sooner than later, Mina," he whispers into my ear, his breath sending a soft shiver down my spine. I lean into him, feeling the steady rise and fall of his chest as he adjusts my grip on the pen. The nib scratches lightly against the thick parchment, each line more jagged than I intend.

"Did your parents not spend any time on the finer points of being a dragoness?" He bites his bottom lip, exhaling roughly as he clarifies, "What I mean to say is, did your mother teach you anything about running a nest—or flight?" His brow arches, a hopeful flicker in his crimson-flecked amber eyes.

"She tried ... but my father insisted the gauntlet and training came first." My voice drops, shoulders tensing at the memory. Klauth moves my hand gently, guiding the pen in slow, deliberate motions. I catch the faint sound of other students murmuring around us, chairs scraping, but I focus on the faint rasp of our pen strokes.

"Well," he says softly, kissing my temple in a surprisingly tender gesture, "if you'll permit me, I'd like to teach you enough that you won't have any difficulties." His tone is warm, threading through the quiet atmosphere of the room.

He releases my hand, and I attempt the decorative script on my own. My pen glides over the parchment, forming swooping loops and elegant lines that resemble, if not match, Klauth's effortless flourish. My fingers tremble slightly at first, but with each stroke, I find more confidence. "How's that?" I ask, turning to gaze into his mesmerizing eyes. A faint reflection of the sputtering lanterns dances across them.

"Very good, my treasure. Let's try the next section. Take your time— don't rush," he encourages, pressing a light kiss to my temple again, the warmth of his lips sending a small thrill through me.

"I'd rather be sparring," I admit with a soft laugh, the tension easing from my shoulders. Each carefully crafted letter feels more challenging than parrying a broad sword, yet strangely satisfying. I push forward, letting the gentle scratch of the pen fill the silence. Occasionally, Klauth's hand slides over mine to correct my grip, a subtle reminder of his patience.

Eventually, we reach the signature line. I write out Willamina, pausing at the surname, heart thumping in my chest at the weight such a choice carries.

"Try writing both, my treasure," Klauth whispers next to my ear, his breath brushing the tiny hairs at my nape, sending a warmth trickling down my spine. "See which one you like better? I promise I will not be upset, no matter which one you choose." He kisses my shoulder before leaning back, giving me the space to decide.

I take out a separate sheet of paper and try writing all the surnames for shits and giggles.

Willamina Havock

Willamina Ragnar

Willamina Whitlocke

Willamina Husk

Willamina Crosse

Willamina Dagon

Willamina Xander

Willamina Mrithun

MY EYES LOCK on the sheet of paper, the thin pages rustling under my fingertips as I examine how my name looks written alongside each of my mates' surnames. There's a stale chalkiness lingering in the air— Finlay must have been writing on the board before class. Around me, the gentle hum of murmured conversations forms a low backdrop, but my attention narrows on the ink scrawled in front of me.

I shake my head, glancing up at the four names that tug at my focus more than any others: **Havock**, **Ragnar**, **Whitlock**, and **Mrithun**—the last one generously supplied by Thauglor, though I wish he hadn't. My fingertips brush over the page, feeling the slight grooves where I've pressed the pen too hard. Then I rewrite my name again, pairing it with only those four. Finally, I narrow it to **Callan's** and **Klauth's** surnames.

Willamina Ragnar
Willamina Whitlocke

A COMFORTING WARMTH spreads through my lower back as Klauth rubs gentle circles there, his touch effortlessly calming the tight coil of anxiety in my belly. I can sense the faint heat his dragon form radiates even in this human guise; it's like standing near the mouth of a forge.

"I can't decide," I sigh, my exhale catching the faint scent of old paper and dust. Klauth leans closer to peer at the two names I've painstakingly circled.

He inclines his head toward the full sheet with all eight surnames, the overhead lights reflecting off the paper. "I recognize three of these. Which mate is Whitlocke?"

"Callan, the gryphon," I say quietly, letting my pen drag over the sheet in a slow, deliberate line. I write it out once more. Then, I scribble a quick note with **Ragnar** at the end of my name and stare at the result, my heart thumping as I weigh each option.

Klauth's gaze sweeps over my scrawl. "He has a very aristocratic surname. If I wasn't concerned about how the other dragon dens would take it, I would say choose his." His remark surprises me. The subtle dryness of his voice mixes with a warmth that is entirely his own.

I turn in my chair—a slightly stiff, squeaking auditorium seat—to look at him. "We'd have to announce your awakening if I use yours." I rest my palm against his cheek, the skin there so much hotter than mine, and look up into his crimson-flecked amber eyes.

"Our bond would have to be acknowledged by the temple of Bahamut," he says softly, "as well as the others in the bond." His gaze drops to an ancient ring on his pinky. The metal is darkened in places, tiny etched symbols winding around the band. He slides it off his pinky finger and onto my ring finger. It's snug, but oddly comfortable, like it's molding itself to me. "That's the royal seal of my bloodline. My family line ended when I went into the cursed egg. It will be reborn through you." He leans down to kiss me, the press of his lips igniting a spark that chases away the stale air of the classroom. I find myself sinking into that moment of warmth, letting out a soft sigh.

A sudden voice slices through the room. "Miss Havock, do I need to call the general and tell him about your indiscretions?" Finlay's sharp tone booms from the front of the auditorium, and I feel the weight of every classmate's gaze fall on Klauth and me in the back row.

I straighten, the seat squeaking as I shift. "Should I summon him for you?" I tilt my head, letting my voice carry. My dragoness stirs, impatient with the interruption. Before Finlay can retort, I reach through the tether linking me to Abraxis, sending a gentle **come here** pulse. Heat flares beneath my skin when he replies, and I smirk, leaning back against Klauth.

"You love playing with fire, my treasure," Klauth whispers against my ear, his breath hot on my skin.

"You're a red dragon," I murmur with a teasing grin, "you'd be the expert on that." I lean up and brush a kiss under his jaw. My nose catches a hint of something smoky—remnants of his earlier shift, perhaps.

The door on the stage swings open, revealing Abraxis. The speed at which he arrived suggests he was waiting close by. Footsteps echo across the wooden boards as he advances.

"General, did you know your young mate is having a dalliance with that male up there?" Finlay points a bony finger in our direction, practically shaking with indignation.

Abraxis's gaze coolly sweeps through the auditorium. "He's one of her mates, so yes, I'm well aware." His blunt tone leaves Finlay momentarily speechless. The general ascends the stairs, heading toward us. "How's class?" he asks, his voice dropping a bit when he's near.

"Survivable." I can smell the faint leather of his uniform and feel the powerful aura he carries. My fingers flex around the paper I'm still clutching. "We're working on my penmanship—and I'm trying out everyone's surnames." I hand Abraxis the list, feeling the edges of the sheet scrape my palm.

He arches a brow at the names. "I mean, for the good of the nest, the ancient surnames would do best. Selfishly, I want you to keep mine." He shifts his attention to Klauth, offering his hand. "Thank you for yesterday. I took your guidance to heart and will make the needed changes going forward."

Klauth accepts the handshake, the mutual respect radiating from them both. I feel the tension in the row before us, classmates no doubt craning their necks for a better view.

My gaze darts from one dragon to the other. "We need to go to the temple of Bahamut to have the bonds acknowledged before Mina has her first clutch," Klauth says. His tone is hushed, but I sense the gravity in every syllable. Abraxis's eyes widen.

"That means revealing yourself to all dragon kind," Abraxis whispers, leaning closer. I can almost taste the adrenaline in the air—thick, electric.

"It's a sacrifice I'm willing to make for our nest and mate." Klauth's voice is resolute. "All that belonged to me before my capture will be returned to me, per tradition. Including ownership of the lands and buildings this academy is built on. This was all my territory, plus the lands north of the dragon dorms for about thirty miles."

My breath catches, and I fumble in my bag for a rolled-up map, the worn parchment crackling as I smooth it out on the armrest. "Thirty miles north ... That touches the mountains where my nest is built. Which means my territory extends another twenty-five miles. Combined, that's..." My eyes widen at the magnitude. "We control nearly thirty percent of the continent."

"**Our** territory, my treasure," Klauth says, kissing my temple. His lips are warm, pulling me out of my startled haze. We both look up at Abraxis, whose expression is thoughtful. I recall he hasn't inherited his father's den yet, so he's effectively landless for the moment.

"When is all of this happening?" I ask, my pulse skittering with unease. Something cold nips at the edges of my mind, reminding me that when Thauglor hatches, Abraxis's father's lands might revert as well.

"The next temple verification is in five days," Abraxis says, pulling out his phone. The soft glow of the screen lights up his face. "I'll fly over and put our names on the list."

I stand, the stiff chair scraping against the floor, and wrap my arms around Abraxis. The faint musk of his jacket mixes with a hint of metal —probably the buckles on his uniform. I try to raise my arms to his neck, craving the press of his cheek against mine. Abraxis stops me and adjusts so my hands only make it around his waist. A warning growl resonates in his throat, low enough that the rest of the class might not catch it, but I feel it reverberate against my chest.

"Mina..." His voice is a caution, a firm reminder of some boundary he's set.

My dragoness bristles, but I force a tight smile. "Fine..." I settle for hugging him around his waist, feeling his heartbeat under my cheek. I nuzzle my nose under his jaw, inhaling the clean, spicy scent that's uniquely his. The arrangement feels awkward, so different from our usual easy closeness.

Abraxis runs his fingers through my hair, letting a soothing warmth slip into that space between us. "Finish your lesson. I'll see you later," he says, stepping back.

"I love you," I whisper, holding his hand for a moment. The soft brush of his thumb over my knuckles reassures me.

"I love you too, Mina." He nods to me and offers a polite bow of the head to Klauth before turning to leave.

A quiet shiver races down my spine as I watch him go. Everything about that exchange felt ... strained. Though I know it's for our own good. My scales prickle beneath my skin in protest.

"Good girl, my treasure," Klauth murmurs, pressing his lips against my temple again. There's a faint hint of sulfur, a reminder of his ancient dragonic heritage. My pen scratches against the paper one last time as I sign the invitation I'd been drafting: ***Willamina Ragnar ...*** The name sits on the page, and I can practically hear the unspoken possibilities echo in the quiet hush of the auditorium.

slight furrow of her brow by the pale glow of the floating orbs that line the path.

"I don't think any of you lived in there. Or am I wrong?" Mina motions toward the night-dark house perched on the shore.

"You're correct," I reply, my voice low. "We either stayed in our rooms at Shadowcarve, or when new students arrived, we used to babysit in the northern dorms. Young dragons are temperamental." My words echo in the stillness as we near the footbridge to the temple.

"I'm glad to see the old bridge has been maintained all these years," Klauth remarks. He runs his hand over the weathered stones, and I hear the soft scrape of his palm against the coarse surface.

"It had to be partially rebuilt about ten years ago after a horrible storm," Abraxis points out, showing the newer section where the stones are much lighter than the original masonry. I can almost imagine the fierce winds and pounding surf that must have torn through here, the chaos that left part of this bridge in ruins.

We cross under an ancient arch that leads us onto the bridge proper. It's several hours after sunset, and we have everyone in the nest with us. Vaughn stands slightly apart, gazing warily at the structure stretching out over the dark water. I sense the ripple of unease in the group; non-dragon shifters aren't usually allowed in the temple. There's a collective tension in the air—like a coil wound too tight.

We ascend the gleaming white marble steps, which reflect the faint starlight and cast strange shapes along the ground. The chill of the stone seeps through my shoes, and a shiver traces up my spine. Finally, we reach a broad landing marked by ornate golden doors. Abraxis knocks three times, each rap echoing in the silence. I catch the faint smell of incense drifting from within, a sweet, smoky scent that mixes oddly with the brine in the air.

"Why do I feel like we're about to be put on trial?" I whisper, my voice hushed, as though something in this sacred place demands quiet. My shift moves uneasily under my skin, muscles tightening in response to the unknown.

"Because we are," Klauth answers. His voice sounds heavier here, absorbed by the thick marble walls. "Mina will be separated from us once we prove our bloodlines. While she's separated, she'll be asked to summon a mate at their request. As long as she can do that, most of the bond is proven."

"Most of the bond?" My brow furrows, and I look between the three dragons. My heart thuds in my chest, sending adrenaline coursing through my veins.

"Beyond who I am, they will ask to test my connection to Mina." Abraxis's gaze flickers to her, and she nods in confirmation. There's a heaviness in their shared glance, like some unspoken fear.

"What else?" My stomach churns, the tension drawing tighter.

"They will ask who the dragoness set as the dominant drake." Mina pales, stepping back into Ziggy's arms. The subtle scent of her anxiety —something faintly electric—reaches my heightened senses. "You cannot escape the process," Klauth continues. "If you do, they will not validate the bonds."

I study Mina's face, noticing the flicker of indecision before she speaks. "Abraxis and I talked about it." She sighs and drops her gaze. "We're still working on our issues, and if they test us, we'll fail. So Klauth will be named the dominant drake in the nest." She bites her bottom lip so hard I see a bead of blood bloom there, and the metallic tang wafts faintly through the air.

"I know that was a tough decision, Mina. I am proud of you for doing it logically," Callan says, his reassuring smile a brief balm on her nerves.

I watch Mina's reaction. She's clearly torn about disappointing both Abraxis and Klauth. Before any of us can say more, the golden doors swing open with a creak that seems to reverberate through the night. A priestess in long white robes stands before us, torchlight glinting off the polished marble corridor behind her.

"Follow me, please," she whispers, then turns and strides inside. The echo of her shoes on marble clicks like a metronome, punctuating each step deeper into the temple.

Mina clings to Ziggy's side, her tongue flicking out to taste the blood on her lip. Five sets of footsteps echo through the corridor, though Mina, Balor, and Ziggy move so silently that only the faint rustle of cloth betrays their presence. The priestess glances over her shoulder, ensuring we're all still following, then leads us into a grand chamber.

Solid onyx pillars rise on either side, holding up a ceiling lost in shadows. Torches set in ornate sconces cast flickering orange light across black marble walls. Each pillar is engraved with intricate carvings of ancient dragons, their snaking forms frozen in stone. The carvings shimmer with faint flecks of gold, and I catch the distinct smell of old incense mingled with a hint of burned wax.

I notice the depiction of the Goddess Tiamat, her dragon form eerily similar to Mina's. Klauth, walking beside me, also stops, glancing back at our mate, his features set in a mask of concern and curiosity. Nine priestesses stand on a set of stairs leading up to the massive statue of Bahamut, their white robes stark against the darkness.

"The dragoness needs to step forward," the elder priestess says, her voice echoing around the cavernous space. She takes a measured step down from the line, the other priestesses parting to let her through.

Mina moves without hesitation, raising her chin defiantly. Klauth follows, gently removing the shawl that had covered her shoulders. The summer dress she chose reveals the shimmering scales across her skin—ridges of pearlescent color that catch the torchlight. They trail from her shoulders up into her hairline, an unmistakable sign of the strength of her dragoness. If needed, they can pull down the back of the sundress to show how far the scales extend.

The elder priestess circles Mina like an art collector examining a masterpiece, her gaze lingering on each patch of scales. I hear the faint rustle of her robes against the polished floor, and the air feels heavy with impending judgment. The cut of Mina's dress also exposes the mate bites each of us has left on her, the small crescent scars shining faintly under the shifting light.

A hush falls over us as we wait for the priestess to speak again. My pulse thrums, and the cool air of the temple seems to press in on all sides. Though I can barely breathe, I force myself to remain still, my gaze locked on Mina. Every sense is heightened—every sound, every flicker of light—and all I can think is that the next few moments may define our fates forever.

The polished marble floors reflect dancing torchlight, casting flickering shapes across the ancient stone walls. I catch a faint hum of distant chanting—priestesses praying, perhaps—though the hush in this chamber is almost tangible, as if the space itself is waiting for a verdict.

"Who is the dominant drake?" the elder priestess asks, her voice echoing in the stillness. The timbre of her words resonates against my chest, sending a slight quiver through me.

"Klauth," Mina says without hesitation.

"Klauth is imprisoned, never to take to the skies again," the priestess asserts confidently, her tone reverberating in the silence.

"Yet I stand before you," Klauth says calmly as he moves beside Mina and raises her left hand. The soft rasp of their clothes brushing together makes my pulse spike. "My mate wears the signet ring of my family as proof of who I am."

The priestess takes Mina's hand. I hear the faint clink of her ornate bracelets as she lifts Mina's fingers toward her gaze. She snaps her own fingers, and the sudden sound makes me jolt. A scribe steps out of a dark corridor—his footsteps tapping lightly on the stone floor— carrying an immense tome bound in cracked leather. The pages rustle as the priestess flips through them, the dry whisper blending with the quiet flicker of torches.

She brings Mina's hand closer to the book. "The ring is the signet ring of King Klauth Ragnar, the high king of the Marzana Empire." I watch torchlight dance across the polished gold of the ring. The priestess and her companion lower themselves to one knee, the metallic echo of jewelry touching stone sending a sudden chill through me.

My heart pounds in my chest at the implications. Klauth has exposed himself so the nest can be verified—taking a significant risk by doing this now. The tension in the air is thick enough that I can almost taste it, a metallic tang against the back of my tongue. The priestesses all bow to Klauth and now Mina as well.

"Please rise. Let us finish what we have come here to do." Klauth extends his hand to the elder priestess. The material of his dress jacket rustles softly when she accepts, and he helps her to stand.

"My future queen, what is the name of the drake that sired you?" the elder priestess asks, turning to Mina. I sense Mina's hesitation before I see it. There's a subtle stiffening in her posture, and I notice the small scales shifting at the back of her neck, a sign of her discomfort.

"Abaddon Bladesong of the Risedale nest," Mina says, her voice clipped and tense.

"And the female that bore your egg?" The elder priestess tilts her head, and the scribe's quill scratches faintly against parchment as he readies to transcribe her response.

"Layla Laraunt of what was the Tyr nest. She was the last female born of the iron dragons there," Mina answers quietly, her weight shifting nervously. A waft of the musty air moves past us, carrying the subdued scent of old ink and parchment.

"Yes, it was sad what happened to that nest," the priestess says under her breath, as if recalling a distant tragedy. She steps away from Mina and moves to Abraxis. Her robes sweep the floor with a soft, dragging sound that sets my teeth on edge. "Who is the drake that sired you?"

"Vox Havock of the Blackhaven nest. The female that bore me is Cerce Aslaug of the Freyja nest. She is a bronze dragon–red dragon mix," Abraxis replies, bowing slightly. The torchlight catches the proud tilt of his jaw, illuminating the faint gleam of his obsidian wings and horns.

I notice the priestess doesn't question Klauth's lineage—no one dares to doubt the legitimacy of a legendary line so long thought dead. A hushed reverence hangs in the air at the mere mention of his ancestry.

"Very good. I will take the female with me. My priestesses will take each male and separate you from each other. They will gather all the needed information, and then you wait for Mina to summon you to prove the bond." The elder priestess gestures for Mina to step forward, but Mina remains rooted in place, her gaze locked on Klauth. I can almost feel her trepidation rolling off her like a wave of heat.

"Go with her, my treasure. You will be safe." The minute he speaks, she nods, a subtle relaxation in her stance, and then moves to follow the priestess. Her footsteps are soft but resonate in the hush as she departs, the tension in the room easing just a fraction.

Klauth steps closer to us, his voice a low rumble. "They were testing if her claim of me being the dominant drake was true. Thankfully, she waited for me to tell her it was safe to follow them."

A wave of apprehension twists my stomach. I know everything from here on will be a test of our nest's strength. The priestesses approach, dividing us with purposeful steps. Each of us looks at Klauth, waiting for his nod of approval. When it's my turn, I bow to him—heart still pounding from the surging adrenaline—then follow the priestess down a dimly lit corridor leading to places unknown. The scents of damp stone and ancient parchment accompany me, along with the echo of my own uneasy footsteps.

inspects each mark, and the scratch of his quill against parchment sets my nerves on edge. My skin prickles where his gaze lingers.

"Which drake made this bite?" he asks, using the feather end of his quill to gently tap the front of my throat. The soft bristles tickle, but the spot still throbs faintly, reminding me of Abraxis's sharp teeth and his possessive nature.

"Abraxis," I answer, tilting my head up to give him a better view. My hair shifts over my shoulders, releasing a whiff of lavender oil from earlier bathing rituals.

"And these repeat bites are his?" He motions to my one shoulder, where the skin feels tender.

"Yes." I try not to think about how the skin there still tingles whenever Abraxis is near.

"An adolescent black dragon does that when their strength is threatened." The scribe's observation sends a chill slithering down my spine. I can practically feel the worry emanating from my dragoness, an unspoken tension coiling low in my gut.

'What is wrong, mate?' Klauth's voice resonates through my mind, a comforting, electric warmth along our bond.

'I am sure you already know,' I reply silently, not daring to let my attention wander for too long. My pulse thrums in my ears, and the musty dryness of the chamber seems to thicken around me.

"This bite?" The scribe's quill grazes the back of my neck gently.

"Leander, the Nightmare," I say, my voice barely above a whisper.

'Abraxis's multiple bites on your shoulder.' Klauth's concern hums through our bond.

'I did the same to him,' I admit, recalling the feverish intensity of our last altercation.

'*You reacted to how stressed he was, his insecurity,*' Klauth murmurs, and some of the tension eases within me. I focus again on the priestess as she steps closer.

She studies me intently. "Who were you speaking to?" she asks, her penetrating gaze making my pulse flutter anxiously.

"Klauth felt how stressed I am about being separated from my entire nest in a new place. He was making sure I am alright," I reply, keeping my tone even. I let a half truth slip, hoping it's enough to keep her from prying deeper.

"He was a just ruler in his time. Shame what happened to his betrothed," the priestess continues, her voice echoing softly. There's a faint tang of incense in the air, a bitter note that sets my teeth on edge.

"It is a shame that the wyvern attacked a female on a nest. It was the act of a coward." I keep myself composed, though my heart twists at the memory. I feel the weight of the scribe's eyes on me as he waits to record which mark belongs to which mate.

"Let's test the strength of the bonds to your mates." The priestess glances down at her list. "Summon the gryphon to you." She settles onto a high-backed chair behind an ancient desk, the wood creaking under her weight.

I inhale slowly. The air tastes faintly of ink and old leather. I focus on Callan's bond, sending a gentle caress down it, then give it a slight tug. A ripple of energy runs through my body, and I can sense him moving closer. Within minutes, Callan enters. He's at my side in an instant, his arms warm around me. Relief floods me, and I release the tether, hugging him tightly. The smell of fresh mountain air clings to him, a sharp contrast to the musty chamber. He kisses the underside of my jaw, and my skin tingles where his lips brush.

"Summon the basilisk," the priestess says without looking up from her notes.

I give Callan a tender smile before shifting my focus. My heart beats faster as I grip Balor's tether and pull. A thrilling spark flares to life in my mind, and I sense him heading straight for me. Within moments, Balor leans in the doorway, his presence commanding. His gaze sweeps the room, then he steps forward, the soft scrape of boots on stone announcing his approach. He kisses the underside of my jaw, leaving behind a hint of something metallic—like the scent of minerals in a deep cave—and hugs me firmly.

"The gargoyle." The priestess tilts her head, a calculating glint in her eyes. She's hunting for a weakness in our bonds, I can feel it.

I breathe in, letting the gritty stone smell of the room fill my lungs as I focus on Vaughn. A gentle caress, then a tug. The tether thrums with life. Seconds later, Vaughn practically sprints into the hall, nearly skidding past the door before regaining his composure. A soft laugh slips out of me, the tension easing for a heartbeat. His arms wrap around me in a crushing hug, and he presses a chaste kiss under my jaw, his body cool and solid like carved marble.

"The displacer beast," she calls out next, arching an eyebrow.

A grin stretches across my face as I tug on Ziggy's bond. The moment I do, he appears in front of me in a blur of shadows and feline grace, the space around him rippling with displaced air. He nuzzles against my jaw and peppers me with light kisses, his enthusiasm lighting up the stale room like a burst of fireworks. My giggle echoes off of the walls.

"The Nightmare." She frowns at the text on her parchment, then at me.

Ziggy steps away, joining my other mates. I sink deeper into my mind, reaching for Leander's bond. It resonates with a dark, velvety warmth that sends gooseflesh prickling over my skin. I tug gently and feel him draw near. Moments later, he appears, his heavy footfalls echoing in the corridor before he steps inside. There's a faint smell of smoke about him, like distant embers. I open my arms, inviting him close, and when he kisses under my jaw, I let my eyes flutter shut in relief.

The priestess actually chuckles, her gray eyes gleaming as she observes us, then returns to scribbling notes. "Summon the black dragon."

My stomach twists into a knot. My heartbeat quickens, and I swallow hard before reaching for Abraxis. Our bond feels taut, like a thread on the verge of snapping, but I stroke it carefully, then tug. Tension swirls in my gut, matching the dryness of my mouth. When Abraxis walks in, every gaze fixes on him. I hear the rasp of his scales in my mind as he draws close, and my dragoness inside me shifts uneasily.

Pressing the bridge of my nose under his chin in a sign of submission, I catch the faint sulfuric tang of his breath—like a warm updraft from a deep cavern. His dragon rumbles softly, and he hugs me, kissing my forehead. The bond between us thrums with both caution and promise.

The priestess finishes scribbling and looks at me again. "Summon Klauth."

I carefully ease away from Abraxis. The dusty air of the chamber crackles with anticipation as I concentrate on Klauth. The moment I tug his tether, lightning seems to spark under my skin, skittering up my spine. Within moments, Klauth appears at the doorway, a kingly aura surrounding him. When he steps closer, I throw my head back, exposing his mate mark. My eyes drift shut, and I clasp my hands behind my back. The brush of his lips against the mark sends a shiver down my body, and his arm curls around me in a protective embrace.

"My precious treasure," Klauth rumbles softly, his voice radiating warmth. "You submit to no one unless you want to." He gently caresses my face, guiding my gaze to meet his. For a moment, the cool chamber, the priestess, and the scribe seem to fade. All I sense is the electric hum of our bond, the reverberation in the very air around us, and a promise that I'm not alone in this place.

I release the breath I didn't realize I was holding and let my forehead rest against his broad chest. The faint scent of incense tickles my nose, mingling with the slightly metallic tang lingering on his shirt—a stark reminder of the tension in the air. We stand in a dim, vaulted chamber, the echo of our breathing somehow louder than the crackling torches lining the walls.

Across the room, the elder priestess shuffles through a stack of yellowed papers, her gnarled fingers tracing each line of text with meticulous care. "From what I can see, the bonds are firmly in place," she says, setting the pages aside. Her keen gaze shifts to Abraxis. "You show signs of stress, of feeling unsure about your place in this bond."

At her gesture, I step forward. She gently brushes my hair from my shoulder, exposing Abraxis's fresh marks. The sudden touch sends a jolt along my spine, the delicate scales at my nape prickling in response. She tuts softly. "This is what a threatened male does to prove he's in control—or, as the young ones say, 'I was here first.'"

I glance from Abraxis to Klauth, my heart thudding in my chest. Abraxis began biting more often once I received Klauth's egg, long before Klauth was physically in the picture. My bottom lip stings under the pressure of my teeth, but I keep quiet, waiting for the priestess to continue.

"We have verified all the bonds. We have also started the process of restoring the lands and title that belong by right to King Ragnar— especially now that he has a viable mate to carry on his bloodline." Her gaze locks on me, and the scales along my spine rise in instinctive defense. A chill seeps into my bones; I still have three known enemies out there, and this is no time to be carrying or laying eggs.

"Thank you." Klauth's voice rumbles softly as he steps beside me, his arm draping over my shoulders.

"We'll need you to return so we can complete everything," the priestess says, consulting a scroll with faded ornate lettering. "We plan to announce your sovereignty over what was once known as the

Marzana Empire during the winter formal. The coronation for you and your queen will happen then."

My throat tightens. How in the world did I go from being an assassin in training and the unwanted daughter … to now a queen of a long-forgotten empire? My pulse thrums in my ears, and internally, I'm screaming. If I didn't have a massive target on my back before, I certainly do now.

Klauth presses his lips gently to my temple, and a soft purr of reassurance vibrates through him. "We'll talk as a nest when we get home," he murmurs. "Certain things are already in motion. We can't stop them now."

He turns and nods at Ziggy, who steps forward with his easy, lopsided grin. "Come on, Mina," Ziggy says, looping his arm through mine. The movement makes me aware of every taut muscle in my body, as if bracing for a fight. "Let's go home."

In the space of a single heartbeat, we leave the hush of the priestess's hall behind. The breath of cool air that hits my face feels like a promise of momentary peace. Hopefully, once we're all together in the suite, we can make sense of this madness—and the new crown looming over my head.

"That's the understatement of my existence." I sigh, wrapping my arm around his before sliding my hand down to lace our fingers together. His warmth grounds me for a moment, and I give his hand a reassuring squeeze.

Balor stops us beneath a drooping willow tree. The branches trail against the ground like silent sentinels, shielding us from the bustle of campus. He tilts my chin up. "Talk to me, Mina. I can't help you if you don't tell me what's wrong." When he kisses me softly, the faint taste of mint on his lips mingles with the crisp air. Then he rests his forehead against mine, as if trying to absorb all of my stress.

"I don't know what to do anymore." I close my eyes, letting out another shaky breath as I focus on the rhythmic sound of Balor's breathing. "Vox has been trying to reason with Abraxis. Abraxis doesn't feel Klauth should be head drake of the nest—he wants that role for himself. But a head or dominant drake is supposed to put the good of the nest, or flight, before his own desires." My words come out in a rush, and I pull away to hug myself, feeling a chill that has nothing to do with the weather.

Balor's arm encircles me again, drawing me back in. "What do you want, Mina?" He cups my cheek and makes me meet his gaze. "What do you feel is best for the nest?" His lips brush the tip of my nose in a tender gesture, and he offers a small, encouraging smile.

"Klauth is a great wyrm—his drake is over a hundred and thirty feet long. He can protect the nest and me in ways Abraxis's dragon can't." My eyes drop to the ground, and a swirl of brittle leaves crackles under my feet. "Abraxis is nine years older than me, so I feel closer to him in that sense. But that doesn't mean we'll be safe from our enemies if he's the one in charge." I nibble on my bottom lip and let out a shaky breath. "I love them both equally, no matter what Abraxis tries to convince himself."

"Have you told him that?" Balor asks, tucking me under his arm. The warmth of his body and the steady thrum of his heartbeat soothe some of my anxiety as we continue walking.

"Many times. He doesn't want to believe it, and I don't know why." My eyes flick ahead, noticing the looming silhouette of Malivore. Its darkened windows and stone arches always give me a strange sense of foreboding. My stomach twists in knots.

"He's been in love with the idea of you since he was nine," Balor says, his tone thoughtful. "He's spent twenty-three—almost twenty-four—years living with the fantasy of his mate. Maybe reality isn't lining up with the dream he created in his head."

His words sink in, resonating with my own suspicions. "Yet another male's expectations I don't live up to," I murmur. That old pit of grief yawns wide inside me, and the icy breath of depression wraps itself around my chest. It always comes back at the worst times.

"It's not like that, Mina..." Balor's protest is gentle as we enter our suite. The stale, slightly musty smell of the hallway mingles with the faint scent of dust and old furniture.

I just look at him, offering a sad smile before perching myself on the arm of the couch, bracing for whatever torture this nest meeting might bring. My pulse pounds in my ears. Tonight feels like a crossroads—one where all our hopes, fears, and rivalries collide in a storm. I'm not sure any of us can fully control.

I STAND AGAINST THE WALL, letting the cool stone at my back anchor me, while Leander moves front and center of the room. The low glow of the overhead lights casts long shadows across the floor, making the space feel both intimate and tense. I've deliberately placed myself a few steps away from both drakes, making sure neither feels I'm favoring the other. My pulse thrums in my ears, and the faint scent of candle wax and old parchment lingers in the air—remnants of tonight's studying and earlier gatherings.

"I've been doing a lot of reading on managing a large nest," Leander begins, his gaze drifting over everyone. His voice carries a certain measured calm, but I sense an undercurrent of nerves. "It's suggested we have check-ins regularly. So that's what this is. Mina, I've had the guys all put anonymous concerns on slips of paper."

He lifts what looks like a plain pillowcase, its corners darkened by shadows. The shifting of paper within makes a faint crinkling sound that seems unnaturally loud. "I'm going to shake it up, then have you draw out the questions. If you want to read them aloud, that's fine. If not, I can do it."

I nod, a silent agreement, feeling a subtle flutter in my stomach. There's a sense of dread gnawing at the edges of my thoughts—I'm not entirely sure what issues might come up.

"Okay, here we go."

Leander shakes the pillowcase, and the soft rustle of paper feels more like a death knell than simple questions. I swallow hard as he opens the bag and extends it toward me. My fingertips brush against the rough cloth, and I close my eyes, plunging my hand in to grab a single folded piece. The edges of the paper are crisp against my skin as I pull it free and open it.

I clear my throat. "What do we do if it's not our night and we need Mina?" I read aloud, my voice echoing slightly off the stone walls.

Leander manages a smile and answers first. "Go to the person whose night it is and ask if, before bedtime, they can share their allotted time —just for a little bit. But sharing time isn't meant to be abused by one person."

He looks at me, brow furrowed, silently asking if I want to add anything. I give a slight shake of my head. The tension in the room lifts a fraction.

"For example…" Ziggy jumps to his feet, his movement sending a ripple through the charged air. "If Callan or Abraxis get called to the front again."

I cringe at the thought, my heart thudding as I recall the last time they left for some urgent summons. Ziggy notices my discomfort and mouths *"sorry"* before continuing. "They can ask to switch or share the time they have left with whoever has that night, so they can be close to Mina before they leave."

Chewing my bottom lip, I speak up. "Why don't we just do an emergency switch if that happens again? Whatever time they have left can remain theirs, without sharing. The person who loses that slot will take either Callan's or Abraxis's night—whichever comes first." I drop my gaze to my hands, tracing the faint scars there.

Leander's voice cuts through the hush. "Is that a solution everyone can agree on?"

A chorus of assent fills the room, though it's subdued. "Okay, passed," he says, relief softening his tone. "Next concern." He brings the pillowcase back to me, and I feel a twist in my gut as he holds it open.

This time, the paper I pull out seems thinner, almost delicate. My hands tremble as I unfold it. "It's still not safe enough for Mina to lay eggs. What are we going to do for her next cycle?" I read, my voice hitching. I can't help the tiny flinch that follows.

"I've been thinking about it a lot," Callan says, moving to stand near Leander. His steps are quiet, but I still catch the faint scrape of his boots on the stone floor. "We wear protection and cycle in and out of Mina's space. As long as she's … occupied, she shouldn't shift and become dangerous."

His words spark a tense chuckle from me. "If two drakes and a basilisk can't contain me, the world is in deep shit." My attempt at levity is shaky; I'm trying not to add to Abraxis's worries by mentioning his name or Klauth's in that context.

Leander rattles the pillowcase once more, the noise somehow sharper this time, and holds it out. My heart thumps painfully against my ribs as I draw the next slip. I sense everyone watching me, the air thick with anticipation. Unfolding the paper, I pause. My throat feels suddenly tight.

"If you could do it all over again, what would you change?" I read, my voice cracking. A tear slips down my cheek before I can stop it. My breath hitches as I turn away. "This isn't fair. The things I would change … they weren't my choice."

Silence floods the room. I lower my head, letting the tears fall in hot tracks down my cheeks. My chest aches, and I want nothing more than to disappear. Then Abraxis's voice, soft as a breath of wind, breaks through.

"Mate?" he murmurs, contrition clear in every syllable. "Please look at me. I'm sorry. I shouldn't have asked that question."

I force my gaze to meet his, blinking through tears. "I wouldn't have waited so long to complete the bond with you. I was scared I wasn't enough." My eyes flick over his shoulder to Balor. "If I had known, I wouldn't have let you linger in the shadows for so long. You're probably my most selfless mate."

Drawing in a shaky breath, I turn to Callan. "I know what it's like to feel you're not enough. I grew up with that feeling every day of my life. I still feel it when my mate is so stressed he bites me continuously … then I do it because I'm stressed that he's stressed."

Ziggy hands me a tissue, and I blow my nose, trying to compose myself. "I wouldn't change who's in my life, just how they got here." I meet Abraxis's gaze again, searching his face. "It doesn't matter if you're the lead drake or the second one. You were my first mate, and no one can take that from you."

I lean forward and press a gentle kiss to his forehead, then shift my attention to Klauth. My eyes narrow with intent as I stare at him. "Once you're king again, you'll take over command of the continent's armies, right?"

He holds my gaze, the tension between us electric. "Yes. What's going on in that pretty little head of yours?" Klauth steps closer, and out of the corner of my eye, I see Abraxis stiffen, as if he already understands my plan.

I straighten, my spine tingling. "I know what I want instead of my father's head on a pike as my mating present."

"And what's that, mate?" Klauth's half-smirk suggests he already knows.

"Mated drakes are no longer forced to serve until their females lay a clutch. Once they have a mate, service becomes optional." The command in my tone surprises even me, but it's something I refuse to budge on.

"I never agreed with that rule anyway," Klauth replies, giving a small shrug. "Yes, it will be changed once I'm crowned. Though I'll need to amend it so the bond has to be verified by the Temple of Bahamut for legitimacy." He glances between me and Abraxis, then nods.

"Thank you," I whisper. I shift my focus to Leander, whose shoulders look a bit more relaxed now.

"I think we've had enough excitement for one night," he says, setting the pillowcase aside. "Let's pick a movie and hang out for the rest of the night as a nest."

The idea is a relief. I can almost taste the tension in the air, as sharp as the ozone before a storm. But the questions in that bag can wait until tomorrow. As I stand, Ziggy offers me Thauglor's egg, and I cradle it against my chest. Its warmth seeps into me, comforting in a way that nothing else can right now. I smile softly. At least I have one drake in my life who isn't openly jealous of the others—or if he is, he hasn't said so yet.

The room shifts around us, each mate moving closer, and for a moment, the swirl of uncertainties and fears fades beneath the steady hum of our bond. I hold the egg tighter, silently promising myself—and them—that no matter what questions come next, we'll face them together.

tacticians, who's propped against his console with a cocky slant to his posture.

"Today, B Team is going to attack A Team's barracks," Leander announces, his authoritative voice reverberating against the metal walls. "You have all the intel you'd normally receive in a war scenario."

I move to Klauth's side, arching a brow at him in greeting. "How's the day going?"

He barely glances at me before handing over a crisp, cream-colored invitation. "Mina drafted this for your parents earlier." It's a formal announcement of his coronation and the distribution of titles.

"Titles?" I mutter under my breath, leaning in closer. My heartbeat kicks up as I think about how this might change our dynamic.

Klauth's voice is calm but tinged with amusement. "Yes, Mina wants everyone in the nest to have titles. You and the others will be King Consorts to Her Royal Majesty. If anything happens to me, you or Thauglor step in as the next King—then the basilisk, and so on." He waves his hand in a lazy circle, as though the idea of ranking royalty is casual business.

My jaw tightens in surprise, and I peer over at Mina—then at Idris, who's fiddling with his station. "Why is Idris even here?"

"No one else wanted to face our mate. Idris made the mistake of stopping by to check on her for you," Klauth says dryly, arching an unimpressed brow at me. The tension in the air is palpable, pressing in on my chest.

I sigh. "I'm sorry. With the priestesses needing your attention so often, I figured Idris could fill in if you had to step out." I shrug, trying to convey that I meant no harm. He nods slowly, then turns and leaves shortly after.

Leander slips program cards into the machines, the soft click-click of each card echoing. "You have ten minutes to review your information and set up offense or defense," he instructs. "Then I'll start the battles —two at a time. Winners will face off in our next class."

Mina's fingers fly over the keys with a confident rhythm, the tap-tap-tap blending with the whir of the simulation consoles. She hits the last button hard, flips down the metal cover, and locks it in place. The clang of metal on metal sends a faint shiver up my spine; she carries herself like someone who knows exactly what she's doing.

"There's no way you're done already," Idris scoffs, leaning sideways to peer at her screen.

"Focus on your squad; let me worry about mine." Mina's voice is as cool as sharpened steel. She fixes Idris with a stare that lingers a second too long before scanning the room. When her gaze lands on me, my chest warms despite the grim setting. "Hi, Abraxis. When did you get here?" She offers a small, quick smile.

"Just a moment ago," I say, returning her smile. "You're actually facing my tactician from my outpost."

She smirks, tilting her head in Idris's direction. "So if I beat him, that explains why your battles are always close calls—or maybe I'm just smarter than he is?" Her teasing tone makes Idris bristle, and she waves at him with an almost mocking sweetness.

Idris sneers, leaning back against his console. "Females are not meant for war. That's why your scales are softer, your talons smaller and weaker."

The air crackles with tension, and I can practically taste the ire rolling off Mina. My pulse spikes, and I instinctively shake my head at Idris, silently begging him to back down. He doesn't.

In one fluid motion, her emerald, and silver scales creep over her hand. The razor-sharp silver talons extend, catching the overhead light, and she drags them across the metal frame of Idris's screen. The screech of tearing steel sets everyone's teeth on edge. Sparks fleck the air like fireflies before the shredded metal crashes to the floor with a clang. Idris's face goes pale, his eyes wide.

"Yeah, those rules don't apply to me," Mina says coolly. With a flick of her wrist, the scales, and talons retract, leaving her hand smooth once more.

Idris stares at the quarter-inch plate steel as though it's a fallen comrade. His gaze slides to me, and my gut twists. Mina's newfound ability to shred metal is concerning—she's leaning more toward her iron dragon ancestry than her father's green.

Still, beneath my worry, a dark pride stirs within me. She's strong—maybe stronger than any of us realized. It also makes sense how she managed to cut through the scales on Balor's basilisk. And though I'm here to observe, I can't shake the feeling that, in so many ways, Mina is the one truly in command of this room.

ALMOST AN HOUR HAS ELAPSED and Mina has been reading a book on the history of the continent for most of the hour. "Okay, so I have to admit, this is the battle I have been waiting to see. Mina versus Idris, who is General Havock's personal tactician." Leander hits the button and explosions echo in the silent room. The mini war wages for half of the time that the other battles took before it goes dead silent.

Mina leans back, still reading her book, not even paying attention. The light turns on over Mina's side and she glances up briefly before returning to her book. "Congratulations go to Mina!" Leander announces and Mina smiles and waves, then packs her bag as if nothing happened.

She walks over to me and rolls her eyes. "Can we please find something to challenge me? I'm bored as all hell."

Idris comes to join us and looks between the three of us. "This is your mate?" His eyes jump from Mina to me.

Before I can answer, Mina moves and wedges herself between me and Klauth as he walks back in. "And his too…" She smiles, looking up at Klauth like he hung the stars and moon just for her.

"Forgive me…" Idris bows and leaves the room.

"I'm going to walk our young mate to her poison's class." Klauth says.

Mina watches the last students leave before she throws her arms around Leander's neck and kisses him. "See you later. Love you." She nuzzles him and touches the bridge of her nose under his jaw. His nightmare vocalizes and Mina smiles before coming to me. "See you later baby … Love you." Her velvet soft lips press against mine and I sigh, hugging her to me. I remain still to see what she's going to do. Mina presses the tip of her nose under my jaw briefly before tilting her head back. This is a pleasant change. I nuzzle her cheek, then kiss her forehead. "Love you too baby, don't be late for class." I pat her ass to send her on her way.

"Please, it's Balor. I can show up whenever and he'd be happy I was there." She smiles and her statement isn't wrong.

I watch Mina slip out of the room, the echo of her footsteps fading down the corridor. The moment the door clicks shut, Leander sidles up beside me, and we both stand there in a heavy silence, staring at the spot where she disappeared. The academy's ancient walls, dimly lit by flickering overhead lamps, seem to press closer, cloaking us in a hush that weighs on my chest.

"How's therapy going?" Leander finally asks, his tone hushed and careful. We move over to his desk to review the latest performance scores. The old wood creaks under our touch, and the smell of dust and aged parchment makes my nose twitch.

I swallow, my throat suddenly dry. "The priestess accusing me of abusing Mina—because of how much I bit her—still haunts me," I admit, picking at a scar along my wrist. "Apparently, I felt threatened by the thought that ancient dragons might hatch, and the fact Mina is stronger than me." A shiver crawls up my spine as I voice that. No matter how many times I repeat it in therapy, it never gets easier.

Leander nods, glancing at me with sympathy in his eyes. "That was a big confession, Abraxis. I'm proud of you." He shrugs, then focuses on the data spread across his desk. "On another note, Mina outperformed your tactician by a whopping fifty-nine percent efficiency. Maybe that guy needs a refresher from Callan's class?" He gestures toward a nearby simulator, metal edges gleaming under the overhead lights. "Here, you can watch the replay from Mina's perspective."

I drop into the squeaky chair, feeling its worn leather protest beneath me. Leander sets up the scenario with deft fingers, each click of the keys echoing in the otherwise quiet room. It's the same battle we barely survived a few weeks ago—every detail is mapped out in the sim. "Can we have Mina run it like she was the attacker next class? I'll get Idris to come back and face off against her." My voice comes out tight with curiosity and unease. If my tactician can't match her raw instincts, we have a bigger problem than I realized.

"Of course. What're you thinking?" Leander moves beside me, the soft rustle of his jacket filling the silence. We both stare at the flickering images on the screen.

A dull ache spreads through my jaw as I clench my teeth. "I'm wondering if we were given an inexperienced tactician on purpose— maybe someone wanted to get me and Callan killed." I pace, the floor cold beneath my boots, then glance back at the sim. "Look at how we got swarmed. Wyverns and green dragons rarely attack head-on. Drow hunted down Callan in broad daylight, using the forest to shield themselves from the sun."

Leander snorts, raking a hand through his hair. "I was attacked and tossed in the academy's prison like a piece of meat—left for dead. Vaughn got taken out when they stole his amulet." He jots down a list of occurrences on a notepad, each scratch of the pen echoing in my ears.

"Damn … Didn't Ziggy say Mina told him they wanted to turn her into some kind of dracolich? Her father basically sold her body to a mage to create an 'ultimate weapon.'" My stomach twists in knots, and I exchange a panicked glance with Leander before we both bolt for the door. Balor's classroom is only a few steps away, and Mina is his only student during this period.

We rush inside, immediately spotting Mina, and Balor huddled over a thick tome. The scent of ink and old leather assaults my senses. I clear my throat, and Klauth—standing watch—fixes us with a glare as we beckon him into the hallway. Eventually, he sighs and follows us, arms crossed in annoyance. We shuffle into Balor's cramped office next door.

"What's so important, youngling?" Klauth demands, voice rumbling with irritation.

Leander blurts out, "They want to turn Mina into a dracolich," and then proceeds to fill Klauth in. The explanation takes a good twenty minutes; Klauth's stern expression barely changes as he listens. The tightness in my chest grows as we detail the past two years of conspiracies, close calls, and betrayals.

When Leander finishes, Klauth lets out a slow breath. "I see. One issue with that plan: she'd have to willingly tie her soul to a phylactery to escape a true death." He glances out the open door, eyes lingering on Mina across the hall.

I pinch the bridge of my nose, forcing myself to remain calm. "Even so, knowing her father tried to sell her soul puts Mina in a lot of danger."

Anxious energy crackles through me, making my wings twitch against my back.

"We will be more vigilant," Klauth says, squaring his shoulders. "For now, at least, I can remain at Mina's side."

"For now?" I echo, arching an eyebrow.

He inclines his head. "Once I'm crowned again, I'll have to manage the continent's affairs. I've already agreed to have Mina's property overhauled—exactly as she wished. Aside from what Warwick's people can do, we've got engineers coming in to modernize and upgrade the private shelter I built for Mina." Klauth tilts his head at an angle I know irritates her to no end.

Leander clears his throat. "Did Mina approve this?" He voices my question before I can ask.

"Approve it? She suggested it." Klauth gives a faint smirk. "Restoring my home would be too resource-heavy." He gestures across the hallway. "Come on, let's speak with her. She hates it when we plan these things without her input."

We follow him back, expecting Mina to explode at any moment, but she barely looks up when Klauth addresses her. "My treasure, we have a matter that needs clarification."

"Oh? What is it?" She sets down a pair of glass vials, their liquid contents reflecting the overhead lights in shifting colors.

"Regarding where we should rule from," Klauth begins. "Where would you prefer?"

I tense, fully expecting him to simply dictate terms, given his personality. But Mina surprises me by answering lightly, "My lands. Most of the infrastructure is already in place. We just need to update the lower levels, add a throne room, and enlarge the war room." She tilts her head and smiles. "Klauth suggested having contractors modernize our private dwellings. I agree it would be nice to have hot water and soaking chambers, like your mother has, Abraxis."

Suddenly, a golden eagle swoops through the open window. The rush of wind from its wings tousles my hair, and Mina calmly covers her forearm with a thin layer of scales just before it lands. My gaze narrows. "Is that my dad's familiar?"

"Yeah," Mina says, untying a small scroll from the eagle's leg. "Since emails and texts can be intercepted, we've switched to using our familiars." She unrolls the parchment and skims the contents, her expression unreadable. "Perfect. Your dad's sharing his plans for his home with the contractors. I already gave Vox a list of things from your father's estate that I want in mine." She hands me the note, scribbles a reply of her own, and secures it back to the eagle's leg. It takes off silently, leaving a swirl of loose feathers drifting to the floor.

"When were you going to tell me about all this?" I snap, my pulse hammering. I hate being in the dark—it makes me feel powerless.

Mina's eyes flash, her pupils contracting to dangerous slits. "Look at your messages, Mr. Havock." Her voice carries a low, dragonic growl, and the hair on my arms stands on end. Hastily, I pull out my phone. It's still on silent from this morning's therapy session. My stomach drops when I see a dozen missed messages in the family chat—exactly what I needed to stay informed.

"I'm sorry, Mina," I mutter, lowering my head. "I messed up. My phone was on silent for therapy. I've been going every day these past four days ... trying to be a better mate and bond brother." Shame coils in my gut, and I feel my wings droop.

Mina steps closer, lowering her head until our gazes meet. "I'm proud of you, Abraxis, for going." Her tone softens. "I didn't want to push you, because I know you're sensitive about being seen as weak." She nudges Klauth with her elbow, eyes shining with amusement. "Guess what? He started therapy yesterday, too. Klauth, you need to head there now if you don't want to be late. Love you." She leans up and kisses him, sending him on his way.

"I'm going to finish up with Balor, then we'll head home." Mina turns to me with a gentle smile. "Do me a favor and start some steaks, maybe?" That small gesture—a simple request—warms me from the inside. Despite everything, the tension in my chest eases, and for a moment, the world feels right again.

I sigh, thinking about how I've been relying on Abraxis's mom in my mother's absence. She's been phenomenal through all of this—patient, knowledgeable, and far less judgmental than I expected. Still, part of me aches for my actual mother's presence.

"Mr. Martz..." Arista's smooth, calculated voice drifts across the amphitheater. A flicker of mischief lights her eyes, and I tense against the cold, hard edge of my desk.

"What is it, Arista?" Mr. Martz asks, turning away from the projection of a dragon's nasal plates flickering on the screen at the front of the room.

"Is it true that only pure bloods are being invited?" Arista's tone drips with faux innocence as she tosses a glance over her shoulder at me. "And the new king will look for a female to be his?" Her eyes narrow, and I have to stifle the urge to let my power crackle in the surrounding air. I want to roast her where she stands.

"There are several requirements for the invitation," Kai chimes in from the front row, his voice echoing off the high walls. "But being pure blood isn't one of them. And from the missive, the future king already has a powerful mate. He's not looking for another."

"Hear that, Mina?" Arista taunts, her gaze swirling with the fire of her drake. "No chance you're going, nor will you horde another male for your collection."

Balor's warm laugh resonates against my back as he lounges beside me. The faint scent of leather wafts over me from his fighting leathers. "I'd be more worried about the third-year purge than the formal if I were you," he says, kicking his feet onto the seat in front of us and leaning back.

Mr. Martz sighs at the flickering projector. "Care to come down and explain that to the class, Mr. Husk, while I fight with this blasted machine?"

"Gladly." Balor stands, the heavy clunking of his boots echoing in the amphitheater. My eyes follow the broad line of his shoulders, and I catch the glint of my mate mark on his neck.

"The third-year purge is a single night," he begins, voice low and confident, "when all vendettas can be settled without repercussions. Diplomatic immunity doesn't apply, even if you have it. It happens the night before winter break, so be ready." He smirks as Arista's face pales.

A male two rows back from Arista's group raises his hand, voice cracking with interest. "Faculty isn't allowed to interfere, right?"

"Correct," Balor replies. "As much as some of us might like to strangle the life out of you, we can't join in or provide shelter." He crosses his arms, and the leather strains, reminding me of the raw power he keeps so carefully leashed.

"What's the containment area?" I ask, imagining Arista's entire nest quivering under my wrath.

"The campus," Balor says. "Staff will be relegated to the healers' quadrant or staff housing. All kills must be reported to one of the approved teachers." He scribbles a list across the board. None of my mates' names are on it. "That's all." He climbs back up the steps, each footstep reverberating through the silent room, and settles next to me again.

"Interesting post-birthday present," I muse, drumming my fingers lightly on the worn armrest. I know the others have probably forgotten my birthday with everything going on, but I also know that Balor's is tomorrow. I already have a plan for him.

"Every three years, the third-year purge happens," he murmurs, bending close to brush a kiss across my temple. "We're just lucky it's near your birthday."

My hand drifts to Thauglor's carrier, my fingertips tracing the soft fabric. Soon, mate number eight will hatch, and our family will finally be complete. "I'm leaving Thauglor with you for the purge," I say, my lips curling into a feral grin.

Balor snorts. "Oh boy, that look tells me something just clicked for you."

"Klauth isn't staff…" The whisper of an idea grows in my mind, and I can't contain a low chuckle as the rest of Mr. Martz's lecture passes in a blur. There's a buzzing in my veins now—the same electric anticipation that comes every time I'm granted free rein.

I mentally start my list. Names, faces, all the ones I want to tear apart. Year three means student against student, and from what I've seen at this academy, they aren't kidding around. The night before winter break can't come soon enough.

I place my foot on the narrow wooden beam and inhale, feeling my lungs fill with the musty air of the ancient temple. Torches flicker along the cold stone walls, casting dancing shadows that make the beam look smaller than it already is. A faint scent of incense tickles my nose—something floral and spicy, likely meant to cleanse the space of dark energies. Not that it does anything for my nerves.

"Again, my queen. Walk on the beam, hold your head high, and keep your shoulders back. You're a—what's it called? A Shadowblade? This should be easy for you." Priestess Hellen's voice echoes from ten feet below me, the authority in her tone prickling my skin.

I straighten, trying to ignore the tremor in my legs. "I don't usually cross a mock parapet in a full-length gown and heels," I mutter, cheeks warming. My breath comes in short, shallow puffs that swirl the incense-laden air.

Taking a deep breath, I place one foot in front of the other. Every muscle screams with tension, and the echo of each hesitant click of my heel against the wood sends a pulse of anxiety through me. The skirt of my gown drags along my ankles, so I lift the edges slightly. I have to force myself not to sway my hips like I usually do in heels, because any sudden shift might tip my balance.

Below me, Balor, Abraxis, Leander, and Ziggy hover with a net, ready to catch me if I fall—as I have before. Their concern weighs on me, and I fight the urge to hurry and spare them any more stress.

"Come on, Mina, you've got this!" Callan calls from the sidelines before a sharp crack of wood meeting flesh cuts him off. He's supposed to be balancing books on his head for posture practice, but it appears the Priestess just reminded him to keep quiet.

A low chuckle slips from my lips. "Deep breath, my treasure," Klauth purrs, standing at the far side of the platform with his arms outstretched. The faint scent of his cologne reaches me—a mix of sandalwood and something darker. "The sooner you get here, the sooner I can hold you."

My heart thumps. I focus on his voice, letting it guide me across. The torchlight catches on the polished wood, momentarily blinding me, but I push forward. "Just a little bit more, my treasure," Klauth coaxes, his voice low and soothing.

I step off the beam and practically collapse into his arms, my pulse racing. "Ugh, that was horrible," I groan, clinging to him. His chest is warm, and I catch the steady rhythm of his heartbeat.

"You still have to walk back the other way, yet, Mina." Priestess Hellen's tone is merciless as it drifts up to us. "Abraxis, wait on the other side. Vaughn, replace him so your mate doesn't splat on the ground."

Vaughn slides into position below, giving me a reassuring grin. The soft rustling of robes and clank of metal echoes in the cavernous space as everyone shifts into place.

Klauth presses a comforting kiss to my temple and turns me gently. "He's been working very hard to improve. Walk to him the way you walked to me," he whispers. A breath of warm air caresses my ear, sending a ripple of tingles down my spine.

On the opposite side, Abraxis crosses his arms, a confident smirk lighting his features. "Come on, baby, you've got this. Six-time gauntlet champion won't let a wooden parapet and heels stop her."

His words pull a small laugh from me. "You've got a point there, my love." The beam no longer feels so daunting. Each step grows lighter, fueled by the memory of why we're doing this—training, discipline, and partnership. My mind flickers back to my childhood: cold, loveless halls, and parents who never showed me a single ounce of warmth without an ulterior motive. It's no wonder I struggle in relationships now, always waiting for the other shoe to drop. But these men ... they talk me through every doubt, every nightmare.

We've been putting in the work, especially after therapy sessions they insisted I start. And here, in the temple, my usually overwhelming visions are silenced. It's a strange relief, but it also cuts off my connection to Thauglor, a being I sense in the corners of my mind. My steps falter as a prickly feeling creeps over my skin—something is off.

"What's wrong?" Balor's voice echoes from directly below.

"Something's shifted..." My eyes roam the temple. The fluttering torchlight is the same, the thick, incense-tinged air unchanged, but a sudden hush has fallen, as though the temple itself is holding its breath. I hear a distant twang followed by a sharp whoosh. I whip my head toward the sound just as something pierces my shoulder. A burst of white-hot pain steals my breath. The arrow nearly punches through me, and I reel from the shock.

I glimpse the attacker for the briefest moment before Ziggy disappears, presumably to hunt him down. Abraxis launches into the air, powerful muscles straining as he scoops me from the beam and glides me over to Klauth. I register frantic shouts—Priestesses rushing us into a hidden chamber. The walls here are damp and cool, the floor slick with condensation. I can taste copper in my mouth, and my vision swims.

I stare at the arrow embedded in my shoulder. Thick, dark blood stains my gown. Klauth's hand trembles near the shaft, but I shake my head. "Don't touch it. It's made from dragon's bane. It's highly poisonous to dragons."

"Shit..." Klauth and Abraxis exchange panicked looks, both clearly torn about pulling it out.

I struggle to keep my voice steady. "Leander, get hot water. Ziggy needs to grab my green bag from my bedroom. Hurry—while I'm still awake." My throat feels tight, and the pain radiates through every nerve, making my head spin. I force myself to focus on Klauth and Balor. "Mix Macabate at twenty percent, Arkasu at thirty, Laumpor at forty, Blabert at ten. It should fix everything."

My words slur as I fight the toxins searing my veins. I feel the air shift as Leander returns, the steam from the hot water drifting across my arms. It smells metallic, like overheated stone and a hint of linen from the clothes.

"Soak two rags in the hot water, then grip the arrow and snap off the fletchings or the arrowhead," I instruct, voice wobbling. My eyelids grow heavy. My body wants to shut down and heal. The world blurs around me.

"Someone hold her," Leander orders as Callan directs Ziggy to find the ingredients.

There's a sharp crack. The agony of the arrow moving rips a scream from my throat, and darkness immediately rushes in. The last thing I hear is my own ragged breathing and my father's voice echoing in my mind: *Be faster.* Then everything goes silent and I sink into the dark, willing sleep to claim me, if only to escape the pain.

I'M NOT sure how long I've been unconscious, but my nose tells me exactly where I am. The crisp mountain air carries a faint tang of snow and stone, and I catch the comforting warmth of my scent mingled with Ziggy's and Balor's. My skin tingles against the rough scales and coarse fur that line my makeshift bed, and I realize they must have brought me back to my nest high in the mountains.

A low groan escapes my throat as I try to shift. Ziggy's displacer beast —a hulking creature with dark, mottled fur—wraps a thick, rubbery tentacle around my waist, carefully lifting me upright. My head throbs, and the world tilts for a moment, forcing me to squeeze my eyes shut.

"She's awake," I hear Callan shout, his voice echoing along the newly renovated corridors. Moments later, a stampede of footsteps booms toward me, sending vibrations through the stone floor.

I slowly blink and let my gaze wander around the main chamber. Thanks to the contractors, it looks more like a palace now than a hollowed-out cavern. Smooth walls gleam faintly under soft overhead lights, and plush carpets cushion the cold stone. Everything has been transformed with elegant arches, gilded accents, and velvet drapes. Balor's basilisk shifts beside me, its serpentine form dissolving until only the man remains, kneeling at my side. His gaze, a molten crimson, roams over my face with desperate concern before relief softens his features.

"How are you feeling?" he asks, just as the others gather in a semicircle behind him. Their combined presence is a comforting weight on my senses.

"Other than this pounding headache, I'm good," I answer, and glance down at my left shoulder, where a tight bandage wraps my skin. "How bad was it?" My gaze flicks between Balor and Klauth, who are just as knowledgeable about poisons as I am.

Klauth's voice is tinged with anger and relief all at once. "A lethal dose, my treasure. One that would have killed a lesser dragon." He steps aside so Abraxis can move closer.

"How long was I asleep?" I manage, though the grogginess threatens to pull me under again.

"Four days," Leander replies. I look at Balor, feeling a pang of guilt.

"Sorry I missed your birthday." My shoulders slump with regret.

Balor's expression softens. "You surviving is more than enough of a birthday present," he says, then glances at Ziggy behind me. "That one wouldn't let go of you for more than an hour at a time."

I twist around to meet the malevolent green eyes of Ziggy's packlord displacer beast. My heart tightens with gratitude. "Thank you, Ziggy. Can you shift back? I want a hug." A yawn slips past my lips, and I lower my gaze to the bandage again.

There's a subtle crackle in the air, like static brushing over my skin, followed by a rapid ripple of pressure. In the next instant, Ziggy appears in his human form and scoots closer. He gently pulls me into his lap, wrapping muscular arms around my waist and pressing his chest against my back.

"I was so scared," he whispers, his breath tickling my ear. I exhale a shaky sigh.

"Me too, Ziggy. It's not my first time being shot with dragon's bane." I look pointedly at Abraxis and Klauth. "Dad shot me once while we were practicing dodging arrows—told me to *move faster* before I passed out. No one treated the wounds. I slept for a week without the poultice you made for me."

Klauth's roar reverberates through the chamber. "He didn't treat you at all?"

Abraxis interjects as he offers me a cup of steaming bone broth. "Sadly, it sounds exactly like her father." His gaze flicks to mine, eyes gentling. "We'll start you off with broth and work up to real food. It's Saturday, so we're free for the next two days."

I nod, the aroma of the broth—savory and rich—coaxing my stomach awake. I take a careful sip; the warmth slides down my throat and settles in my belly.

"The house looks incredible," I say, surveying the polished walls, plush rugs, and ornate furnishings.

Leander gives me a proud smile. "I gave Klauth access to your online wish board. Cora had a shared inspiration board you two were working on for the combined flight. So we based the design on the colors and themes you liked."

My eyes sweep over the room, taking in the subtle mix of shimmering gold, rich burgundy, and soft cream. "I love it," I say quietly, finishing the last of the broth. A wave of exhaustion surges through me. "Is there somewhere I can lie down? I'm still so tired."

Callan steps forward, his eye glowing with an eager warmth. "I have just the place for you."

Abraxis bends down and scoops me into his arms, cradling me gently as he carries me through a short hallway. We enter the egg chamber— a circular space where the ceiling arches high, and the walls are lined with softly glowing crystals. In the far corner stands a large gryphon nest piled high with downy feathers. My eyes widen at the luxurious sight of it.

"Did you pluck yourself bald lining this?" I ask Callan, marveling at how plush and inviting it looks.

"Yup, several times," he replies. "My feathers grow back quickly if I eat and rest, so over three days I filled it just for you." He shifts into his gryphon form—a regal creature with tawny feathers and piercing eye—and prances over to the nest before leaping up and settling in. He lifts one wing, inviting me into his warmth.

My mates each press a kiss to my forehead or cheek, and I'm passed to Callan's waiting embrace. The softness of his gryphon feathers cushions me like a thick, luxurious blanket. The scent of fresh hay mingled with his musky gryphon scent, envelops me. My eyes flutter closed, and I nuzzle into his side.

Safe in their care, I sink back into sleep—my head pounding less, my breathing finally steady, and the comforting hum of their presence anchoring me in the darkness.

until our faces are nearly touching. My breath mists the air between us. "Look deep into my eyes and listen to my voice."

A cold sensation creeps into my skull as my eyes shift into their basilisk form. My tone drops, taking on a resonant hum that vibrates in my chest. "Who hired you to shoot the female?"

His eyes go vacant in seconds. Blood trickles from his lower lip as he mumbles, "Demi hired me to kill the future queen."

"Does anyone else know the future queen's identity?" I press, tension coiling in my gut.

"No," he whispers, breath hitching. "Word got out that the future royal family is training in the temple. A priestess named Elain leaked it."

I glance at Ziggy, who disappears without a word—likely off to tell Hellen or settle the priestess matter himself. I don't particularly care which; the priesthood handles their own, and I have no sympathy for those who betray us.

Turning back to the fire drake, my fangs extend, and I sink them into his shoulder. My necrotic venom floods his bloodstream, guaranteeing he'll rot from the inside out. He thrashes and howls as his flesh sizzles beneath my teeth. My nostrils fill with the stench of decay, and I watch impassively; he nearly killed the one I love.

Moments later, Ziggy reappears in a rush of displaced air. He looks at the convulsing prisoner, then at me. "Ready?"

I nod, stepping away from the doomed fire drake. Ziggy folds time and space around us, the dungeon dissolving into a swirl of darkness.

When reality solidifies again, we're standing in the restructured courtyard of the Risedale nest. The raw scent of fresh mortar and newly cut stone mingles with the crisp air. I spot Mina on the back of Callan's gryphon, her eyes bright as she surveys the upgrades. She cradles a baby in her arms, Thauglor's carrier strapped securely to her back.

"How are you feeling?" I ask, keeping my voice gentle as the Callan pads closer.

"Better. Have you seen Cora's baby up close?" Mina's voice is soft, and she nuzzles the child, her dragoness purring deep in her chest.

"Not yet." I step closer, the baby's sweet, milky scent replacing the bitter tang of the dungeon in my nose. "He's a sturdy little man. What's his name?" I press my forehead gently to Mina's arm, relieved to see her safe and whole.

"William." Her eyes glimmer with tears she refuses to shed. "Cora named him after me."

A gentle warmth spreads through my chest, chasing away lingering anger. "That's a fine name for him. He's named after his very strong aunt." Mina leans in, her lips brushing mine in a tender kiss. The darkness from before fades a little more. I help her slip off of Callan's back.

"It's times like this I want my own," she murmurs, gaze drifting down to the baby's chubby cheeks. "A whole nest of babies, everywhere. But we're not safe yet, and I still have to finish school." She sighs, a slight tremor in her shoulders.

"As soon as it's safe," I promise, helping her dismount from Callan's gryphon with care, "we'll give you as many eggs as you want." A wry chuckle escapes me. "Until then, practice makes perfect."

A pretty blush warms her cheeks as she glances up at me. "I fully endorse that idea," she whispers, slipping her arm around my waist as we head inside to the lower living quarters.

The Risedale nest looks nothing like it did during Mina's first yearly as a dragoness. New corridors branch off from the main tunnel, lined with softly glowing lanterns. Reinforced stone arches overhead, making the place feel vast and secure.

"How do you like the changes?" Klauth asks, stepping out of a room down the hall.

"It looks amazing. Are my gardens intact?" Mina's teeth catch her bottom lip, worry etched in her brow.

Callan chuckles. "Come and see."

We pass Cora, who takes her baby back from Mina, then continue on to a set of wrought-iron bars that seal off the gardens. A faint breeze carries the scent of growing herbs and damp earth. Klauth unlocks the gate, and we follow Mina inside.

"I expanded your poison herb garden," I say, nodding toward a larger section where exotic plants sway in a breeze that filters through a natural vent above.

Mina's expression lights up. "I see that. It looks terrific." She slips past the gate, running her fingertips over the leaves.

Abraxis trails behind us. "To think she started tending this garden at about six or seven years old," he comments quietly.

"It's insane, the things her father put her through," Callan mutters, his voice grave as we watch Mina tend a cluster of dark purple blossoms.

In the far corner, three metal rods stab up from the ground like silent sentinels. I raise an eyebrow. "Do I even want to know what those are for?"

"Abaddon, Lysander, and Arista," Klauth says simply, his smile cold. "I promised Mina their heads would end up on pikes."

Mina glances over. "If my visions are accurate, Dad dies as his dragon, so a pike won't work." She points to a natural skylight overhead. "But dropping his cleaned skull through that hole? That might be satisfying."

"I'll make a bigger pike," Klauth replies, eyeing the rods speculatively.

Mina approaches Ziggy and whispers something. In a flicker, they disappear. Moments later, Ziggy returns alone, grabs my arm, and the world twists. The gardens vanish, replaced by a cavern with warm, humid air that clings to my skin. A hint of sulfur wafts through the darkness.

"Enjoy," Ziggy says, then fades, leaving me standing on slick rock. The rush of water echoes off the walls, guiding me deeper.

At the end of a winding tunnel, I find a wide chamber with a natural hot spring. Steam rises in gentle wisps, and the mineral-rich water glistens under the faint light spilling in from a crack in the ceiling. Mina's dragoness form sprawls in the center of the pool, her scaled limbs moving lazily in the water as she preens.

A stray pebble skitters under my boot, and her head snaps up. At once, she shifts, returning to her human shape and swimming to the water's edge. "Are you going to join me?" she asks, tilting her head just so, eyes entirely human but still holding that dragonic intensity.

"If that's what you want," I answer, unzipping my fighting leathers. I take my time, letting the rustle of fabric and the slight scrape of leather on rock tease both of us. Her eyes darken with hunger.

"How did I get so lucky to have so much eye candy in my nest?" she purrs, voice echoing softly against the dripping walls.

"Lucky, I guess." I grin, then run and leap into the water, creating a spectacular splash. The hot spring's warmth envelops me, easing away the ache in my muscles. I swim closer, catch her around the waist, and press a soft kiss to the corner of her mouth. "What made you decide to come here?"

She exhales a contented sigh. "It has healing properties, and I want to be at my best. Plus, I've been trying to spend equal time with everyone, and I have two very selfish drakes to manage." She laughs, low and melodic, and lays her head on my shoulder. "So I chose you right now."

I stroke her damp hair, relishing how the mineral-rich water of the hot spring seems to make each strand silkier between my fingers. Steam drifts across our skin, curling around us in hazy tendrils. The heat soothes my muscles, but it's her warmth—her body pressed to mine—that chases away the last trace of chill in the night air.

Mina's lips graze my jaw, playfully nibbling in that teasing way she knows drives me mad. A soft, satisfied sound vibrates in my throat as I guide us through the shallower edge of the spring. The smooth rocks beneath the water offer just enough friction to push off and float. Gently, I maneuver us so we're half-submerged, the steaming water lapping at our waists.

I roll on top of her, supporting my weight on one arm while the other slips around her ribs. With a careful tug, I draw her onto a flat stone ledge at the perimeter of the spring. Leaning down, I capture her lips in a hungry kiss, pouring every ounce of my devotion into it. Her taste is a heady mix of salt and mineral water, intoxicating enough to make me forget we're not alone in the world.

My sly little minx of a mate shifts beneath me, aligning her hips with mine. *Who am I to resist?* Slowly, I press forward, feeling each piercing drag through her welcoming heat. A deep, resonant purr escapes her, echoing off the rocky walls of the spring as I bottom out. The flutter of her core around me is nothing short of divine.

"Move, baby..." she murmurs, nose tucked under my jaw, her breath warm against my neck.

I grin against her lips, withdrawing at a torturously slow pace before driving in again, deeper. Her frustrated whine is as sweet as the humid air around us. My shoulders flex with each measured thrust. Her fingers curl against my skin, urging me to go faster, but I keep my rhythm. This is part of our reconditioning—**I** decide how this plays out. Besides, there's a dark thrill in seeing her perched on the brink of surrender.

"Please, Balor..." she moans when I adjust the angle just enough to keep her from reaching her peak.

"Patience, my love. Good girls get orgasms; bad girls get edged," I murmur, nipping her shoulder lightly. The second she whines again, I still my hips, letting her feel the weight of my control. When her protests subside, I pull out completely and shift onto my knees, steam swirling around my torso. "Hands and knees, love," I instruct, tipping my head.

She obeys in record time. The sight of her bared, glistening skin is almost enough to break my composure. Still, I move with deliberate slowness, entering her again and gripping her hips. Then, I unleash a punishing rhythm—each slap of skin on skin echoes in the confined space, droplets splashing against the hot rocks. My Jacob's ladder piercings catch every sensitive spot, and she soon shatters around me. Her wail reverberates off the stony walls, a symphony of pure, unrestrained need.

I slow when I feel her knees wobble, and together we sink into the water once more, settling onto our sides. Our bodies remain joined, the heat of the spring enveloping us. Carefully, I roll my hips, letting the piercings brush all her best places. I bite down gently on her shoulder —just enough to make her gasp. Her core clenches in response, sending another spike of pleasure through me.

Mina curls my arm tighter around her, guiding my hand to rest just beneath her breasts. Her heartbeat thrums against my forearm like a caged bird. "Someone's very close..." I whisper, tracing the shell of her ear with my lips before nipping at her earlobe.

"Come with me, baby, please..." Her voice trembles as she arches back, trying to meet my gaze. I kiss her cheek and angle my hips, fully aware it will send us both careening over the edge. We rock together, the motion fanning the steam around us in ghostly swirls. Mina cries out first, her body clenching so hard that I lose myself, pulsing in time with her erratic shudders.

In the aftermath, we remain cocooned in each other's arms. The mineral-rich water soothes our overheated flesh, and the lingering steam presses in like a warm blanket. My beloved mate is still trembling in my embrace, the center of my world. I'd raze everything—turn it all to stone—if it meant keeping her safe.

I float lazily in the warm mineral spring, water lapping at my shoulders, while Mina clings to my side. A gentle steam rises around us, creating a veil of heat that clings to my skin. The subtle scent of earth and wet stone fills my lungs each time I breathe in. Mina's voice, hushed and concerned, breaks through the soothing ambiance as she confides her worries about the coronation.

I offer her the plans the guys and I have discussed, hoping they'll ease her mind. "It'll work," I assure her, letting my hand rest on her bare shoulder. She looks at me with those dark eyes of hers, filled with a mixture of doubt and hope.

Before I can say more, Ziggy's voice echoes from the edge of the spring. "Are you guys coming home soon? Dinner is almost ready." His tone bounces off the cavern walls, a jarring reminder we can't stay hidden here forever.

"Who cooked?" I ask as I help Mina onto the smooth rock ledge. Droplets cascade off her body, and I catch the faint scent of her floral shampoo mixed with the mineral tang of the spring.

"Abraxis and Klauth. We're still in the Risedale nest, having dinner with Cora and Warwick," Ziggy explains, his figure flickering closer in an instant. The temperature dips slightly when he appears—his presence always brings a subtle chill.

"That sounds great," Mina says with a grateful smile. Her hand grips mine, and I feel the coolness of her damp skin against my heated palm. The moment she drags me forward, Ziggy places his hand on my shoulder.

In the blink of an eye, we phase back into the Risedale nest's dining room. The sudden shift hits me like a gust of wind; the room's light and warmth replace the humid darkness of the spring. Poor Warwick yelps, nearly toppling off his chair in surprise. The savory aroma of roasted meat and spiced vegetables assaults my senses, making my stomach rumble.

Klauth rises from his seat at once, his stern gaze locking on me. He motions for me to follow him out of the dining room and into a narrow hallway. Each step I take echoes on the polished floor, and I catch a whiff of wood polish and parchment as we enter what appears to be an office space.

"What's wrong?" I ask, noting the tension in Klauth's broad shoulders.

"The priestesses have sent Priestess Elain to Blackhaven for interrogation," Klauth says calmly, though his eyes flicker with intensity.

I narrow my gaze. "That's not the only reason we're here, is it?" I recognize his tell—the slight tilt of his head that always betrays him, just like Abraxis has his own.

"Did Mina claw or bite you?" Klauth demands no hesitation.

I scoff and arch a brow. "No, she submitted exactly like she's supposed to. I remembered the assignment." My tone carries a trace of annoyance; I hate being tested.

"Good. Let's go enjoy dinner," Klauth says, but I can't miss the way his eyes shift. "Mina picked her two dresses for the Winter Formal. She'll ride Leander's Nightmare in the processional, like last time."

He lifts his head, casting a wicked glint in his gaze. "For Mina's safety during the coronation, I want you shifted. You and Ziggy will stay at her side at all times—one to defend, the other to ensure a quick escape. Will you do me that honor?" He extends his hand, and I stare at it briefly, considering.

"Anything you need for Mina or the safety of this nest, I'll do without question." I let out a half laugh. "I'm no hero. They sacrifice the girl for the world. I'm the thing that goes bump in the night. I'll watch the world burn to keep Mina safe and never regret it." I clasp his hand firmly, the air crackling with unspoken resolve.

Klauth nods, a faint smile curling his lips. "On that, we agree completely. Turn everyone to stone if you have to, as long as Mina lives." He pats my back, his palm warm through my thin shirt. "Now, let's eat before our mate comes looking for us."

As I follow him back toward the dining room, the scents of roasted garlic and spiced wine grow stronger. I think about the stories everyone tells of Klauth, painting him as a monster. He might be capable of monstrous acts, but he protects his mate above all else—and that's not a monster. That's a damn good mate.

"Everything changes today." I bite my bottom lip, torn between the two gowns that represent two starkly different roles I'm about to play.

"It doesn't have to," Cora says, soft but firm. "You're still you, no matter what." She looks up at me and kisses my cheek, her sweet perfume lingering in the air.

I let out a shaky laugh. "I'm finishing school. That part I refuse to give up on." My voice wavers. "But the council said I can't run the gauntlets anymore." A subtle chill creeps up my spine at the memory of the council's final decree.

Cora carefully sits William down on a soft blanket on the couch, arranging pillows around him so he can't roll off. "You never wanted to be a weapon, right? So maybe this is a good thing." She offers me the black gown, her smile gentle. "Now, come on. I get to be your hand-maiden tonight."

I roll my eyes, but I'm grateful for her levity. "Okay, fine. Let's do this." I peel off my sweatshirt and leggings, the cool air brushing my bare skin. As Cora helps me into the gown, the corset tightens around my ribs, making my breathing shallow. "I keep forgetting these stupid things have corsets." I glance down at my breasts, which feel like they're seconds from spilling out. "My boobs look huge," I mutter, horrified at the cleavage. Abraxis's necklace rests right above the apex, drawing even more attention to them.

Cora laughs and sets about fixing my hair, pinning up braids and adding the delicate adornments Cerce gave me. Each polished inch of my horns gleams under the light, reflecting a faint pearlescent sheen. I tug on the long black gloves that slide over my forearms, the fabric smooth and slightly cool against my skin.

"We have ten minutes to get you on Leander's back before the procession," Balor announces as he steps into the room. He's wearing a finely tailored black suit that catches the faint flicker of torchlight from the hallway.

I nod, heart thudding, and slip my arm through his. My heels click against the stone floor as we head toward the staging area. An undercurrent of charged excitement hangs in the air—whispers, hushed conversations, the metallic tang of polished armor.

"Klauth thinks something is going to happen, doesn't he?" I hazard a glance at Balor, my voice low.

"That's an understatement. He wants me and Zig shifted for the coronation, which speaks volumes." Balor's mouth twitches in a grim half-smile. "I think Zig will walk you down the aisle to Klauth."

"If you two are shifted, how are you being crowned?" My brow furrows as I imagine the ceremony with Balor's basilisk and Ziggy's displacer beast in place of my mates.

"Easy. It'll still be done while we're in our shifted forms," Balor explains, patting my hand reassuringly. We enter the staging hall where a line of mounted riders awaits, their horses shifting restlessly. The air is thick with the scent of leather and the unmistakable musk of the stable. At the front stands Abraxis and Leander in his nightmare form.

Abraxis lets out a low whistle when he sees me, his eyes flashing with primal interest. "You look absolutely stunning, Mina."

Leander bows, and Balor helps me settle into a sidesaddle position on his nightmare's back. My gown drapes elegantly over his flank, though Balor fusses with the skirt to keep it from tangling. When Leander rises to his full height, I realize just how small I feel perched on him—but also how safe.

"See you soon," I say softly to Balor as he moves away. Turning to Abraxis, I force a smile despite my racing pulse. "Nervous?"

"No... not at all." Abraxis huffs out a laugh, a faint edge to his voice. "I'd rather go to war naked than do this. But it'll buy us more security and get me off the front lines."

"That is one of the bonuses." The toll of the bell rings out, resonating through the wide hall and signaling the start of the procession. I swallow, tasting my fear and excitement.

Just like last year, we have to ride out at the head of the procession and stop in front of the royal box. Klauth will offer me a single flower—his choice. Leander will have to rear up for me to accept it. In return, I'm supposed to give Klauth one of my hair ornaments. But I have other plans. I've cut one of my braids loose to give him instead—an unmistakable token, binding me to this new path in a way that feels both exhilarating and terrifying.

The heavy doors swing open, and the cool night air rushes in. My pulse thunders as we prepare to lead the procession outside. I catch Abraxis's eye one last time. There's no going back now, and the darkness of this night seems to shimmer with countless possibilities—and threats—just beyond the threshold.

THE THUNDEROUS CLOPPING of hooves against the stone reverberates through the courtyard, instantly commanding silence from the gathered onlookers. My pulse thrums in time with the steady cadence of Leander's footsteps as he walks, in his shifted Nightmare stallion form, side by side with Abraxis's heavily armored warhorse. Flames lick across Leander's mane and tail, causing the surrounding air to shimmer in the humid night. The tang of smoldering ember mixes with the cold bite of metal, curling into my lungs in a heady rush.

Though every fiber of me itches to scan the crowd, I force myself to keep my gaze forward—chin high, shoulders back. This is as much a performance as it is a test. Abraxis, regal and unyielding in the saddle, tilts his head in acknowledgment of the spectators, while I grip the front of Leander's saddle, the heat from his blazing mane warming my gloved hands.

We approach the royal box in a synchronized march; Leander's fiery hooves spark against the flagstones in unison with the clang of Abraxis's warhorse. The crowd's hush deepens, a tense current of curiosity and awe. A wisp of incense drifts my way from somewhere off to the left, mingling with the sweet fragrance of roses—the chosen symbol of this entire farce of a ceremony.

My gaze lands on Klauth, seated in the royal box alongside my other mates. Even from this distance, I sense the weight of his scrutiny, as though he's taking my measure in real time. A whisper of excitement and dread slides across my skin. Any misplaced step could risk everything we've planned.

Leander draws nearer to the box, his nostrils flaring to release plumes of steam in the night air. At my soft cue—my palm brushing his shoulder—he slows, lifting his head. Abraxis's warhorse matches the tempo, a testament to the endless hours of practice we've poured into these precise movements.

We draw alongside the royal box, and Leander rears up, his flaming hooves striking at the air. The spectators gasp in unison, and adrenaline jolts through me, heightening every sensation—the roar of the crowd, the crackle of his mane, the frantic pulse in my ears.

"My treasure," Klauth calls, offering a crimson rose so close to the shade of his scales that it sends a shiver rippling through me. I feel the weight of a thousand gazes, but I school my features into a calm mask. Removing one glove, I accept the rose with careful grace, inhaling the delicate perfume as though committing it to memory. I hand Klauth the hair ornament and the braid of my hair. His eyes flair for a moment before he nods his head at me.

Leander's flame-wreathed hooves drop back to the ground, and we ease into the procession line. Hugging the rose to my chest, I exhale, trying to calm the pounding in my veins. The most nerve-wracking part of this spectacle is over. Now we must head behind the scenes so I can prepare for the sham wedding and the public bite exchange. The knowledge that the purge begins in four days hangs over me like a storm cloud, electrifying the air.

But for this fleeting moment, I hold tight to the rose and cast a small, measured smile. Leander, Abraxis, and I have played our roles to perfection—at least for now. Tonight's performance only sharpens the eyes already fixed on me, but there's no turning back. As we move away from the royal box, I grip the rose tighter, each fiery flicker from Leander's mane illuminating my next step into the darkness that waits.

Cora, Cerce, and Ziggy meet us in the staging area, where the other horses are being led into their stables amid the earthy tang of hay and the soft whicker of restless animals. I can feel the cool night air brush against my skin as I listen to the steady rustle of leaves and distant murmurs from the academy's corridors.

"We don't have a ton of time," Ziggy says, his voice low and urgent, as he stretches up to help me off Leander's back. The contact with the cool ground jolts me, and I can taste the dust and adrenaline on my tongue. I grab my gown—a heavy, dark fabric that brushes softly against my skin—and we take off running, the sound of our hurried footsteps echoing off stone walls. Ziggy laughs, a sound that mingles with the night's crisp air, shaking his head as he phases us into the changing room.

Inside, the space smells of polished wood and faint incense. We burst into laughter, marveling at how Ziggy's quick thinking saved us time. With practiced ease, he unties the corset of my black gown. His fingers, warm and precise, work quickly as he helps me step out. "I am so sorry you have to go through this," he murmurs, gesturing to the elaborate outfit change and the intricate web of ribbons and boning that await me.

"That makes two of us. I hate gowns," I grumble, and even as I speak, my dragoness rumbles deep within, emphasizing my displeasure.

"At least you look phenomenal in the gowns," Ziggy insists, his eyes gleaming with genuine admiration. "This one almost exactly matches your scales. Vox's seamstress really outdid herself." He threads the ribbons with meticulous care, cinching me into the corseted top of the gown. I watch, almost hypnotized, as my emerald and silver scales peek through along my forearm. I compare their iridescent shimmer to the delicate hues of the fabric. "She did a wonderful job matching the colors," I agree softly, shifting slightly as I let my eyes roam over the interplay of light on the gown and my skin. I make my scales recede and draw in a deep breath.

"Are you nervous?" Ziggy asks as Cora and Cerce catch up, their voices light and teasing as they fuss over my long, green-and-silver hair. Their touch is gentle, and I can smell the faint aroma of lavender in Cerce's hair, mixing with the cool scent of the changing room.

"I'll have you at my side every step of the way. I know you'll never let anything happen to me." I lean forward and press a warm kiss to Ziggy's lips, feeling a comforting steadiness in his embrace as I smile at him.

"Almost done," Cerce calls out, her voice echoing softly off the tiled walls as she sets ornate combs into my hair, expertly sweeping it up into a classic French twist. Ziggy catches my glance and takes it as his cue to shift into his large, sleek black packlord displacer beast. His fur, depending on the angle, either as dark as pitch or glimmering with a hint of blue-black.

"Five minutes, m'lady," a deep, resonant voice calls down the hall, each word heavy with expectation.

"Go take your places; Ziggy and I will be fine," I say, offering a small smile that barely conceals my unease about what's coming.

"I'll see you on the other side," Cora says, her smile warm as she steps forward to give me a gentle hug before departing. Cerce lingers, her eyes bright with pride as she says, "I am so proud of you. You are doing what is best for the nest and the continent," she presses a soft kiss to my cheek before leaving.

Ziggy and I move into position, waiting for the double doors to swing open. I run my fingers through his thick fur, its soft, velvety texture grounding me as my heart races. With each measured step, I remind myself that once we pass through those doors, my life will never be the same. My thoughts drift to the coming year and a half at the academy, and the purge looming in four days. I am painfully aware of my three clear enemies—two definite, and an entire nest of fire drakes whose presence prickles the air with menace.

Thauglor, I remind myself, lies hidden in my poison garden, nestled among the most toxic plants I own. The sharp, almost metallic scent of their poison hangs in the air. It's a silent warning that any who dare reach for him will find death swift and merciless.

Tonight, all of my mates are being made consorts—except for Klauth, of course. I draw in a steady breath as the heavy doors before us creaks open, revealing a grand hall lined with polished chairs and bathed in the soft glow of flickering chandeliers.

We take our first few measured steps out, my gaze locked on the dais at the far end of the aisle. There, Balor's basilisk is coiled behind the thrones, its head held high as if it were a silent sentinel keeping a watchful eye on us. To the right of Klauth, Abraxis stands tall, surrounded by the rest of my mates. I am relieved to have Ziggy by my side. I keep a reassuring hand on his back as we proceed. Every sound

—the murmur of disapproving voices, the rustle of fabric, and even the distant hum of anticipation—reminds me of how surreal and fraught with danger this entire event feels.

I am a mixed-breed dragoness, looked down upon by the pure bloods —not just because of my non-purebred status but also because I am half green dragon. Klauth and Abraxis, however, have never held my bloodline against me. I dare not meet the eyes of the onlookers. I can almost hear their whispers of discontent as I walk down the aisle.

"The King deserves better!" Arista's voice suddenly rings out, cutting through the murmurs and silencing the crowd. Every head turns, shock and indignation etched on their faces. "He deserves a pureblood mate!" she yells, her words laced with venom as security moves in to remove her from the hall.

I ignore her outburst, my focus unyielding. What she fails to realize is that he chose me two years ago. His egg ignited for me, burned bright, and demanded my attention. He soothed me when no one else could.

We ascend the five stairs, each step echoing softly under the weight of tradition, until I finally drop into a low curtsy before Klauth. I close my eyes and bow my head, waiting for him to retrieve me, per custom. I feel the warmth of his body before the tip of his fingers gently graze my jaw. I rise, then lower my head again in the practiced rhythm we've shared countless times. Taking my hand, he leads me toward the priestess as the ceremony is about to begin.

gifting a delicate braid of her hair. I tuck it carefully into my pocket alongside my handkerchief, the vivid color of the braid peeking out like a secret promise.

"It's time to move to the next area, Sire," Vox intones. His voice measured as he gestures down the corridor. His retinue, steadfast and silent, shadows our progress—a show of security that clearly irks Lysander. I reply with a cool, deliberate "Lead on," and stride ahead into the next room.

Immediately, my eyes are drawn to the thrones, carved from solid stone in the traditional style. The chill texture of the stone under my fingertips as I pass by reminds me of the enduring legacy of our people. The dais, set about five steps above the lower level, commands attention, while the smaller audience area hums with an expectant murmur as guests take their seats.

I sense Mina's unease about what is coming—a tension that mirrors the low rumble of an impending storm. I don't blame her. I have allowed this charade to continue solely to secure certain immunities for my mate. In these halls, to harm a royal invites immediate death, and with her ever-growing list of enemies, this measure is our next logical safeguard.

Once every guest is seated, I watch as Cerce and Cora from Abraxis's family slip in through a side door. Mina stands ready, every inch the picture of poised defiance. My heart thunders in my chest as I will the doors to open, each agonizing moment stretching out like miles. The faint scent of burning torches and the cool draft from the open corridor heighten my anticipation.

The guard at the door meets my gaze, and with a subtle nod, I signal him to swing open the double doors. They move in perfect unison, revealing the grand hall beyond. There, amid the flickering light and the soft hum of whispered conversations, Mina appears—a vision in a gown matching the exact coloration of her dragoness. She steps forward gracefully, her hand resting on Ziggy's back, her head held high. The hall fills with both appreciative praise and skeptical murmurs; some still question my judgment in claiming a green dragon as mine.

What they don't understand is that Mina and I chose each other over two years ago. I recall how her voice once sang of forever, of redemption and sanctuary. A song that promised a nest strong and safe for herself and any future offspring. In its final, haunting notes, she vowed revenge against those who dared harm us. No woman should ever feel unsafe, and in that moment, I felt the raw power of her bloodline and knew she was the one.

Suddenly, a female voice rings out, slicing through the murmurs and silencing the crowd. "The King deserves better!" Shock and indignation flash across every face. "He deserves a pureblood mate!" The words, laced with venom, reverberate against the stone walls as security moves in to escort the madwoman from the hall.

I ignore her ramblings and fix my gaze on Mina, who too dismisses the outburst with quiet determination. Each step she takes toward me sends my pulse racing faster, echoing in the quiet spaces between the heavy beats of the ancient floorboards. When she finally stands before me, she yields completely—a deep curtsy that is more profound than I had expected. I trace a fingertip along her jaw, feeling the warmth of her skin, and she rises gracefully. Lowering her head in the practiced manner we've shared countless times. She allows me to take her hand as I lead her to the next stage of the program.

The priestess steps forward, her voice steady as she reads from an ancient tome about our heritages. My lineage is unveiled before the gathered crowd, prompting a few gasps. I am King Klauth Ragnar, high king of the Marzana Empire—the lands beneath our feet claimed by ancient rite. Then, her gaze shifts to Mina as she recites her full birth name. On her mother's side, she is descended from Gruaghlothor, the supreme ruler of the ferrous dragon clans; on her father's, from Aglaraerose, the undying one. Abraxis and I exchange knowing looks as we absorb the weight of her bloodline. A fact underscored by the array of scales trailing down her back and spine, cited by the priestess as irrefutable proof of her heritage.

"To properly crown your queen, mate bites must be exchanged and witnessed," the priestess declares. In response, Mina steps forward and stands before me, offering her throat where my first bite already marks the side of her neck. I lean in, pressing a soft kiss to the familiar scar before sinking my teeth in. My voice, deep and resonant like a distant drum, rumbles in a soothing cadence to calm any lingering anxiety. I trace a gentle path over the wound with my tongue, sealing it before pressing another tender kiss.

The priestess approaches once more, inspecting the bite on Mina's throat before speaking softly, "M'lady, if you would be so kind." Mina dips her head in deference to the priestess and then draws closer to me. As we have practiced, she gently presses the bridge of her nose against my jaw, her hands resting on my chest. I envelop her in a warm embrace, then grip the back of her head to guide her mouth to the spot of her original mark. She purrs softly, and I feel the delicate pressure of her teeth as they meet my skin. "Do it, Mina—mark me," I whisper just for her.

I feel her teeth slowly press against my skin, the warmth of her bite igniting a hum that makes our bond flare brighter. With deliberate care, she withdraws her teeth and licks over the wound to seal it, then steps back, lowering her head in quiet humility. I resent she must adhere to these ancient traditions, but they are as unyielding as the stone beneath our feet. The priestess smiles approvingly as she inspects my mark.

Drawing Mina close to my side, I follow the priestess as she steps before the gathered masses. "I am proud to announce that the Aurelian Isles now have a king and queen!" Her words boom through the hall, eliciting cheers that reverberate off the high ceilings. "King Klauth Ragnar and Queen Willamina Ragnar—may you rule well!" She gestures to the other mates on the stage and beckons Mina forward. "Will you be so kind as to mark your king consorts?" With a nod, Mina moves among them, one by one, giving her ceremonial bites. Balor and Ziggy are the last to be marked, their reactions a blend of pride and quiet acceptance.

When Mina finishes, we are instructed to proceed to the ballroom, where the celebration continues amid the soft strains of music, the rich aroma of spiced wine, and the warm glow of countless candles. In every sense, the night pulses with life—and with the unyielding promise of what is coming.

THE ENTIRE NEST hangs back as our guests flow into the ballroom, their excited chatter mingling with the soft hum of distant music. I scan the room, my heart thumping in sync with the pulsing bass, and ask, "Is everyone okay so far with what's happening?" I meet each of my bond brothers' eyes, gauging their moods under the warm glow of the chandeliers.

"I hate how Mina had to act submissive to all of us," Balor declares, his tone rough as he leans back with a dismissive smirk. His words slice through the ambient noise like a sharp blade.

A low, simmering growl builds in my chest as I think about it. "It's one of the first things I'm abolishing. Females should be treated as equals," I retort, my voice barely rising above the soft strains of a string quartet now tuning up in the background.

"Hey..." Mina's gentle voice interrupts as she reaches up, her hand warm and soft against my cheek. Her eyes meet mine with a calm assurance that belies the storm inside. "It wasn't that bad. I didn't have to do anything degrading, so it was livable." A smile tugs at her lips as she glances around the room. "Watching Arista get kicked out was more than worth it." Her words ring out, laced with mischief, and then she looks toward the door. "We should get out there soon."

I slide a folded sheet of paper from my pocket, its crisp texture contrasting with the velvet drape of my jacket. The paper outlines the evening's events in meticulous detail. "The first official dance is Mina's and mine. Second is Abraxis, then Balor, and finally, free-for-all with everyone else." I say this with a measured calm, my fingers tracing the printed lines as if reading my destiny.

"Why is Balor third?" Vaughn asks, tugging at his tie as he straightens up. His voice carries both curiosity and a hint of irritation.

I offer a wry smile. "It's tradition that in a nest, a succession is made. If I die, Abraxis is next in line. If he dies, then it's Balor—until either my son or Abraxis's son is old enough to rule." My gaze drifts toward the ornate doors leading to the hall. An attendant stands there, his polished shoes clicking softly on the marble floor. "Let's get this done. After tonight, I can fly wherever I want, whenever I want," I joke, a rare note of genuine freedom in my laugh. "We will head back to our nest in the mountains tonight. I don't trust the others yet."

At that, Mina moves to my side, her hand slipping onto my arm as if it were a lifeline. The attendant opens the door with a gentle creak, and I lead our nest into the resplendent room. The ballroom dazzles under a cascade of sparkling lights, each chandelier beam refracting like a million tiny diamonds dancing across the polished floor. The music shifts—a slow, haunting waltz fills the air—and I guide Mina into the center of the floor.

I remember how Abraxis mentioned Mina has been taking dance lessons in Finlay's class since last year. Holding her close, I feel her warm breath against my ear as we glide effortlessly around the floor, our steps as familiar as old memories. "I would love to know what's going on in that brilliant mind of yours," I murmur, bending down to whisper.

A soft smile plays upon her pale pink lips, the delicate scent of her perfume mingling with the rich aroma of spiced wine in the air. "I'm hoping that when all of this is said and done, we can bring about real change for our people." She arches her head and puckers her lips in invitation. I lean in and kiss her, our moment punctuated by the sudden burst of cheers from the surrounding crowd. "The betrothal system has to go," she declares between kisses.

I press a gentle kiss to her temple, savoring the warmth of her skin. "It's one of the first things on the chopping block," I reply, kissing her again as we eventually drift apart, passing her off to Abraxis for the next dance.

Callan sidles up next to me, bumping my shoulder with a knowing grin. I raise an eyebrow as he comments, "They're doing better. Abraxis is handling his insecurity, and Mina isn't trying to destroy the world just because he's feeling insecure and anxious." His words, casual yet piercing, hit the nail on the head.

"They spent the other night together—and not a single fresh bite on Mina," I note, tilting my head as I watch them from across the room. "I call that an improvement."

Callan's eye widens slightly before he leans in, lowering his voice. "The therapist telling him he was physically abusing her—biting her so much—it hit him hard. Don't tell him I told you that part."

Shaking my head, I draw in a deep breath, the cool air mingling with the heady scent of incense. "Mina already told me. She didn't realize he was abusing her. Hell, he didn't know he was doing it. It's a stress reaction from a young, insecure drake. It wasn't intentional or malicious."

Before I can dwell further, Abraxis and Mina return to the dance floor, and Balor sweeps in to lead Mina away for another dance.

"Have I missed anything?" Abraxis asks as he approaches, his tone light but laced with curiosity.

"Nothing important—just enjoying how happy Mina is," I reply, deftly steering the conversation as a member of the wait staff approaches with glasses of wine. The clink of crystal against crystal punctuates my toast. "Here's to a better tomorrow," I say, raising my glass.

"Here's to the purge. May Mina's talons be sharp and strike true," Abraxis retorts before taking a long, deep drink. The bitter tang of the wine reminds me abruptly that the purge is scheduled in three days—a thought that sends a shiver down my spine.

"Well, since I'm neither staff nor an instructor, I guess I'll be on Mina watch," I add, knocking back the remaining wine. I draw in a deep, steadying breath, the taste of wine and apprehension mingling on my tongue.

How did I manage to forget that the purge is starting so soon?

from my raids on hidden caches around the campus. I load my leathers with ten throwing knives, along with my dual short swords, a gift from Ziggy. While rummaging, I find my handheld drow crossbow and secure the bolts into the forearm bracer designed for it.

"Can I help you?" Abraxis enters the space, holding up the tape I use on my horns. His tone is calm yet probing.

"Sure, start at the tips, then wind down to the base," I instruct, closing the trunk and settling onto its worn surface. The leather creaks softly beneath me as Abraxis carefully wraps the tape around my horns. I reach into my pocket and pull out a miniature map of the campus, its creased edges a testament to many nights spent studying it.

"Remember, you cannot shift fully—partial is allowed," Callan reminds me while flipping through the rule book. His voice carries a weight of authority as he recites, "The containment area is the campus; no one is allowed to leave. Anyone caught outside is automatically thrown into the dungeon to be sentenced at a later date." He looks up, and I nod in understanding.

"Gotcha. I'm going to go get into position." I slip the hood over my horns and tie my mask securely into place. Approaching the mirror, I retrieve a small pot of black paint and carefully coat the skin above the mask, the bristles of the brush whispering over my skin. Balor steps in then, spraying me with a scent-neutralizing mist that carries a crisp, almost clinical odor.

"You know we can't help her during the purge," Callan interjects, his tone laced with caution.

"The purge hasn't started yet. The sun is still up," Leander says from the doorway, his silhouette framed by the last light of day.

"So technically, I could ask Ziggy to drop me somewhere as long as the sun is up?" I arch a brow, glancing at Callan, who is a stickler for the rules.

"Technically, yes..." He arches his brow over his empty eye socket as he scrutinizes me.

"Excellent! Ziggy, we're burning daylight—let's go!" With that, he grabs hold of me, and we phase onto the roof of the Aurelian Conservatory.

"Why here?" Ziggy whispers, his voice soft and full of curiosity, as I nudge him into the shadows.

"I can see both the Northern and Southern Dorms from here. It will be easy to spot them moving about," I explain, pulling down my mask momentarily to kiss him. I press him against the wall, my black leather concealing him in the dim light. A soft purr escapes his lips as his hand finds the small of my back, drawing me flush against him.

We break apart slowly, our eyes lingering on one another. I kiss him once more before spraying myself with a small bottle of scent neutralizer. "I love you," I whisper, the words almost lost in the rustle of night.

"I love you more," he replies with a wink before vanishing from sight.

I close my eyes for a moment, savoring the lingering warmth of his affection—a happiness that always seems to cling to Ziggy. When I open my eyes again, a steely, predatory focus takes over. I pull my mask back up, secure my hood in place, and slide on my black gloves. Keeping to the shadows, I find the best possible vantage point to watch the campus, every sense alive to the night's sounds and scents. All I need now is for the sun to set completely and for the games to begin.

THE LAST LIGHT fades over the mountains, and the bells toll, signaling the beginning of the purge. Students burst from the dorms, their hurried footsteps echoing along cold stones as they scatter in search of hiding places. Some have already started to hunt—faces twisted in feral determination. They kill anyone who dares come too close. I watch my guys and several others leave Malivore, heading toward the teachers' housing to wait out the purge.

The only ones I don't see emerging are the fire drakes. I creep along the roof of the Aurelian Conservatory, my boots barely whispering against the cool slate. I make sure no one else has dared to follow the brilliant idea I had. My eyes shift over to my dragons as I take in the scene below. The frantic shuffling of students, the ragged breaths mingling with the chill night air, and the scent of fear and smoke that hangs heavy in the darkness.

It feels like an eternity before the first fire drake slinks out from the northern dorms. Serra steps into the gloom and immediately slashes at the first student who crosses her path, her blade catching the meager light. I reach back into the pouch at my lower back and extract some fresh poison I harvested today. Monkshood, otherwise known as wolf's bane—contains aconitine, a potent neurotoxin and cardiotoxin. I dip the tip of an arrow into it, then load it into my mini crossbow.

When Serra pauses, I take my shot. The arrow finds its mark in her abdomen. I watch, impassive, as she crumples to the ground clutching the deadly shaft. Her agonized cries reverberate through the night, drawing Graham to her side. I quickly dip another arrow in the monkshood tincture and fire again—this time nailing him squarely in the ass. The muted thud against his flesh is confirmation of my precise aim. I keep low, shifting positions to maintain a perfect line of sight, and then scale a small tower. My back presses against the cold stone as I watch, every sense attuned to the unfolding chaos.

Serra dies quickly, the combined effect of the neurotoxin and cardiotoxin halting her heart with ruthless efficiency. Graham, having been hit in the muscle of his ass, will endure a slower, more agonizing end. Soon, Cillia emerges, her steps tentative in the chill night as she investigates alongside Demi, who follows not far behind. They find their nest mates lying dead outside the northern dorms. Their mistake was looking low, on the ground, instead of up, where the actual threat lingers.

Across the dorm, I see Arista leave, heading south toward Malivore. Vaughn, technically is not a student this year after losing his amulet, has taken refuge with the guys at the teachers' housing, waiting for the madness to subside.

A question pulses in my mind. Do I hunt Arista, who is alone at the moment, or pick off these two fools from up here? I decide—I'm going after Arista. After all, I'd like the second half of my year to be easier than the first.

I SPRINT to the back of the building, my heart thundering in my ears as I press my body against the cool, rough stone. I dig my talons into the weathered surface and scale the wall with a steady, determined grace. Once on the ground, I crouch low, every sense alert. I listen to the distant echoes of footsteps. The rustle of leaves in the chill night air, and the soft hum of the city beyond.

I make my way to the tree line, running along its edge while staying within the boundaries of shadow and light. The crisp scent of damp earth mingles with the faint odor of burning wood, a reminder of last night's bonfire. I crouch low once more, watching the chaotic scene unfolding around me before I sprint toward the Malivore building. My gut churns with unease. I know Arista is headed for my suite. Whether she's hunting me or one of my guys, it spells trouble.

Using my talons again, I scale the stone face of the Malivore building. My fingertips grazing the cold, rough surface as I ascend. I perch on the roof for a moment, the cool night air nipping at my skin, and listen intently. Seconds pass as I soak in every sound — murmurs of conversation, even the soft scuffle of my breath—before I continue along the roof until I am directly over my balcony.

Inside, I hear movement. I hang upside down at the glass door, my eyes straining in the dim light, and watch as she moves inside my suite. The sound of her deliberate steps sends shivers down my spine. The moment she heads down the hall toward the back rooms, I drop silently and ease the door open. I slip into the suite, slide the door shut behind me. Quietly, I hit the breaker just inside the pantry in the kitchen, plunging the apartment into darkness.

I count my heartbeats in the silence before she returns to the main living space. A flicker of movement draws my attention—a small ball of fire dancing over her hand, casting eerie shadows that stretch like claws across the walls. With every step she takes, I move in tandem, silently positioning myself for the kill. I toss an empty can into the living room; its clatter distracts her just long enough. When she turns, illuminated by the pulsating glow of the flame, I step forward.

Her face pales under the fiery light as I raise a single finger to pull down my mask. "You stole something from my mate ... I want it back," I murmur, my voice low and dripping with menace. I study her panicked eyes as they dart around the room.

Without warning, her hand dives into her pocket, and she slaps an amulet onto the nearest table. "There. I'll leave now," she stammers, attempting to push past me. I block her path, my nails shifting into deadly talons as I slide my hand up her throat.

"That's not what I want," I purr, stepping behind her as the door to my suite swings open and Demi enters with Cillia.

"What do you want?" she whispers, motioning for her nest mates to halt. My talons press against her soft throat, and I feel her pulse pounding like a frantic drum beneath my fingers. "The time I lost with my mate, back," I reply. In a swift, brutal motion, I pull back hard and fast, nearly severing her head from her shoulders. Blood erupts, splattering in a macabre arc as she crumples to the floor.

Before Demi and Cillia can react, I hurl my knives with precision. They sink deep into the sockets of their eyes with a sickening, wet thud. Their bodies collapse just inside the door, and I arch a brow, a bitter smile curling my lips as I survey the carnage.

'Mate, are you okay?' Klauth's voice echoes in my mind, and I allow myself a small, triumphant smile.

'Yes, tell Vaughn I have his amulet. We're not living here any longer—the stains will never come out of the carpets,' I remark, my gaze lingering on the blood-soaked floor.

'The stains?' Klauth's tone is teasing, and I can't help but laugh.

'Yeah … I killed Arista in the kitchen. Demi and Cillia ended up with blades in their eyes in the living room. Now I need to drag the bodies out into the hallway,' I explain calmly, starting with Cillia's limp form.

'Three out of five—not bad, mate,' Klauth's pride resonates in his words.

'Serra and Graham are dead outside the northern dorms. Five for five,' I add as I move Demi next in to the hallway. I pause, scanning the corridor for any sign of pursuit, before returning to drag Arista's body out last.

'I shall tell the others. I can't send Ziggy to you—it's against the rules. You still need to come and record your kills,' Klauth's voice drones, almost bored in my mind.

'Will do. See you soon,' I reply. I step back into the apartment and scatter baking soda over the blood on the tile, watching as it soaks in and helps blot the crimson stains. On the carpet, I pour peroxide, silently praying it won't leave a permanent mark.

Before leaving, I slip out into my poison garden, the scent of decaying vegetation and toxic blooms thick in the air. I retrieve Thauglor's egg with careful precision, nestling it into the single leather carrier I carry.

Then I return to the kitchen, grab Vaughn's amulet, and slip it into my pocket before locking up and departing the suite. I claim my trophy and walk down the hall, heading to exit Malivore and meet up with my mates.

I leave my talons exposed as I navigate the dim hallways of Malivore. When one student charges at me, I simply raise my empty hand, and they falter, eyes widening before they turn and run back the way they came. The journey, which feels like it should have taken days, consumes the better half of the night. I recall my mother's words with a dark chuckle. *Time flies when you're having fun.* Tonight, I have five fewer enemies to worry about. Now, with only two remaining, I wonder how I'll handle them when the time comes.

His words are as precise as the click of a clock, each syllable punctuating the growing tension.

Just then, Samara glides past, her presence both graceful and predatory. "We're about to end the purge," she announces, her voice as smooth as dark velvet. I watch Finlay shift into his phoenix form—and fly out the open door. I can almost hear the rush of wind as he makes his way to the bell tower to ring the bell. We all fall silent, our ears straining until the deep, resonant tone of the bell echoes across the campus, reverberating in the hollow spaces of our anticipation.

"Now we wait," Callan states as he moves to the window, his eye scanning the darkness for any sign of Mina. The sound of his measured footsteps on the creaking floorboards blends with Leander's restless pacing inside.

"Waiting is the worst part," Leander grumbles, his voice low and heavy with impatience.

In a far corner of the room, Samara, and several other professors huddle over record books. Their pens scratch methodically on paper as they tally the kills. "It's morbid we do this," Anipe purrs softly, her voice almost a caress as she flips her book open to a clean page and neatly writes the date at the top.

I notice Lysander is nowhere in sight—a detail that sets my nerves on edge. Soon, a half dozen students file in, each documenting their claimed kills, most only listing one or two. I watch Klauth's smirk widen as he listens to the meager records, a silent acknowledgment of our grim reality.

After almost an hour, the heavy wooden door creaks open and Mina enters. Her fingers are tangled in Arista's vibrant red hair, a striking contrast against the dull room. As she strides over to Samara's table, I catch the faint scent of blood and iron in the air. Without ceremony, she plops Arista's severed head down on the table. "Willamina Ragnar, five kills: Arista, Serra, Cillia, Graham, and Demi.

Two by poison, two by knives in their eye sockets and one…" Her voice trails off into a twisted grin before she tilts her head, adding, "One you can say lost her head." The purr in her tone sends a shiver down my spine, and the hairs on the back of my neck stand at attention.

"Recorded, your grace," Samara intones, lowering her head in respectful deference as Mina returns a graceful bow before approaching us.

"I wish to go home," Mina declares, her voice low and laden with a bittersweet finality. I can see her canines still distended, a visual promise of the hunger beneath her composed exterior.

Concern tugs at me as I step closer. "Mina, are you okay?" I ask softly, my voice nearly drowned out by the distant echoes of my restless thoughts. From past experience, I know she gets amped up after fights, her adrenaline mixing with something darker.

"You know how I get, Ziggy…" she purrs, moving closer. Her scent envelops me—a heady blend of musk and desire that makes my pulse quicken.

"Let's get everyone home so we can talk together," I suggest, pulling her into a tight embrace. I press my lips to her neck, feeling the heat radiate through her skin as I run my hand through her hair. I watch, transfixed, as her scales shift color, shimmering with an intensity that mirrors the storm of emotions inside me. The start of the magenta that warns of her yearly is clear. When Abraxis and Klauth exchange a glance, I point to her neck, and they immediately understand. The start of her cycle is upon us.

Before I know it, Balor, Klauth, and Abraxis are at my side. I phase the four of them to the nest deep in the mountains. As I phase back to the school, Leander, Callan, and Vaughn are waiting, their anxious faces illuminated by the dim corridor lights. I pull them along and, together; we phase back to the nest.

When we arrive, I can hear one of our own already taking care of Mina's needs.

"Her scent is stronger than ever," Balor remarks as he rounds the corner into what has become our makeshift living room. The smell is pungent and intoxicating, lingering in the air like a forbidden perfume.

"Who's in with Mina?" I ask, my voice low and curious as I head over to grab a drink from the counter.

"Both dragons ... Mostly so Klauth can get Abraxis to have Mina fully submit to him," Balor explains, sipping his drink slowly as if it holds the answers to the universe. "We need to settle the nest, and if she continues challenging one of the dragons, we'll never find peace."

"So most of the issues are because Abraxis let Mina get away with shit?" Vaughn interjects, tilting his head as he looks at all of us while clutching a glass of water.

"The short version, yes," Balor replies, his gaze fixed on his drink as though it might reveal more secrets.

I climb onto the worn arm of the couch and peer down the darkened hallway toward Mina's room. "So, how is this going to work?" I ask, glancing over at the others with a mix of apprehension and determination.

Callan, ever practical, strolls over while handing out boxes of condoms. "We go in by twos. Someone will have to stay with the last person after their turn."

"With two viable drakes in the nest, this is going to be far worse than last time." I mention as I settle myself on the couch, waiting to see what happens next.

Four hours later, Klauth emerges from the dim corridor with Abraxis, who looks as if he's just returned from war. I clutch two cold bottles of water in my hand, the condensation slick against my skin, and ask, "What happened?" as I offer them both a bottle.

"It was far worse than even I expected," Klauth growls, his voice rumbling low and dangerous as he fixes a steely glare on Abraxis. His words slice through the heavy, sweat-laden air. "Regaining her respect is going to be difficult now that she knows she's stronger than this one." He jerks his thumb sharply in Abraxis's direction.

Abraxis's face twists with raw frustration. "How many times do I have to say I'm sorry and admit I fucked up?" he barks, his voice rough and desperate, the sound echoing off the cold stone walls.

Klauth's tone shifts to one of command as he fixes his gaze on me. "Ziggy, you and Balor go in together. Establishing dominance shouldn't be an issue, since neither of you are dragons." With that, he strides over to Thauglor's egg resting on a cluttered table. As he picks it up, I notice its surface pulsating in a slow, almost violent rhythm— each beat sending a shiver down my spine. "You better hatch it before our mate's next cycle. I swear if I have to wrangle this again alone, I will punt your egg off a cliff."

Thauglor's egg throbs in his hand as if protesting its fate. "Don't yell at me because your descendant didn't make our mate submit last cycle. I wasn't even hatched yet." Klauth shakes his head and disappears down the hall in deep conversation with the egg, leaving an unsettling hum in his wake.

Balor's steady voice cuts through the tension. "Are you ready?" he asks while gathering drinks and food from the table. The scent of stale alcohol and charred meat lingers in the air, mixing with the underlying aroma of sweat and anticipation. I take a long, steadying breath and reply, "I'm as ready as I'll ever be. At least if I'm in danger, I can just phase out of the room." A mischievous smirk curves my lips as I exchange a knowing look with Balor.

"That's cheating," Balor teases softly, his tone half-amused as he watches my reaction.

"True, but I don't have armored scales. You do," I reply, my voice low and teasing, as I pull open the door to Mina's room. The corridor beyond smells faintly of lavender and damp fabric. Inside, Mina lies sprawled on a rumpled pile of blankets, her features softened in sleep. We slip in quietly, the soft rustle of our movements almost swallowed by the hush of the room. We have to be careful not to disturb her too abruptly.

Glancing to my right, I raise an eyebrow. "Didn't you only have four piercings when I took you?" I murmur to Balor, the humor in my voice barely concealing the heat rising within me.

Balor chuckles, rubbing the back of his neck as he replies, "Yeah, I didn't think it looked right with only four, given the length." With a casual shrug, he rolls a condom down his erect length. The slight crinkle of the latex is audible in the quiet.

"Gotcha. I thought about it..." I murmur, indulging in a slow, deliberate stroke that sends warm tingles of desire coursing through me. "I like mine naked." My gaze drifts past Balor to where Mina stirs softly beneath the covers. The cool air of the room mingles with the heat of my anticipation as I race to the side of the bed and gently turn her to face me.

"Hey, baby..." I purr softly, leaning in until my lips meet hers. The taste is faintly sweet and warm—a delicate reminder of sleep and vulnerability.

"Hey, Zig..." she murmurs, glancing over her shoulder as Balor slides in close, teasing her with a subtle touch at her entrance. "Mmm, someone knows what I need..." Her voice is low and inviting as she caresses her throat. She tilts her head back to expose the sensitive skin there.

"Anything you need, Mina. Anything you want—me, or both of us,"

Balor promises, his tone husky as his eyes flick to me. It's not the first time we've shared a lover, but it is the first time we share our mate.

Her voice drops to a breathy whisper, "I need you, both of you," and that single phrase sends a surge of heat through me. Before I can fully savor her words, Balor moves in, thrusting forward with a deliberate force that makes Mina gasp. The sound mingles with the rustle of sheets and the low hum of our shared desire.

"You have us," Balor murmurs as I drop to my knees. The coolness of the sheets contrasts with the heat of my desire. I gently tap her lips with the head of my cock, guiding her hands over her head. The moment she parts her lips for me, I slide in eagerly, my free hand steadying my movement. "Her mouth feels like heaven..." I purr, each word laced with an unspoken promise. I slowly slide my length in and out of her, savoring the soft, warm taste and the tender texture of her lips.

Mina suddenly pulls back, a soft cry escaping her as she reaches her peak. The sight of her—flushed skin, trembling beauty, and that momentary vulnerability—is almost too exquisite to bear. As I continue, several more deliberate thrusts later, Balor grunts and then sinks deep within her. He pauses, panting as if time has slowed, before eventually pulling back. He cleans himself, discarding the used condom with an almost detached efficiency, and then moves in to join me once more.

I withdraw slowly from her mouth, my skin still tingling with the memory of her warmth, and trail my hands down her body. "Hands and knees, Mina," I purr, my voice soft but commanding as I retrieve another condom. I roll it on carefully, the cool latex embracing my length. Crawling onto the bed behind her, I pause to admire the sight. Her perfectly curved, heart-shaped ass, the glistening folds that catch the low light, and a trail of her own release glistening along the inside of her leg.

"Ziggy, please ... I need you... I ache..." Mina's breathy plea wraps around me like a velvet rope. It ignites the beast inside me with a fierce pride that our mate desires us so deeply.

"As you wish," I reply, crawling closer. I shift my tongue, its wet heat matching the soft, slick warmth of her glistening folds. I lick her in slow, deliberate strokes that draw shivers from deep within her. The rush of her natural sweetness lands on my tongue, making her thighs quiver with delight.

Meanwhile, Balor is already kneeling before her. Mina is already sucking on him with a steady, almost rhythmic motion that fills the room with muffled, intimate sounds. I can barely bear the soft moans and the delicate noises of her pleasure. My hands grip her hips firmly as I slide deep within her, each thrust punctuated by a deep purr that reverberates in my chest. I roll my hips slowly, feeling her muscles spasm around me in pulsing waves. Each contraction makes me fight the overwhelming urge to cum too soon. I wonder how the dragons manage to last so damn long when she feels this fucking good.

Then, a subtle click sounds behind us. I glance over my shoulder towards the door, then turn to lock eyes with Balor. He immediately steps back as my hand slides down Mina's spine. Standing in the doorway is Klauth. He watches as I place two firm fingers along her back, pressing her into complete submission. The instant her chest meets the mattress and her hands fold under her throat, she cums. It's a powerful, shuddering release that crushes my length with its intensity, milking every drop of pleasure from me. I hold her down with one hand as my thrusts turn erratic, each one a desperate bid against the overwhelming surge of pleasure. Finally, I cum hard, feeling as if my soul has left my body.

Gasping for breath, I finally secure the condom and pull out. Klauth holds out a small trash bin with a nod of approval. "You get it ... Yet the other one can't seem to grasp the concept," he remarks with a shake of his head, then moves to the cooler to fetch a bottle of water.

He then crosses to the side of the bed where Mina now lies on her side. "Drink," he instructs gently, offering her a water bottle. She takes it slowly, her lips wrapping around the cool plastic as she sips, her soft, steady breathing filling the brief silence.

"Hey, honey…" Mina murmurs with a sleepy yawn before handing the bottle back to Klauth.

"I'll lie with you, my treasure. Let the others go eat and rest," Klauth says, his gaze passing between Balor and me as if offering a silent escape. We nod, gathering our scattered belongings.

"See you soon, baby," I whisper as I lean down to kiss Mina tenderly, the lingering warmth of our intimacy a bittersweet farewell before I step out into the corridor. As I glance at the clock, a ripple of panic shoots through me. Balor and I kept Mina busy for nearly an hour. Three more days of this relentless cycle lie ahead of us.

Balor exchanges his goodbyes, and together we leave the room, rejoining the others. Abraxis snoozes in an old chair, and the remaining mates have drifted off, their quiet breaths merging with the dark silence of the living room. I brace myself—these next seventy-two hours promise to be the longest, most tumultuous stretch of my life.

growls, his tone rough with the effort of holding his instincts in check. I know that if I push, I might finally claim what I want. But I'm too tired; that burning fire in my chest has dwindled to embers. I feel my inner dragon settle into a deep, drowsy sleep as I glance at Klauth, resigned.

"It's over…" he murmurs softly, just as I feel Vaughn's growl signal his release along my shoulder. Slowly, Vaughn shifts back to his human form, releasing my hands and running his fingers through my hair with deliberate care. "Your scales are back to normal," he remarks quietly, then pulls out and secures the condom before discarding it.

"How are you, my treasure?" Klauth asks, opening his arms wide. I move slowly and melt into his embrace. The warmth of his body and the faint trace of his cologne wrapping around me like a familiar lullaby.

"Tired. I want a bath and a nap," I murmur, my voice heavy with sleep as I nuzzle his shoulder. He scoops me up effortlessly, and I feel the soft rustle of his clothes against my skin.

"The guys have your bath ready, so let's get you cleaned up," he says, kissing my temple gently as he carries me out of my room. We navigate several winding turns until we reach a natural hot spring carved into the mountain in my home. "We got lucky—a natural spring runs through this mountain, giving us hot water year-round," he explains. The air here is steamy, filled with the tang of mineral-rich water and heated stone. While the soft murmur of water trickling over rock creates a soothing symphony.

I yawn and take in the scene: all of my mates, except for Vaughn, are gathered in the hot spring. Their faces lit by the gentle glow of the heated water. "A hot bath will feel so good," I murmur, snuggling into the warmth and letting out a long, relieved sigh. The aches of my fertile period weigh on me, but the comforting heat promises relief.

"Do you want me to help bathe you?" Abraxis asks softly from the edge of the tub, his voice blending with the soft lapping of the water.

"Just a bath—I'm too sore for anything else," I reply. Klauth hands me over to Abraxis, who wades into the water with me. The heat seeps deeply into my muscles. I feel the tension melt away like wax under the summer sun.

"Hey, beautiful," Leander greets as he comes over and presses a tender kiss to my temple. I murmur a quiet "Hey…" and close my eyes while Abraxis supports my floating form. I feel Leander's gentle hands massage my shoulders. His touch is both firm and caring, as the mingled scents of warm water and sandalwood drift around us.

"Bath, then food, Mina," Callan announces, holding a soft washcloth as he cleanses the arm nearest him. The cool fabric against my warm skin is refreshing, a small comfort amid the lingering heat.

Balor soon appears, carrying a glass of juice with a straw. "Drink, baby…" he teases, tapping the straw to my lips. I laugh, feeling my cheeks warm as I reply playfully, "Stop giving me reasons for my mind to wander into the gutter." His mischievous smile confirms he's delighted by my reaction. I savor the cool sweetness of the juice as it refreshes me.

Finishing the drink, I roll my eyes with a smile. "Seriously, stop tempting me," I say, though exhaustion is already pulling me under. The gentle ministrations of my mates, the enveloping heat of the spring. The soft murmur of water lull me into a blissful drowsiness—a welcome respite in the darkness of this night.

Winter break ends far too soon for my liking, and we have to return to the academy. Most of the students remain blissfully unaware of what transpired before the break—except for whispers about the purge. As Vaughn and I slip into the bustling cafeteria for a quick bite, the warm, buttery aroma of toasted bread and freshly brewed coffee mingles with the low murmur of conversation. I can still taste the lingering bitterness of secrets in the air.

Klauth, being the king of the Aurelian Isles, is buried in political duties while I'm stuck in class. His absence is a constant, aching reminder of what I could be doing. I settle next to Vaughn as Marri's voice cuts through the hum of chatter.

"How's it feel to be back?" he asks, his tone teasing but curious.

"It's tough readjusting to a daytime schedule," Vaughn replies, and as I lean into him. I feel the reassuring warmth of his body and the steady thrum of his heartbeat through the fabric of his shirt.

Before I can lose myself in the comfort of his presence, Lyla leans forward. "We heard about the purge results. Thank you," she murmurs, her voice barely above a whisper, as if sharing a dangerous secret meant only for our ears. Her earnest eyes search mine, and I can almost taste the relief in her tone.

I lean in closer, my voice equally soft. "For what?"

Brawn chimes in, pulling Lyla onto his lap and planting a kiss on her cheek. "The fire drakes supported the Nagas' advances. Now that their biggest backers are gone, there's been less trouble." His words blend with the clatter of trays and low laughter around us, punctuated by the faint taste of cinnamon on his breath.

I shrug, my gaze drifting down to the waffles neatly arranged on my tray. They're perfectly golden, still steaming, and the sweet, buttery aroma mingles with the scent of freshly ground coffee. "I guess it was a win-win for everyone," I say, more to myself than to anyone else.

Glancing to my left, I notice Balor seated there. His intense eyes scan the room with a quiet vigilance that makes my pulse quicken. Leaning forward, he brushes my cheek with a gentle kiss. "You need to eat, Mina. We have first years who need more training, and I was hoping you'd help." His tone is both commanding and tender, and his breath, warm against my skin, sends a comforting shiver down my spine.

Across the table, a pair of gargoyles—faces chiseled like ancient stone —lean back, their cold, unyielding stares fixed on Balor. "You have a basilisk in your nest?" Marri asks, glancing from Vaughn to me. His words hang in the air like a challenge, echoing off the hard surfaces of the room.

Vaughn bursts into laughter. "Balor is the shit, man. If you need something—or someone—messed up, he's your guy. I swear, he's deadlier than most of the dragons in the nest." His boisterous tone, laced with crude affection, makes Balor's chest puff up with pride.

"Thanks, man..." Balor replies, patting Vaughn on the shoulder. His gaze drifts back to me as I rest my hand on the smooth, cool surface of the egg carrier. "How's Thauglor today?"

I flip open the carrier and peer at the black egg inside. Its shell is smooth and unyielding, dark as if it holds a fragment of the void itself. "He's good," I say, smiling as I run my fingers reverently over the shell. As I caress it, I feel it warm under my touch—a slow, rhythmic pulsing that sends a shiver through my fingertips, reminiscent of a distant, steady heartbeat.

Balor leans in, his voice dropping to a whisper. "Do you know when he'll hatch?" I use our hand signals to tell him 'not here'.

I draw in a deep breath and stand, the clamor of the cafeteria momentarily fading as I address Vaughn. "I'll see you in archery last period," I say before leaning down to press a firm, lingering kiss to his lips. His taste—a blend of mint and rich coffee—grounds me during swirling uncertainty.

"See you soon," Vaughn replies softly. Moments later, Balor takes my hand, and we step out into the cool corridor. Outside, the campus buzzes with early-morning activity. The sound of rustling leaves and distant footsteps is a backdrop to my quickening heartbeat.

I scan the surroundings before pulling Balor close and whispering into his ear, "He's going to hatch because I'm in danger. It's not clear who it's from. My gut says Lysander." I pull back to study his eyes, and for a fleeting moment, I catch a flash of reptilian slits behind his gaze before he slides on his sunglasses, concealing that wild intensity.

"Do we know when?" he asks as he pulls me against his side, his grip both protective and possessive as we head toward the Arcanum campus.

"It's warmer—that's all I know," I reply, my voice barely concealing the undercurrent of worry. Then, without warning, movement off to the side catches my eye. I shove Balor away just as a blade whistles through the air. Its cold, gleaming edge embedding itself in the rough bark of a nearby tree with a harsh, metallic thunk.

Before I can react, Balor is in motion. In a blur of controlled fury, he seizes the ambush drake by the throat, lifting the creature off the ground with terrifying speed. "Who sent you?" he bellows, his voice echoing off the wall as he slams his body against it. The sickening crack of bones reverberates, and my blood runs cold.

The ambush drake croaks, voice raw and broken, "She killed Demi..." Its words hang heavy in the charged silence.

"And Demi has tried to kill my mate several times," Balor growls, lowering the creature so that its feet touch the ground. "Kill or be killed—that's what the purge is for." His voice is rough, laden with a dangerous promise that sends shivers down my spine.

The creature manages a sneer. "The purge is over, teach..." it rasps, dripping contempt.

"That's true," Balor retorts, his free hand rising to lift his sunglasses onto his head, "but you just tried to kill my mate. Your life is forfeit." In that instant, I watch in horrified fascination as the ambush drake's face slackens. Its skin beginning to harden in a creeping wave that starts at its eyes and cascades down its body. I've never seen a basilisk's stone gaze at work. Seeing it in action is far more chilling than any tale.

"Fuck!" Balor screams, wrenching his fingers from the creature as he runs a rough hand through his hair. His eyes dart from me to the stone figure, his voice thick with anger and regret. "I never wanted you to see that."

I rise onto my tiptoes and press my lips gently against his, careful of the egg carrier wedged between us. A low, contented purr, deep and resonant as my inner dragoness awakens, vibrates in my chest. "You are not a monster, Balor. You ... are a very good male—a wonderful mate and my best friend," I murmur, framing his face with my hands as I look up into his soft, earnest eyes.

He leans down to kiss me again, his lips warm and reassuring against mine. "The things I can do, Mina ... my temper is uncontrollable when it comes to you. I'd turn this entire campus into a statue garden if it meant keeping you safe," he murmurs, his fingers threading through my hair with a fierce tenderness.

I laugh softly, wrapping my arms around his waist. "I never thought hearing about mass genocide could be romantic. But if anyone ever hurts you," I add, lifting my face to meet his gaze, "I'd light up the sky with the fiercest lightning strike I can muster and burn them all to ash."

Balor's eyes soften as he bends to press his forehead against mine. "We will do whatever it takes to keep the nest and our family safe," he whispers, before kissing my forehead. His words are a vow as solid as the stone of the ambush drake now frozen in our midst.

Hand in hand, we make our way toward my first-period science class —a pointless requirement for someone with mates, yet necessary for graduation. As we walk, I squeeze his hand. Some students give us a wide berth while others lower their eyes in deference, acknowledging the new reputation I bear.

"I'm your personal guard from now on," Balor declares with a wry smile. "Well, Ziggy and I are. We've been relieved of our teaching duties—except for my one class and anything involving the gauntlets."

He opens the classroom door for me, and I step in ahead of him, moving to my usual seat at the far back against the wall. The room smells faintly of chalk and old books, and the low hum of the projector mingles with the quiet rustle of turning pages. Balor sits beside me as we watch Kai stride onto the platform at the head of the class.

"Most of this class is for the unmated dragons and other species today," Kai announces in a calm, measured tone. "For those who are mated, please read chapter six on your own." His lecture on pheromones and their effect on males begins. I can't help but let my mind wander between the day's lessons and the tumultuous events that have already shaken my world.

reverberates through the room, and I catch a whiff of its musty pages as they settle open.

Anipe tilts her head, her eyes narrowing as she examines the tome. "My people adhere to the same right of inheritance," she says softly before her gaze shifts to me. "Your mate is now our queen, yet she still attends classes like a commoner. Why hasn't she tried to test out and graduate early? She's clearly the smartest student on campus." Hearing her praise for Mina fills me with a fierce pride, even as the charged air prickles with unspoken disapproval.

"She believes she needs the education here and doesn't want to be treated any differently," I add, my voice firm yet tinged with concern. I glance at Abraxis—his silent nod confirms it—and I see Leander and Ziggy offering their quiet assent. Their subtle gestures mingle with the low hum of tension that vibrates in the room.

Lysander's gaze sweeps around as he demands, "Where is Mr. Husk?" His voice is sharp, echoing off the stone like a challenge.

"He's on guard duty," Ziggy replies. As he speaks, his eyes suddenly flash with an eerie green light—a glow that sends an unexpected chill down my spine.

Lysander isn't having any of it. "He has classes to teach," he snaps, slamming his hands down on the table. The resounding thud rattles the heavy silence.

A low growl escapes Abraxis as he fixes Lysander with a steely stare— the first time I've ever seen him openly defy that man. "He has fifth-period archery and weapons training three days a week. When he's teaching, one of the others stays with Mina." His words are accompanied by a subtle unfurling of his wings. The soft rustle of the leathery skin a clear warning that fills the room with a palpable charge.

Finlay's measured voice cuts in next. "Do we have the final total from the purge?" He holds up the ancient tome as if to record the last counts, and I catch the faint scent of ink and worn paper rising from its pages.

Isobel—the resident green hag with a voice as rough as gravel—steps forward. "Three hundred and nine. Willamina Ragnar…" She enunciates the new last name with a crisp finality, then looks at Abraxis, who simply nods. "Had the highest kill count of five." Her words hang in the air, heavy and foreboding, as the reality of the purge's toll settles over us like a dark shroud.

Lysander snarls, turning his back on the table. "She wiped out an entire nest of fire drakes. Do you have any idea how much trouble her killing spree caused us with Arista's father?" His voice, raw with anger, seems to make the very air vibrate.

I can't hold back. "You know as well as I do that diplomatic immunity means nothing during the purge." I slam the rule book onto the table, its pages fluttering open to the exact section that outlines the rules. "If he was so worried about his daughter, he should have taken her out of school for the days around the purge." The impact of the book echoes, and a few startled glances ripple through the room.

Lysander roars again, "She wiped out an entire flight," his words sharp and unforgiving.

"If you had done your damn job, she wouldn't have wiped them out," Abraxis retorts, jabbing a finger at Lysander. The charged atmosphere forces the other staff members to step back, their eyes darting nervously between each other.

Kai arches a brow as he confronts Lysander. "I've brought my concerns to you, too. You didn't do anything about it?" His tone is icy, laden with the weight of unspoken accusations.

Lysander dismisses the challenge with a scoff. "It's a moot point. She was bred to be a weapon." In his arrogance, he turns his back on the table, exposing himself to further reproach.

Before I can even process the next moment, Ziggy vanishes from his seat and reappears in front of Lysander. His eyes burn brighter than I've ever seen them, the glow almost blinding in its intensity. "Mina is not a weapon. She is a living, breathing person. Just because you and her father do not value females doesn't mean the rest of us follow your sexist views," he growls, his voice resonating with a fierce, protective energy. Instinctively, I yank him away, fearing what might happen if Lysander's notorious stone gaze falls upon him.

The low, rumbling growl from Ziggy's chest draws every eye in the room. Normally, he's the calming presence we rely on, but now he stands defiant—a spark of rebellion amid the suffocating tension. I can almost taste the acrid fear and anger that hangs in the air.

A sharp knocking at the door interrupts our simmering conflict, and we all fix our eyes on it. The rhythmic rap feels urgent, and I sense something is about to change. I watch as Abraxis's features shift ever so slightly—a corner of his mouth lifting in a way that tells me Mina has arrived. Another knock sounds before a silver talon slips through the narrow gap between the door and its frame, deftly lifting the latch. The door creaks open, and in steps Mina, with Balor on her arm. Her presence fills the room. Her eyes blaze a fierce, golden light, narrow and penetrating, while her every movement exudes an effortless, dangerous grace.

"Why is my Ziggy so angry?" Mina purrs, though the gentle lilt in her voice does nothing to hide the rage simmering behind those glowing eyes. I watch, transfixed, as sparks—like quicksilver lightning—seem to dance along her horns. Her gaze sweeps the room, finally locking onto Lysander in a challenge that makes the hairs on the back of my neck stand up.

"Just a misunderstanding, your highness," Lysander spits out, turning his face away as if to hide his discomfort. His words, cold and dismissive, send a chill through me.

Mina's smile is a slow, dangerous curve as she replies, "Doubtful..." The way she holds her head, defiant and unwavering, reminds me painfully of Klauth in those rare moments when he loses control.

"Your Highness..." Anipe addresses her softly, and Mina turns with a cool smile that barely masks the fire in her eyes.

"Please, it's just Mina while I'm here. Most of the student body doesn't know about the change. I'd like to keep it that way for as long as possible." She smirks, then fixes her gaze on me for a fleeting moment. "Then again, are you all aware that Abraxis, Callan, Balor, Ziggy, and Leander are my King Consorts?" She leans back against Balor's broad chest, her hands resting lightly on the egg carrier slung beneath her breasts. The other staff members' gazes dart around the room as they exchange incredulous glances.

My heart pounds in my ears as I silently ask, *What has my mate done?* The disbelief in the room is almost tangible—a heavy, oppressive force that makes every breath shallow.

Mina continues, her tone laced with sarcasm. "Hmm, judging by your faces, it seems our headmaster didn't pass that information along like he was supposed to." She fixes her steely gaze on Lysander, then turns to Finlay. "We learned in our first year of etiquette class that when a new monarch ascends, proclamations are to be sent out. Something I handled personally with Finlay's help." For a moment, she studies her hand, then her eyes settle on Klauth's signet ring glinting on her finger in the low light.

"I wonder why they weren't distributed as they were supposed to be?" she muses, every word dripping with biting sarcasm.

Trying to defuse the tension, I offer, "The staff is aware now." My voice is soft, but I feel the weight of her distant, troubled eyes as they betray a storm brewing within her.

Mina blinks slowly and nods. "I'll see everyone at home later. I'm needed elsewhere." With that, she turns and strides out, Balor following with a storm of anger etched into his features. I watch them go, my thoughts churning with concern, wondering what could have set both of them off at the same time as the echo of their footsteps fades into the oppressive silence of the room.

MINA ISN'T in the nest above the Risedale compound tonight. Instead, I find her in the main meeting room with Vox, Warwick, Abraxis, and Klauth. The room is dimly lit, the low hum of conversation blending with the lingering scent of aged wood and stale coffee. I feel a prickle of anticipation mixed with unease as I step further inside.

"So, the threat seems to be the headmaster, if I'm understanding correctly?" Vox asks, accepting a drink Mina has poured. The cool glass in his hand contrasts with the warmth of the liquid. I catch a subtle tang of lemon zest underneath its bitter edge.

Mina's eyes narrow as she replies, "Yes. He was railing against the right of inheritance as well." At that moment, she tilts her head in the opposite direction to where Klauth leans, a silent counterpoint to his unspoken assertion.

Abraxis sips his beer slowly, the froth dissipating into the air as he comments, "This one announced we are all king consorts to the staff," his free hand gesturing toward Mina with deliberate emphasis. His tone carries a mix of irony and bemusement that ripples through the room.

Mina huffs and rolls her eyes. "It was apparent that the announcements Finlay, Klauth, and I wrote weren't handed out by Lysander." With a playful shove, she nudges me into the chair behind her before striding over and settling on my lap. The sudden closeness sends a surge of warmth through me—a comforting intimacy that contrasts with the cool, calculated atmosphere of the meeting room.

I lean in and press a soft kiss against her cheek, tasting a whisper of mint from her perfume. "But you didn't name Vaughn as a king consort to the staff. Why?" I ask, my voice low and curious as I search her eyes for the answer.

Klauth, leaning casually against the cool wall, fixes his gaze on all of us and says, "That was my request. He can be turned to stone and then shattered if anyone thinks he can be used against Mina." His words settle over us like a heavy shroud, punctuating the charged silence that follows.

Vox nods, his eyes scanning the table cluttered with half-empty glasses and scattered documents. "Makes sense. What's the next move?" he inquires, his tone deliberate.

Mina's gaze drifts to the egg carrier resting on the table, its surface smooth under the ambient light. "Well, no one saw us leave the campus, so they probably think we're all in Malivore," she whispers, her voice laced with mischief and concern. "Thauglor's time is approaching." Her eyes flick briefly to Iris before she flies over to rest on her lap, as though drawing strength from the familiar.

Abraxis leans forward, his impatience barely concealed. "What aren't you telling us?" he demands, his eyes flitting from me to Mina and back again.

Mina's gaze hardens for a split second. "I don't want to talk about it," she replies curtly before her head snaps in Klauth's direction.

Klauth glances at Ziggy before returning his attention to Mina. "My treasure, you look tired. Why don't you let Ziggy take you and the others back to your nest to rest? I'll join you shortly." His voice softens as he steps forward into the muted glow of the room. With deliberate care, he pulls Mina to her feet and kisses her softly on the forehead—the gentle warmth of his lips a stark contrast to the cool air—before releasing her into Ziggy's care.

I watch, a mix of longing and apprehension knotting in my stomach, as Mina smiles and murmurs, "Okay, my love, see you soon." In the blink of an eye, she and Ziggy vanish into the ether, leaving behind a bittersweet echo of their presence and the fading aroma of her perfume that lingers in the stillness of the room.

"We need to wait for the others," I murmur, sliding into the hammock and arranging my pillows just so. I carefully lift Thauglor's egg, its warm, smooth surface pulsing beneath my fingertips, and set it beside me.

"It's that bad?" Ziggy inquires, climbing into the hammock and wrapping his muscular arms around my waist. I feel the steady thump of his heart pressed against me—a reassuring, rhythmic counterpoint to the tension coiling in my stomach.

"Lysander will try to kill me," I confess, fixing my gaze on the flickering flames. The fire's heat, mixed with the acrid tang of smoke, makes my throat tighten as I imagine his lethal intentions.

"How? His stone gaze and venom won't work on you," Ziggy reasons, gently rolling me so I can rest my head on his chest. His voice is soft and steady, though a trace of disbelief lingers beneath it.

"He's going to constrict around me," I say, closing my eyes to better hear the steady beat of his heart. In the background, the creak of footsteps and indistinct murmurs signal that the others have arrived in the living room.

"So what didn't you want to say in front of the others?" Leander asks from the arm of the couch, his tone laced with both curiosity and concern.

I sit up and swivel the hammock to face everyone. With deliberate care, I rest Thauglor's egg on my lap, feeling its erratic warmth pulse through my fingers. "Lysander is going to try to kill me by constricting around me while I'm still human," I declare, my words trembling with apprehension.

"He knows his venom and stone gaze don't work," Balor remarks as he accepts a drink from Callan. The soft clink of glass punctuating his sentence, accompanied by the faint, spicy scent of the liquor.

"Exactly why he's going to constrict around me," I add, my eyes fixed on the egg's insistent pulsations, like distant drumbeats heralding impending doom.

"Why don't you shift and destroy him as your dragon?" Klauth suggests, placing a drink before me with a muted thud.

I trace the egg's smooth surface with a fingertip before replying, "I'm not sure. The vision is part of a waking dream—it never finishes for whatever reason." I sigh and take a tentative sip of the tart juice in my hand, its sharp flavor a brief distraction from the dark dread churning inside me.

Balor shifts his weight from foot to foot, the soft tap of his boots betraying his unease. "We need to find a spot where I can shift, so that I can coil around you, Mina, and help you figure out what to do," he says, his voice edged with anxiety.

"I don't like the idea that you can't shift," Abraxis interjects, glancing sharply at Klauth. "Is there anything that can block our shifting?"

Klauth paces, his boots scraping quietly against the worn floor. "Several herbs can slow down the ability to shift," he muses. "I'm not sure if there's anything to completely stop it—unless he has someone with a knack for dark magic working for him."

My blood runs cold. I leap from the hammock, clutching Thauglor's egg as if it were a lifeline. "Isobel..." I whisper urgently, locking eyes with Abraxis as a startling thought rockets through me. "What if she's working with Lysander? Both have openly defied some of the dragon accords in the past." My voice trembles, and I watch Klauth come to an abrupt halt in his pacing.

"Let's move the furniture around—get it all against the walls," Klauth commands, shoving chairs and tables with determined force. The creak and scrape of wood fills the room as he speaks. "You're about the same size as Lysander's basilisk, right, Balor?"

"I'm bigger," Balor replies, arching his brow in a silent acknowledgment as if connecting dangerous dots in a grim puzzle.

"Then you're immune to another basilisk's stone gaze?" Klauth asks, as he and Abraxis work together to drag the couch to the wall. The soft rustle of fabric and low thuds of shifting furniture underscore the urgency in his tone.

"Stone gaze and toxin," Balor states firmly, glancing at me before returning his steady gaze to Klauth. "I'm going to be the only one able to get close to him."

"Thauglor is going to hatch to save me," I declare, looking down at the egg resting in my arms. "But I'm afraid he'll get turned to stone trying to rescue me." I shift my gaze to Balor, who stands in the center of the room, his body tense with anticipation. Reluctantly, I hand Thauglor's egg to Klauth. Its warm pulses, a silent reminder of the uncertain future, and step into the center of the living room.

"How does it happen?" Callan asks as he circles us, his footsteps echoing softly on the hardwood floor.

I close my eyes and let the vision replay in my mind, each detail etched with painful clarity. "He comes up behind me and coils around me quickly, then turns his head to stare at me—trying to turn me to stone." My voice is barely a whisper, and as I speak, Balor mimics the lethal motion, his coils outlining the crushing embrace with unnerving precision.

"What else happens?" Ziggy prompts, and I force the vision to replay in slow motion. "I hear Thauglor's dragon roar in the distance..." The deep, resonant bellow vibrates in my mind, as real as the heat from the fire. "Lysander tightens his grip around me again, making it harder to breathe." I feel my chest constrict as if the imagined coils are closing in on me. "Then something distracts him from behind—a flash of black scale—and that's when I wake up." The memory shatters like fragile glass, leaving my heart pounding in my ears.

As I open my eyes, I lock gazes with the blood-red, serpentine eyes of Balor's basilisk, their predatory glimmer sending a chill straight to my core.

"Where are your dragon mates?" Leander asks, stepping closer as he studies how Balor's coils have pinned my arms to my side. His voice is laced with concern and urgency, the soft rustle of his movement underscoring the tension.

"I don't know," I admit, my voice strained. "Whatever is blocking the shift is also keeping me from reaching Klauth. I suspect Thauglor's inability to sense me triggers his hatching." I stare into Balor's eyes, lost in thought. "There used to be an ancient tradition—a scale exchange between mates," I continue, recalling whispered legends of bonds sealed with scales, the memory sending a shiver along my spine.

I glance over my shoulder at Klauth. "It was once common practice," he murmurs, eyes widening as he realizes why I mentioned it. "We can sense parts of ourselves, even if we can't sense your dragon." He exchanges a long look with Abraxis before returning his gaze to me.

"Where I am, a dragon can't fit—he chose it on purpose," I say, my eyes drifting to Balor's glistening scales before meeting the wary stares of my dragon mates. "Will Balor's scale become part of me? I'm somewhere underground wherever I am, yet his basilisk could reach me if it learns my location. I think that's why the vision remains incomplete— because all the pieces aren't in place yet." My voice trembles with the weight of the uncertainty, each word heavy as lead.

Abraxis's eyes blaze with anger, Klauth resumes his pacing, and Balor uncoils from around me, shifting back as the room fills with a suffocating tension and dread.

"You would wear my scale?" Balor cups my face between his rough, warm hands, his touch both gentle and insistent as he searches my eyes for any hint of hesitation. The cool night air mingles with the heat of his skin, and I feel his gaze probing deep into me.

"Why wouldn't I? I intend to take scales from both of my dragon mates so that they can rain fire down wherever I'm held prisoner. If you can get to me—wherever I am—it only makes sense." My voice is low and determined, each word carrying the taste of hope and love.

"Basilisks are looked down upon by most of dragon society," Ziggy says softly. I watch him absentmindedly pick at an invisible speck of lint on his shirt. His tone is quiet, yet laced with an edge of disdain. The sound of his fingers brushing the fabric punctuates the heavy silence around us.

"Shit's gonna change, damn it," I growl, locking eyes with Balor. Anger blazes in my chest like a wildfire, and my teeth clench in a silent snarl. "I will not let anyone be looked down upon ever again just because of their species."

My voice trembles with passion as I continue, "I'm looked down upon because I am half-green dragon, deemed untrustworthy because of the color of my scales." Even as the rumbling growl in my chest deepens, I taste the metallic tang of fury and defiance.

Balor draws me flush against his chest, and I feel the solid warmth of his body against mine, his heartbeat drumming steadily in my ear. "What do we need to do to implant the scales? And do we need one from Mina as well?" His voice is steady and urgent as he tries to change the subject. He turns toward Klauth, silently seeking confirmation.

Klauth's response is measured, his tone calm despite the tension. "We need a scale from Mina, and all that has to happen is we cut our flesh and implant the scale. In theory, the scale will only live on a true mate."

He shrugs his broad shoulders and shifts his hand slowly as he searches for a scale to gift me. I can almost feel the weight of his conviction in the careful way he moves.

"Here, let's start with mine." I shift my left arm, the cool air caressing my exposed skin as I search for a scale that gleams with potential.

With a steady breath, I extend the talons on my right hand. I feel the slight resistance of my skin as I use the tip of my talon to rip a scale free from near my thumb. The scale catches the dim light with its iridescent green and silver hues. Cradling it, I carry it over and offer it to Abraxis.

"You want to gift me your first scale?" Abraxis's eyes flicker with surprise and a trace of admiration as he glances from me to Klauth, then over at Balor before finally meeting my gaze again.

"It's why I'm standing here, silly. Open your shirt so I can stab you and place the scale." His compliance is immediate—he quickly unbuttons his shirt, the fabric rustling softly as he exposes his chest. I choose a precise spot, pressing my talon against his skin until it cuts him. He hisses softly, a sound that blends with the quiet tension of the room, and I carefully plant the scale. I watch, mesmerized, as his skin knits around it with a smooth, almost hypnotic speed.

"Wow ... It feels like the bond is stronger now." Abraxis smiles, his expression softened by awe, and then he pulls me into a passionate kiss. His lips are warm and insistent, and I feel a surge of reassurance in his embrace—a certainty I haven't felt in far too long. I smile into the kiss and wrap my arms around him tightly before reluctantly pulling away.

"Your turn." I say, tilting my head as I peel open the leather of my jacket to reveal the upper part of my chest. The cool air brushes over my exposed skin. Abraxis shifts his hand and studies the delicate scales by his wrist, eventually plucking one free with deliberate care. He hesitates, his talon hovering uncertainly over my chest. Taking his hand in mine, I press his talon against my skin until it cuts me. He jerks his hand back, as if I've committed the ultimate sin, but I persist. I carefully press the tender flesh against the wound, feeling my skin knit quickly around the scale as if sealing our bond. A quiet smile spreads across my face as I murmur, "The bond definitely feels stronger."

Klauth steps forward then, holding out his own scale with a reverent smile. The scale shimmers in the dim light, its cool surface a promise of connection. "Will you honor me by accepting my scale?"

"Of course." I reply, my voice a blend of determination and vulnerability. Unlike Abraxis, Klauth shows no hesitation as he drives his talon into my chest. I feel the sharp prick of pain, followed by a rush of warmth as he places the scale into the freshly cut wound. I watch in awe as my flesh quickly knits around his scale. The sensation akin to a powerful wave washing over me.

The surge nearly knocks me off balance, and Klauth's muscular arms steady me as he murmurs reassuringly. "Wasn't expecting that to happen, my treasure." He teases softly as he unbuttons his shirt. I search for a scale for him, my fingers grazing over his skin as I select one that gleams with promise.

With a decisive motion, I dig my talon into his chest. The sharp sting of the incision is immediate, and as I pull my talon away. I swiftly press the fleshy side of my scale into the opening. Klauth blinks in surprise as he fixes his gaze on the thick, green, and silver scale now embedded in his chest. Before he can utter a word, he pulls me into a warm, enveloping hug and presses a tender kiss to my forehead.

When he pulls away, I stride over to Balor, the air between us charged with unspoken promise. "You don't have to accept my scale, Mina," he says softly, holding it up as if weighing its worth. I smile mischievously and choose a completely different, secret place for it.

I turn and lift my silver and green hair up, revealing the smooth curve of my neck. "Find a place along my hairline on the back of my neck. I don't want Lysander to know I have your scale," I whisper, my voice low and conspiratorial. I close my eyes and lift my hair aside, feeling each strand brush softly against my skin as he begins his careful work.

"Brilliant and beautiful." He kisses the back of my neck, the warmth of his lips igniting a pleasant shiver, before finally finding the perfect spot for his scale. Then he calls out, "Klauth, I need your assistance—I don't have talons like you do."

"Of course." Klauth's reply is quiet but resolute. A thick silence settles over us for a moment before I feel the precise, sharp pain of his talon digging into my skin once more. The sting is immediate, yet oddly soothing, as I sense the second Balor's scale beginning to heal in its new place.

I pluck one last scale of mine and watch Balor as he pulls his tee shirt up over his head. I stare at his defined chest before picking the place over his heart. I dig my talon in, then sink my mostly silver armored scale into the hole I made. We watch his skin knit around it, healing almost instantly. I rest my hand over my scale on his chest, hoping against hope this is enough.

My entire body buzzes like a live wire, each nerve alight with the electric connection to my three mates. "Hopefully, this is enough to save me later," I murmur, my voice barely audible over the pounding of my heart. I glance around at them and meet wary, searching eyes. Deep down, I know they're uncertain whether this plan will work, but right now it's the best shot we've got.

Vaughn: Where is everyone?

Leander: Risedale, where are you?

Vaughn: Malivore. When did you guys leave?

Callan: Right after the faculty meeting this morning.

Mina: Ziggy, can you go get Vaughn, please?

Ziggy: Already there.

like an unexpected specter. I drop my phone onto the worn wooden floor. His presence sends a jolt of adrenaline through me.

"We were waiting for you to finish classes before I came back and got you," he says, his voice calm yet laced with mischief. He pivots smoothly and strides into Mina's room, the soft rustle of his steps mingling with the faint hum of the building. I catch the sound of canvas bags crinkling as he retrieves two of them—bags I know Mina must have asked for. "Grab whatever you need. We're sleeping at the Risedale nest tonight," he adds before continuing on his mission. One by one, he moves through the rooms, gathering packed bags and depositing them in the living room. The clatter of zippers and rustling fabric punctuating the silence.

I retreat to my room, where the stale air carries the faint odor of old books and a lingering trace of cologne. There, I find the bag Abraxis had insisted we pack just in case—a weighty reminder of the uncertainty ahead. Shaking my head, I change quickly; the texture of the cool fabric against my skin is a brief distraction from the gnawing tension. Slinging my bag over my shoulder, I head back into the living room, only to find that the pile of bags and Ziggy have both vanished. Left alone, I cross the room to the fridge. The chill from its interior contrasts with the warmth of the anxiety building inside me as I gather the food Mina prepared for tonight's dinner. The soft clink of jars and the crinkling of plastic provides a small, comforting rhythm amid the chaos.

I can't help but wonder what happened at the meeting to send everyone rushing to the nest. The fluorescent lights overhead flicker as I secure the last tray in the cooler bag—just then Ziggy reappears, a half-smile tugging at his lips.

"Good thinking, Vaughn. Mina was just complaining she wasn't going to have her wings she wanted for tonight," he teases, his tone light yet carrying an undercurrent of urgency. He helps me pack the sides, his deft fingers moving quickly, and soon enough, we vanish from Malivore.

Arriving at the nest—I find Mina hunched over a canvas, her brush dancing feverishly across its surface. The scene she's captured is nothing short of nightmarish. It appears as though she's painted herself ensnared in the twisting coils of a monstrous basilisk, with the head of a second basilisk looming menacingly. The acrid scent of turpentine and bitter paint fills the air. "What did I miss?" I manage to ask, my voice trembling with disbelief as I struggle to comprehend the horror unfolding before me.

Leander steps closer, his footsteps soft on the creaking floorboards, as he surveys the three canvases Mina has hastily taped together. "She's been having half visions. Apparently, all the pieces weren't in place for it to play out," he explains in a low, measured tone, his words mingling with the ever-present smell of oil and paint.

I furrow my brow and ask, "What changed?" My gaze shifts from Leander to the canvases. On the left, the painting reveals what looks like a basilisk lunging towards the next canvas. In the center, a basilisk—rendered in sinuous, chaotic lines—twists around a figure that eerily resembles Mina. On the right, the white-faced dragon's snarling maw and flaring nostrils threaten with silent menace. The detail sends a chill crawling up my spine.

Before I can dwell further, Abraxis ambles over, a drink in hand. The cool glass meets my fingertips as he passes it to me. "We exchanged scales," he states casually, as though discussing the weather.

I blink, trying to process the significance. "What does that have to do with anything?" I ask. The convoluted nature of their kind—especially when it comes to dragons' freaky mating rituals—often makes my head spin.

"Eyes on me," Klauth commands suddenly, his deep voice reverberating in the charged air. He unbuttons his shirt deliberately, the fabric whispering against his skin as he reveals something glinting on his chest.

I can't help but snort, "Dude, I don't go that way, so don't start..." My protest dies as I notice the unmistakable shimmer of one of Mina's scales, embedded on his chest like a secret badge.

"Dragons—and those of the dragon's extended family—can exchange scales," Abraxis explains matter-of-factly. He pulls at his collar, revealing another of Mina's scales on his chest. His tone is clinical, as if discussing an odd piece of family heirloom.

"So what does that do?" I ask, watching as Mina's hand glides over the canvas, her fingers stained with paint and lost in the intensity of her vision.

"Even when external forces dull the bonds between us, we can sense the missing of a part of ourselves," Klauth says. "She has one of ours on her as well."

I arch a brow, a mixture of curiosity and relief washing over me. "So it's like a tracker of sorts?"

Abraxis nods, his eyes never leaving the painting. "It strengthens our bonds with Mina. We can sense each other more acutely than before. In case her vision comes true, we'll be able to locate her faster."

I scoff, the tension in the room thickening as I challenge, "But that's a second basilisk. Won't you be turned to stone?" I scan the room—and catch Balor stepping silently out of the shadows, his presence as foreboding as the scene on the canvas.

"I won't be," Balor replies evenly, moving to examine the painting. His eyes narrow as they lock onto the depiction of the basilisk coiled around Mina. "I'm the second basilisk—the one coming to attack Lysander coiled around her. I just have to get him to attack me and give her time to ... shift if she can." His gaze shifts over the canvases from several angles, as if he's deciphering a hidden message in the chaos of brushstrokes.

My curiosity isn't sated yet. "Who's the white dragon?" I ask, glancing between Klauth and Abraxis.

"Thauglor," Klauth answers quietly, his voice steady as he watches Mina work.

I tilt my head in confusion. "I thought he was another black dragon?" I probe, eyes flicking to Abraxis.

Abraxis chuckles softly, a sound that almost seems out of place in the tension. "As we age, our faces turn white." He glances at the painting, then pulls out his phone. The cool screen reflects in his eyes as he shows me one of Mina's older paintings—a close-up of a dragon's eye and the graceful curve of a horn. The horn is black as pitch, while the face is white as freshly fallen snow. In the deep reflection of the dragon's eye, I can just make out the unmistakable image of Mina's own dragon form.

In the dim light of the nest, every sound—the soft shuffle of feet, the whisper of fabric, and the distant hum of anxious conversation—reminds me that tonight, nothing is as it seems.

I watch as what feels like hours pass before Mina finally steps back from the easel in our living room. Her paint stained fingers lingering on the intricate details of the image she's been working on. The dim lamplight casts long, wavering shadows across the room, mingling with the pungent aroma of turpentine and oil paint. She tilts her head slowly, her eyes locked on the stark portrait of Thauglor's side. The soft, rhythmic murmur of her concentration fills the quiet space with a hypnotic cadence.

"Hmm..." she breathes. The sound is barely more than a soft hum. It's as if she is deciphering secrets hidden within the canvas.

Before she can add more, I step up silently behind her. Feeling the gentle rustle of her clothing against my arms, I pull her close until her back nestles against the steady warmth of my chest. "What's puzzling you?" I ask in a low, steady tone, my voice barely disturbing the still air.

Her eyes remain fixed on the canvas, dark and searching. "I'm guessing Thauglor digs down to where I am," she replies, her tone threaded with a quiet challenge as she narrows her eyes to scrutinize the image. In that moment, a subtle inner fire ignites in her gaze. I can almost feel the electric tension as her fingers twitch with restless energy.

Without missing a beat, Ziggy moves swiftly—the soft scuff of his shoes on the creaking wooden floor punctuating his actions—as he sets up another canvas. Together, we help Mina settle back onto the worn stool she'd been occupying. The room is alive with the gentle rustle of movement, underscored by the distant clink of glass from the kitchen, merging into the constant, underlying hum of our home.

Now, her pencil dances across the surface of the new canvas, each delicate scratch whispering a burst of creativity. She sketches what appears to be a gaping maw on the side. The jagged teeth of a dragon rendered with chilling precision, glistening as though still slick with saliva, each stroke vivid against the pale, almost ghostly background. A spray of green, thick and viscous in texture, bursts from the maw on the canvas.

The next strokes bring forth the image of a basilisk, its contorted form twisting as it lunges at the dragon. Its flesh depicted in agonizing drips, as if melting away under unseen pressure. On the far side, Mina's delicate rendering of her own dragon reveals a solitary wing flared out protectively, like a living shield deflecting the corrosive spray.

I can almost feel the heat in the way Abraxis asks, "Why endanger your wing?" The question hangs in the charged air like a whispered challenge.

We watch, entranced, as she adds the final delicate details to the canvas. When she finally sets down her pencil—with a soft, final click against the wooden easel—she tilts her head once more.

"Where am I?" Balor asks, his tone a curious blend of intrigue and caution as he studies the melting form of the basilisk, his eyes narrowing in thoughtful appraisal.

"Under my wing on the other side," Mina replies softly, her voice carrying a distant, echoing quality that seems to reverberate off the living room walls. "My scales are impervious to acid damage. And the leather of my wings—laced with tiny scales—shares that resistance." Slowly, she turns to face Balor, and I catch a flicker of understanding in his eyes as the lamplight softens his features.

"So I save you and then you save me? Sounds good," Balor jokes, his voice light and teasing as the tension momentarily dissolves.

"Yeah, and Thauglor saves both of us," she adds. Her hand slips down to the leather of the egg carrier nestled beneath her breasts. "Lysander and the elders are pissed that I hid the fact that Klauth hatched. I made them look like fools, handing them his empty egg as if it had simply gone dormant." Her gaze drops to the floor, and her voice softens, laden with regret.

Before I can respond, Klauth interjects with a smooth, authoritative tone as he retrieves a crisp, folded letter from the inner pocket of his impeccably tailored jacket. "The grand council has recalled the elders and is putting them on trial for crimes against dragon kind. The King is having both them and the headmaster investigated." His words cut through the murmurs in the room, and his smirk—sharp and precise —serves as a cold reminder of the power he wields. Behind that smirk,

I know he is not only the King but also the master puppeteer of our household.

"I'd say the King is making a wise move investigating the corruption in our midst," I remark, accepting the letter with steady hands as I scan the list of crimes printed in stark, unyielding type. The words leap off the page—chief among them the charge of forcing females through both gauntlets. It's a practice that blatantly contradicts the original tenets of our guidelines.

"There are fewer and fewer females being born each year across the board," I note, my voice low and measured as I hand the crinkling letter back.

"Just this past year, most of the deaths were female," Abraxis states, his tone thick with disgust that seems to reverberate in the heavy air.

Klauth's eyes shift slowly from Abraxis to Mina, his gaze hard and calculating as he recalls, "On the original draft for the house guidelines, females were exempt from the gauntlets—except for Shadow-carve." The room seems to quiet further, as if the very air is holding its breath at his words.

"Yeah, we see how well that worked out," Mina practically snarls, her tone biting. "I'm not like the others—I was trained for it." She exhales, a heavy sound laden with conflicting emotions, and her gaze drops once more. "I don't want to be a weapon." Her eyes follow the shifting interplay of shadows and light on her hands, now transformed into talons that gleam with razor-sharp precision. "But I am a weapon of my father's creation." The glint of her talons is both beautiful and terrifying in its unwavering clarity.

With fluid ease, I shift into my gargoyle form, my body contorting in a way that feels both natural and alien, and scoop Mina into my arms. I wrap my expansive wings around us in a protective embrace. Their soft, rhythmic rustling acting like a comforting lullaby that soothes her instantly. Whether under my care or Abraxis's, she finds solace in the gentle embrace of our wings.

"Shhh. You can be whatever it is you desire to be. We'll make it happen, Mina. You want to be a general—I'm sure the King would have some say in that," I murmur, a gentle laugh escaping my lips as I watch her reaction. "I'm sure there's a way you can sweet-talk him into it." My words carry a promise of certainty amid the dark uncertainty that surrounds us.

Mina giggles from within the cocoon of my wings—a delicate, almost musical sound that momentarily softens the room's tension. She peeks out to glance at Klauth, whose eyebrow arches in silent amusement, before ducking back down; her laughter echoes softly. "Oh, I know the exact thing to do … I'd rather be a tactician than a general. Most generals are assholes."

Abraxis nearly chokes on his drink at her remark—the clink of glass punctuating the moment as he coughs. "She nailed that one on the head," Callan declares, his booming voice underscored by a hearty slap on Abraxis's back, the sound resonating in the charged air.

Mina pops her head out from beneath my wings once more, her eyes twinkling with playful mischief. "You know, you were in asshole mode until Klauth hatched," she teases, wiggling a finger at him with a light-hearted precision. "Don't pretend you weren't. We know the truth." Her voice blends humor with challenge, the words hanging in the space between us.

"Fine, I was an asshole—anything else?" Abraxis smirks, his eyes dancing with mischief as he meets her gaze, the banter a welcome distraction from the heavier matters at hand.

"Demanding, angry, controlling, anxious, and…" Mina begins, then suddenly freezes, her breath catching as a slow, knowing smirk curves her lips. "Lysander is on his way to the nest," she announces, the words dropping like a whispered prophecy into the heavy air.

In a heartbeat, she slips out from under my protective wings and seizes Abraxis and Ziggy with confident precision. "We'll be back," she declares, her voice firm and decisive, and in an instant, they vanish to attend to their tasks back in Malivore. They leave behind only the echo of their departure mingled with the lingering aroma of turpentine.

I exchange a glance with Klauth and Balor, the tension in the room growing ever more palpable as shadows lengthen. "What do you think that's all about?" I ask, my voice laced with a quiet curiosity that resonates in the stillness.

"Probably he's trying to figure out why Mina hid I hatched. With her being queen, she doesn't have to answer him. Hell, she could kill him the second he steps into her nest—as only a dragon would," Klauth remarks, his voice a blend of playful mischief and grim determination as he pours himself two fingers' worth of whiskey. The amber liquid catches the light—a silent testament to the gravity of our circumstances.

As shadows dance languidly across the room, the weight of Mina's choices presses down upon us, as tangible as the dust motes swirling in the fading light. With all the changes that have swept through our lives in recent months, the question is no longer what Mina will do—it's what she won't do to get an answer.

As the thunder of my heartbeat subsides, I concentrate once more. "My nest feels off. Something has been changed," I say, my voice low and trembling with uncertainty. I sweep my eyes slowly across the room before meeting Ziggy's. His eyes glowing a mesmerizing shade of green that reflects both calm reassurance and unspoken urgency.

"What was changed?" Ziggy asks, but before I can reply, Abraxis strides over to the door. I catch the soft creak as it opens and feel a cool draft sweep into the room as he steps outside.

I resume my patrol, moving through the interior with deliberate care, each step heightening my awareness of the subtle disturbances. Approaching the kitchen, the disquiet grows stronger—a prickling tension that tightens in my gut. On the counter, bathed in the flicker of a solitary lamp, I spot salt and pepper shakers. I don't recall ever purchasing such items; their presence is foreign, even jarring, against the familiar textures of my home. Without hesitation, I snatch them up, the cool metal clinking between my fingers, and stride to the balcony. I slide open the door, feeling the crisp night air brush against my skin, and hurl the shakers down into the dew-kissed grassy lawn below. The immediate discomfort eases, though a lingering unease still nestles in the corners of my mind.

Before I can resume my careful prowling, the front door swings open again. Abraxis re-enters, this time with Lysander in tow. A low, primal growl stirs within me—a sound I quickly suppress. "Miss Havock..." he begins.

"Ragnar—Queen Ragnar," I correct him firmly, standing tall with my shoulders squared as I fix him with an unyielding stare.

Lysander narrows his eyes as he regards me. "Queen Ragnar, may I inquire why you gave me a dud egg?" he asks, his tone mingling with amusement and reproach.

'Do I have to answer Lysander's questions?' I silently protest as I lean on the bond I share with Klauth for guidance.

'No ... *You are his Queen—you answer to no one but me in public. Otherwise, you answer to no one,*' Klauth interjects smoothly, and I can almost feel the curve of his smile in his measured words.

Lysander fixes his gaze on me, waiting for my retort. I sigh and reply in a bored tone, "There's only one male I answer to, and it's not you." I tilt my head, watching a flicker of irritation pass over his features as Abraxis muffles a laugh and looks away.

"I am still the headmaster of this academy!" he declares, his voice booming off the stone walls. I smile in return.

"For now..." I let the veiled threat hang in the air as I lock eyes with him. A low, rumbling purr—a deep echo of my inner dragon—rumbles through me as I watch the colors in Lysander's gaze shift from defiance to reluctant submission. I sense his desire to launch into a tirade, yet he remains silent, simply turning and leaving my nest. I narrow my eyes as the door thuds shut behind him.

"You like pushing buttons, don't you?" Abraxis teases, drawing me into a warm embrace. The deep, resonant rumble of his drake—a vibration that settles something deep within me—brings a small sigh of relief.

"No more than he enjoys doing it to me," I reply with a playful arch of my brow, meeting his amused gaze.

"Oh, calm down, Brax. Mina did exactly what you would have done if you were in her place," Ziggy chimes in with a light laugh. He holds up an odd little knickknack. It's a curious trinket etched with intricate designs. I gesture for him to toss it out the sliding glass door. With a swift motion and a cheeky wink, he complies.

"Does everything feel better now?" Abraxis asks, studying my face for any lingering sign of discomfort.

I close my eyes and breathe in deeply, letting the cool air fill my lungs as I stretch my senses across every inch of my space. In those quiet, closed-eye moments, every creak of the floor, every whisper of wind against the window becomes an extension of myself. Satisfied that nothing is amiss, I open my eyes and murmur, "Everything is okay now." A contented smile curves my lips, reassured that my sanctuary is secure once more.

Ziggy moves to lock the front door—the click of the bolt echoing in the stillness—then returns with his hands extended. "Let's go home," he whispers. I take his hand and give it a reassuring squeeze. Within seconds, as our hands remain clasped, we phase back to my nest, the familiar contours of home gradually materializing around us.

Back in the living room, I find Cora and Warwick with their baby seated on the couch alongside the others. "Hey, little man," I coo softly, and the baby's eyes light up as he reaches for me with innocent eagerness.

"Oof, settle down, William—Auntie Mina will pick you up," Cora teases with a gentle laugh as she passes the squirming bundle to me.

I cradle William in my arms and rock him slowly, the rhythmic motion a soothing balm in the quiet room. His tiny hand pats gently against the soft fabric of my blouse, and he instinctively attempts to latch on, as if seeking dinner. "Whoa, little man, those don't work," I giggle, carefully adjusting his position and swaying with him in a tender, timeless dance.

"We were coming to invite you to dinner with us in the compound—in the main kitchen area," Cora explains with a warm smile as she watches me cradle her son like the most precious treasure. "Mom is taking over the kitchen tonight to cook, and she wants our nests to blend together."

I turn to Klauth, tilting my head ever so slightly. "Can we?" I ask, my tone taking on a devilishly playful lilt as I lean in with the baby still in my arms. I glance up at him from beneath long, fluttering eyelashes. "Please?" I pucker my lower lip in a silent plea, fully aware of how diffi-cult it is for him to resist my requests.

Klauth leans forward and presses a lingering kiss to my forehead, his warm breath a soft caress against my skin. "If that will make you happy, then we shall go," he whispers. I smile and lift my face to meet him, returning his kiss with gentle affection.

"My brother isn't the lead drake anymore?" Cora inquires, and I cringe at the question, a flash of discomfort crossing my features.

"For the safety of the nest, it's best that the elder be in charge," Abraxis admits, his tone measured yet resolute. "He's stronger and larger than I am—both defensively and offensively, he surpasses me on every front." I can sense the weight of his reluctant honesty in every word.

ZIGGY MANEUVERS the nest into the shadowed corridors of the Risedale compound. I tread carefully through halls that once echoed with laughter and secrets—each step stirring memories, both unsettling and familiar. One part of me tingles with apprehension, my scales prickling like a swarm of tiny needles, while the other part welcomes me home. The cool, damp air carries the musty scent of ancient stone and worn wood, mingling with a faint trace of long-forgotten incense.

I still cradle the sleeping baby and the snug egg carrier pressed against my stomach. Holding them fills me with an unexpected contentment. At this moment, every burden is lifted, and everything is perfect. The baby's gentle, rhythmic breathing soothes my frayed nerves. I marvel at his cherubic face: soft cheeks and full, delicate lips, each feature igniting a tender warmth deep inside me.

"Penny for your thoughts?" Leander's low, melodic murmur drifts toward me as he settles beside me on the cool bench. His presence is a balm against the residual chill of the corridor.

I nod, determination and vulnerability mingling in my eyes. "I want this," I reply, gently gesturing to the baby in my arms. "But I need us to be safe first. I can't bear the thought of my hatchlings being hunted or stolen—to be used against me." My voice trembles as a single tear escapes, glistening in the dim light and tracing a slow path down my cheek. The ache in my heart deepens as I imagine a future where my offspring are prey to those who would see us destroyed. Leander draws me into his embrace, his warm body pressing against mine, and his lips rest softly against my temple.

"Why do you cry, mate?" Klauth asks, his tone laced with quiet concern. I lift my gaze, meeting Klauth's compassionate eyes as he offers me a steadying hand.

I accept his hand and adjust my hold on the baby with delicate care before Cora steps forward to take him. "I ... I'm afraid of having a family that will be hunted," I confess, my lower lip quivering as I search Klauth's eyes for understanding.

"What else?" he murmurs. His fingers trailing lightly along my cheek before leaning down to press a gentle kiss against my lips—a promise of solace and strength.

"I want it—I want it all," I admit, my voice gaining strength as I speak of dreams and desires. "The hatchlings, the snuggles, even the little fire starters darting around, stirring delightful chaos. But it's not safe." More tears fall, and Klauth tenderly brushes them away with his thumb, his touch warm and reassuring.

"We will give it to you, Mina," he vows, his words echoing softly in the quiet room as he kisses my lips once more. Leander boldly leans in, his mouth trailing a fervent path down my throat while Klauth continues his tender ministrations. The combined sensations send my pulse racing, my heart thundering against my ribcage as if it might burst.

Both men eventually pull away, leaving me panting and struggling to regain control of my emotions. The intensity of their combined affection feels as if it could overwhelm me entirely. I step back into the dining room and take a seat near the head of the table. As the others file in, a quiet reassurance settles within me—like a solitary ember glowing amid cold, unyielding stone.

Cerce emerges from the kitchen, carrying the first tray laden with steaming dishes whose savory aromas mingle with the soft clink of porcelain. She offers me a warm, motherly smile before slipping back into the busy kitchen. I survey the table and sigh softly as reality returns—I have a flight. Once, I never wanted this responsibility. Even now, part of me resists it. But here I stand, the dominant dragoness presiding over a growing flight.

"How many others have come to join us?" I ask, glancing toward Vox and Warwick. Their eyes meet mine with a mix of deference and pride.

"Several couples from my parents' flight wish to join us here—with your permission, of course," Warwick replies, his tone respectful as he bares his neck in a silent gesture of submission.

"I want to meet the potential couples with my mates," I declare, flexing my hands as my talons catch the soft light of the chandeliers overhead. "There is much to be done here for the good of the flight." I watch my talons shift, the movement a quiet testament to the power and responsibility I hold.

"Very fair of you, my queen," Warwick murmurs, bowing his head in deference. I glance over at Klauth and Abraxis, both nodding their silent approval with pride gleaming in their eyes.

My attention drifts to Cerce as she takes a seat next to Vox. Then Vox lowers his head to me, and I tilt my head, waiting. "Anything I need to know, Vox?"

"Nothing of note, except that three of our younger couples would like to join you," he says, his voice measured and observant as he watches for my reaction.

"The same applies to them—we must meet them first before they are allowed to join," I reply firmly, exchanging a proud smile with Abraxis and Klauth.

"Your mom would be proud," Cerce adds softly, and I stifle a low growl —the comment pricking an old wound.

In that moment, Ziggy appears beside me, clutching the letter I have folded and unfolded a million times. I silently motion for him to pass it to Cerce. As Ziggy hands over the letter, my eyes drift downward to the egg carrier nestled under my chest. Its quiet presence captures my attention, and I almost turn when Cerce gasps—a reaction that reminds me of the past. I know she sees why I growled: my mother once rejected me for bearing my father's green coloring. It wasn't my scales that took after her, nor my horns and strength—it was the green that branded me with my father's legacy.

Here I stand, the dominant dragoness of a burgeoning flight. I have seven devoted mates, with an eighth waiting to hatch from his confinement. Part of me swells with pride at all I have accomplished. Yet another part remains wary—always alert for the silent threat of betrayal, as if a new knife might suddenly appear in the dark at my throat.

room, noting the mix of eager and indifferent faces. Mina's gaze meets mine, intense and curious, as I stride across the classroom. I pick up a piece of chalk and draw a mock battlefield on the board, every scratch against the slate punctuating the silence. "Who wants to pick a side?" I ask, my eyes scanning the rows.

A male student at the front hesitates before stepping up. He taps the right side of my drawing, and I ask him, "Do you want offense or defense?" He mumbles, "Offense." I then query, "Who wants defense?" My eyes drift over the class, and I catch a sly smirk on Mina's face as not a single hand rises. With a confident grace, she stands and strides to the board.

I pass out cards to Mina and Brennen. I watch as Mina's smirk deepens the moment she glances at her card. She places it deliberately on the desk, then takes the chalk and begins redrawing the board. Every movement is precise, as she erases all traces of my initial work and replaces them with her own calculated defense strategy. Brennen pauses, his eyes following her every fluid motion. He shakes his head, clearly impressed or perhaps exasperated, then turns back to his own side to adjust his lineup accordingly.

"Time's up," I call out, my tone firm as I refuse to glance back at them. They both settle into their seats, and I direct the class's attention to the coded markings along the edge of the board. "Anyone want to tell me who wins according to how it's set up?"

A heavy silence falls over the room as I scan their faces. Finding no volunteers, I furrow my brow and start drawing decisive lines, methodically crossing out units. When I step back, Mina's defense still stands. I face the class again and announce, "I need someone to double-check me." Two nervous students approach the board, their footsteps soft against the worn linoleum, and they inspect my work meticulously.

Satisfied with their validation, I turn back to the class. "Can anyone tell me why Mina's defense held?" The room stirs, and after a moment of hesitant glances, another male student rises and approaches the board.

He explains, "Brennen tried overpowering the defense. He didn't account for the tank-like formation of the black dragons on the front line. The blues in the secondary line could volley their attacks over the black dragons, while the black dragons maintained an acid cloud that halted both land and air assaults." Zac finishes his explanation and returns to his seat with a self-assured nod.

I add, "Sometimes the best offense is a well-set defense. Know the strength of your troops and move them accordingly. Sometimes the old ways aren't always the best." I erase the board, the chalk dust billowing briefly in the cool air, and catch Mina's gaze as she's absorbed in a page of her book.

"Moving on," I continue, "we'll be hitting the simulators on Thursday. So study up on the species guide and the guide to the flora and fauna of the Aurelian Isles." I draw a large circle on the board, dividing it into three distinct sections with swift, clean strokes. "Next class, you will find a bucket with numbers in it at the door. Take one as you walk in. When we move to the simulation room, these numbers will correspond to the circle to assign you to a station. The color will indicate offense or defense."

I notice Mina tilting her head slightly as she processes the instructions, her eyes narrowing in thoughtful challenge. I already know that later we'll be discussing who she wants on her team. After graduation, if she decides to serve as she originally planned, she'll need a team. As the top student in her class, she has the right to pick her base team.

The bell rings, its shrill tone mingling with the murmur of departing students, and I watch as the class files out. Mina slowly packs her books, and several classmates drift over to talk to her. She lingers by the board, animatedly explaining her changes and the reasoning behind them.

While she's distracted, I slip away to join Balor. We lean our shoulders against the cool, rough wall at the back of the room, our eyes following Mina's animated interactions. I lower my voice and ask, "Going home or heading to your next class?"

"My class for a bit then home," he replies quietly, his gaze never leaving Mina as she uses a pointer stick to further illustrate her choices.

I lean in, barely loud enough for him to hear over the low hum of the emptying classroom, "Why does she seem off tonight?"

Balor's response is measured, his tone laden with concern: "Cora laid an egg as her dragoness this time." The simple statement carries the weight of unspoken worries. I know Mina's attention shifts subtly toward her friend—someone her own age who is finally nurturing the family she desires.

I sigh heavily, running my fingers through my hair. "It's not safe … We all want that full nest, the little ones scampering around everywhere." The thought leaves a bitter taste in my mouth.

Balor continues softly, "Mina wants to go see the eggs. She's curious to see how much bigger they are than the one she helped Cora deliver." His eyes drop to his feet, avoiding mine as if the truth is too heavy to face.

I rest a hand on his shoulder, my voice tentative. "You think she's going to push for eggs next cycle?"

He meets my gaze, his expression hardening as he speaks, "I think she's going to use her nest as bait to lure her father out. She's clever enough to know he won't surface until he believes she's defenseless. I know she craves eggs, and I know she'll manipulate her own nest to lure him out. And I know she'll destroy him utterly if he dares come near her children." His words are cold, and a chill runs down my spine at the intensity of his conviction.

I whisper, almost to myself, "A dragoness is at her most dangerous when she's protecting her nest..." and steals another glance at Mina.

Balor nods slowly, his voice low, "Exactly. According to Klauth, a dragoness changes when she's about to lay eggs—their scales harden, their talons sharpen, and their temperament turns volatile." He shivers, glancing at me before shifting his gaze back to Mina.

"What about their breath weapon?" Even now, the mere thought of it sends a shiver through me—Mina's breath weapon is the most dangerous I've ever seen.

Balor adds, "A hundred times worse ... Klauth said that Mina's is much stronger than it ought to be for a dragoness her age." At that, he freezes mid-sentence, then offers a tentative smile over my shoulder.

Mina slides between us so that her back brushes lightly against my chest. She asks playfully, "What did I miss?"

Balor stammers, "Um..." before I interject quickly, "We were talking about dragon breath weapons." I try to mask the full depth of our conversation.

Mina turns to look at me, her eyes knowing all too well that I can't hide the truth. "And?"

I confess in a low voice, "Eggs—and how dangerous a dragoness becomes when she's defending her nest." Mina nods slowly and sighs, the weight of unspoken worries lingering between us.

"I'm going to visit Cora after class," she announces, her voice steady despite the underlying tension. "She and Warwick dug a small nest at the base of the mountain within the compound. It's just big enough to shelter Cora completely, and Warwick is going to be forced to shift and settle outside it to shield her from the elements." Shaking her head as if in resignation, she gathers her things and leaves the classroom. Without missing a beat, Balor turns and runs after her, clearly troubled by something more.

I stand there in the fading light of the classroom, the echoes of our conversation mingling with the scent of chalk and distant footsteps, wondering how much more dangerous our world can get when the stakes are as personal as a nest.

Mina waits for me at the end of the day, her silhouette outlined by the fading light, and leads us out to the flight field. The cool evening air carries the scent of damp earth and distant wood smoke as Balor approaches from Malivore, his arms burdened with well-worn leather bags.

When we reach the field, Mina smoothly hands off Thauglor's carrier before beginning her shift. Gone are the days when her transformation seemed slow and unnatural; now it's fluid and swift. I watch, mesmerized, as she rises gracefully, every muscle rippling beneath her skin, then lies down and stretches out, inviting us to climb onto her back. Her scales shimmer in hues of emerald and silver, now edged with a jagged armor that catches the last glints of sunlight. I gesture to Balor, urging him to take a closer look. We agree, her scales have changed.

We settle ourselves by leaning our backs against her frill, feeling the subtle vibration of her power under our hands. "All set, Mina!" I shout at the top of my lungs, my voice echoing across the open space. Slowly, she rocks to her feet, unfurling enormous wings that beat against the cool air and propel us farther away from the academy with each powerful stroke.

Up ahead, the colossal red form of Klauth dominates the sky—a blazing silhouette against the twilight. Mina roars, a deep, resonant sound that vibrates through the air and shakes her very form. Balor and I cover our ears instinctively, startled by the force of her call. Klauth answers with a thunderous roar, then slows to a smooth glide.

When Mina catches up, she emits a series of low rumbles before wobbling in mid-air and finally landing on his massive, scaly back. With a graceful roll of her shoulders, she signals that it's time for us to dismount. I cling to one of the tall spines along Klauth's back as I watch her shift back.

"Klauth is going to check the borders before we head home. I'm going to take a seat on his head, so settle in and enjoy the ride," Mina announces, her voice carrying both authority and excitement. She flashes a warm, enigmatic smile and plants soft kisses on both of us before ascending along Klauth's broad back toward his head.

Balor whistles low, his tone a hushed murmur of awe as he surveys the ancient creature. "He's well over a hundred and thirty feet long. I see why Mina hopped on his offer for a ride," he says, clearly impressed as he traces the sinuous ridges of Klauth's back with his gaze.

"It's terrifying how massive dragons can become," I remark, my eyes sliding from his formidable back down to the undulating tail that follows.

Before I can process my thoughts further, Mina races down Klauth's back and grabs Balor by the shoulders. "Shift and coil around several spines and protect Leander," she commands, her eyes burning with a fierce, dragonic intensity as she shoves Balor toward the center of Klauth's back.

"What's happening?" I ask, my voice trembling with a mix of fear and awe as the glow in Mina's eyes intensifies like molten gold.

"Wyvern ... I've already called for Abraxis and Vox to bring any males without nests to defend," she replies. In that moment, she leans in and kisses me—a kiss that nearly steals my breath. Her hand lingers on Thauglor's egg, its cool surface contrasting with the heat of her touch. She leans forward again to kiss the side of Balor's basilisk face. I step into the protective coils, clutching the egg carrier tightly to my chest. Its worn leather is a tangible reminder of the precious cargo within.

I watch in awe as our mate dashes off Klauth's back and leaps into free fall, shifting seamlessly in the air. The atmosphere changes instantly; the sharp tang of ozone mingles with the acrid scent of brimstone wafting from Klauth's breath. Overhead, the sky ignites in a brilliant flash as Mina exhales a bolt of lightning shrouded in a mysterious, hazy aura.

"Are you seeing that?" I shout, craning my neck to witness the spectacle. I glance to Balor's basilisk, which coils tighter around me protectively, its sinuous body a living shield. Its serpent-like head nods in silent affirmation as we watch Mina strike down attackers one after another with relentless ferocity.

I feel the burning anger radiating through our bond—a fierce, almost tangible heat that promises it will be a long time before she finds calm again. Her inner dragon is unleashed in full force as she protects the egg I hold so dearly. Questions churn in my mind. Why are wyverns so close to our border? Are they testing us? What is their motive? And the one question that haunts me—could her father be behind this attack?

appear on the scene. Pumping my wings harder, I slice through the cool air, my eyes scanning the darkened landscape for any further threats.

'Mate? How are you moving so fast?' Klauth's voice echoes inside my head. I hover in place, the wind buffeting against my scales, and scan the area—I don't see the others. Then it hits me: I'm less than a mile from my nest.

'How did I get to the border of my territory?' I wonder aloud, my eyes darting over rustling trees and the dim outlines of distant hills.

'You're at the border?' Klauth's tone is laced with shock. *'Some iron dragonesses can bend time with their swift movement—a gift lost around the time of my birth. I never witnessed it in my youth.'* With that, I land in a soft clearing at the edge of my territory, waiting for them as the night air settles around me.

I have no idea what I did or how I did it, yet here I am—almost home—confounded by the mystery. My eyes keep flitting between the swaying trees and the star-flecked sky, searching for answers. Klauth's booming roar cuts through my thoughts, and I launch back into the sky. The question: *How did I get here?* Echoing in my mind.

We circle the compound several times before Abraxis and Warwick land first, their heavy steps stirring dust from the rocky ground. Klauth touches down next, his presence enough to send a shudder through most of the population. I complete one final circuit before shifting just as I'm about to land. When my feet finally meet the cool, rough rocks, I sprint across the courtyard, following the familiar, comforting scent of Cora. But I skid to a halt when I see Cerce's dragoness form lying before the den.

She lifts her head slowly, eyes meeting mine, and I feel my inner dragon stir uncontrollably at the look in her gaze. "I would like to pass, Cerce," I breathe. The last thing I want is to shift and attack my mate's mother.

"Mina, we can come back later," Abraxis offers, his tone laced with concern. I shake my head firmly.

"No, this is my territory. My mountain." A low, rumbling growl vibrates deep in my chest as I fix Cerce with a steely stare. "You don't want me shifting right now, Mom ... My dragoness is angry and not in the mood to be gentle." I watch as her scales prick and stand on edge, glistening in the faint light.

"Cerce, step away from Cora," Vox commands from over my shoulder. His tone is cold, and she bares her teeth at her mate—a silent alarm that something is terribly wrong.

"Fuck, something is wrong," I mutter. I shift on the spot, raising my frill and flaring my scales to appear even larger. I swing my head from side to side, sizing her up. I know I'm bigger than Cerce—it's plain to see. Lowering my head, I roar a challenge. She may lead her flight, but here, she's merely a guest. I feel a charge of static, like lightning rolling over my scales, as I struggle to suppress the urge to strike.

"Mom, Mina is in a foul mood. We fought wyvern on the way here—please move..." Abraxis begs, his voice trembling with worry.

The sound of his pleading makes my temper spike. I pivot sharply and snap my jaws near him, and he tumbles to the ground with a thud. Before I can fully process my actions, I turn back to see that Cerce has already shifted back to her human form, now cradled in Vox's arms. My inner dragon softens; I croon in a low, soothing timbre, letting my song wash over Cora to calm her. After several long, tense minutes, Cora rises and drifts away from the nest.

I settle near the opening of the den and snake my head inside. As I tilt my head, I quickly assess the situation. Four eggs lie before me—two are soft-shelled and lifeless, one has a hardened shell but holds no promise of life. Only one egg is viable, though its shell is slightly malformed. Carefully, I extend a taloned finger, plucking the three dead eggs away and nudging the good one to the center.

As I remove the lifeless eggs, Cora shifts back to her human form and breaks into tears in Warwick's arms. I glance over at Klauth. *'Offer her the egg chamber off of the main hall for her egg,'* I instruct silently.

I watch as Klauth moves forward, resting a hand on Warwick's shoulder. "Mina is offering the egg chamber off of the main hall," he announces, and both men turn to me for confirmation.

"I didn't hear her say anything," Cora protests as she approaches my dragoness. "You'll let me use your egg chamber?" she asks, her eyes pleading.

My dragon rumbles its assent, reminding her she may use the chamber where I was hatched. The chamber above is part of my private residence—reserved only for me and my bloodline. When my dragoness finishes her rumbling, Cora nods gratefully.

"I understand. Thank you," she murmurs, smiling as she carefully steps past the dead eggs, gathering her only viable egg before heading inside.

I seize Warwick by hooking a talon around him, halting his advance. In one swift motion, I shift back, standing toe-to-toe with him. "If Cora lays another egg this year, I will personally ensure you never have use of your favorite part again." My talons extend from my human hands as I tap the back of one against his groin.

"Understood, my queen..." Warwick replies, bowing his head and quickly retreating.

Before I can shift to dispose of the eggs, two young drakes scurry forward to clean up. I arch an eyebrow as I watch them tidy and then clear out the nest. Lowering my head slightly in acknowledgment, they smile and wave before disappearing back inside. I stand for a long moment, staring at the now empty cavern as silence settles in.

"Why did Mom challenge you?" Abraxis asks softly from behind, wrapping his arms around me. The warmth of his embrace steadies my racing heart.

I lean back against him and sigh heavily. "She was worried about Cora. She didn't want me to get upset about the eggs again." Slowly, I pivot in his arms, resting my head against his shoulder as my arms wrap around his waist. "Klauth told me about another dragoness—one who was essentially bred to death. Too many hatchlings in too short a time can deplete a female." I close my eyes, letting the familiar comfort of his hold ease the turmoil inside me. For once, my inner dragon isn't railing against me for taking what seems like a submissive stance with my mate.

"I was going to talk to him about that," Abraxis admits quietly. "But we also have to remember that my sister willingly went into season again. She's just as much to blame." He presses his lips gently to my forehead before leading me inside, and I let his warmth carry me away from the storm of the night.

I walk into the lower part of the compound, and a chill creeps along my neck, setting my scales on edge. The cold stone beneath my feet and the faint odor of damp earth stir memories I'd rather forget— childhood days steeped in loneliness and pain. I pass the main sitting area, its low murmur of conversation and shadowy corners whispering warnings, and head toward the egg chamber.

Inside, the air is warm and heavy. Cora stands there in the dim light, cradling her son in her arms as she gazes at an onyx egg resting in the egg cradle. I step into the doorway and murmur, "Hey."

"Hey," she replies in a soft, resigned tone. Her voice trembles like a distant echo in the cavernous room. "I just wanted William to have a sibling. He's the only hatchling in the compound, and it's so lonely for him." I watch as her eyes soften while she leans down to check on her sleeping babe, the quiet rhythm of his breath mingling with the low hum of the room.

"We grow fast. I get it," I say, stepping closer. My fingertips hover over the egg's smooth, dark surface—barely touched by the colors of her mate. It's a bit larger than a big watermelon, cool and weighty in my hand. "Was it easier when you were your dragoness?" I ask, tilting my head as I search her face for any sign of regret or relief.

She laughs—a soft, bittersweet sound that fills the silence. "Oh gods, tons easier. The wait sucked, but it was painless." With a gentle smile, she kisses her son's forehead, the gesture both tender and melancholic.

"It was what—three days from conception until you laid the eggs?" I probe, piecing together what I'd overheard from Klauth.

"About that. We counted, I think, a little over two days after it was finished," she replies, her smile tinged with nostalgia. I furrow my brows and, almost instinctively, brush aside her hair to search along her neck for scales. "What are you looking for?" she asks, a trace of amusement in her eyes.

"Scales. You don't have any," I reply, sliding her hair aside again, double-checking what I know to be true.

"You're the first female I've seen with scales in human form, Mina. I don't think it's a common trait," Cora says, her tone a mix of wonder and caution as she takes my hand and leads me out of the egg chamber.

I bite my bottom lip as we return to the main sitting area, where murmurs and subdued laughter fill the space. Klauth catches the puzzled expression on my face and arches an eyebrow. "Am I an oddity for having scales in my human form?" I ask, glancing between Cora and him.

"These days, probably," Klauth replies. "Back in my time, only the most powerful dragonesses bore scales in their human form." He then turns his gaze to Vox. "Do you know of any other females with scales in their human form?"

Vox paces the room, his boots echoing on the stone floor, then stops to lift Cerce's hair. He reveals three delicate scales along the back of her neck. "Nothing compares to what Mina has. She nearly has armor in her human form," he observes, his voice low and measured.

I think to Klauth, *'I can cover my ribs, stomach, and arms with scales when needed, not just my neck.'*

Almost immediately, his voice resonates in my mind, *'No one outside our bond needs to know that.'*

Before I can dwell further on our secret, Ziggy suddenly bounces in front of me. My heart jumps, and I squeal, nearly stumbling backward. "Shit, Ziggy!" I exclaim.

He boops my nose with a soft, playful nudge. His purr vibrates against my skin as he chides, "It's not nice to talk only to Klauth in front of everyone." In a swift, unexpected move, he dips me backward and plants a quick kiss on my lips before helping me steady myself and trotting off.

"You two share a mental bond?" Vox asks, his eyes narrowing with curiosity. I glance over at Klauth, who leans casually against the wall.

"Yes. I am a great wyrm—it's a gift that comes with age. I share it with my mate for her safety," he grumbles, his deep voice blending with the low ambient sounds of the room.

"That must be very handy," Vox adds, glancing first at Abraxis and then at me.

"It is. It comes in handy when I run the gauntlets and need someone to keep an eye on me. Besides, it saves me from having to rely solely on

Ziggy," I reply with a smile, snuggling closer to Callan as he ambles past me.

Callan's gryphon emits a high-pitched whistle—a sound that sends a delightful shiver through me. I purr softly, nuzzling his cheek and the underside of his jaw, feeling warmth flood through me. My eyes close as I melt into his arms. The comforting warmth of his embrace mingles with the ambient murmur of the room. "I've never heard a gryphon make those noises before," Warwick comments. Instantly, my scales prickle with a protective heat, a fierce instinct rising within me at the mention of Callan.

"My shift makes that sound for its mate—just as a happy dragoness purrs, a gryphon calls to his mate," Callan explains, his fingers threading soothingly through my hair.

"The room feels scary..." Cora murmurs, pressing herself closer to Warwick as if seeking solace.

"Your mate spoke of Callan in a way that angered Mina. What you feel now is the presence of her dragoness—a force that can fill a room and intimidate those weaker than her," Klauth declares, stepping forward to stand shoulder-to-shoulder with Abraxis.

I hear a soft "oof" and a cough before turning to see everyone's concerned faces. Warwick clutches his ribs, holding himself near Vox. "I'm sorry if my statement angered you. I meant no disrespect," he says, his voice earnest. I nod in acknowledgment, feeling the tension ebb slightly.

"Forgiven," I reply, glancing over at Balor and then Leander. "Dinner should be just about ready." The two flank me with knowing smiles. Leander hands me Thauglor's egg carrier, its cool leather contrasting with the warmth of my skin as I strap it on. Being in charge of a flight isn't easy, but in this dark, unpredictable world, it's a responsibility I've learned to embrace.

master. I glance at the clock high in the tower; his observation is right —Mina is almost fifteen minutes late.

Leander descends from the observation room, his eyes scanning the space before arching a brow at me. I shake my head. "That's not normal."

Just as I'm about to call for my familiar, the heavy wooden gates groan open and Mina strides through, flanked by Balor and Callan. Both look disheveled—as if a storm had whipped through them—yet even in their unkempt state, there's an air of purpose. Mina adjusts the egg carrier strapped under her chest, then retrieves the bow I left for her, her fingers steady despite the tension simmering beneath the surface.

I lean toward Balor and Callan, whispering, "What happened to you two?"

"Mina happened," Balor replies, exhaling slowly, his breath thick with lingering frustration. "She was still pissed off from earlier."

Callan scoffs, shoving Balor lightly. "This idiot said, I can't tell if you want to fuck or fight..." His tone drips with incredulity.

"Oh ... I guess we know which option she chose," Balor retorts, and my gaze drifts over to Mina, who is striking targets at the farthest range with cool precision. The rhythmic twang of her bowstring punctuates the silence.

"In the middle of my class, no less. Next thing I know, she's dragging Balor out the door," Callan continues, running a hand down his face, as if trying to erase the memory of chaos. "I go to my office, thinking they've left— and find this asshole with Mina bent over my desk, my papers, and books scattered like leaves in a storm. My office looked like a hurricane had hit."

I let out a quiet laugh as I watch Mina in action. "Oh, act innocent, Callan. Who sat Mina on the arm of the couch and fucked her there? Hmm? It wasn't me..." Balor teases, and I glance at Callan in shock.

I shift my attention between them and then back to our mate—Mina—who remains absorbed in her target practice. "Did she get into a fight? Lose her temper? Cross Lysander's path?" I fire off questions, my voice edged with concern.

"Honestly, not sure," Balor replies, his eyes tracking Mina's every movement.

I turn to Callan. "What do you know, Callan?"

"Klauth reached out to her during class. A flight of green dragons was seen heading toward your parents' den," he explains, raising his hands as if holding the weight of his words. "Klauth sent Warwick to alert them, and Mina wasn't happy he wouldn't let Ziggy bring her to them." Callan's gaze drops, and I nod slowly, absorbing his tone.

"Did she say why?" I ask, watching as Callan pales, his eye drifting away.

"I said, I am no different than I was yesterday. And unlike your family, I am immune to the acid. Your father's flight will lose warriors because Klauth is being stubborn." Her voice is as cold and resolute as the academy's silent halls, and now she stomps over to stand in front of me, the fire in her eyes a clear warning.

"Where is Klauth right now?" I ask, choosing my words carefully.

"Risedale—in a meeting," Mina replies, tilting her head in that slow, disarming way that makes the hair on the back of my neck stand on edge.

I quickly text Ziggy to come get us, even though a knot of dread tightens in my stomach—I know I might be making a big mistake. Moments later, Ziggy manifests before us, his presence filling the space with quiet authority as he glances between us.

"Why do I think the big guy is going to be pissed?" Ziggy says, arching a brow before moving to envelop Mina in a firm hug.

"I'll handle him later," she declares sharply. "We need to go to Risedale." Her gaze hardens as she addresses Callan and Balor. "You two finish up here. Ziggy will collect everyone later." There's no room for argument in her tone.

Before I can protest, she grabs me, and in a flash, Ziggy phases us to Risedale. I stagger slightly, the sudden shift leaving my stomach in knots. "I still can't get used to that," I mutter, half to myself.

"Oh, stop, you big baby," Mina teases as we move, her voice echoing with both exasperation and affection. "He moved slower because he has you with us this time." Her words distract me as we approach the meeting room.

We linger just inside the door. Inside, Mina's posture is perfect—shoulders back, chin high—as she strides toward Klauth. The room is filled with a heavy, unspoken tension; the quiet murmur of low voices fades as she draws near. She barely acknowledges the men at the table with him, her focus fixed upward. I watch her tilt her head back, her eyes locking with his. Not a single word is exchanged, but the oppressive air around us shifts as if charged by an unseen battle of wills. One by one, the men at the table retreat hastily as the pressure mounts.

Lightning ripples through Mina's hair—a shimmering, dangerous aura that seems to defy the silence of the room. I find a strange relief in not hearing their clash. Sometimes, the mere intensity of their stares is more terrifying than any outburst. Their faces are impassive masks, with only the erratic flashes in Mina's hair betraying the fierce internal conflict.

"Fine..." Mina growls, breaking the charged silence. Without another word, she removes the egg carrier and straps it to Ziggy's chest, her movements decisive and full of purpose. Then she leaves the meeting room as abruptly as she entered.

Klauth approaches and rests a firm hand on my shoulder. "Come on, we have to go save your parents." He winks at me—a fleeting spark of reassurance—before walking past.

I blink several times, still in shock, and then look to Ziggy. "She actually won," I whisper, awe and disbelief mingling in my voice. I shrug off the lingering tension and dash after Mina and Klauth, my footsteps echoing through the silent, tomb-like halls of the academy as I follow into the uncertain night.

KLAUTH CONVINCES us to ride on his dragon for the quick trip to my parents' den. The wind bites at my face as we take off, the roar of Klauth's dragon echoing off distant stone walls. Mina sits perfectly still, her eyes fixed on the horizon like a sentinel.

"Shit," she mutters, and without warning, she takes a running start and leaps off Klauth's back. I watch in awe as her own dragoness erupts into existence—a magnificent creature of raw power. Lightning ripples over her shimmering scales as she speeds away, faster than I ever thought possible.

A dozen green dragons, including Abaddon, swarm toward my parents' den. The air vibrates with their menacing growls and the acrid tang of burning flesh. Mina roars, unleashing her lightning with precision upon the invaders. She dives after her father, barely missing him as he narrowly escapes the snapping of her jaws.

I leap off Klauth's back and shift into flight, determined to help Mina drive off the attackers. Klauth unleashes torrents of fire, the scorching heat melting the green dragons' skin into raw bone. Amid the chaos, I lose sight of Mina for several heart-pounding moments before glimpsing her locked in combat. Her talons are entwined with those of a green dragon hybrid—though I suspect the other part might be black.

Mina strikes the creature with lightning, but nothing happens. Her eyes widen in terror as she grapples with this new, formidable foe. *"Shit..."* I think, and dive toward them—but I'm blindsided by another dragon that comes out of nowhere. I tumble midair, my senses reeling as I try to right myself. After several frantic flaps, I regain control and see Mina still locked in a desperate struggle against the new male attacker.

Klauth, noticing the danger, heads straight for her. Before he can reach her, Mina's eyes flare brighter, and she releases a breath weapon that carries a strange, hazy blue-purple tint—a gas mingled with lightning. The effect is immediate; the male dragon struggles to keep his eyes open. In that instant, Mina strikes decisively, tearing his throat out. She opens her talons and drops his lifeless body into the tree line before taking off once more.

I turn and fly in tandem with her as we force the remaining green dragons away from the den. The air is filled with the mingled scents of burnt scales and scorched earth. I scan the skies for Abaddon, but there's no sign of him.

Mina lands first, followed by me and then Klauth. Even as we come to a stop, her eyes dart continuously over the horizon—flickering between the fierce intensity of a dragon and the vulnerability of a human.

Soon, Warwick lands and strides over. "I thought you weren't coming. We were getting slaughtered," he says, his tone edged with worry.

Klauth huffs. "Your queen went to war for this den. She won," he replies, his gaze lingering on Mina before he walks over to her.

"Your dad is in the infirmary. He was hit pretty bad by green dragon acid," Warwick adds hesitantly, glancing at Mina. "The healers need green dragon acid to create a healing salve."

I exchange a glance with Klauth. "I don't know if Mina can produce it. Her dragoness has lightning," I remark, watching as Klauth and Mina approach.

"What happened?" Mina asks, her eyes shifting between me and Warwick.

"Vox was injured and the healers need green dragon acid," Warwick says before I can intervene.

Mina's gaze drops to the ground as she nods slowly. "Abraxis and Klauth will have to harvest it from me. My dragoness will bite anyone who gets too close. Get the healers to bring glass containers." She pauses, waiting until Warwick leaves, then fixes both of us with a determined look.

"I will show you where the acid glands are in my mouth," she instructs, glancing briefly at Klauth. With a deep sigh, she continues, "There are two glands in the back of my mouth—one that produces a sleep toxin and the other, acid. Get extra jars and harvest both. I have a plan."

I step away and shift into my black dragon, landing carefully on the cool cobblestones. Laying down flat, I open my mouth wide. In a move that both amazes and unnerves me, Mina climbs completely into my mouth and walks along my tongue.

"Right here," she says, touching a spot near my back upper molar. "This is where the acid is produced." She walks a few steps forward and presses near the middle molar on the top. "And here is where the sleep toxin is produced." With deliberate care, she retraces her steps back to the opening of my jaw.

Once she's clear, I shift back and study her uneasy expression. "What's wrong?" I ask softly, opening my arms to her. Without hesitation, she dives into my embrace, clinging tightly.

"I shouldn't have three breath weapons," she confesses, her eyes darting toward Klauth.

"Do you want me to shift with you? To keep you under my wing while Abraxis harvests the acid? Would that make you feel safer?" Klauth asks in a tone far gentler than I've ever heard him use with her.

"Yes," she whispers, "but we need to warn the others not to come close while I'm so nervous." She meets my gaze, then looks back up at Klauth. "Please relay my concerns. One wrong move and my dragoness will kill without a second thought." Klauth gives her a reassuring kiss on the temple.

I fire off a quick text to my mom, warning the den not to come out until the jars are delivered. Her reply is swift. Warwick will bring out the jars. The healers, it seems, are afraid of Mina.

"I have the jars," Warwick calls, holding up a box. The glass containers clink against each other as they shift in his grip.

"Good, leave them here and then head inside. Mina is uncomfortable, and Klauth is going to shift with her," I remark casually, as if this were an everyday occurrence. Then again, Klauth waited a thousand years for a mate like her—there's not much I'd put past him at this point.

Mina steps closer and locks eyes with me. "Do you remember where I touched?" she asks, and then, in the oddest moment, she grabs my face and stares deep into my eyes. "Do not break eye contact. I'm going to try something." Her voice reverberates through my mind, and all I can do is watch as my perspective shifts.

I suddenly see from her point of view—inside my mouth. She points out where the different glands are, explaining which is which. When she pulls back and smiles, I feel disoriented. "What was that?" I ask, my voice trembling as she steps back.

"A happy little present from Klauth," Mina replies, before she shifts into her dragoness form. Her dragoness turns to face Klauth, and he shifts, rising high above her—easily triple her size. Mina lies down, and soon Klauth follows, draping a protective wing over her and drawing her close.

"Okay, Mina, I'm going to start with the acid," I announce as she lays her head down and opens her dragon's mouth wide. I carefully advance, finding the first gland hole. I search further back for the acid gland, and when I locate it. I open the jar and position it over the hole. A small dribble of fluid appears, then a modest gush follows. Once the bottle is nearly full, I step back and walk halfway toward the building.

A healer rushes out to grab the jar, then runs back inside. I quickly secure two more jars to extract the sleep toxin from the slightly swollen gland—likely rarely used. Repeating the process, I fill both jars, stepping back as Mina shifts and examines the blueish-purple fluid.

"I'm going to hide this in our home, then join you to check on your dad," Mina declares. She closes the distance between us and kisses me passionately. My heart thunders in my chest, each beat echoing like the first time our lips met. I hold her tightly, and my dragon rumbles in contentment. "I love you, Abraxis," she whispers before backing away toward Klauth.

"I love you too, Mina. See you soon," I reply softly as she climbs up to perch behind Klauth's crown of horns. I watch them take off into the dusky sky before turning to head inside. Moments like these make me question why she fights so fiercely—when all I want is to hold her close. But my dragon reminds me, Klauth is the dominant drake. Mina is safer with him than she ever will be with me.

I take a deep breath as I head inside my parents' den, silently praying that my father isn't too badly injured.

"Yeah … That was probably the only time I said '*oh shit*'—aside from when my dad tried to kill me the second time," I say, my hand absently stroking Thauglor's shell as if seeking comfort.

"He hums like Klauth did," Vaughn observes. He shifts until he stands directly behind me, his muscular arms wrapping around me and pulling me close. I feel his steady heartbeat and warmth press against me, a welcome distraction from my racing thoughts.

"Yeah, he knows when I'm stressed. I don't like that whatever hybrid that male was remained unaffected by my weapon," I confess, pausing as the weight of the revelation settles on me.

The lab door creaks open and Balor appears, visibly shaken. "What happened?" I ask, my voice trembling. I rush over and guide him to the worn couch, the fabric soft under my touch. Vaughn quickly brings over a glass of cool water, and I urge Balor to drink as I try to steady my own churning thoughts.

Balor's eyes lock with mine, his bottom lip quivering slightly. "It's part basilisk." We stare at each other for several heartbeats, and then reality slams into me like a tidal wave. If Balor and I have a child—the one in the painting—it will be more powerful than the male I killed.

My mouth drops open, and my chest feels as if a heavy weight has settled on it, making each breath a struggle. I stumble, collapsing onto the nearest chair as I repeat the thought over and over. That male—the one I killed—was half basilisk. I try to force the pieces to make sense, but they slip away like mist.

"Why do Balor and Mina look like they are in shock?" I hear Abraxis ask before I even see him. Klauth walks in with him, followed by the rest of my mates.

"The male that Mina ripped the throat out of was half green dragon and half basilisk," Callan explains, his voice low and heavy with disbelief.

"Shit..." Abraxis echoes, shock written plainly on his face.

Then, a deep, rhythmic purring sounds behind me. Before I can process it, a tentacle wraps around me and lifts me gently. Ziggy, who is sprawled on the floor, shifts so that I'm pressed against his soft, black fur. The instant I feel his warmth, the dam holding back my tears breaks, and they flow freely down my cheeks. I have just killed a male who could have answered all the questions we have about what could be.

Leander comes over and settles beside me, resting his head on Ziggy next to mine. He pulls me into his arms, and his soothing voice whispers, "Let it out, baby. Ziggy and I will be here however you need us. No questions asked, no words needed." He leans forward and kisses my forehead. A gentle promise of comfort. I nod, running my fingers through Ziggy's fur, grateful for these two—the feelings guys in the nest—who never push me to speak before I'm ready.

We lie together for what feels like an eternity before I steady my breathing. Slowly, I pull away and notice Klauth deep in conversation with Balor about the discovery. As I draw closer, tears well up again, blurring my vision and weighing my heart with guilt.

"I'm so sorry, Balor—I didn't know what he was ... If I hadn't killed him..." My voice falters, unfinished. Before I can continue, Balor rises swiftly and presses his lips against mine, silencing my confession with a fierce tenderness.

The unmistakable heat of Klauth's body behind me sends my pulse into overdrive. Part of me yearns for these two together, their raw dominance igniting a dangerous, liquid heat that pools deep within my core. Balor withdraws just long enough to press a gentle kiss against my forehead.

"If you hadn't killed him, he would have killed you," he murmurs, his voice hoarse with emotion. "I'd rather have no answers and hold you in our arms than face burying you for trying not to kill him." His words reverberate as Klauth trails soft kisses along my shoulder.

Lowering my eyes, I nod slowly. "Go with Balor for a while. You both need each other right now," Klauth instructs before his lips find my neck over his mate mark. "Head to the hot springs and relax—you both deserve it." He shakes hands with Balor and moves past us toward the door.

Heavy is the head that wears the crown. I've barely seen Klauth these past few weeks, except on our rare date nights and fleeting encounters in passing. Balor gently lifts my hand and presses soft kisses against my knuckles. "Let's do what boss man said and go relax in the hot springs," he says, forcing a smile as he tries to be strong for me.

"I know it's not easy," I reply, wrapping my arm around him as we leave my lab and make our way down the quiet hall toward the sanctuary of the hot springs.

"Nothing worth keeping ever is," he adds, pulling me closer to him. Our footsteps echo softly in the hallway.

We step into the room where the hot springs bubble gently, their warmth a soothing balm against the chill of lingering tension. I find a safe spot to set Thauglor's carrier down, then undress to prepare for a swim. The moment the steaming water embraces me, a deep, restorative breath fills my lungs.

I glance around and spot Balor accepting a cooler from Callan, whose wave carries a hint of reassurance before he leaves. "What's in the cooler?" I ask, swimming to the edge and waiting.

"Drinks and snacks," Balor explains with a strained smile as he scratches his forearm, his fingers tracing nervous patterns on his skin. "We're worried that after all the energy you've spent, you need to eat."

"Is something wrong?" I ask, watching him rub his hand against his arm again.

He shrugs, his eyes darkening momentarily. "I was going to leave this morning to go into one of the deep tunnels to shed. But…" He pauses, then adds, "I'll be alright. For now, let me take care of you."

I watch as Balor strips down and carries a drink and a snack into the soothing water. "You need to eat, Mina," he insists, holding the offerings out to me. I hesitate for a moment, the steam curling around us like whispered secrets.

"Only if you let me help you peel away your shed," I reply, biting into the snack stick and studying his reaction carefully.

"Fine, after you eat," Balor laughs softly, the sound echoing against the stone walls of the cavern. "Usually I drag Abraxis with me because of his talons, but I'm sure you'll do a better job than he usually does." His laughter mingles with the gentle burble of the hot springs, and I smile as I finish chewing the meat stick.

"I can only imagine," I tease. "Why don't you shift and let the hot water loosen up your scales?" I lean back against the edge of the pool, the heat seeping into my skin.

"My skin—" he begins, then nods as he assesses the size of the pool. "A soak would help." He shifts into his massive basilisk form. Now I can see his scales in their dull, lifeless sheen and the whitened caps over his eyes, blocking his vision. Instead of floating as he did when carrying me, his immense body sinks, leaving only his nostrils above the water's surface.

This is going to be a challenge. I'm used to the tactile struggle of prying dragon scales off with our talons—this is an entirely new adventure.

I float around the hot springs for what feels like forever, the water warm and thick against my skin, until Balor bumps me gently with his nose. "Okay," I murmur, my voice low and playful. I push myself upright in the water, feeling it lap softly under the curve of my breasts as I wade closer to the carved stone stairs. I shift my hands, and my silver talons catch the flickering light from the distant fireplace, glinting like shards of broken glass in the dim room.

Balor slithers to the low end of the spring, making room for me on the cool, worn steps. With deliberate care, I use the tips of my talons to lift the edge of his peeling skin. Each inch of movement is methodical. I don't want to miss a single patch as his heat receptors cling stubbornly, unwilling to let go of the cones of old skin. A soft laugh escapes me as I peel away another layer, the sound mingling with the gentle burble of the spring. I set the freed cones aside on the edge of the pool.

"I feel like I'm picking your nose," I tease, chuckling to myself as I free six small cones—not counting the two around his actual nose. As the skin parts, I approach the first of his eyes. I retract my talons and slide my hands on either side of the eye, and with a soft pop, the old eye cap detaches. I lean in, careful and precise, until the next eye yields, repeating the process until the eyes on one side are clear.

"I'm going to start on the other side now," I say. Balor turns his head so that the opposite side faces me. I resume my work, removing the caps with a careful rhythm. "I guess it's easier without having to worry about turning me to stone accidentally," I chuckle. The thought of Abraxis—trying to do this with his eyes closed—bringing a brief, mischievous smile to my face.

After all six of Balor's eyes are free, I shift my focus to the skin along his bottom jaw. Inch by inch, I peel it back, feeling the subtle texture of the aged skin as it gives way past the coarse spikes on his head. Once I have cleared that section, Balor slithers out of the water and begins rubbing his body along the cool stone wall, the friction easing the remaining layers of skin off.

When every piece of old skin is free from his body, I gather it along with the bits that tore off, piling them neatly beside the pool. Balor slips back into the hot spring, sinking once again into the comforting heat. I follow his lead, easing myself back into the water, and recline on the carved stairs to relax. The gentle warmth, the quiet drip of water against limestone, and the rhythmic sound of my breathing create a small haven of calm amid the chaos in my mind.

Lying on the warm limestone stairs, I close my eyes. In moments like this, I am profoundly grateful that some of my mates know precisely when not to push me. Even though I know we need to talk about what we discovered today, deep down, I understand it has hit him as hard as it hit me. For now, I let the soothing heat and gentle sounds of the springs silence the spinning thoughts in my head.

Outside of our own kind, we're shunned by most species, and it's no wonder. When we breed outside our kin, our children often emerge malformed, cursed to remain half-shifted for their entire lives.

When I sense that my scales have hardened from the heat, I surface and shift back to my human form. I find Mina lying on the middle stair, her head resting on the edge of the step above her. "Babe?" I whisper softly, my voice barely audible over the gentle hiss of the steam. She smiles as she opens her eyes to look up at me, and in that moment, I'm captivated by the love radiating from her gaze—it steals my breath away.

Slowly, I bend down and kiss her lips, savoring the delicate taste of her skin. I nibble lightly on her full bottom lip and smile. "Penny for your thoughts?" I murmur against her lips before settling onto the stair below her.

Mina exhales a heavy sigh and then slides down to sit in my lap. "I feel horrible for killing that male," she confesses, her fingers twisting nervously in her lap. "But I understand—it was better he was him than me." She glances down at her hands, as if searching for answers in their familiar lines.

"We at least know that when our child is born, they'll be safe from most dangers," I say, kissing her lips again in an effort to be the strong one for both of us.

She nods and hugs me tightly, her arms warm against my back. "It's okay to be sad or scared, Balor. It's just us here. You can be the big, scary basilisk outside of this room." I feel her breath hitch, and her body shudders slightly as she clings to me.

My arms wrap around her, holding her close as if my embrace could mend her wounded spirit. I remember the one therapy session we shared—she confided in me about the emotional abuse she endured. Where tears meant punishment and crying became a silent, guarded defense. That memory still burns as I hold her, promising silently that we can both be strong and scary outside of here.

She pulls back just enough to meet my eyes as I feel a single tear roll down my cheek. Gently, she leans in and kisses it away, a tender act that speaks of unspoken forgiveness and understanding. Deep inside, I mourn silently for the one regret I dare not voice. How I wish I could have asked him about his own upbringing.

"My big, terrifying basilisk," Mina teases with a soft smile, her voice warm against the chill of the night. Her words spark a laugh from deep within me, a sound that feels both unexpected and healing.

"I'm so terrifying," I murmur, half in jest, feeling a tear continue its slow journey down my cheek. I cast a sidelong glance toward the heap of my shed lying against the wall.

Mina traces my jaw with the delicate tip of her finger, her touch light and curious. "I never thought in a million years we'd be here, like this," she whispers. Her eyes wander over my face, down to my chest, and back up again, and a soft laugh escapes her lips. "Can I be honest with you?" Her gaze shifts, flickering between human and dragon, vulnerable and raw.

"Of course," I reply, caressing the side of her cheek. She closes her eyes briefly, as if savoring the quiet intimacy of the moment.

"If I wasn't afraid of getting you killed, I would have asked you out before I met Abraxis," she admits with a smirk, shaking her head after the confession. "You were one of the first males not afraid of what I am. You felt dangerous and safe at the same time. I wanted to get to know you better, but I was terrified of what my betrothed might have done to you." She tilts her head, studying my reaction, searching my eyes.

I am shocked, to say the very least. "Most are afraid of me, too. Can I be honest with you?" I counter, my voice low and earnest.

"A truth for a truth, of course," Mina says, leaning back against the wall so she can face me fully.

"I knew you were mine the minute our eyes met," I confess, feeling a weight lift off my chest as I speak. "The way you looked at me—I swore you knew. When I saw you with Abraxis for the first time, I realized you didn't even know he was your mate. So, I buried the bond. I know it was stupid, that I could have confessed after you bonded with Abraxis, but then Callan..." I pause, the memory of dejected Callan stinging like a fresh wound. To throw my hat into the ring then would have only driven him further away.

"You sacrificed your happiness for your friend," Mina whispers, kissing my lips so softly that my heart flutters from the gentle contact.

In that tender moment, wrapped in each other's embrace and the soft warmth of the hot spring. I realize that even amidst the darkness and the scars of our past. We have found something precious—a shared truth that binds us in a way that is both dangerous and beautiful.

Some hours later, we emerge from the hot springs, our skin still warm and damp, to find the kitchen alive with the sounds and scents of dinner preparation. The polished surfaces gleam under the soft glow of the overhead lights. The aroma of sizzling herbs and roasted vegetables mingles with the lingering tang of salt from the springs. In the center of it all, Abraxis is busy cooking, his focused expression softened by a hint of a smile.

Mina glances at me, her eyes curious, then back at Abraxis. "Are you feeling okay?" she asks softly, one eyebrow arched in quiet concern as she steps closer to him.

"Klauth and I figured out that most of our birthdays are clustered together," Abraxis explains casually, and I steal a glance over at Klauth. He nods, confirming the truth in Abraxis's words. "So tonight we're celebrating Klauth's, Leander's, and Callan's birthdays. Next month are Vaughn's, mine, and Thauglor's. While yours and Balor's are separated by a few days." Abraxis's tone is light, and I lean back against Balor, letting his familiar warmth soothe me.

"Our birthdays already passed," I murmur, wrapping my arms around Mina in a quick, affectionate hug. I remember the small trinkets we left on each other's pillows, tokens of celebration and remembrance.

"What can I do to help?" I ask, nudging Mina gently toward one of the birthday boys in the nest.

"Maybe set the table?" Abraxis shrugs, his casual demeanor at odds with his usual command. It's rare to see him leading the nest like this. Mina is typically the one in charge.

I move to the dining area and begin setting the table. The clink of cutlery and the soft rustle of napkins filling the quiet space. Soon, Leander steps up beside me. "Klauth had a long talk with all of us while you were off with Mina," he whispers, his voice low as we arrange the plates. "He said that a dragoness dominates a nest when she feels unsafe. Our goal is for each of us to take over one aspect of the nest so that Mina can settle in better." His words resonate with the gentle clatter of tableware and the subdued hum of conversation.

"What's my role in all this?" I ask, setting the next plate carefully before looking back at him.

"You and Ziggy are on Mina protection detail," he explains, glancing briefly at Callan and then at Abraxis. "They're getting called back to the front again. This time, it's on our border—not over the line like before. Klauth is holding our troops within our borders to prevent the fighting on the other side from spilling over." Leander looks down, then away, as if the weight of his words presses on him.

"Mina doesn't know, does she?" I whisper, a trace of worry creeping into my tone.

"She told us about it last night. We sent scouts, and what she said was true," he sighs, shaking his head in quiet resignation.

Just then, Klauth's deep voice cuts through the murmuring, "We are trying to keep this light, gentlemen," as he places a centerpiece crafted from dragon glass in the middle of the table. The glass catches the light, scattering flecks of red and amber across the white tablecloth.

"Mina is going to lose her mind if they leave tonight," I murmur, turning to face Klauth. His calm demeanor makes me feel both reassured and uneasy.

"She just wrote three things she's seen and sealed the envelopes. Each envelope contains a trigger—a contingency plan, in case one of those events occurs," he explains, tilting his head as he gazes past me toward Mina. She stands beside Abraxis, helping with dinner, her presence steady amid the rising tension. Klauth's measured tone contrasts with the urgency in my mind.

"So she's seen the war, and three possible events, and she's prepared instructions for each?" I ask, feeling as if he might sprout a dozen heads with the complexity of his explanation.

"Yes. Veil walkers are rare—and stronger than any intrinsic force to ever roam the continents. Mina explained she can almost fast-forward her vision. When she senses multiple outcomes, she can walk through all of them," Klauth continues, leaning forward to adjust the centerpiece again as if to emphasize the gravity of his words.

"I thought Callan and Abraxis wouldn't be sent away after you were crowned. Did I misunderstand that?" I stop, setting down a plate, and turn fully to face him.

"They are going because they want to," he replies, his eyes hard to read. "I can't say exactly what Mina saw—things may change if I do.

But Abraxis will single-handedly eliminate part of a larger threat in this battle." Klauth pauses, scanning the room before sighing. "He will fall. Mina will feel him get hurt and rush after him. That gives me the right to protect my mate by any means necessary." He arches an eyebrow and offers a wry smile.

"Oh shit, so that means when Mina feels Abraxis get hurt, you're going to follow her into battle and even the odds," I whisper, my eyes widening at the implications of what's about to unfold.

"Abraxis has one job. Not to die," Klauth states firmly, then turns and walks away. I watch his retreating back, my mind racing with the weight of his words. Moments later, he crosses the room to take Mina in his arms and kisses her, his actions as deliberate as his plans. In that instant, I realize that this man has plans for everything. No wonder he ruled the continent until his capture.

Ziggy planted for me. The scent of damp soil and the delicate perfume of young Japanese maple trees fill the air, while a small water feature burbles softly. Fancy fish dart through the clear water, their movements both calming and restless.

I chuckle softly as I stroke Thauglor's egg, now resting on a weathered bench. "The fire drakes and ambush drakes will try to attack us here, but they'll never make it up here with us." I smile as the egg pulses in response. The gentle vibration is a reassuring reminder of the bond we share.

"It still amazes me how you interact with us in the eggs," Klauth says, settling onto the bench in front of me. His tone is contemplative as he watches my every move.

"It's not like I'm talking to a lifeless chicken egg," I reply with a shrug, lifting Thauglor and setting him on my lap. The warm, smooth surface of his shell contrasts with the warmth of my hand.

"That is true. Still, I see what Abraxis meant—you really never let go of his egg," Klauth teases, tilting his head as he studies me.

"You are a brilliant tactician. Tell me, what would be one of the major ways to destabilize my nest?" I ask, curiosity lacing my tone. I watch the morning light dance across his features as I continue, "If it were me, I'd steal the egg. Second, I'd steal Cora's child—or egg—or both. Third, I'd destroy Shadowcarve." I slide Thauglor back into his carrier and stand, feeling the weight of my own words settle over me.

"Someone steals Thauglor, and I would go on a rampage that might set the world on fire," I confess, beginning to pace as my eyes drift toward the water feature, following the graceful movements of the fish.

"Someone steals Cora's child or egg—I'd be too busy managing Abraxis to lose my temper completely. I'd be angry, but not utterly detached," I muse, letting the image of swirling fish distract me for several minutes as I ponder the intricacies of my vision.

"And Shadowcarve's destruction?" Klauth asks, just as I notice the rest of my mates walking toward us.

"It's where I found my true family," I say, my gaze falling and then meeting that of my mates who are still here. "It's where I first had the freedom to decide for myself. Shadowcarve is the first place where I could make choices for me—and no one else." A genuine smile spreads across my face, and my heart sings with the truth of those words.

Klauth leans in, kissing my forehead before pulling me close. "It's almost time."

I close my eyes, focusing on Abraxis as I try to force a vision of the unfolding chaos around him. I picture him on a battlement, watchful and resolute. One key event remains unseen.

"What do you see, Mina?" Vaughn's voice cuts through the quiet like a shard of glass.

I open my eyes and reply, "Abraxis is waiting, watching the fighting raging around him. The manticore are clashing, and some green dragons are attacking the base, testing its defenses." I meet Vaughn's gaze, the weight of my words hanging between us.

The sound of powerful wingbeats fills the air, and soon Vox's black dragon soars above us before landing gracefully in the courtyard. He shifts his posture and strides over, tilting his head as if in silent inquiry.

"Vox, what are you doing here?" Balor asks, closing the gap to shake his hand.

"Would you believe I felt a pull to be here? That I sensed Mina needed me?" Vox replies, his tone laced with confusion as he glances between me and Klauth.

"Apparently, your dragon acknowledges my mate as the dominant dragoness in the region. Only a dominant dragoness can summon other dragons to her," Klauth says with a smile, kissing my temple.

"I did call for you, Vox," I state firmly, stepping three paces away from Klauth to stand tall in front of my father-in-law. "You've been made aware of what I can do, yes?" I offer no further explanation.

"Yes, Abraxis told me what he said I needed to know," Vox laughs lightly. "It made no sense how he said it, but I assume there's a reason for all the secrets." He smiles at me, and I nod in silent agreement.

I gaze at the position of the rising sun and sigh. "Before it reaches its apex, you need to get Cora and her clutch up here." My eyes shift, diving back into the vision. "Six black dragons must be stationed up here, ready to cover the lower courtyard in acid. Especially along the mountain's rock face—set it on fire at the right time, and the attack will end swiftly." I blink several times, emerging from the vision, and turn to Leander. "You will be the one to signal when."

"What was that? You sounded detached..." Vox steps back, nervous about what I just revealed.

I shake my head firmly. "If you love your son and want to see his progeny thrive, you will stop asking questions that could get me killed." Swallowing hard, I move closer to Vox. "They will kill everyone in my nest—or in my part of the continent—just to be safe. I am the weapon my mate wields." I say it in a measured tone, hoping to settle Vox's worries. As long as he believes the males of the nest are in control, he will remain calm.

Vox steps forward, kissing my forehead before leaping off the cliff and shifting. I can tell by the direction he's flying that he's heading back to Blackhaven to retrieve the black dragons first.

Leander steps in front of me and cups my cheeks gently in his hands. "What did you see?" he asks, his voice filled with a mix of concern and quiet understanding.

"Vox meant well, but he made the mistake of mentioning the visions in front of an elder," I admit, drawing a deep, steadying breath. "The elder suspected Vox wasn't telling the whole truth and went to Arameth—the grand dragon council. They immediately ordered the extermination of the Risedale nest." My gaze shifts to Klauth as I continue, "Mages intervened between them and the dragons they'd brought... and we died together." I pause, the weight of loss heavy in my words. I won't mention that he fell first—those massive spears knocked him from the sky. Klauth was struck down first, thinking himself invincible, while I lived long enough to die knowing all my mates perished before me. My body fell from the sky, landing atop Klauth, and we took our last breaths together.

Suddenly, I feel a mental gasp. *Oh, shit...* I think I accidentally shared the vision. *'You did, mate. I'm sorry I wasn't strong enough to save us all,'* comes a whispered apology through our mental bond.

"Will Vox say anything?" Ziggy asks as he moves closer, apparently unaware of what I just revealed.

"I said I was a weapon for my mate to wield. I didn't specify which mate. Let him believe it's Abraxis if it keeps us safe. He won't risk not having his name go on to another generation," I reply, staring at the ground for several moments. Then I lift my head and ask, "What's the biggest thing you can move, Ziggy?" I tilt my head, eyes challenging him.

"Balor shifted—why?" he asks, puzzled.

"Because when Klauth and I go in to level the field, you and Balor need to protect Abraxis. When he's able to shift back, you need to get him out of there," I instruct firmly.

"What will Leander and I be doing?" Vaughn's gaze shifts between us, seeking clarity.

"Protecting my nest and Thauglor. Leander will signal for the fire to rain down and ignite the acid," I say, locking eyes with Leander, who nods in understanding. He knows the vital role he must play in this operation.

I glance once more at the rising sun, its light growing bolder as the shadows of the nest stir. We have hours left before everything is set in motion, and every moment is charged with the weight of what's to come.

THE GUYS KEEP SHOVELING food toward me while I devour every bite, the tang of spiced stew mingling with the bitterness of dread. The surge of lightning I need to summon courses through my veins—a force more immense than anything I've ever drawn upon. Klauth too is gorging himself, every bite charged with grim determination for what is coming.

I pause mid-motion as I feel Abraxis shift; a cold tremor ripples through me. My hand clenches so tightly that the glass in it shatters, scattering tiny shards that sting my skin. I freeze, breath catching, and watch in horror as the vision changes. The third option—the one I have dreaded—is unfolding in real time.

"We need to go now..." I roar, my voice echoing off the cold walls as I dash from the room. This is the vision that if I don't move fast enough, Abraxis dies.

I burst through the front door into our courtyard, where the night air is thick with the scent of damp stone and distant smoke. Six black dragons sit perched on the edge of the cliff, their dark eyes glinting in the sparse light. "The enemy is coming. Leave nothing to chance," I yell at them, the urgency in my tone mingling with the metallic tang of impending danger. Klauth, Balor, and Ziggy finally catch up with me. "Cover the courtyard in acid, then watch it burn," I command, my eyes hard as I meet theirs. "I'm going to shift and get us there fast. Tuck in close to my frill and hold on for dear life."

My gaze flits between Klauth and Ziggy as I continue, "Klauth will tell you when to phase to Abraxis—it'll be when we're directly over him. Get out as fast as you can after that; there won't be much left of the valley once we're done." I stare into Klauth's crimson-flecked amber eyes, and he nods without a word.

"Won't Klauth get us there faster?" Balor asks, edging closer with concern in his tone.

"No," I reply with quiet confidence. "I've learned what being a veil walker means. I can bend time—that's how I move so fast." I lean in to kiss him deeply—a moment of tenderness amid the chaos—before pulling away to shift. I gently lay my dragoness down in the courtyard, waiting as my mates scramble to climb on. The instant they are securely in place, I rise and sprint toward the cliff's edge. My wings snap open, their leathery surface whipping against the cool night air, and I feel the low hum of lightning thrumming in my veins.

'Here goes nothing,' I whisper.

I reach deep inside, finding the tether to Abraxis pulsing like a lifeline. Instead of pulling on it, I follow its call. Pure power floods through me, and the sharp scent of ozone fills my nostrils—reminiscent of the aftermath of a lightning strike. I feel no pain from my mates clinging to me, reassuring me I'm not harming them. The ground below blurs into a dark smear as each powerful flap of my wings carries me leagues in mere seconds. The burning heat of Abraxis's tether intensifies, urging me on.

I **need** to be faster.

dragons. It's an ability long forgotten, a power that sets her apart from all others.

Mina launches off the cliff into a momentary free fall, the wind whipping past us in a deafening roar. The instant she beats her wings, I catch the sharp tang of ozone in the air, the scent electric and alive. Along her flattened frill, I watch lightning race down to her tail. It pulses first at her horns, then leaps along her frill before streaking to her tail, a dazzling display of raw power. With every beat, the cycle of power intensifies, the air humming with energy, and the ground below melts away into a blur of colors and shifting shapes, the world falling away beneath us.

"Are we safe here?" Ziggy asks, his voice barely audible over the rush of wind as the clouds smear past us, his words nearly lost in the chaos.

"As long as you don't fall off, yes," I reply, staring at him briefly before looking to the horizon, trying to find my bearings. The landscape below is a dizzying patchwork of green and brown.

I sense her urging in our bond, her desperation palpable: *'I have to move faster.'* Her words are a plea, a prayer whispered into the void.

'My Treasure, we are halfway there by my estimation,' I add silently, attempting to soothe the worry consuming her, to ease the fear that grips her heart.

But then I hear her desperation. The words are a knife twisting in my gut. *'He will die if I'm not fast enough. The Drow will attack him while he's down and wounded and kill him. I need to move faster.'* Her voice turns into a whine as she pumps her wings harder against the biting wind, the muscles straining with the effort.

"Are we going faster than before?" Balor suddenly asks, his eyes darting around, the question hanging heavily in the air between us.

"Drow will hunt Abraxis once he hits the ground," I explain, my gaze shifting from Balor to Ziggy and back, the gravity of the situation etched on their faces. "She's afraid we won't make it in time. Kill anything that is not from our nest. I'll deal with the bodies later."

"You've got it," Balor responds, glancing ahead toward Mina's head, his expression grim and determined.

Then we hear her roar—an earth-shaking sound that seems to split the sky, the force of it vibrating through my bones. My vision blurs for a moment as I see a black dragon fall from the sky, the sight a punch to the gut. She has seen Abraxis fall. The realization is a cold, sickening weight in the pit of my stomach. "Get ready—he was just shot down. Get him back to Risedale as fast as possible," I command, staring at Ziggy until he nods, the understanding clear in his eyes. "Get ready." Balor shifts at my order, his body coiled and tense, and with another thunderous roar from Mina, Ziggy, and Balor vanish into the void, the air shimmering in their wake.

"Time to hunt," I say to myself, my heart pounding as Mina slows her pace ever so slightly, the change in speed almost imperceptible. The moment her speed drops, I leap from her back, plummeting in freefall and shift. My body twists and contorts as I transform, the rush of wind deafening in my ears.

The first crack of lightning rends the sky, its branches splintering in multiple directions and striking several targets. The air sizzling with the smell of ozone and charred flesh. I catch sight of movement in the trees—shadows converging toward where Abraxis fell. I unleash a searing burst of fire. The flames leaping from my maw in a torrent of heat and light. The flames are so hot they melt stone as they cascade around our enemies. The scent of burning flesh and singed hair filling the air. Banking hard, I circle around where the others protect Abraxis, breathing fire again to encircle them in a blazing ring, a barrier the Drow dare not cross. The heat is a palpable force against my scales.

Mina's roar burns with pure rage, a sound that makes my scales rise in response. The fury in her voice is a tangible thing. I glance down to see Abraxis limp in Ziggy's arms. His body is broken and still, before Balor shifts back and they vanish from sight, the air shimmering in their wake. I cannot gauge his condition without distracting Mina, so I trail behind her as she charges toward the outpost, striking everything that moves in her path. The ground trembling beneath her fury. The anger I feel through our bond rivals the heat of my own flames, a searing, all-consuming rage that threatens to engulf us both.

Movement to the right catches my eye, and I twist just in time to avoid a barrage of huge bolts. The projectiles whistle past me in a deadly hail. As I turn to roar at Mina, the warning dying on my lips. I watch in horror as two bolts strike her side and she's shot out of the sky, her body plummeting toward the ground in a sickening arc. My heart seizes in my chest, a cold, paralyzing fear gripping me. I unleash my breath weapon toward the source of the attack. The flames leaping from my maw in a torrent of heat and light. Screams echo in the valley as I incinerate everything in my path. The stench of burning flesh and melted metal filling the air.

Once I'm certain the threat has been neutralized, the valley is silent save for the crackling of flames. I fly toward Mina and land beside her, my claws digging into the scorched earth. Her massive form lies on its side, a bolt lodged beneath her wing. The sight of it is like a knife to my heart. I detect no scent of blood, only the acrid tang of burnt metal, a small mercy in the face of what could have been. I move closer and nuzzle her gently with my maw. My breath is warm against her scales. Her body trembles beneath me until her head snaps up, and she roars, the sound a defiant cry against the darkness.

I release the breath I didn't know I was holding as I see her move. The relief washing over me in a dizzying wave. She lifts her wing, and the bolt's tip is pressed against her scales. The metal glinting dully in the fading light. Only splintered fragments hold it in place, a testament to the strength of her armor.

'I'm okay, Klauth. It didn't penetrate my scales—just knocked the wind out of me,' she says through our mental bond, her voice a soothing balm to my frayed nerves.

I stretch my neck and bite the bolt, wrenching it free from her scales. The metal is bitter on my tongue. 'You are truly amazing, my treasure. I can only hope our progeny inherit half the strength you possess.' I nuzzle her side, carefully plucking away splinters with my teeth.

'Is it over?' she asks slowly, turning her head to scan the smoldering valley. The landscape is a hellish patchwork of ash and embers.

'Yes, the guys have Abraxis far from here. We just need to summon Callan and then head back to Risedale.' I carefully stand and lie down beside Mina, sheltering her smaller form under my wing. The warmth of her body is a comfort against the chill of the night. 'Call for Callan and rest for a bit. I'll fly us home.' I feel the pulse through our bond as she summons him, the connection between us a living, breathing thing.

Mentally, I hear Mina yawn, her soft exhale mingling with the steady beat of our hearts. The sound is a gentle lullaby in the stillness. She lowers her head to rest it across my foreleg, her scales smooth and warm against mine. I stare down at the most powerful dragoness ever to grace this dark continent. The sight of her is a miracle amid the chaos. I am blessed beyond measure to call her mine. To be the one she chose to stand by her side, to weather the storms and face the darkness together. And as I hold her close, our hearts beating as one. I know that there is nothing in this world or the next that could ever tear us apart.

WHEN MINA FALLS ASLEEP, her dragoness releases her form. A very human Mina lies sleeping under my wing, her body small and fragile against the expanse of my scales. I scoop her up and feel the soft rhythm of her breathing against my black talons. A gentle pulse amid the chaos of the burning valley, a reminder of the life I hold in my grasp. The surrounding forest, scarred by battle, blazes fiercely, its flames licking the night sky in a dizzying dance of light and shadow. The acrid scent of smoke mingles with the cool night air, the smell sharp, and stinging in my nostrils.

In the distance, Callan shifts back to his human form, his features sharp, and alert in the flickering light. He quickly climbs onto my back, his movements swift and sure. I had hoped he would take Mina with him. But it seems I will carry her with her body cradled against my chest like a precious treasure. Once he's secure, his hands gripping the ridges of my scales. I rise onto three powerful legs and launch into the night; the wind rushing past us in a deafening roar. The rush of air against my wings and the steady throb of Mina's breathing in my grasp soothes something deep within me. It's a reminder that I almost lost my mate today. A realization that sends a chill down my spine. Softly, I croon a quiet melody, just loud enough for Mina to hear as I hold her close to my chest. The sound is a gentle lullaby in the night's chaos.

I cannot fly as fast as Mina once did, her speed a marvel to behold. But my broad wingspan carries us swiftly over the fiery remains of the forest. The landscape below is a hellish patchwork of ash and embers. As we breach the valley, the heat intensifies, the air shimmering with the force of the flames. The burning treetops glow like embers against the dark sky, a haunting sight that sears itself into my memory. Below, I see fire drakes prowling at the edge of the burning acid. Their silhouettes blurred by the dancing flames, their eyes glinting with a feral hunger. I hover for a moment, my heart pounding, then unleash my breath weapon on the pack. The flames leaping from my maw in a torrent of heat and light. The sudden burst of power silences any warning calls as I swiftly subdue the fire drakes skulking near Mina's territory. Their bodies crumpling to the ground in a smoldering heap.

Once the territory is secure, the air is still heavy with the scent of smoke and charred flesh. I steer toward the upper courtyard where the black dragons take flight at my approach, their wings beating a hasty retreat to grant me room to land. Balor and Leander rush out. Their voices laced with urgency as they see me cradling something precious to my chest, their eyes wide with fear and concern. I gently release Mina into Balor's arms, her body limp and unresisting. I feel Callan shift as he launches off my back, his movements swift and agile. As soon as he's clear, his feet hitting the ground with a soft thud, I shift back and lean in to check on her, my heart in my throat.

"What happened?" Leander asks, concern heavy in his tone as Balor carries Mina inside, his steps careful and measured.

"Abraxis was shot down, and Mina went on a rampage," I reply evenly, the words heavy with the weight of loss, the memory of her fury still fresh in my mind. "Then I was nearly shot down, and Mina was shot down, too—the bolts couldn't penetrate her scales." I fix my gaze on Balor, letting my words sink in. The gravity of the situation etched on his face.

"Bolts meant to take down a dragon couldn't get through her scales," Callan adds, carefully examining Mina, his fingers gentle and probing.

"Exactly." I follow Balor into Mina's private chambers, watching as he meticulously removes her leathers, the fabric stiff with dried sweat and dirt. Not a single scratch mars her skin—only two large bruises on her ribs where the bolts struck her dragon's form. The skin is mottled and angry. We stand in stunned silence, absorbing the miracle that these deadly weapons only bruised her, the realization a cold comfort in the face of what could have been.

"Abraxis wasn't so lucky. The surgeons are working on him as we speak," Balor says softly, gently pulling the blankets up over Mina, his touch tender and reverent.

"How bad is it?" I ask, watching the color drain from his face. The sight is a knife twisting in my gut.

"By all accounts, he should be dead," he murmurs, his voice laced with sorrow as he guides us out of Mina's room, the words hanging heavy in the air between us.

"But?" I arch a brow, feeling as if I'm trying to pry open a crocodile's mouth with a toothpick. The tension in the room is palpable.

"We're honestly not sure how he's still alive. He's lost a lot of blood, punctured a lung, and we're uncertain if his dragon will ever fly again." He glances down briefly, his eyes haunted by the weight of his words. "The second bolt almost severed his left wing, as if it was aimed that way on purpose."

His words strike me like a blow, the air rushing from my lungs in a painful gasp. Death, in its brutal finality, might have been kinder than a life spent watching our skies instead of flying. It is a fate worse than any I can imagine. "Where are Ziggy and Vaughn?"

"Sitting with Abraxis's parents," Leander offers quietly, his voice heavy with the same sorrow that grips us all.

My eyes dart between Balor and Leander as I decide, the weight of it settling heavily on my shoulders. "Balor, please stay with Mina. Leander, let's go check on Abraxis." Balor nods solemnly and slips back into Mina's chambers, the door closing softly behind him. The walk to check on the youngling feels like stepping in front of a firing squad—each step heavy with the burden of impending consequence. The air is thick with the scent of blood and the hum of urgent voices. Abraxis's decision may have cost him everything, and I can only hope it hasn't cost us all. The thought is a cold, sickening weight in the pit of my stomach.

SEVERAL HOURS CRAWL by as I sit vigilant in the makeshift infirmary, my senses assaulted by the surrounding chaos. The room pulses with hushed voices and the soft pad of hurried footsteps against the cold tile floor. My nostrils burn with the sterile, chemical bite of disinfectant that cannot mask the metallic tang of blood hanging thick in the air. Across from me, Vox cradles Cerce's limp form, his knuckles white with strain. While Warwick supports Cora, her head lolling against his shoulder. Their faces are carved masks of shock and sorrow—eyes hollow, jaws clenched tight enough that I can almost hear their teeth grinding.

We've already relayed what happened to Mina. The weight of disbelief presses down on us like a physical presence. It makes the air dense and difficult to breathe, a suffocating fog that clogs my lungs with each labored intake.

"Even the strongest iron dragons can't survive a direct hit by a bolt," Vox declares, his voice cracking like brittle glass. The raw mixture of awe and despair in his tone scrapes against my nerves. The words seem to vibrate through the room, settling heavy in my gut like stones.

Leander's phone pings, the cheerful electronic tone jarringly inappropriate against our grim setting. He swipes quickly, then turns the screen toward Abraxis's family. I watch intently as blood drains from their faces in real time, leaving behind a sickly pallor that makes the overhead fluorescents seem even harsher. Their eyes widen, pupils dilating with silent horror that no words could capture. The collective, sharp intake of breath is deafening in the stillness. The enormous bruises testament to her surviving the impossible.

I have my suspicions about why Mina has become what she is now. The first is that having a great wyrm as a mate transformed her dragoness when we exchanged bites—a fiery, unspoken pact that scorched through her veins and altered her very core. Somehow rewriting ancient code embedded in her DNA. The second reason is far darker. When she was murdered by her father, something essential inside her shattered beyond repair. Now, she moves through the world built like a flying fortress, every muscle taut beneath her skin, eyes constantly scanning for threats. Her inner dragoness no longer dares to feel safe, not even for a moment.

I can't blame her for that fear. It's unthinkable—males hunting a female driven solely by their twisted desire for power. Yet someone tried to shoot my mate down today, tried to extinguish the very light that gives me reason to continue this torturous existence. My chest constricts painfully at the thought, making each heartbeat a struggle.

My eyes drift to Abraxis's family, their faces contorted with grief. Their despair mirrors my silent dread, a reflection so perfect it makes my skin crawl. I wonder, as cold sweat beads along my spine, if the worst is yet to come. How will we help Mina keep her will to live? She has other mates, including myself, but he was her first, her cornerstone. The foundation upon which she built her new life. And as much as Abraxis can be a prick, with his cutting remarks and arrogant posturing. Mina's love for him burns fierce and bright, a tangled web of loyalty and pain that I can see written in every line of her body when she speaks his name.

his hands. With gentle urgency, Callan helps me reposition Abraxis, whose body is marred by multiple surgical sites. The bandages stark are a white against his pale skin. Every cautious movement releases a faint scent of medicine and sweat, each moment weighted with the silent promise of hope.

Once I am satisfied with his new position, I take the dropper and administer tiny sips of bone broth past his parched lips; the liquid glistening in the dim light. "I'll feed you while you feed him—deal?" Callan offers as my other mates slip quietly into the room, their footsteps muffled on the soft carpet. The rich, savory scent of steak fills the air as Callan theatrically waves a hunk of meat in my face, the juices dripping onto the floor. My stomach rumbles with hunger. Reluctantly, I bite into it, the hearty flavor a brief respite as I raise the dropper again to Abraxis's closed mouth, the glass cool against his skin.

"He should have woken up by now," Leander murmurs softly, his tone both gentle and mournful. The words hanging heavily in the air. A low growl builds within me, a primal sound that vibrates through my chest. I fix him with a determined stare, my eyes blazing with fierce resolve. "He needs time. He will wake up—he doesn't have a choice." I close my eyes, focusing on the deep, shared bond between us, feeling the tender threads that connect our souls. I pour every ounce of my will into him, willing him to come back to me. For a fleeting moment, I sense his heart shift its rhythm—a tentative staccato of hope.

"Mina, the doctor said if he doesn't wake up in a week, he won't," Klauth warns, his words heavy with resignation. The sound grating against my ears. I feel a burning anger rise within me, a surge of protective instinct that sets my blood on fire, as if my very skin were rising with defiant scales. "He will wake up, even if I have to drag him back from the brink myself. Null will not take him from me—he will wait his turn to hold him." I gaze at his slack face in the half-light, tracing the elegant lines of his features with my eyes. In that fragile moment, I swear I see a tear glimmer at the corner of his eye, a silent plea for help.

"He's strong, a fighter. If anyone can cheat death, it's Abraxis," Balor asserts confidently as he takes a plate from Callan and offers me a chunk of steak. The rich, iron tang of the steak mingles with my anxiety as I reluctantly accept it. The flavor bursts on my tongue, a momentary distraction from the pain that grips my heart.

I close my eyes and press both my hands against his chest, feeling the faint, irregular throb of his heart beneath my palms. "Null will not have you," I murmur, channeling every ounce of my shared vitality into him, willing my strength to become his. Even with seven mates sharing our life force, I know I have more power than any other living dragoness. I will spare every bit for my wounded love, a sacrifice I make willingly.

As fatigue sets in, a heavy weight that settles in my bones. I pull my hands away and resume feeding him the nourishing broth, the liquid warm and soothing as it slides down his throat. Every drop feels like a silent promise, a vow that I won't give up on Abraxis until he chooses to. Until he returns to me or slips away forever. Even the doctors marvel at his unlikely survival, their eyes wide with disbelief. But I refuse to surrender, my determination as unyielding as the scales that line my spine.

A sharp knock at the door shatters the quiet, the sound jarring and loud in the stillness. Vox, Cerce, Warwick, and half a dozen familiar dragons from our flights stand in the doorway, their expressions etched with concern, their eyes filled with a shared sorrow. "Klauth told us of an ancient rite of benefaction—our essence can heal another," Vox says, his gaze softening as he looks at his son. The lines of his face deepening with grief.

Klauth steps to my side, resting a steady hand on my shoulder, his touch a grounding presence in the chaos. "It's our last hope, my treasure," he murmurs, kissing the crown of my head before Vox takes Balor's seat opposite me. The chair creaks beneath his weight. "I gift my son a spark of my essence so he can return to us," Vox declares as he lays his hands on Abraxis's bare chest. I feel a cool surge of energy pass into him—a silent current that sends shivers down my spine.

"Come back, my precious boy," Cerce whispers as she places her hands on him, her voice thick with unshed tears. One by one, each dragon who has crossed Abraxis's path bestows a spark of life. With every gift, I feel his strength growing. Tears well in my eyes as I watch his battered body absorb the healing essence, the sight of a miracle unfolding before me.

When the last dragon departs, their footsteps fading into the distance. Klauth sits across from me, his eyes soft but determined as he surveys Abraxis, taking in the full extent of his injuries. "We don't always see eye to eye, Abraxis," he breathes. A trace of regret in his tone, the words heavy with unspoken emotion. "But one thing is clear: keeping you safe for, Mina, is what matters most." He tilts his head and sighs, the sound weary and resigned. "I gift you a spark of my essence. Return to our mate; she is grieving herself to death over you."

My heart clenches as I look up at him. My eyes are wide with a mix of gratitude and disbelief, and I whisper, "You gave him more than a spark." Klauth's hands move over Abraxis's chest, his touch gentle and sure. I feel a powerful surge ripple through him, a current of energy that takes my breath away. My eyes widen in shock.

"We need you, Mina. If preserving Abraxis's life means sharing centuries with you, then sacrificing a few years is a small price," Klauth declares, his voice steady and sure. Leaning over, he presses a tender kiss to my lips. The touch is soft and lingering, before leaving the room with a final nod, his footsteps echoing in the silence. I have been at Abraxis's bedside for what feels like an eternity, the hours blending together in a haze of fear and hope.

I finish feeding Abraxis while my mates help reposition him. They gently turn him onto his side, elevating his head with care, and placing a soft pillow between his knees, the fabric cool and smooth against his skin. I curl up close, my head resting near his fragile chest as I listen to the soft, irregular beats of his heart.

In the fading light, I silently pray to Tamara, the goddess of healers and mercy, my lips moving in a fervent plea. I beg her to return Abraxis to me, to spare his life and give us more time together. Exhaustion overwhelms me, a heavy weight that settles in my bones, and sleep finally drapes its heavy veil over my eyes, as relentless as my determination to keep him alive. As I drift off, I cling to the hope that tomorrow will bring a new dawn, a chance for a future with the man I love by my side.

I FEEL the warmth of someone's embrace, a steady, comforting weight against me. I long for five more minutes in this cocoon of safety, the desire to linger in this moment almost overwhelming. Yet when I next stir, my eyes fluttering open, I find myself alone, the space beside me cold and empty. Ziggy must have slipped me out of Abraxis's hospital bed, his touch gentle and careful. As I scan the room, blinking away the lingering haze of sleep. I notice he hasn't shifted me in the least—and Abraxis is nowhere to be seen, his absence a sharp ache in my chest. I reach for his tether, my fingers closing around the coarse texture, the sensation stronger and more reassuring than anything I've felt in days. Following it through the dim corridor, the air heavy with the scent of antiseptic and the faint, metallic tang of blood. I make my way into the sitting room, my footsteps muffled on the plush carpet.

Finally, I see him: Abraxis sits propped up in a worn recliner, a rumpled blanket draped over his lap, the fabric soft and worn. My eyes sting with unshed tears, and my bottom lip trembles as I gaze at him. I drink in the sight of his face, the planes, and angles so achingly familiar.

"Hey, baby," he murmurs weakly, his voice rough and low, the sound sending a shiver down my spine. I rush to him, my heart pounding in time with the quiet thrum of the room.

I scour his features for any sign of harm, my eyes roving over every inch of his face, searching for the slightest sign of pain or discomfort. Tears silently stream down my cheeks, the hot, salty trails a testament to the depth of my relief and the lingering fear that still grips my heart.

"How?" I whisper. My voice catching, the word sticking in my throat as my eyes land on Klauth. Who now wears a knowing smile, the expression both comforting and unsettling.

"It's the cost of benefaction," he explains in a low, measured tone, his voice a soothing rumble in the stillness of the room. "It isn't done lightly—it means trading years, a debt paid in time. I convinced several dragons to give years to Abraxis. Each one made that choice willingly." His hand shakes Abraxis's briefly, the contact brief but meaningful, before he fixes his gaze on me, his eyes intense and piercing.

"Usually an elder surrenders their life so that the younger dragon can live," he continues, his words heavy with the weight of centuries. The knowledge of countless sacrifices made in the name of love and loyalty. His eyes move from Abraxis then back to me, the depth of his understanding evident in his gaze.

"You're the eldest of the den," I murmur, my voice barely audible, the words a whisper.

"It would be counterproductive to surrender my life," he replies, his eyes drifting over our extended family gathered in the room. Their faces etched with both relief and sorrow, the air thick with the mingled scents of sweat and tears. "We'd be no better off, and you'd still be short a mate. So I asked several dragons to lend their years to Abraxis. Each was a personal decision made in honor of what we're fighting for."

"Now, Grumpy just needs to rest and finish healing," Ziggy says with a gentle smile, his voice a soothing balm to my frayed nerves. "Glad to have you back, Brax..." Murmurs of agreement ripple through our family as a few approaches, offering soft words and light handshakes for Abraxis.

When the visitors finally leave, the room falling silent once more. I inhale deeply, steadying my nerves, the scent of Abraxis filling my lungs, a reminder of his precious life. "Did we win?" he asks, his voice fragile, the words a tentative hope in the stillness. My jaw drops as I take in his weary eyes, the sight a reflection of the toll this battle has taken on us all.

"Yes," Klauth declares with a smirk, his voice firm and unwavering. "You dismantled most of their forces. While you slept, Mina and I handled the cleanup." He reaches into his jacket, the fabric rustling softly, and withdraws a leather box. The surface is smooth and cool to the touch. Opening it reveals three medals, each gleaming dully in the low light. The metal is warm against my skin as I reach out to touch them. "I promote you to supreme general of the Aurelian Isles. You will lead from the war room, making every major decision on both defense and offense. Eight legions will answer to you. None, but I outrank you on this continent." Vox gasps at the honor now given upon his only son, the sound sharp and surprised in the quiet of the room.

"There's also the Crimson Heart," Klauth continues, his voice softening with respect, the words heavy with the weight of sacrifice. "For your valor and sacrifice on the field—you knew the odds of survival were low, yet you went anyway to save lives. And you receive the Seal of Thauglor. You are now recognized as the most formidable black dragon on the continent."

"Wait—a medal named after Thauglor?" I ask, glancing from the black talon medallion to Klauth's steady gaze, my brow furrowed in confusion.

"Apparently, Blackhaven has produced some of the most formidable warriors our kind has ever seen," he explains, his voice rich with history and pride. "Thauglor once held the title that Abraxis now bears." With that, he shakes Abraxis's hand once more. The contact is firm and meaningful before departing, his footsteps fading into the distance.

Vox and Cerce exchange their farewells, their voices soft and emotional, leaving Abraxis and me alone, the silence heavy with unspoken words. "Are they all truly gone?" he sighs, looking up at me as I settle beside him on the worn arm of the couch, the fabric rough beneath my fingers.

"Not a single wyvern survived. Even the drow who fired the bolts have perished," I reply softly, my eyes drifting to the mug of bone broth clutched in his hand. Its steam mingling with the cool air, the scent rich and nourishing.

"Who else got hit?" he asks, his voice laced with concern. I hesitate before slowly standing to remove my sweatshirt, the fabric soft and warm against my skin. Balor moves closer, his presence a silent comfort. He carefully unwraps the ace wrap from around my bruised stomach and ribs, the fabric smelling faintly of antiseptic and worn leather, the scent sharp and familiar.

"It looks worse than it is," I assure him, closing my eyes as I lean into Abraxis's touch, his fingers gentle and soothing against my skin. "The doctors say not even a rib is cracked." My scales were marred by splinters from the bolts—extracted by Klauth's dragon—have somehow repelled the worst of it. The damage was minimal compared to what could have been. Guilt wells inside me, a hot, bitter knot in the pit of my stomach, as I realize I escaped nearly unscathed. While we still wonder if Abraxis can fly. The uncertainty is a heavy weight on my heart.

"You need to take care of yourself, Mina," he says, sadness etched in every word. The sound is like a knife twisting in my gut. "You matter more than I do."

"That's where you're wrong," I counter, my voice trembling with both pain and determination as Balor re-wraps my side, the fabric tight and secure against my skin. "No one's life is more important than another." The mingled scents of sweat, leather, and the faint, bitter tang of blood remind me of the cost of every sacrifice.

I climb onto the recliner's arm carefully, mindful of Abraxis's injuries, and curl around him, drawing him close, my body molding to his. "I saw you get shot down," I murmur, the memories searing into my mind, the images vivid and painful. "I watched you fall from the sky— there was no sound, just a sudden burst of red, the color stark against the blue." My hand finds his, our fingers intertwining, and the contact sends a familiar shiver through me, a reminder of the bond we share.

"It felt like a piece of my heart was torn away and hurled over a cliff," I confess, my voice raw with emotion. The words are a confession of the depth of my love and the agony of nearly losing him.

"Mina didn't leave your side unless she went to the bathroom," Vaughn recalls softly, his tone both teasing and tender. I sigh and run my fingers through Abraxis's tangled hair, each strand a reminder of the fragility of our existence, the preciousness of every moment we have together.

I watch him intently, every shallow breath and slight twitch of his features etched into my memory, the sight a reminder of how close I came to losing him forever. The past week has been torture—every nerve on edge, every moment a battle against the encroaching dark- ness. All our petty squabbles vanish now. The past conflicts and disagreements fading into insignificance in the face of what we've been through. I nearly lost my mate because he felt compelled to prove himself. The weight of his own expectations and the need to protect us driving him to risk everything.

I vow to do better, to be the mate he deserves, the partner he needs by his side. I will make sure every mate feels as deeply cherished as the next. Each mate is a vital piece of the tapestry that is our love, our bond unbreakable and eternal. Once Abraxis is healed, I have plans—plans that will bind us closer, that each of my mates will treasure for the rest of their lives, memories to hold close in the darkest of times.

For now, I am simply grateful that Abraxis is alive, his heart beating steadily beneath my palm, his breath warm against my skin. He may be as grumpy as he wants, his mood a reflection of the pain and trauma he's endured. But as long as he draws breath. I have hope— hope for a future together, hope for a love that will endure through the ages.

from the relentless storm of our lives, a moment of solace in the chaos. Together, we've taken turns ensuring she finds refuge in sleep. I smooth her tangled hair away from her face. The silken strands slide through my fingers, and tuck her in with care, the blankets a soft cocoon around her form. Then, I slip into bed behind her, drawing her close. I hold her while she sleeps, her breath a soothing rhythm against my chest.

In the deep hours of the early morning, my body ignites with a feverish energy. A surge that electrifies every nerve ending, setting my skin ablaze. Every inch of me awakens with a desperate hunger, as if my very flesh craves the touch of another, a primal need that consumes me. I feel a deliberate, wet caress tracing along my hardening length, igniting sparks that spread like wildfire through my veins. My pulse races under the expert, teasing pressure. Each touch stirring a torrent of desire that makes time itself falter, the world narrowing to this singular sensation.

Before I can fully comprehend the feverish passion. The next thing I feel is warmth—a slick heat wrapped around my shaft like a silken glove, engulfing me in its embrace. Weight settles on my hips, and lithe hands roam all over my chest, mapping the contours of my body with a reverent touch. A soft purr escapes my lips, the sound a throaty rumble in the stillness of the room. The best sex dream ever. It feels so real, so vivid, as if I could reach out and touch the fantasy. My Mina, my mate, rides me slowly, sliding up and down my shaft, teasing me with each deliberate movement, each roll of her hips a sweet torture.

"Mhmmm," I murmur, my voice thick with desire as I pull her close. The heat of her skin searing against mine. As soon as she's pinned beneath me, I find myself drifting back to sleep, the line between dream and reality blurring. Teeth graze my shoulder, Mina's bite jolting me back to awareness, and I move, my body responding instinctively to her touch. The longest, most intense sex dream ever.

"Ziggy?" Her soft giggle cuts through the haze of passion, jolting me into a lucid state, my eyes flying open. I stare down at her in disbelief, startled to see her beneath me, her eyes gleaming with mischief and desire, the sight a revelation.

"Good morning, love," I whisper, arching a brow as I try to reconcile the vivid, burning passion of our shared dream with this startling reality, my mind reeling.

She laughs softly, the sound a melodic tinkle in the quiet of the room, and rolls her hips beneath me. The motion sending shockwaves of pleasure through my body. "Move, baby—I need you. I want you, Ziggy," she murmurs. Her voice is a sultry purr that vibrates against my skin, igniting a fire in my blood. My mind stutters for a moment, struggling to process the shift from dream to waking. I reach down and lift her leg gently, draping her calf over my forearm, the position intimate and possessive. "Sneaky mate, attacking me in my sleep," I purr, thrusting forward hard and then stopping, my body trembling with the effort. Her whine is music to my ears, a desperate plea that fuels my desire.

"Please, Ziggy..." she begs, her lips pressing a trail of scorching kisses along my jaw, each one a brand upon my skin. I roll my hips with a slow, deliberate rhythm, savoring each nuanced movement as her soft gasps mingle with the cool hush of the morning. Every brush of her body against mine, every whispered promise that falls from her lips, sets my senses ablaze. I can feel her core pulsing around me—a delicate flutter that keeps me poised on the edge of oblivion.

Mina's lips drift along the column of my throat as I lift her leg higher, changing our angle with careful intensity. The new position allowing me to sink deeper into her welcoming heat. Within moments, we come undone together, our release crashing over us like a tidal wave, sweeping us away in its undertow. I bury my face in the tender crook of her neck, inhaling the musky perfume of her skin. Every touch blurs into a fevered need to bite her again, to mark her as mine. The temptation to claim her in every way intensifies, a primal urge that thrums through my veins. Yet I temper my hunger with soft, lingering kisses along the slope of her shoulder. I slow my movements so that each sensation can be savored.

With gentle tenderness, I roll to the side and pull her into my arms, our bodies fitting together like pieces of a puzzle. "Sleep, baby," I murmur, my voice low and resonant with love, a soothing balm to the frenzy of our passion. "Morning will come too soon before we know it."

Her eyes, heavy with the weight of sleep yet bright with affection, meet mine as she whispers, "I love you, Ziggy." The words are a balm to my soul, a promise that echoes through the chambers of my heart. She nestles closer, her head resting against my chest, seeking refuge in the safety of my arms.

"I love you too, Mina," I reply, pressing a soft, lingering kiss to the crown of her head, breathing in the sweet scent of her hair. As I close my eyes, the world outside seems to fade away, the troubles that plague us receding into the shadows.

THE NEXT MORNING, I awaken to find Mina gone, the sheets beside me cold and empty. A small note rests on my pillow. The paper is crisp beneath my fingers as I pick it up. It bears a hand-drawn heart with a smiley face right in the center, the ink slightly smudged. I smile as I read her words, her familiar handwriting a comforting sight, and exhale a soft, contented sigh. The scent of her lingers on the pillow.

A steady knock at my door snaps me from my reverie. The sound echoing in the quiet of the room. I quickly pull on my shorts. The fabric is rough against my skin, and make my way to answer it, my bare feet padding softly on the cool floor.

Balor leans against the doorframe, his usual smirk playing on his lips, his eyes glinting with a hint of mischief. "Mina wants to get Abraxis into the hot springs. We need you to phase him in," he announces, his tone low and measured, the words hanging heavily in the air between us.

"Okay," I reply, my voice still rough with sleep. "Let me get changed, and I'll be right there." As I head back into my room. I hear footsteps trailing quietly behind me, the sound of Balor's approach muffled by the plush carpet.

"So, Mina ended up in here?" he asks, arching a brow as he studies my face, his gaze piercing and knowing.

I meet his eyes, unflinching. "We both know you can smell her on me. What's wrong?" My voice is cautious, the air thick with concern, a palpable tension settling over the room.

"She's not acting like herself," he murmurs, his words laced with worry, a frown tugging at the corners of his mouth.

"What do you mean?" I ask, recalling the events of last night—the heat of Mina's touch, the urgency of her kisses. She had started everything, just as she always does between us—intense and unpredictable.

"She's not fighting anymore. She just kisses until we take control. No more struggles for dominance," he explains, his voice low and troubled. His words send a shiver down my spine, a cold, unsettling feeling. I freeze mid-step as I pull on my swim trunks, the fabric suddenly heavy in my hands.

"Do you think Abraxis nearly dying did it?" I ask, tilting my head as I search his eyes for answers.

"I think so. He's not a threat now. But she's realized he doesn't have to be because she loves him," Balor replies, exhaling slowly as he gazes at something on the rug, his expression distant and pensive.

"Let's go help her get him into the hot springs. It'll do him some good." I give him a friendly slap on the shoulder, the contact brief but reassuring, and stride past him toward the main sitting area.

There, Vox and Klauth are supporting Abraxis as they move, their movements slow and careful. Now, for the first time, I get a good look at his wings, and the sight steals the breath from my lungs. The once-pristine leather is now marred by several rows of stitches and bandages. His left wing, in particular, is heavily wrapped, a haunting reminder of the battle he nearly lost.

"Can I help at all?" I ask, catching up to the group, my voice low and urgent. I notice Mina's bottom lip quivering as she watches Abraxis, her eyes glistening with unshed tears. I guess it's the first time she's seen just how bad his injury really is, the full extent of the damage laid bare before her.

"I think having you phase him into the water would help," Vox suggests, glancing over his shoulder at me, his expression grim. "Part of his therapy is in the water—taking the weight off him."

"You need to go back to school, Mina," Abraxis chides gently as we guide him into the chamber where the hot spring steams in the dim light. The air is heavy with the scent of minerals and damp stone.

"I've already tested out of the third quarter. Samara made sure I could. I'll go back during the fourth quarter when I'm sure you're okay," she replies firmly, stepping in front of him and resting her hand on his chest, her touch gentle but insistent.

"Mina, you need to finish school," Abraxis sighs, leaning his forehead against hers, the gesture intimate and tender.

"I will. I already told you—I tested out of this marking period. You need me here," she insists. Her hands gently framing his face as she presses a soft kiss to his forehead, her lips lingering on his skin. "Please, let me take care of you." I've never heard Mina beg outside the bedroom. Seeing the strongest dragoness on the continent pleading to care for her mate sends a chill down my spine. It's a cold, unsettling feeling that settles in the pit of my stomach.

Abraxis gives a weak nod, the movement slight and pained, and then turns to me with a wry smile. The expression not quite reaching his eyes. "Mind giving me a hand, old friend?" he laughs softly as I approach, the sound hollow and strained.

"Of course," I reply, my voice steady and reassuring. I step forward and carefully slip an arm around his back, positioning myself under his uninjured right arm. The muscles tense beneath my touch. Within seconds, I phase us into the deep end of the hot spring. The warm water enveloping him, its soothing heat easing some of the pain etched into his scars, the lines of his face relaxing slightly.

Mina swims over, her movements graceful and fluid, her eyes scanning us with equal parts determination and fear. The emotions warring on her face. "I need to change the old bandages once they're soaked— they'll peel off easier then," she murmurs, gliding behind Abraxis. Her hands hover over his wounds, hesitant to touch. She bites her bottom lip, the gesture a sign of her anxiety. I can see the fear flickering in her eyes, a shadow that refuses to dissipate.

"Let's have you help him float—it might ease his discomfort," I suggest, sliding to his side and carefully placing an arm under his shoulder and lower back, mindful to avoid the wounds.

"Ugh, I hate feeling so helpless," he growls, his voice raw with vulnerability. The admission is a sharp contrast to his usual strength and confidence.

"You were granted a second chance, Abraxis," Klauth says as he walks around the edge of the hot spring, his footsteps echoing on the damp stone. I notice he deliberately avoids calling him "*hatchling*" or "*youngling*" this time, a small mercy in the face of his suffering.

"Mina was threatening Null," Balor adds. His voice is low and grave, and I see Klauth's eyebrows shoot up in surprise, his eyes widening slightly.

"I wouldn't put it past our mate," Abraxis replies, a small, bitter laugh escaping him as he closes his eyes.

Mina moves closer again, her movements slow and deliberate. She gently checks the bandages on his ribs, untying them with trembling fingers. She hums softly—a familiar tune, one that dragonesses often sing to their hatchlings, the melody soothing and comforting. The gentle sound mingles with the soft bubbling of the water, easing the oppressive darkness that lingers in the room, a momentary respite from the pain and fear.

I watch as Mina's eyes widen in horror when she sees just how grievously injured Abraxis is, the full extent of the damage laid bare before her. In that split second, her eyes flare a brilliant, unsettling gold before settling back into their usual guarded shade. The color is a fleeting glimpse of the power that lurks beneath the surface. Every inch she peels away the grimy, bloodstained bandages feels deliberate and slow. The rustle of fabric and the faint, metallic tang of iron in the air heightening my unease, a cold sweat breaking out on my brow.

Callan takes the soiled bandages and drifts them toward the murky edge of the spring where the water laps against the stone. The sound is a gentle whisper in the oppressive silence. Nearby, Klauth methodically collects the discarded clothes and dumps them into a garbage bag, the crinkling noise echoing in the stillness. Vaughn moves with a surgeon's precision as he sets up a makeshift med station. Mina, drawing on lessons learned from past healings, shoulders more than her fair share of the responsibility. The burden of her love etched on her face, a weight that seems almost too heavy to bear.

Once every bandage is removed, we gently lower Abraxis into the hot water so he can lie alone for a moment. The steam rising around him in wispy tendrils. Mina climbs out with measured steps, her movements graceful and deliberate, and begins organizing the scattered medical supplies. I watch as she discreetly slips a piece of paper to Leander. He vanishes from the room with urgent quiet, his footsteps fading into the distance. Nearly ten long minutes later, he reappears carrying a spray bottle filled with a purplish-blue liquid that glimmers eerily under the weak light; the color unsettling and strange.

"I'm ready for you, Abraxis," Mina says softly. She pats the makeshift hospital bed with a tenderness that belies the level of stress she's under, her touch gentle and reassuring.

"I've got you," I reply, my voice steady and calming as I lift Abraxis and guide him to where Mina has set the bed, my muscles straining with the effort. I steady him as his legs wobble, watching his pallid face twist in pain—a moment that sends a chill down my spine. Almost immediately, Klauth is at my side, his powerful arms holding Abraxis upright as if to shield him from the encroaching darkness.

I catch the fear in Mina's eyes as she watches every trembling move-ment, her gaze sharp and assessing. "When you're ready, he needs to lie down," she instructs, her tone a mix of command and concern. The words are heavy with unspoken emotion.

"How do you need me, mate?" Abraxis asks, forcing a smile that doesn't reach his eyes as he glances over his shoulder. The expression is a pale imitation of his usual confidence.

"On your stomach for now," Mina directs, her smile wavering as her bottom lip trembles—a silent confession of the pain she feels, the depth of her love laid bare. Together, we maneuver him until he lies with his head cradled on a soft pillow. Balor and Callan shuffle in, hauling two more tables to support the weight of his injured wings. The clatter of their arrival punctuating our heavy silence, the sound harsh and jarring.

"I'm going to make you sleep for a little bit, baby. Cleaning everything is going to hurt too much," she murmurs, waving for the rest of us to step back, her hand trembling slightly.

"If you think that's best, I love you," Abraxis says with a fragile smile, his words barely audible above the gentle splashing of the water.

"I love you too. Forgive me," Mina replies. Her voice is thick with unshed tears as she sprays the blueish-purple liquid over him. The mist settles on his skin like a fine sheen. Within moments, his eyes close, and sleep overtakes him, his breath evening out into a slow, steady rhythm. I watch as silent tears slip down Mina's cheeks, their paths glistening in the low light. She bites her lip in a desperate effort to hold herself together before turning her attention to his wounds. Her hands are steady and sure despite the pain that radiates from her in palpable waves.

Klauth shakes his head, his hand trailing down his face as if to wipe away his own despair, the gesture weary and resigned. Balor and I step closer when he asks, "What did you see that we don't understand?" Gesturing for the others to assist Mina. We follow him into the cold, echoing hallway, the air heavy with a sense of foreboding.

He sighs heavily before confessing, "I do not believe his wing will support his weight in his human form—unless, by some miracle, the tendon wasn't severed. Even if the surgeons did a good job, there's only a slim chance his dragon could ever fly again."

The tension in his shoulders speaks volumes, the words hanging heavily in the air between us. "You don't think he'll ever fly again—neither as man nor as dragon?" I ask, watching his face intently as one of his eyes twitches in a fleeting moment of vulnerability. The sight is unsettling and strange.

"I promoted him to supreme general, anticipating he might lose the skies. A war dragon that cannot fly is not a war dragon—it's a target. At least with the promotion, no one would question why he isn't fighting," Klauth explains quietly, his voice heavy with regret, the admission a bitter truth. I realize then that this decision was made to preserve Abraxis's honor, a small mercy in the face of a devastating loss.

"Thank you," Balor says as he moves to shake Klauth's hand before returning to aid Mina, his touch brief but sincere.

"When will we know if he can't fly?" I ask, glancing back toward the steamy, shadowed edge of the hot springs.

Klauth stares at the ground and sighs, "The minute he tries." His voice cracks, mirroring the heartbreak in Mina's eyes, the sound a sharp contrast to his usual composure. I recall the dark tales I've read—how flightless drakes were once mercilessly killed so that their mates could be taken. It's a grim reminder of our brutal reality. An icy shiver runs down my spine at the thought.

With the shortage of females and the fierceness that burns in Mina. I connect the dots and look up at Klauth, my eyes searching his for confirmation.

"I've already anticipated the possibility of fending off viable males," he continues, his tone softening as he recounts a plan Mina and he once discussed at length. The words are heavy with unspoken emotion. "She's ready to burn all suitors to the ground." A small, bitter laugh escapes him, the sound harsh in the stillness. "How did she put it? *They try to hurt Abraxis, and the continent loses another drake.*'"

I blink and nod, the image of Mina's determined expression etched into my mind, as unyielding as the dark night that wraps around us, a silent promise of the lengths she will go to protect the ones she loves.

"Are you okay?" Callan's voice drifts from behind me, soft and laced with concern. I collapse onto the cool marble bench, its surface smooth beneath my trembling fingers, the chill seeping through my clothes.

"Define okay," I reply, my voice brittle, the words tasting like ashes on my tongue. "I'm alive. My mates are alive. I have a flight I never wanted—and I'm back in the place I swore I'd burn to the ground." I slowly turn to face him, noticing the tender way he cradles Cora's son in his arms, the baby's soft coos punctuating the stillness. Forcing a smile that feels like a mask, I extend my arms to take the baby from him. Callan gently slides little William into my embrace. I hold him tight, feeling the warmth of his small body seep into my skin, his soft breathing lulling him into a peaceful slumber.

"I figured you needed baby snuggles. Cora needed a break and couldn't find you," Callan says, settling beside me, his presence a solid comfort in the haze of my thoughts.

"Thanks, Callan," I murmur, pressing the warm, fragile body of the baby against my chest, his heartbeat fluttering like a tiny bird. But as his gentle breaths fill my ears. My thoughts drift to all the ways I've failed Abraxis—raised to be dominant, believing that the weak deserved to be ruled, a queen in a game I never wanted to play.

Before I can lose myself further in the labyrinth of regret, Callan sinks to his knees before me. His eyes searching mine, their depths filled with a quiet understanding. "Where did you just go?" he asks, his voice a gentle prod as he reaches out to cup my cheek, his touch both tender and insistent.

I shake my head and pull back, the motion jerky and raw. "Mina, you know hiding the truth doesn't help anyone." Leander's voice cuts through the stillness of the garden as he walks in with Cora, their footsteps soft on the lush grass.

I lower my head, nuzzling the sleeping child until Cora takes him away, her hands gentle and sure. "It's all my fault," I confess, the words tearing from my throat, my voice trembling as I meet Cora's steady, questioning gaze.

"What's all your fault? I don't understand," she asks, rocking her son slowly as if trying to soothe not just him but me, too, her brow furrowed with concern.

"It's my fault Abraxis got hurt. It's my fault he charged into battle, desperate to end one of the rising threats against me." I run my fingers through my tangled hair, the strands slipping through my grip like memories I can't hold on to, my scalp aching from the pressure. "He loves me so completely, and I fought it. I was terrified of ending up like my mother. Instead, I made the nest unbalanced." My voice cracks as I lower my eyes, half-sobbing, the tears hot and bitter on my cheeks. "I was scared that loving him so much would cost me everything—my freedom, my identity. I'd become nothing more than the weapon my father always intended."

My confession lingers in the air, the silence heavy and oppressive, until two warm hands settle on my shoulders, their touch gentle, and grounding. I curl forward, burying my face in my palms, my tears seeping through my fingers as I listen to the sound of quiet footsteps retreating, the gathered crowd dispersing until only those two comforting presences remain. I know without a word who they belong to. Abraxis and Klauth have found me, their bond to me a tether in the storm of my emotions.

"I don't blame you for anything, Mina," Abraxis murmurs softly as he sinks down beside me, his voice rough with pain and regret, his warmth seeping into my side.

"You almost died because of me. I may have doomed us both," I reply, turning to face him through a veil of tears, his features blurred and indistinct. I've never allowed myself to be this vulnerable. Yet here I am —raw and exposed, my heart laid bare.

"You saved me," he insists, his hand lifting slowly to cup my cheek. His touch is gentle despite the bandages that crisscross his wing, the fabric rough against my skin.

"I nearly got you killed," I whisper, unable to meet his gaze. My eyes fixated on the braced and bandaged wing—a living testament to my failures. The sight of it is like a knife twisting in my gut.

Klauth sits on my other side, his hand resting lightly on my thigh, his touch a silent comfort. He plants a soft kiss on my cheek, his lips cool and tender, his silence speaking volumes.

"Mina, I chose to go off script," Abraxis continues, his fingers intertwining with mine, his grip strong and sure. "I dove into battle to wipe out the wyvern. I read the three letters you told me not to read until the time was right, and I chose a path—my path." I search his face, my vision clearing, and with a slow nod.

"I didn't have to fight with you about control, about being afraid of becoming like my mom," I murmur, my voice thick with regret, the words sticking in my throat. "I was scared, utterly and completely terrified."

Klauth's soft voice breaks through once more, a soothing balm to my fractured soul. "I'm proud of you, Mina, for admitting your fears. Spend some time with Abraxis. Show him what you created out there in the courtyard." With that, Klauth rises and departs, his footsteps fading into the distance, leaving Abraxis and me alone in the hushed garden. The silence is broken only by the gentle rustle of leaves.

Steadying my shaking hand, I rise and offer Abraxis mine, my palm clammy and cold. "Are you up for a walk?"

"I would love that," he replies, his voice warm and rich as he rises to his feet and takes my hand. His touch chasing away the chill as we leave the garden behind.

We navigate the refurbished halls, our footsteps echoing on the polished floors, until we reach the heavy doors leading to the courtyard. I shove them open, the wood rough beneath my hands. A burst of sunlight washes over me, warming my skin with a gentle caress. "I almost forgot what the sun feels like," I murmur, closing my eyes and tilting my face upward. The light seeps into my bones, chasing away the shadows.

"When was the last time you basked in the sun for more than a moment?" Abraxis asks softly, leaning in to press a tender kiss against my cheek, his breath warm on my skin.

I turn slowly, the truth heavy on my lips, the words tasting like bile. "When I went on that rampage—before I was shot down." The memory of the bolts striking me, the searing heat of the impact. The sudden, jarring pain of being knocked off balance washes over me like a tidal wave, my breath catching in my throat.

Before he can speak, I take his hand and lead him to a quieter corner of the gardens. A place where a pond reflects the sky like a mirror and weathered benches invites quiet contemplation. "Klauth and Ziggy dug this spot so the flight would have a place to breathe, to find solace."

I guide Abraxis to a stone bench, its surface cool beneath our touch, and help him settle down before I ease myself beside him, my body molding to his. Resting my head on his strong shoulder, I feel the rough texture of his wing brush against my cheek—a tender, familiar caress in this twilight of pain and regret. For a moment, the searing ache of separation and the heavy burden of my guilt swell within me until tears threaten to spill once more. I grip his arm tighter. The sound of my shallow breaths mingles with the soft rustle of fabric as I cling to the memory of his protective embrace, the scent of him filling my lungs.

"It's beautiful, Mina," Abraxis murmurs, his voice low and resonant like a distant echo in the darkness, his words a lifeline in the storm of my emotions. I can barely form a response, managing only a silent nod as I swallow back the lump in my throat.

In a hushed tone, I add, "You know, your dad designed it as a mating present for us." The words feel delicate—as if they could shatter the fragile quiet around us. I share them like a secret meant only for our ears, a glimmer of light in the darkness.

"Mom probably pushed him to do it," he replies softly, his head settling over mine, our warmth intertwining, our hearts beating in sync.

Abruptly, his phone pings—a sharp, insistent sound that slices through our reverie, the noise jarring and unwelcome. With a resigned sigh, he retrieves it, the device cold and impersonal in his hand. "Time to see the doctor. Want to come with me?" He kisses the crown of my head, his lips soft and warm, and for an instant. I feel a small, flickering hope igniting in his chest, the sensation like a candle flame in the night. Though he never says it aloud, I know he needs me by his side, a silent plea in his touch.

"Yes," I reply, my voice steady as I wait for him to retract his good wing, the movement slow and careful. I extend my hand once more, our fingers interlacing, and together we make our way back into the labyrinthine corridors of the lower levels. The halls winding and whispering secrets until we reach the infirmary on the compound's cold, north side. The air is heavy with the scent of medicine and disinfectant.

"My Queen," the doctor says with a respectful bow, his staff echoing his formality, their eyes averted in deference.

I dismiss the title with a gentle wave, my hand cutting through the air. "Please, just call me Mina."

"We're taking the brace and bindings off his left wing today," the doctor announces in a clinical tone that makes my heart skip, his words like a punch to the gut. A sudden chill runs down my spine as I mentally tally everyone's whereabouts: Iris is with Thauglor, Klauth is in the upper nest in a meeting. Callan and the others went to Shadow-carve, and Vaughn lingering on campus—apparently enjoying a gargoyle holiday for the next two days.

Abraxis steps forward and smiles, the dim light catching the crinkles at his eyes, the sight of it a balm to my frayed nerves. "Were you talking to Klauth?" he teases, tilting his head in amusement, his tone light and playful.

"Actually, no. I was running a mental inventory of where everyone is right now," I explain, my eyes drifting over his shoulder to watch the doctor approach with a pair of surgical scissors, the metal glinting coldly in the stark light. "Let's sit you down for this," I say, signaling a nearby assistant who promptly brings a tall stool for Abraxis, the legs scraping against the tiled floor.

The snip of the scissors cutting through the gauze sounds thunderous in the quiet room. It echoes like a distant explosion in my ears. The sound setting my teeth on edge. I watch, heart pounding, as the bandages tumble onto the side table. The same gauze I applied the previous night, my fingers trembling as I wound it around his wing. The doctor's careful removal of it feels ominous, laden with unspoken dread, each layer revealing more of the healing skin beneath.

"We're going to remove some of the sutures today from the leather," the doctor explains, his tone neutral as he reveals the healing progress. The sight of the neat stitches is a stark contrast to the ragged wound they once held together. "You healed up nicely, but unfortunately, there will be white spots where the sutures were—scar tissue, General."

Abraxis offers an easy smile that belies the situation, his lips curving upward in a show of nonchalance. "I'll take white spots over torn flight leather any day," he remarks, his tone light and reassuring, the words a brave front. I wonder if his relaxed demeanor is for my sake or if he truly feels so at ease. The thought nags at the back of my mind.

I take his hand, drawing closer to catch every detail of the doctor's demonstration, my eyes roving over the exposed wing. From my vantage point, Abraxis's wing appears nearly flawless, a testament to my level of care, the sight of it filling me with a fierce pride. "You did wonderfully, Mina, taking care of your mate's wing," the doctor compliments, his eyes kind, his smile warm and genuine. "I think you did better than some of the wound specialists I've seen. If you ever want a job, just say the word." His words are a soothing balm to my battered soul. For a moment, hope flutters in my chest like a trapped bird.

I shake my head, smiling back, the expression feeling foreign on my face. "No, thank you. I only learned how to care for my mate. The females who came to tend his wound angered me—this was the safer alternative for everyone." I step aside to get a better look at his left wing, tracing its lines and scars with anxious eyes, my gaze lingering on the puckered flesh.

"It appears to have healed better than I originally expected, General," the doctor observes, now standing before us, his hands clasped behind his back. His smile is gentle as he instructs, "I want you to stretch and start using the wing, but non–weight bearing. Stretch it, flex it, but do not attempt to fly." He concludes with a lighthearted promise, his tone teasing, "I'll see you in another week, same time."

I watch as Abraxis gingerly stretches his wings, the movement slow and cautious. His right wing unfurls fully like a banner in the wind, the sight of it breathtaking. While his left lags, moving slowly until it opens only halfway, the muscles straining with the effort. I smile encouragingly, murmuring, "We just need to re-stretch it slowly. It's been resting for almost a month and a half."

Abraxis nods and leads me out of the infirmary, his steps measured, his gait slightly uneven. "This is going to sound weird," he begins, coming to a stop before me, his eyes searching mine. "Can you take us flying? I want to feel the wind in my face."

I return his smile and nod, the motion feeling more natural now. "Anything you want, my love. Just promise me you won't try flying," I say, raising an eyebrow in playful caution, my tone stern but laced with affection.

"I promise—I won't risk damaging my wing further. I want to fly on my own again someday. Besides, one day, I want to take our hatchlings out for their flights. I kinda need both wings for that." His smile radiates honesty, the sight of it easing the knot of worry in my chest. And I believe him.

Shifting as we step outside, I lie down on the cool ground. The grass ticks my scales as I invite him to climb onto my back, my scales smooth and warm beneath his touch. The fresh air envelops us like a comforting blanket, and when I feel him settle in, his weight is solid and reassuring. I rise and take off, my wings beating powerfully as we soar into the sky. Catching a thermal—a warm, rising current—I glide effortlessly, the wind caressing my face; the sensation is exhilarating. I sense the pure joy radiating from Abraxis, and in this moment, I'm grateful to be able to do this for him.

Mina and Idris sit, then carefully routes the cable back to my desk, where the unfolding battle will soon illuminate the big screen.

Klauth arrives next, his presence marked by the glint of a silver diadem atop his head. As he steps in, Mina pauses and smiles up at him—a fleeting moment of tenderness amid the looming storm. Wordlessly, he retrieves a velvet pouch from his coat and places the diadem, a gift from Ziggy, onto her head. "I agree with Zigmander—this one is perfect for you. It compliments your horns nicely," he murmurs, his voice dripping with both admiration and a hint of mischief. He leans forward and kisses her forehead. He takes a seat beside Abraxis, his every movement radiating a cool, dangerous confidence.

I shake my head slightly as I launch the first two battles, my eyes never leaving the screen. Every click and clatter of the keys blends with the low, tense hum of combat, and I can almost taste the metallic tang of impending defeat and victory. Occasionally, I glance over at Mina, who looks up at the performance board as I update the statistics with swift, precise keystrokes. She reaches into her bag and retrieves a small note-book, scribbling something down with intensity. I suspect she's assembling her team for the war games—a silent, determined strate-gist in a sea of chaos.

The class progresses as it must: wins, losses, and flashes of temper from those who fail to perform as expected. Midway through, a letter arrives for Mina. She waves a courier over, and with a subtle nod, I take the note from the outstretched hand. The crisp paper carries the seal of the council. As I read, a shiver runs down my spine. Mina is barred from actively participating in the war games. Instead, she is permitted to command her troops from the base. I cross the room and show her the note, my heart pounding in my chest.

She pauses her reading on the finer points of diplomacy. Taking the card from me, she flips it between her fingers, the paper rustling softly. With a swift motion, she pulls a pen from her pocket and writes her consent. She adds the stipulation that her team will be chosen from any class year between one and three by her hand. With a flick of her wrist, she sends the card back to the courier, who departs without a word.

Abraxis waves me over as I start the next two simulators, the screens flickering to life. "What was that about?" he asks, his voice low and laced with suspicion.

"The council is barring Mina from the frontline of the war games," I explain, leaning in as I update the display with new data, the keys clacking beneath my fingers. "They've offered her control of the legion instead. She accepted—but with the condition that she selects her team from her year and the two years younger." I arch a brow, silently questioning the logic behind her request.

I lean forward as Klauth interjects, his voice slicing through the stale air of our Art of War class. "Tactically, it's brilliant," he declares, his tone both approving and chilling. He reclines in his chair with a slow, eerie smile that sends a tremor down my spine. I watch as he crosses his arms, and even Abraxis mirrors his guarded gesture, a barely perceptible tension thick in the room.

Abraxis scans our classroom before announcing, "We'll have another answer soon. I believe Mina's match is up next." In that instant, a sinking dread coils in my gut. If our suspicions are correct, then Idris is not the skilled tactician we believed him to be. We have been set up, and someone on the council is planning to kill us both. The weight of betrayal presses down like the suffocating darkness outside the high, narrow windows.

Abruptly, Abraxis stands and clutches a card with a smooth, cold edge meant for the simulator. "Here's the rematch we have all been waiting for. Mina vs. Idris." I hear the soft slide of the card into the slot, a sound that echoes ominously as he returns to his desk. The simulator hums to life, its low mechanical vibration mixing with the murmurs of anxious students. The air smells faintly of burnt ozone and metal—a foretaste of the impending clash.

Mina remains absorbed in her worn diplomacy book until a beep signals the simulation is ready. With a swift, almost careless motion, she drops the book onto the cold floor beside her and slides Thauglor's egg back into its carrier. Her fingers dance over the keyboard, each click reverberating in the hushed room. All eyes lock onto the unfolding match between Mina and Idris. Whispers ripple through the class about Mina facing an actual war-proven tactician. I catch sight of Balor, Ziggy, and Leander casually leaning against the wall behind Abraxis and Klauth, their presence adding to the heavy tension.

Every nerve in my body screams that this match holds the answers to our long-standing border disputes. Mina's final keystroke echoes sharply as she slams the metal cover over her keyboard. With deliberate care, she locks the padlock in place. I step forward, retrieve the key from her hand, and return her book. Deep inside, I'm convinced she's destined to win; no one has ever bested her, and even as a veil walker, she seems to foresee the outcomes before they unfold.

Mina leans back in her chair and resumes reading, her calm facade belying the storm beneath. To an outsider, she appears indifferent, but we all know better. Mina is methodical, precise—she commands the field like a seasoned ruler. Idris, meanwhile, hesitates at his terminal, entering and then erasing orders. Mina's head tilts ever so slightly as her fingers tap the edge of her book in silent protest, the rhythm a subtle yet powerful rebuke.

I murmur to Klauth, "I wonder what happened?"

"He changed his mind about troop placement. The results will be the same," he whispers, his voice low and dangerous. I nod, feeling the weight of his words as palpably as the chill in the room.

Eventually, Idris slams his cover shut, the sound reverberating like a death knell. I approach, and he reluctantly hands me the key, which I place on the desk with a clack that seems too loud in the tense silence. "Okay, let's let this play out!" I announce, my hand slapping the execute button on the side of the simulator.

At the start, the match appears evenly balanced, but as the simulation unfolds. I notice Mina has held back roughly a quarter of her forces. Even with only seventy-five percent of her strength deployed, she is steadily containing Idris's maneuvers.

"If I win, Your Highness, I'd like a special dinner at the fort," Idris taunts, leaning over his terminal to scrutinize Mina. His voice drips with condescension, the words slithering through the air like poison.

Mina places her book atop the keyboard cover and smiles—a smile that is disarmingly sweet yet laced with lethal confidence. "In about five minutes or less, I'll have your job," she replies, her eyes sparkling as she peers around the divider, her gaze sharp as a blade.

The first explosion booms through the simulation, a deep, resonant sound that shakes the room. Mina's smile widens as she stands to watch the unfolding chaos on the big screen. I can see her orchestrating a devastating maneuver. A contingent of black and red dragons release a wave of acid breath ignited by the red dragons' fire, so potent that the attackers disintegrate before our eyes. In fewer than four calculated moves, she obliterates the enemy forces, her precision as cold and brutal as the coldest winter.

The replay mirrors a recent, harrowing battle—the very one in which Mina and Abraxis were ambushed. I watch as the last remnants of the invading forces crumble away. I note the blank, almost emotionless mask on Mina's face as she stares unblinkingly at the screen, her eyes reflecting the flickering light.

"How?" Idris almost shouts, rising abruptly so that his stool topples to the ground behind him with a harsh clatter.

Mina whirls around, her voice low and feral. "You are not qualified to call the shots for an outpost." Her eyes burn with a fierce intensity as she fixes Balor with a glare, the air crackling with her authority. "Send him to Blackhaven—I want answers." In that moment, I see the transformation in her: the weight of command and the responsibility for her people awaken something primal and formidable within her.

"General, you seriously can't let your inexperienced mate do this," Idris protests, attempting to sway Abraxis to his side, his voice tinged with desperation.

Abraxis's eyes narrow as he crosses his arms, his tone icy. "My mate has beaten you not once, but twice. Your inability to out think the enemy has cost us hundreds of lives over the past three years." He glances sharply at Balor and Ziggy, his command ringing through the room. "Do as your queen said. Take him to Blackhaven." With that, Balor and Ziggy vanish into the shadows, leaving behind a lingering silence.

I quickly dismiss the class, my heart pounding, and join Mina to watch the replay in slow motion. As the simulation resets, I ask quietly, "What made you hold back those two specific species of dragons?"

Mina moves to the whiteboard, her chalk tracing crisp, deliberate lines. "Out of the species available at the fort, these two possess the strongest offensive and defensive capabilities," she explains, her voice measured and clinical. "Realistically, green dragons are useless—their scales are soft and their talons small. Their breath weapons are impressive, but they lack any real defense. Blue dragons can absorb a normal hit of lightning, but they crumble under fire, acid, and my breath weapon. They're best as a secondary line." She stands before us, a strategist in full command, every word dripping with cold logic.

Mina murmurs, almost to herself, "I didn't program that." She glances at me, then adjusts a line of code with a deft touch before pressing start, her brow furrowed in concentration.

"I wonder why it did that?" I whisper, more to myself than anyone else, my mind racing with possibilities.

We watch the replay together, the tension palpable as Balor and Ziggy reappear. This run is even more efficient—her score is a perfect ten out of ten. "That's better," Mina murmurs, a slight smile touching her lips as she packs her things, the rustle of paper and the clink of Thauglor's egg carrier punctuating the silence.

I turn to Abraxis and Klauth, my voice low. "Our mate—if she were in charge, most of what happened might have been avoided." I lock eyes with Balor and Ziggy and restart the simulation, the hum of the machine filling the air once more. Mina resumes her seat, her hands resting flat on Thauglor's egg as she stares intently at the screen. I can almost see the inner fire in her eyes, mirroring the fierce glow of the screen.

"Klauth, is she doing what I think she's doing with him?" I ask, nodding toward the way she cradles Thauglor's egg, my heart skipping a beat at the implications.

Klauth moves closer, his eyes fixed on her as if she were a work of art, his voice low and almost reverent. "I'll be damned. She's sharing her sight with him."

"What else can our mate do because of being bonded with you?" I ask, my eyes darting between Mina and Klauth, my mind reeling with the possibilities.

He smiles, a dark, knowing curl of his lips. "I'm not sure. She's the first of her kind, and as far as I know, I am the only great wyrm on either continent at the moment." He rests a hand on Mina's shoulder, then abruptly tilts his head upward, as if listening to a distant voice. "Thauglor is teaching her more about what black dragons are capable of." He withdraws his hand and scans our group, his gaze sharp and commanding. "We need to find out what Vox uncovers from your tactician. In the meantime, all hands are on guard for Mina."

Klauth turns to leave, shaking hands with Balor and Ziggy as if sealing our fates, the weight of the moment pressing down on us all. Their duty is clear: one might turn the world to stone, the other whisk her

away in seconds. Either way, Mina will be safe, even as the shadows of
impending danger loom ever closer.

know the extent of his injuries. It's none of their business to know how vulnerable he truly is.

I pore over the list of troops assigned to the outpost, the parchment rough beneath my fingertips as I set up several formations for them. My notes detail the reasons for each formation, the ink smudging slightly as I press the pen to the page. I refuse to take any chances, meticulously reviewing the whys and when's of each strategic move. The only factor I hadn't accounted for is the massive earth dragon stationed here—the oldest drake, nearing wyrm status. His scales are a deep brown, like the bark of an ancient oak, and his eyes hold a wisdom that commands respect. He takes the time to explain his capabilities, and I listen intently, absorbing every detail.

With this new information, I amend the plans already in place, making him the focus of the compound's defensive line. His scales may rival even my own in strength, so holding him back until the end is the wisest course of action.

"How are you holding up?" Balor asks, his voice low and gentle as he guides me back into the planning room. The diorama of the area sits on a large table, the landscape meticulously crafted to mimic the surrounding terrain.

Once we're inside, Ziggy closes the door behind him, the latch clicking softly. "Currently, I'm fine," I say, my gaze fixed on the diorama. I trace my fingers over the miniature buildings, feeling the smooth wood beneath my skin.

"But?" Ziggy prompts, his tone knowing. I freeze, my hand hovering over the tiny replica of the outpost.

"You're taking after Leander, you know that?" I force a smile, but it feels brittle on my lips. I glance at Ziggy before placing colored pins on the field, marking troop positions and potential threats. "I don't believe Abraxis will ever be able to fly and fight like he used to." My hand trembles as I set the next few pins, the metal cool against my skin.

"What makes you say that?" Balor's question hangs in the air, heavy with unspoken concern.

I move to the whiteboard, the marker squeaking softly as I draw a basic wing structure. When I finish, I point to the main flight muscle stretching from the shoulder to the base of the wing. "This muscle...it's missing a sizable chunk," I say, my voice wavering. I clear my throat, trying to steady myself. "Without it, flight is nearly impossible. That's not to say he can't strengthen the accessory muscles to compensate, but..." My words trail off as I adjust the drawing to reflect the damage.

Balor and Ziggy step forward, their eyes examining the diagram with grim understanding. "I see what you mean," Ziggy murmurs. "That's a significant portion of muscle to lose."

I turn to face him, meeting his vibrant green gaze head-on. "I need you to take Abraxis anywhere he needs to go. He cannot be seen as weak. They'll kill him—especially if another drake tries to force its way into our nest." My words are sharp, tinged with desperation.

Balor nods slowly, his expression somber. "Basilisks do the same—eliminate a weak male to claim the female," he says, his eyes dark with understanding.

"Will Klauth or Thauglor protect him?" Ziggy asks, a flicker of hope in his voice.

I shake my head, my hair brushing against my cheeks. "Dragons believe only the strong survive. It's against the dragon codex to interfere in a dominance challenge. I can't intervene either. It would only make Abraxis appear weaker if his mate has to step in." A heavy sigh escapes my lips, the weight of the situation pressing down on my chest.

But then, a thought strikes me, and I slowly turn to face Balor, one eyebrow arched. "You...you could fight in his place if a challenge arises. Basilisks are part of the dragon family. You can accept the challenge on his behalf." A laugh bubbles up from my throat, a glimmer of hope sparking in my heart.

"That smile is concerning," Balor says, a wary edge to his voice.

"Not everyone is immune to your stone gaze," I remind him, a wry smile tugging at my lips.

"Where's Thauglor?" Ziggy asks, curiosity coloring his tone.

"Klauth has him," I reply, a hint of amusement in my voice. "Abraxis is at the hot springs, letting the water take some of the weight off his wing, while Leander tries to help him stretch the muscles." I've made it clear to everyone in my flight that what happens within the nest stays strictly within the nest.

I return my attention to the diorama, my gaze roving over the intricate details. I've done all I can to prepare the outpost. The troops have their orders and contingency plans in case the situation changes on the fly, as it so often does. "Ziggy, take us home, please."

In a heartbeat, we're back in the Risedale nest, the familiar scents of home wrapping around me like a comforting embrace. But my mind is torn, pulled in countless directions. Do I go to Abraxis, offering what comfort I can? Do I seek out my other mates, trying to steal a few precious moments with them? And always, the looming shadow of the war games hangs over everything, a constant reminder of the challenges to come.

There's so much to do and so little time to do it. The weight of responsibility settles heavily on my shoulders as I stand there, caught between duty and desire. The future is an uncertain path stretching out before me.

I STAND IN THE KITCHEN, the low hum of evening settling around me like a comforting blanket. The air is filled with the rich aroma of herbs and simmering broth, a welcome distraction from the tangled web of worries that plague my mind. On the counter sits Thauglor's egg, nestled in the rough, earthy clay holder I crafted during art class. Its presence is a tangible reminder of the life trapped within, a glimmer of hope amidst the gathering darkness.

Lost in thought, I barely notice when Vaughn and Leander arrive home, their footsteps echoing softly on the hardwood floor. It's only when Leander's arms wrap around my waist, warm and solid against my skin, that I'm pulled from my thoughts. "Are you sure you don't want me to cook, babe?" he asks, his voice low and filled with gentle concern.

I sigh, letting my eyes drift closed for a moment as I savor the comfort of his embrace. The steady beat of his heart resonates through me, easing the tempest in my mind. "I wanted to cook for everyone," I murmur, a faint purr escaping my lips as I tilt my head back to rest against his shoulder.

"My poor mate," Leander whispers, his breath warm against my temple. "I can tell your thoughts won't leave you alone. The weight of the world is on your shoulders." He presses a soft kiss to my skin, and I set the knife aside, melting into his arms.

"I'll be okay, Lee, I promise. There's just...so much going on, and with war games starting soon..." My words trail off, heavy with the burden of responsibility.

"You're not fighting in the war games, remember? You can only lead from the outpost," Callan's voice echoes in my mind, a stark reminder of the limits placed upon us.

I spin within Leander's embrace, my eyes scanning the faces of my gathered mates. The tension in the room is palpable, the air thick with the mingled scents of fear and anticipation. "But what's the point of even going if I can't participate? What if the war room is attacked? Am I not supposed to defend myself?"

Stepping away from Leander's comforting hold, I pace the cool tile floor, each step punctuating the conflict raging within me. The clatter of pans fills the silence as Leander takes over the cooking, a quiet gesture of support.

"You know, and I know," I say, halting mid-stride to lock eyes with the others, "the war games are the perfect time for one of my two villains to make their move." The words hang heavy in the air, a dark possibility that sends a shiver down my spine.

"No, that would be too obvious," I murmur, shaking my head. "Strategically speaking, they'd expect me to plan that way. At least, my father would." My thoughts swirl, a dizzying dance of calculated risks and potential outcomes.

Abraxis's voice cuts through the haze, low and cautious. "So, what do you want to do?" He flexes his wings, the left one moving in a way that makes my stomach clench with worry.

"I need to make clay dragon eggs," I blurt out, the words tumbling from my lips before I can stop them. I blink, startled by my declaration, realizing I've missed saying half of my own internal conversation.

"Can we back that up a step or two?" Vaughn's deep voice interrupts my racing thoughts as he steps into view, shifting seamlessly into his gargoyle form. Before I can protest, he sweeps me up in his massive wings, and panic prickles through my veins.

"Let me out…" I push hard against the enclosure, stepping away with my heart hammering in my chest. I avoid meeting Abraxis's gaze, knowing it would only serve to remind him of his injured wing.

Abraxis moves closer, pulling me gently to his side and wrapping his strong right wing around me. In his embrace, I find a calm that contrasts sharply with the chaos in my mind, like a balm to my frayed nerves. "Mate, what do you need clay dragon eggs for?" he asks, his voice a soothing rumble.

I nuzzle into the curve of his jaw, purring softly. "Bait for my father," I confess. "When I lay my clutch next year, I need the clay eggs ready. I have to paint them to mimic the real ones." Carefully, I nudge Abraxis's wing aside just enough to see everyone clearly. "I want to dig a dummy nest further down the mountains, somewhere between here and Vox's territory."

Klauth's voice cuts in, laced with skepticism and a hint of revulsion. "Okay, so a second nest for the clay eggs. But they won't smell like dragon eggs."

"They will," I insist, my tone firm despite the quiver of uncertainty. "When I lay my real eggs, a viscous mucus is released. We'll roll the clay eggs in that goo so they pick up the scent perfectly." I arch an eyebrow, gauging my mates' reactions in the flickering kitchen light.

Klauth shivers visibly, his scales catching the dim glow. "Accurate, but disgusting," he mutters, his voice low and rough. "It will scent the eggs as long as they don't get wet. So, do I need to dig another nest for you?" His tone carries a teasing possessiveness as he steps closer. His hand reaches out to caress my cheek with a gentle yet insistent touch that sends shivers down my spine.

"Over the summer break," I reply, my voice barely above a whisper. I meet Klauth's eyes, even as I remain cradled in Abraxis's secure hold. The air feels heavy, the tension in the room tightening like a coiled spring.

Ziggy's casual question breaks the silence. "When do you get abducted?"

"That's not clear yet," I admit slowly, feeling the weight of uncertainty settle in my gut. "It means Lysander hasn't made a final decision. Or perhaps I haven't made one yet." I nestle deeper under Abraxis's protective wing, my thoughts as turbulent as the shadows dancing on the walls.

Balor's voice cuts through the stillness as he passes out drinks. "So, what are the options?"

I close my eyes, letting the possibilities wash over me. "Option one: play in the war games and stay at the outpost," I murmur, but no spark of relief ignites within me. "Option two: don't participate in the war games and remain on campus somewhere." The moment the second option leaves my lips, it feels as if the wind is sucked out of me, leaving me trembling.

My mind fast-forwards through a bleak future. I see myself on campus, walking beside one of the assigned fourth years. A wide arc of crimson suddenly explodes into darkness. When vision returns, I am in a cold tunnel, against a rough stone wall, staring at a vast, empty room. The fourth year has vanished, leaving me drenched in his blood. The metallic scent of it clings to my skin, and the echo of my racing heartbeat fills the silence.

I blink, pulling myself out of the harrowing vision. I notice that my two dragon mates have seen everything, their eyes reflecting shock and concern. Panting, I steady my spinning head and cling tighter to Abraxis, careful not to pull him down.

Klauth's voice breaks through the haze. "So if you avoid the war games, that is when you will be abducted?"

"I'm guessing so," I admit, slipping away from Abraxis's wing and beginning to pace the living room. Every step on the cold floor sends a jolt through me.

I turn to Abraxis, my gaze flickering to the bird perched over his shoulder. "How good is Rebel at spying on me?"

"Pretty good. Why?" Abraxis arches a brow, his eyes steady and inquisitive.

"He needs to follow me around during the war games," I explain, my voice growing more confident. "At least then you all will know exactly when I get abducted. He can tail me to wherever they hide me, and Balor can play the knight in obsidian scales to save my ass." Despite the absurdity, the plan sounds practical—a strategy born from the chaos in my head.

Callan's comment cuts through the air. "Tactically, that's brilliant. What are we going to do about Lemon?"

I laugh, a sound that feels both relieved and defiant, as Iris lands lightly on my shoulder. "Iris will handle that. She's got a score to settle with Lemon." I press a soft kiss against her cool, smooth scales and smile back at the group. "Iris will be Rebel's bodyguard."

Abraxis's confession is laced with uncertainty. "I don't know how I feel about that."

"Do you have any better ideas?" I ask, tilting my head as I lean back against Klauth. His arms wrap around me slowly, offering a silent promise of comfort, and I let out a soft sigh.

Balor's declaration cuts through the room. "I think we should run with it. Can you breathe that sleep toxin in human form, or only in your dragon form?" He tilts his head, curiosity mingling with amusement.

Vaughn moves closer, his form shifting to his gargoyle self. "Test it on me. Even if there's acid, my stone skin should protect me."

I fix my gaze on him as he nods slowly. My face contorts with concentration. The bone plates beneath my skin shift slightly, and I feel the roof of my mouth alter as the transformation takes hold. I almost hiss when a purplish-blue gas escapes my lips. Within seconds, Vaughn collapses to the ground, the sound of sizzling fluid mingling with the low hum of the room.

"It works, but there's acid involved," I sigh, watching him sleep on the cold floor, his skin glistening with droplets that burn the floor when they fall.

Leander's quiet voice cuts through the stillness, thoughtful and measured. "It's good to know you can do it."

"True..." I murmur, staring at Vaughn's unconscious form. Tomorrow is bound to be an interesting day. Preparations for the war games begin during third period, and I know I need to give Vaughn every advantage possible.

windows. The harsh daylight casts deep shadows that flicker across the room, echoing the turmoil inside me.

Mina's eyes, fierce and calculating, lock onto Trever. I can see her pupils contract in the bright light, revealing the golden flecks in her irises that only appear when she's focused. "Trever, you're a black dragon, correct?" she asks, her voice carrying a slight rasp that betrays her exhaustion. Trever nods, his expression grim despite the bright light that exposes every detail of his determined face. The thin scar along his jaw twitching with tension. "Position yourself here." Her finger taps a spot on the map, the sound sharp in the hushed room. "And remember—do not speak aloud where I am directing you." His nod is sharp, each detail of his resolve etched in my memory as he commits the orders to memory, the muscles in his neck corded tight.

She turns to Max, her lips moving silently as she mouths "jabber-wock," the word hanging unspoken in the air between them. Max meets her gaze and nods, a spark of wild mischief lighting his eyes, the irises shifting from brown to amber as his excitement grows. "Good. Watch Trever's back. Do your thing, but keep the carnage focused on the enemy," Mina instructs. A slight smile playing at the corners of her mouth, revealing the edge of a sharper-than-human canine. I note, with a mix of curiosity and unease, that I have no idea what species of dragon he truly is. Whatever he is, it brings a rare light to Mina's otherwise shadowed expression, the tension around her eyes briefly softening.

Mina then fixes her gaze on Luc, her tone softening as she hesitates. For a moment, the low hum of conversation seems to pause beneath the booming midday clamor outside the room. Her eyes widen with sudden excitement as she bounces lightly on her heels. The leather of her boots creaks with each movement. "How many of your clan are here?" she demands. Her voice trembles with urgency amid the warmth of the day, her breath coming quicker.

"Six, my queen," Luc replies, his smile gentle and respectful. The scent of cinnamon and cloves following his words as if his dragon nature infuses even his breath. Mina arches a brow, her glance probing. "Are there at least two more in the war classes?" Luc's eyes mirror the anxious intensity that flickers in Mina's, the color shifting like storm clouds, and he confirms, "Yes. Would you like them here?" His fingers tap a nervous rhythm on the tabletop, barely audible but persistent.

"Yes, I would," she replies, her voice steady now. She hands him a small, creased piece of paper with instructions scribbled on it, the parchment rustling as it passes between them.

Next, Mina turns to Quent. "You're from my mate's den, aren't you?" she says, tilting her head as I watch the subtle shift in his eyes. They take on a malevolent green glow that sends a shiver through me even under the midday sun. The sight of them raising goosebumps along my arms despite the heat. "Yes, I am," he purrs, his tone a silky murmur that carries a dangerous edge, like velvet wrapped around a blade.

"Good. I can direct the fight from wherever I am then." Mina scribbles a note, the scratching of her pen against the paper filling the momentary silence. She slides it into Quent's hand before he melts away into the crowd, his departure marked only by a faint waft of sulfur.

"And then there was one." Mina's smile widens as she nods at Crassus, who bows his head humbly, the sunlight glinting off the silver strands in his dark hair. "Defense," she murmurs, barely more than a breath, before distributing envelopes to each of us. The paper is warm from being kept close to her body.

Mina steps closer and presses a small, worn notebook into my hand, its leather cover soft with age and use. The pages inside slightly yellowed at the edges. "In here is every idea I've had about what might happen in the war games," she says, her voice soft yet insistent, her fingertips lingering on mine for a heartbeat too long.

As she leads me out of the cool meeting room, the bright midday light greets us with blinding intensity. The scent of fresh-cut grass and distant smoke fills the air, mingling with the metallic tang of weapons being forged somewhere nearby. Outside, Abraxis awaits us near the training yard, his form outlined against the sun-drenched expanse of the field, his silhouette sharp and commanding.

"We're going for a flight," he announces as he joins us, the midday heat making the air shimmer with anticipation around his body. I glance around; the yard is a chaotic blend of clashing bodies and echoing grunts as students spar under the watchful, steady gaze of Balor. The harsh brightness exposes every twitch of movement and the sweat on their brows, a stark reminder of the stakes. The sun glints off practice weapons like warning beacons.

"Exactly," Mina murmurs as we slip far enough from the prying eyes of the yard, her voice barely carrying over the rhythmic clang of metal on metal. Mina shifts effortlessly into her dragon, her bones crackling and reforming with a sound like breaking branches. She lays down so we can climb on, her massive body radiating heat like a furnace.

"Come on, I'm here to translate for Mina's dragon," Abraxis says with a low chuckle as we climb onto her back, his hands steadying me as I find my footing on her shifting muscles. I settle against her rough frill, feeling the texture of sun-warmed scales beneath my fingertips, hard yet somehow alive, just as she rises and bounds toward the open sky. The rush of air is startling, whipping my face and stealing my breath, and the sunlight dazzles as we ascend. The heat mingling with the tension that radiates from us all like a palpable force.

High above the sunlit world, her dragonic form rumbles like distant thunder. The vibration traveling through her body and into mine, rattling my bones. "She says there are three potential outcomes—none with her directly involved in the war games," Abraxis explains, his tone measured as he listens to another low rumble from her, her chest expanding beneath us with each breath. "The key is knowing when to attack and when to defend. That notebook in your hand is the key to victory. Memorize the three events and react appropriately." His voice carries the weight of absolute faith in her visions, unwavering despite the cost.

My gaze lingers on the notebook, its pages rustling in the wind, carrying secrets and grim predictions. The paper feels almost alive in my grip, warm and insistent. "Her visions led her to create the book?" I ask, my voice nearly lost in the roar of the wind and the steady pulse of the bright sky. I still struggle to understand the inner workings of her prophetic insights, the burden she carries.

Mina rumbles, the sound reverberating through her massive ribcage, catching a thermal and gliding gracefully through shafts of sunlight that turn her scales into a kaleidoscope of color. "Yes. She had three different visions, each with you as the leader of her team." Abraxis leans over and taps the book gently, his finger tracing the worn binding. "The dividers split the three events up." Her rumble deepens, a sound like a distant storm brewing on a hot summer day, resonant and foreboding. "The middle one will be the most brutal. I hope it never comes to pass." His voice drops to a whisper, barely audible over the rushing air.

Abraxis turns his face into the warm wind, closing his eyes as if to commune with the vast, cloudless sky, his skin flushing with the heat and exertion. I watch him, his body slowly angling as the gentle current ruffles the leather of his folded wings, every muscle taut with a silent grief that radiates from him in waves. He moves with a grace that mirrors the sinuous flight of Mina's body.

"It'll get better," I say hesitantly, my voice mingling with the whisper of the wind, the words feeling inadequate even as they leave my lips. I glance down at Mina's iridescent scales, trying not to let my eyes betray the worry in my heart, the knot of concern tight in my chest. For a dragon, losing the skies is a fate worse than death—even under the relentless glare of the sun, a punishment that cuts deeper than any blade.

Abraxis lets out a soft, bittersweet laugh, the sound catching on the wind. "I might try gliding this week," he admits. He shakes his head as he leans against Mina's frill, his fingers absently stroking the ridged texture. "I know why Klauth gave me the promotion—just in case I can't fly anymore." The words hang in the air, heavy with unspoken loss.

Then, Mina roars—a sound so raw and heartbreaking it cuts through the bright air like a physical force, vibrating through my chest and squeezing my lungs. A cry that echoes with the weight of loss. Abraxis turns, climbing up her neck to settle near her horns and ears, where he begins a quiet, intimate conversation with her, his words too soft to hear but his body language speaking volumes. I watch from the outside, knowing that the scars they share run deep beneath their skin. They have weathered hell together and even though their reconciliation came at a terrible cost. The pain of their shared past is as clear as the unyielding sunlight above, impossible to hide and impossible to forget.

LAST NIGHT, we were seized by the senior staff and taken to the outpost we now guard for the games. I recall every detail as if it were etched in my skin. Ziggy and three other displacer beasts herded us with brutal efficiency. Their massive paws were silent against the cold stone, their eyes gleaming with a cold purpose like chips of glowing emeralds in the darkness. The memory of their hot breath on my neck still raises the fine hairs along my spine.

I awake before dawn, the chill in the air biting at my exposed skin like tiny needles, feeling the tug on my tether as Mina stirs me awake through our bond. Her urgency pulses through me, almost tangible, a rapid drumbeat in my veins that forces my eyes open.

I burst from my cot, the thin blankets falling away with a soft rustle, and sprint through the drafty barracks. The soles of my boots slap against the worn flagstones, my footsteps echoing down the cold, shadowed corridors that smell of damp stone and old fear. The air tastes stale on my tongue, tinged with the metallic scent of rusted metal and the lingering sweat of nervous bodies.

"We need to move. Get in position," I shout, my voice cutting through the stillness like a blade, bouncing off the stone walls and amplifying my command. The sound of rustling clothes and hastily buckled armor fills the space as my team responds without hesitation. Each of them racing to their designated spots, their eyes alert despite the early hour, pupils dilated in the dim light.

Clutching my notebook tightly against my chest, its leather cover smooth and worn beneath my fingers. I ascend the rickety stairs to the tower, each wooden step groaning in protest under my weight. Splinters threaten to pierce through the soles of my boots as I climb. At the top, I can survey the horizon, the first hint of dawn painting the sky in muted purples and grays, the air crisp and sharp in my lungs. I flip through the pages, the paper dry and crackling beneath my touch, until relief washes over me. The third option is unfolding before our eyes, just as Mina predicted. The scent of the old ink rises from the pages, familiar and oddly comforting amid the tension.

Within minutes, I bark orders drawn from my little notebook, its pages stained with our fears and hopes, the ink smudged in places from my sweaty fingers. My voice carries across the outpost, firm and commanding despite the dryness in my throat.

Just as I set my defenses, the enemy emerges on the horizon, dark shapes against a bruised sky, their outlines sharpening as they advance. The distant sound of their approach reaches my ears. The clink of armor, the low rumble of voices, the rhythmic thud of coordinated footsteps against the hard ground.

"How did you know?" Quent asks, disbelief lacing his voice as the unfolding events mirror our worst nightmares. His breath forms small clouds in the cool morning air. The scent of cinnamon and something darker, more dangerous, emanating from him as he shifts closer.

"Lucky, I guess," I murmur, the lie tasting bitter on my tongue. I open the notebook, the binding creaking softly. I see Mina's careful handwriting detailing the formation advancing toward us. Her precise strokes are as familiar to me now as my own heartbeat. A lone bird slices through the air, its shadow briefly darkening the page, and I notice a note in the margin urging me to turn to a different section. The paper rustles as I flip to the indicated page, my fingers trembling slightly with adrenaline. There, Mina warns of an attack from behind, her words underlined three times. The pen having pressed so hard it left indentations on the following pages.

"Luc, Crassus—watch the south," I call out, feeling my voice vibrate in my chest. Their silhouettes turn at my command, movements fluid and predatory. "Trever, Max—focus on the primary force coming from the north," I repeat, my voice steady as I relay her precise orders. The surrounding air grows heavy with anticipation, the taste of copper flooding my mouth—the taste of imminent violence.

Frantically, I tear a blank page from the back of the book, the sound sharp in the tense silence, and scrawl a quick note, just as Mina instructed, updating her on the situation. My pen scratches against the paper, leaving dark trails of ink that bleed slightly into the fibers. The scent of ink and desperation mingles as I fold the note, the paper warm from my hands.

"Quent, bring this to Mina—she's at Shadowcarve in Callan's office this morning." He accepts the note, his fingers brushing mine, cold as ice despite the exertion, before disappearing into the shadows. The air shifts as he passes, carrying the faint scent of sulfur in his wake.

Now, with nothing more than that solitary instruction, we settle into a tense waiting game, hoping Mina will soon send more words of wisdom to guide us through the impending storm. The weight of responsibility presses down on my shoulders like a physical burden. The cold air filling my lungs with each measured breath. In the distance, the enemy continues to advance, their shapes growing larger against the slowly brightening sky. I feel the first stirrings of something primal and dangerous awakening within me, ready for the fight that will soon come.

THE DAMP, earthy scent of the forest fills my nostrils as I wait, my heart pounding against my ribcage. It feels like an eternity before Quent materializes from the shadows, his worn boots barely making a sound on the soft ground. He emerges into the mid-afternoon light, a basket and another weathered notebook cradled in his calloused hands. The overcast sky hangs low, its dull gray light softening the edges of the world and casting an eerie pallor over everything. A subtle chill lingers in the air, raising goosebumps on my skin.

Quent's low, husky voice cuts through the heavy silence. "Your mate is terrifying, by the way." He offers me the items with a measured calm, his eyes glinting with a hint of unease.

A wry smile tugs at the corner of my mouth. "She can be," I reply, my voice steady despite the thundering of my pulse in my ears. I run my fingers over the cover of the new notebook, feeling the rough texture against my skin. The pages crackle softly as I flip it open.

An undercurrent of tension mingles with the musty scent of damp earth. I remind myself that we haven't yet reached the crucial moment.

My eyes scan every word on the page with cautious intensity. I trace the instructions carefully, committing the formations to memory. In the distance, the sounds of approaching chaos build into a low, foreboding murmur that sets my teeth on edge. The moment the first sign arrives, adrenaline surges through my veins like molten fire. I dash to the balcony, my voice slicing through the muted light with urgent commands.

"Luc, now!" My shout rings out, piercing the heavy air.

In that instant, the very atmosphere trembles as Luc and his clan shift into position. The outpost fills with the ominous presence of eight bronze dragons, their scales catching the subdued light and glinting like polished metal as they align against the overcast sky.

Then, as the enemy forces surge through the outpost, a deafening roar splits the afternoon. The dragons unleash their ferocious lightning breath, the crackling energy momentarily illuminating the gloom. The stench of charred flesh assaults my nostrils as the enemy is reduced to smoldering heaps. Overhead, Crassus, and Trever's clansmen soar above the battlements on cleanup duty, their grim determination ensuring that no foe is left drawing breath.

I steal a glance down at the notebook, its pages a silent witness to the unfolding carnage. I scrutinize the words, ensuring nothing else escapes my attention.

But on the next page, the breath is stolen from my lungs. It's a note from Mina. The paper crinkled and smudged with what looks like dried tears.

By the time your battle is over, mine is just beginning. Don't let Abraxis do anything to injure himself further. Ziggy is already hiding Thauglor's egg like you did last time, close to where I believe I will be. Balor is the only one safe to come after me. Please don't try to be the hero.

*Thauglor is going to be harder to calm than Klauth was.
He is wrath incarnate, his rage a scorching inferno that
will be nearly impossible to extinguish.*

*Remember, I love you. Protect the soft-skinned mates
and don't let Abraxis fly.*

Mina

Her words settle like a stone in my gut, cold and heavy. She knows what's coming for her again, and she's ready to face it alone. The metallic taste of fear coats my tongue as I stare at her familiar handwriting. My fingers tremble against the page.

"Your time is upon us." I caress the egg, the smooth surface heating beneath my touch before moving the silk aside to press my lips against the shell. It vibrates harshly, almost burning against my mouth, and I smile down at it. "You get to torch the headmaster with your acid." A bitter laugh escapes my throat before I look up at Klauth, his ancient eyes reflecting centuries of patience, before lowering my gaze back to Thauglor's egg. The scales at the nape of my neck rises as a powerful sense of déjà vu washes over me.

Drawing in a deep breath, the musty scent of old books and candle wax filling my lungs, I continue. "I will tug on the bond and force as much power down it to you as I can." I raise my eyes as Balor enters the room, his heavy footsteps echoing on the stone floor. "Balor can only do so much to save me. We need your acid to turn him into a puddle of goo." My eyes remain locked with Balor's, the golden flecks in his irises seeming to dance in the dim light. "My scales will not be harmed by your acid, and I will shield Balor from it. Come swiftly when I call for you; our lives depend on it." I kiss the egg once more, feeling the pulse of life within before wrapping it up and handing it to Ziggy to hide close to where I suspect I will be held. Ziggy vanishes in a swirl of shadow. Tears well up, silently rolling down my cheeks, their salt stinging the corners of my mouth.

Balor moves before the others have a chance, crossing the room in three long strides and holds me tightly against his chest. The scent of earth and pine envelops me as his muscular arms wrap around my trembling form. "I won't let him hurt you. If I die and you live, it's worth it." He presses his warm lips to my forehead, trying to infuse me with his strength, his heartbeat steady and reassuring against my ear.

"No one's dying," Klauth says as he steps closer, the boards creaking beneath his weight, his voice cutting through the heavy silence like a blade.

"I can at least help dig," Abraxis says as he tilts his head, looking at me with concern etched across his features, the light catching on the scales that pepper his jawline.

"True, but back off when Thauglor arrives," Klauth says, and we all look at him, the temperature in the room seeming to drop several degrees. "His first instinct will be to get to Mina, and he will not know if you are friend or foe. Especially injured, you will be an easy target for him." The cold way Klauth says it makes the scales on the back of my neck stand on edge, sending a shiver running down my spine.

Klauth closes the distance between us, the scent of smoke and metal accompanying him, and caresses my cheek with calloused fingers. "I remember you saying the same thing to me. I remember feeling your pain and your fear and desperation through the shell of my egg and not being able to do anything." He runs the pad of his thumb over my bottom lip, the gentle touch at odds with his powerful presence. "I will temper my old friend's rage when he hatches and protect Abraxis." Klauth kisses my lips softly, his mouth tasting faintly of cinnamon and ash. I feel the truth of his words wash over me like a warm tide.

When we finally break apart, I sigh and lean against his chest, feeling the steady thump of his heart before turning to face Callan, whose expression is grim in the flickering candlelight. "My guard needs to be changed. Yannis has a mate that has eggs." I look down at the worn floorboards, knowing that whoever is chosen will more than likely die. The weight of that knowledge pressing down on my shoulders.

"Fin has no mate, and he's an older guard on the campus. He never took a female and has no one that will mourn him other than us." The way Callan says it, his voice heavy with understanding.

"Be honest with him. Don't hide the fact that he may die protecting me," I whisper as I watch Callan leave the room to find Fin. The door closes behind him with a dull thud. It feels like a lead weight is sitting in my stomach as I think about sentencing this male to death, the bile rising in my throat.

"Mina..." Abraxis approaches, his footsteps light despite his size, and looks up at Klauth. I feel Klauth step back, the warmth of his body receding, and Abraxis takes me in his arms and holds me tight. My head lowers and rests on his shoulder as I close my eyes, inhaling his scent of leather and sweet herbs. "Callan won't lie to him. He will tell him about the dangers of escorting you today, and he will be given a choice." I feel the moment Abraxis wraps his wings around me, the leathery membranes enclosing us in a private sanctuary. The right wing stretches over me easier than the left, its leather brushing softly against my arm.

"I still feel bad. He shouldn't have to get hurt because everyone has lost their minds," I whisper against Abraxis's throat, feeling his body tremble under my lips, his pulse quickening at my touch.

"When does it happen?" Abraxis whispers, his breath warm against my ear.

"This afternoon." Sighing, I tighten my grip on his leathers, the material creaking under my fingers.

The sound of the latch on the door opening crashes through the room like an explosion. Abraxis opens his wings, the rush of cooler air making me shiver. I wipe away the tears with the back of my hand before turning to face Fin, who stands tall in the doorway, shadows playing across his weathered face.

"Your mate told me what's happening, and I accept the dangers involved." Fin straightens his posture and smiles at me, the lines around his eyes deepening.

I nod slowly and suck in a deep breath, trying to settle my nerves, the taste of fear burning on my tongue. "You'll escort me to Malivore in about two hours, then. For now, grab something to eat." I reach into my pocket and pull out one of the tokens I was given to hand out to my personal guards to get the better meals. The metal coin is cool and heavy in my palm. "Meet me downstairs at four." Fin bows after accepting the token, the metal clinking as he pockets it, and leaves the room. The door closing with a soft click behind him.

Abraxis takes my hand, his skin rough against mine, and leads me from the room, my emotions churning like a stormy sea. Maybe a distraction is just what I need, something to quiet the dread that pulses through every fiber of my being.

Abraxis leads me down the hall to his office, his footsteps echoing against the stone floor, mingling with my own. The scent of him—leather, pine, and something uniquely his—surrounds me as he closes the door behind us with a solid click that resonates through the room. The heavy wooden door muffles the sounds from the hallway, creating our own private sanctuary. Before I can say anything, he closes the distance between us in two swift strides and crushes his lips to mine. The taste of cinnamon and something darker, more primal, flooding my senses.

Since the accident, Abraxis has been distant and withdrawn, his eyes avoiding mine, his touch hesitant. Part of me feels like our bond is strained, a once-vibrant connection now dulled and muted. It's moments like this in his arms that it burns bright again, flaring to life like a flame fed oxygen. I feel our hearts beating as one again, the synchronized rhythm pulsing through my veins like liquid fire.

His hands find my hips, fingers digging into the leather with posses-sive urgency as he pushes me backwards until the backs of my legs hit his desk. The edge of the desk digging into my thighs. A soft laugh escapes my lips, the sound surprising even me, as he lifts me to sit on the edge. The polished wood is cool against my skin through my leathers.

"My Mina..." he whispers against my lips, his breath hot and sweet, as his hands move to the buttons on my jacket. The metal fasteners click softly as he works them open one by one. Slowly, he slides the jacket off my shoulders, the material whispering against my skin. He tosses it onto the floor, where it lands with a soft thud.

"Are you sure?" I ask when I can catch my breath, my chest rising and falling rapidly. Gently, I rest both of my hands on his cheeks, feeling the slight stubble beneath my palms, making him look me in my eyes. His skin is warm, almost feverish, and I can feel his pulse racing beneath my fingertips.

"Yes, I've missed you. With everything that's about to happen..." He shakes his head slightly before turning and kissing my palm, his lips soft against my callused skin. "Let me love you how you deserve." Dragon slits rise, eclipsing his eyes, turning the warm amber to reptilian gold that glows in the dim light of the office. I smile, my lips curving upward at the sight. He needs this. The skies may have been stolen from him, but I refuse to be.

Reaching out, I unbuckle and unzip his fighting leathers, the sound of the zipper cutting through the silence, and slide them off of him. The material is stiff under my fingers, worn from battle. He reaches up and rips the tee shirt off his body, the fabric tearing with a satisfying sound, and tosses the tattered remains over his shoulder.

My hands rest on his chest, feeling the rapid beat of his heart and the smooth scars that pepper his skin, iridescent in the slanting afternoon light. He pulls the pins from the ace wrap that binds my chest down; the metal clinking as they fall to the desk, letting the fabric pool around my waist. He stopped questioning why I still did it over a year ago. But now, I think it's more a habit than needed at this point.

He arches a brow at me, a silent question in his transformed eyes. I reach down for my leather pants to get out of them; the material clinging to my skin before finally relenting. It feels like forever since the last time he was this spontaneous, this hungry for me. The second we're both bare, he pulls me to the end of the desk and sinks into me with a groan that reverberates through his chest. He curls over me, his body a protective cage, and I feel every inch of him as he moves, filling me completely. My body feels electric, nerves singing with pleasure as I focus on the warmth flooding me through the bond, a connection that pulses with renewed strength.

Abraxis's wings stretch wide. The membrane is taut and veined, and the claws at the apex dig into the wood of the desk with a splintering crack as he rolls his hips, thrusting into me with a rhythm that matches the pounding of my heart. The scent of arousal hangs heavy in the air, mingling with the musk of leather and the faint tang of the scales that line my spine.

Soft moans escape my lips, the sounds torn from my throat against my will. I feel like he's everywhere, inside me, around me, his scent filling my lungs and his taste lingering on my tongue. I've missed this version of Abraxis, the uninhibited version. The man I first fell in love with is back and holding me tight, his fingers leaving marks on my skin that I'll wear proudly. My fingers thread up into his hair, silky strands wrapping around my digits. I pull his mouth to my throat, the skin there sensitive and tingling in anticipation. I want him to bite me. I need to feel our bond burn bright like it used to, a supernova of connection rather than the dim star it's become.

His lips caress my throat, hot and wet, before I feel his teeth sink in, sharp points breaking the skin with a delicious sting that sends lightning racing down my spine. My orgasm crashes over me like a tidal wave, stealing my breath from me as I cling to him. My nails digging crescents into his shoulders as I ride the waves of pleasure that pulse through me in time with his movements.

When he removes his teeth and licks my wounds, the gentle rasp of his tongue soothing the ache, he lowers his throat to my mouth. I take the hint and sink my teeth back into his original mate mark, tasting the salt of his skin and the copper tang of blood. He growls his release into my hair; the vibration traveling through my body as he shudders above me, his muscles tensing and releasing. His hips buck wildly, chasing his own pleasure, the rhythm erratic and desperate. Eventually he slows, then stops moving and just holds me.

We lie on the desk, him on his forearms over me, our bodies slick with sweat and still joined. A soft laugh escapes his lips as he pulls his wings back. The movement causing the desk to creak in protest, and the sound makes me smile, my lips curving against his shoulder.

"Why are you laughing?" I can't help but smile, watching him push the hair away from his face, the strands clinging to his damp forehead.

"I ruined my desk." He motions above my head and I look at the deep gouges in his desk, splinters of wood jutting from the claw marks that now mar the once-polished surface.

"Yeah, you did. It was worth it." I rise up and kiss his chin playfully until he tilts his head down towards me and captures my lips, his mouth moving against mine with lingering passion.

When he pulls back, a sigh escapes his lips, warm breath fanning across my face. "Let's get you ready." He pulls back and his length falls free, leaving me feeling suddenly empty.

I sit up and slide off the desk, the wood now warm from our bodies, and get dressed again, my fingers fumbling with the fastenings of my clothes. "I so don't want to go. I'm tired of being attacked all the time because of what I am." My voice sounds small, even to my own ears. The vulnerability I try so hard to hide seeping through.

Abraxis hugs me to him, his arms encircling me completely, and I melt into his embrace, breathing in the comforting scent of him mixed with the musk of our lovemaking. "It's almost all over," Abraxis whispers, his lips brushing my temple, sending a shiver down my spine, before leading me out of his office and back to the others to get this whole debacle over with. The warmth of our renewed bond is a small comfort against the coming storm.

green eyes of his, like polished emeralds that somehow convey both danger and devotion. My fingers thread through his hair, soft as silk against my skin.

"What I don't understand is why risk killing Abraxis?" Balor says from the other side of the room. His deep voice resonates in the confined space, sending vibrations through the floorboards. He has Abraxis's wing in his hands, helping him stretch it. The leathery membrane catches the light, revealing a network of half-healed scars that makes my heart clench painfully.

"All the truly dangerous attacks happened after I had Klauth's egg." I tilt my head and stare into Klauth's crimson-flecked amber eyes, which gleam like fire opals in the dim light. The air between us feels charged, electrified with unspoken understanding.

"He saw the possibility of stronger progeny with me, so he was trying to eliminate the in-theory weaker male." After the words leave his lips, Klauth pauses, his jaw tightening visibly. "Sorry, I was speaking tacti-cally from an insane male position." Klauth watches Abraxis's reaction, his body tense as if ready to retract his words.

"We're good," Abraxis says, then winces as Balor puts his wing through the motions. The sound of stretching leather fills the momen-tary silence. "It makes sense. Why keep your powerful daughter bound to a regular mixed-breed black dragon? When she could be bred by a great wyrm red dragon with titanium in his bloodline." Abraxis looks down for a moment, his lashes casting shadows on his cheeks, then back up again. "He went so far as to steal your pregnant mother from another male to have you. I wouldn't put anything past that warped mind of his," Abraxis says clinically. The coldness in his tone doesn't match the pain I see flashing in his eyes. I'm glad he's not taking any of this personally, though the slight tremor in his hands betrays his true feelings.

Leander stands and offers me his hand as Ziggy rises from my lap, the sudden absence of his warmth leaving me chilled. "It's time," Leander says softly as he pulls me into his arms and kisses me. His pillow-soft lips caress mine, and I purr so deeply for him that the vibration travels from my chest to his. His shift calls to mine, a primal recognition that raises goosebumps along my arms, and I smile against his mouth. I pour every ounce of my love for him through the bond we share, feeling it pulse between us like a tangible force, warm and golden.

Lee releases me, his hands lingering on my shoulders for just a moment longer. Ziggy scoops me up, making me laugh as he spins us in a circle before kissing me. The room blurs around us, a kaleidoscope of colors and shapes. We purr together; the sound harmonizing in the quiet room, and smile into our kiss. We rub our faces against each other, and I close my eyes, savoring the feeling of being in his arms. The scrape of his stubble against my cheek is a delicious contrast to the softness of his lips. Ziggy is like a golden retriever, so happy and full of love and light. He reminds me of everything good in the world, his scent a mixture of sunshine and fresh pine.

Callan gently takes me from Ziggy, his hands firm yet tender on my waist, and he cants his head at that angle that irritates the living hell out of me, his neck cracking slightly with the movement. He bursts out laughing, not able to hold that haughty look with me, the sound rich and warm in the tension-filled room. We press our cheeks together as his gryphon whistles and calls for me, a high, melodic sound that resonates in my bones, while I purr in response. The sweet sound of his shift makes my heart swell with joy, a feeling of belonging washing over me like a warm tide.

"It still amazes me how their shifts calling to yours makes you smile so brightly," Klauth says as he walks closer to me and offers me his hand, his palm up and inviting. His footsteps are nearly silent on the carpeted floor, a predator's approach.

"If they didn't love me as much as I love them, I would never hear their shifts. So hearing them brings me joy." I step into Klauth's embrace and press the bridge of my nose under his jaw, purring just for him, inhaling his unique scent of smoke and cinnamon.

He bands his arms tightly around me and holds me flush to his chest, his heartbeat strong and steady against my cheek. "Don't take unnecessary risks, mate. I love you too much to lose you," Klauth's deep voice rumbles, the vibration traveling from his chest to mine. It's the first time he's been this open with his feelings in front of the others. The vulnerability in his usually guarded tone makes my throat tighten with emotion.

I pull back and look into his eyes as they shift to his dragon's; the pupils elongating into slits; the amber darkening to burnt gold as the crimson burns bright. "I love you too. I'll see you soon." Standing on my tiptoes, I kiss his lips, tasting a hint of the coffee he drank earlier. Then pull away to move to Abraxis, the floorboards creaking under my feet.

My eyes search his face, taking in every detail, from the small scar above his left eyebrow to the faint stubble darkening his jaw. I see his bottom lip tremble slightly, a crack in his carefully constructed facade. "You are my first greatest love. Nothing will ever change that. I don't care if you can raze the countryside or have to direct the assault from a desk." My hands frame his face, the skin warm beneath my palms, forcing him to look at me. "I love you because you are a good male. You have always placed my wants and desires before your own." Drawing in a deep breath, the scent of him—leather and sandalwood—filling my lungs. I take a step back out of his reach and drop to my knees before him, and lower my head in complete submission. The hard floor presses against my knees, the discomfort a welcome distraction from the fear churning in my stomach. My hands go behind my back, and I take my left wrist into my right hand. I am finally honoring my mate the way I should have from the beginning. The posture is both foreign and familiar to my body.

I hear Klauth gasp, seeing what I have done, the sharp intake of breath cutting through the silent room. "Don't just stand there—you have the most powerful dragoness at your feet in complete submission. Either accept it or don't, and sever the bond," Klauth says, and Abraxis moves closer, his shadow falling over me. I see his shoes before me, the worn leather scuffed and battle-scarred like its owner. His hand slips under my chin, the calloused fingers gentle against my skin, and I rise at his urging. He crushes his lips to mine, and I can finally breathe, the tight band around my chest loosening. His mouth tastes of mint and promises, familiar yet exciting. Something settles deep within me, a puzzle piece clicking into place. The need to fight is gone, replaced by a sense of rightness that floods my veins.

When Abraxis releases me, his breathing ragged and warm against my cheek, he offers me to Balor. I hesitate for a moment, glancing back to Klauth, then Abraxis, before moving. The air feels thick between us, charged with emotion. I wrap my arms around Balor and hold on for dear life, my fingers digging into the solid muscle of his back. Stepping into his embrace is like coming home after a long day, his body radiating heat like a furnace. He tilts my head back, his fingers gentle on my chin, and kisses me softly, his lips tasting of the sweet wine he favors. When he pulls back, his eyes search mine, their depth containing galaxies of concern and devotion.

"I'll see you soon," he whispers, his breath warm against my lips.

Forcing a smile that doesn't reach my eyes, I turn and walk away from my mates, each step heavier than the last. The sound of my boots on the floor marking my departure like a funeral dirge. The weight of their gazes on my back is almost physical, a pressure between my shoulder blades. I can only hope I live to see them again. The thought sends a chill down my spine despite the warmth of the room. The wooden door handle is cool under my palm as I pull it open, the hinges groaning softly, as if protesting my departure.

FIN IS WAITING for me downstairs several minutes early, his tall form silhouetted against the weak afternoon light filtering through the clouded windows. His leather armor creaks softly as he shifts his weight from one foot to the other, betraying his nervousness despite his composed expression. I lightly touch his elbow, feeling the tension in his muscles beneath my fingertips, and walk past him, heading towards Malivore. The scent of weapon oil and metal clings to him, mingling with the faint aroma of fear that all prey animals recognize instinctively.

I want to talk to him, to get to know him in what little time he may have left, my throat tight with unspoken words. But something deep down stops me, a primal instinct that whispers caution. He knows what may happen to him, and he's at peace with it. I can see it in the resolute set of his jaw, the calm acceptance in his eyes that looks too old for his face.

As we pass the Arcanum campus, the gravel crunching beneath our boots in a rhythmic cadence. I hear the distant call of a crow, harsh and grating against the unnatural silence that has fallen around us. The sound raises goosebumps along my arms despite the warmth of the day. Glancing to my right, I see Rebel landing on the ledge just under the roof, his ebony feathers gleaming like oil in the sunlight. At least he's following me like he's supposed to be. I draw a small measure of comfort from his presence, my heartbeat steadying slightly at the sight of him.

Once we're clear of the campus, the scales on the back of my neck stand on edge, a tingling sensation that travels down my spine like ice water. The air around us feels charged, too still, as if the world is holding its breath. "Get ready..." I whisper to Fin to warn him, my voice barely audible even to my own ears. His nod is imperceptible, just a slight dip of his chin. I see his muscles tense beneath his armor, the leather tightening across his shoulders as he readies himself for what's to come. The metallic taste of adrenaline floods my mouth, sharp and bitter.

Out of nowhere, three people charge us as we get closer to the southern dorms, their boots kicking up dust that catches in the sunlight like golden specks. Their faces are contorted with hatred, teeth bared in snarls that make them look more beast than human. The sound of their approach shatters the silence—heavy breathing, the clatter of weapons being drawn, a guttural battle cry that sends birds scattering from nearby trees. Fin draws his short swords in one fluid motion, the metallic ring of steel cutting through the air like a physical presence. An arch of crimson blood flies past my face, warm droplets spattering against my cheek like macabre raindrops, as he decapitates one of the attackers. The wet, meaty thud of the head hitting the ground turns my stomach. But there's no time to react.

The first part of my vision has happened, the recognition flashing through my mind with crystal clarity, then pain blooms at the back of my head as I am struck from behind. The impact resonates through my skull like a bell being rung, white-hot agony spreading outward in pulsing waves. The coppery scent of my blood fills my nostrils as warm wetness trickles down my neck. My world tilts on axis, the ground, and sky trading places in a nauseating swirl of color and shadow. Fin's shout sounds distant and distorted, as if I'm underwater. His face—a mask of horror and rage—is the last thing I see before everything goes black, darkness closing in from all sides like a smothering blanket.

THE FRIGID, damp air seeps into my bones as I lie motionless on the hard ground, straining my ears to catch the faintest sounds around me.

Distant whispers float through the air, their source obscured by the vast expanse separating us. Cautiously, I crack open the eye closest to the earth, surveying my surroundings through the narrowest slit. Recognition dawns as I take in the ancient burial grounds on the peninsula, the crumbling remains of Klauth's castle looming in the distance.

I vaguely recall seeing this place marked on one of the countless maps my father painstakingly created of the campus grounds. Instinctively, I reach out with my mind, desperate to connect with Klauth, but my efforts are met with a chilling void. The silence in my head is deafening, the comforting presence of my mates' bonds now eerily absent. Whatever has been done to me has severed our connection, leaving me isolated and vulnerable.

The crunch of approaching footsteps shatters the eerie calm, accompanied by the sound of voices growing louder with each passing second. "Time to check on our guest." Lysander's cruel tone slices through the air, sending icy tendrils of fear racing down my spine.

"What if the king finds out?" The second voice is all too familiar—Professor Kai Martz, the manticore science teacher.

Lysander's laughter, cold and malicious, echoes off of the ancient stones. "He won't. She's going to have a choice. Accept me as a mate or die by my hands, which will kill the King. Or drive him mad, and the mages will imprison him again. This time, we'll dump his egg in the ocean."

As they draw nearer, I focus on remaining perfectly still, my breathing shallow and controlled. Playing dead was one of the first lessons my father drilled into me, a skill I pray Lysander is unaware of.

"Make her stand." Lysander's hiss sends prickles of dread across my skin, my heart plummeting as the realization hits me.

Fuck... He knows.

mahogany desk. My stomach turns as I see what's clutched in her talons—Lemon's severed head, its fur matted with dark, congealing blood. The metallic tang of it fills my nostrils as Iris deposits her grisly trophy on the polished surface. She prances about, head held high, wings partially unfurled in a display of predatory pride.

"You did a wonderful job, Iris. Excellent kill," Klauth praises, his long fingers reaching for a piece of dried jerky from the glass container atop the desk. The container clinks against the wood as he removes the lid, the smell of preserved meat mingling with the coppery scent of blood.

Across from me, Ziggy's face contorts in confusion, his brow furrowing as he eyes the gruesome remains. "Why did she kill Lemon?" The question hangs in the stale air between us.

"She was told if Lemon went after Rebel, she was to kill Lemon on sight," Abraxis explains, his voice softening as he reaches out to stroke Iris's sleek back. His fingers tremble slightly against her scales. "Thank you for keeping Rebel safe," he murmurs, the tenderness in his tone contrasting with the tension radiating from his body.

Iris turns to Klauth, her sharp chirps cutting through the heavy silence. I watch as Klauth's body goes rigid, his eyes widening, pupils dilating until they almost swallow the iris. "Mina's calm for the most part." His fingers dig into the armrests of his chair, knuckles whitening. "She's been knocked out." His gaze darts frantically around the office, unfocused yet searching. "Three just attacked them."

I lurch toward the door, my heartbeat thundering in my ears, blood rushing so fast I feel lightheaded. The floor seems to tilt beneath my feet as panic claws at my chest. "Where are they?" My voice cracks, betraying my fear.

The sudden weight of Balor's hand on my shoulder stops me cold, his grip firm enough to bruise. His skin radiates an unnatural chill that seeps through my shirt. "They won't kill her. They need her for something." His breath ghosts across my ear as he leans closer, whispering words meant only for me. "It's either to force her to bond with the phylactery, which she has to do willingly, or they're going to make her take another mate. Which means they'll have to hunt and kill us." A twisted smile plays upon Balor's thin lips, a glint of anticipation in his eyes at the prospect of being hunted.

"Thauglor hasn't awakened yet, so she's not in imminent danger," I point out, my gaze falling upon the cream-colored envelope Mina left behind. Before anyone can intervene, I snatch it up, my hands trembling so badly I nearly tear the paper as I extract the sheet within. The faint scent of Mina's perfume—jasmine and something uniquely her—rises from the page, making my throat tighten with longing.

> Leander, I know you couldn't resist looking. Your ability to read a situation and people is your greatest gift. Right now, you need to trust the others in the nest. Put your faith in Balor that he will find and save me. Trust Klauth to help control Thauglor. Abraxis needs you now more than ever. He's going to feel useless. Little secret: Abraxis and Balor have the strongest bonds with me. Klauth's is powerful, but not in the same sense as theirs. Watch them, support them. Above all else, don't let Iris eat Lemon's head—she'll be sick everywhere.
>
> With love,
>
> Mina

I pass the note to Balor, then quickly dispose of Lemon's head, wrapping it in several layers of paper from Callan's desk. My fingers come away sticky with blood, and I wipe them on my dark jeans, leaving faint smudges. As Balor reads Mina's words, his face hardens into an unreadable mask. I've seen him like this only once before when we were cornered during the territorial war, and something primal and ancient surfaced in him.

He hands the note to Abraxis before moving to stand by the window overlooking the courtyard. The glass is cool against his forehead as he presses against it, his breath fogging the pane. Another hour crawls by in suffocating silence, and none of us can sense Mina through our bonds. Fear coils in my gut like a venomous serpent, but we heed her words and wait.

"Why did she mention dusk?" I wonder aloud, my voice startling in the quiet room. The words barely leave my mouth when movement in the courtyard catches my eye. Fin is being carried through the iron gates, his clothing torn and blood-soaked. We rush down the stairs, our footsteps echoing off the stone walls as we race to meet him as he's taken to the infirmary.

"Where's Mina?" Abraxis demands, his voice raw with barely contained emotion. The veins in his neck stand out prominently as he looms over Fin's prone form.

"Taken," Fin gasps, his face ashen, lips tinged blue. The acrid smell of sweat and fear clings to him. "I killed two of the bastards. Kai was with them." Fin's eyes lock with Abraxis's, a deep growl rumbling in his throat, the sound vibrating through the air between them.

"That fucking bastard!" Abraxis roars, his rage palpable in the small room. His body trembles with barely contained fury, his fingernails digging crescents into his palms.

Ziggy's fingers twitch at his sides, his face a mask of determination. "Did you see which way they took her?" The urgency in his voice matches the rapid rise and fall of his chest.

"Towards the ruins. Or the water. The general direction of the ruins from Malivore." Fin's voice softens, his words slurring slightly as his strength wanes. "I did the best I could." He clutches his side, blood seeping between his fingers, the crimson liquid stark against his pale skin. The metallic scent of it fills the room, making my stomach clench.

"Mina will be pleased you didn't die," I offer gently, trying to keep my voice steady despite the fear threatening to overwhelm me. "Rest and heal. We'll find Mina." I pat his shoulder as the medical team whisks him deeper into the infirmary, the wheels of the gurney squeaking against the polished floor.

"We have a direction," I say, turning to the others. My heart pounds against my ribs as determination replaces fear. "Maybe we can get to the shore across from the ruins on the mainland?" I glance at Ziggy, who nods, his jaw set with resolve as we prepare to depart in pairs, the taste of vengeance already bitter on my tongue.

As Ziggy finishes bringing the entire nest to the shore across from the crumbling ruins of Klauth's once-grand castle, frustration simmers in my veins like acid. The sharp tang of salt water fills my nostrils, mixing with the scent of decaying vegetation along the shoreline. Icy wind whips across my face, carrying the promise of rain. Behind us, the setting sun bleeds crimson across the horizon, its dying light casting long, distorted shadows over the landscape. Waves crash against the jagged rocks below with increasing violence, as if nature itself shares our agitation. The thunderous sound reverberates through my chest, each impact a grim reminder of what awaits below—ancient crypts carved into the very bedrock, holding secrets darker than the waters that surround us.

"What are we waiting for?" I demand, my voice tinged with exasperation. My boots sink slightly into the damp sand as I shift my weight, muscles tense and ready for action. In the distance, Abraxis's familiar Rebel, circles over what appears to be the entrance to an ancient cave system, his dark form stark against the slate-gray sky. The harsh cries of seagulls punctuate the heavy silence between us.

Klauth reaches inside his weathered leather jacket, producing a second envelope. The paper is slightly yellowed at the edges, bearing the faint scent of jasmine—Mina's scent. He hands it to me with a solemn nod, his eyes reflecting the turbulent waters of the bay. I open it slowly, the sound of tearing paper unnaturally loud in the coastal quiet. My fingers tremble slightly as I extract another letter penned by Mina, her elegant handwriting instantly recognizable.

> Guys,
>
> I know this must be frustrating, but I need you to have patience. We need to know who all is involved in what's happening at the academy. There are several things I haven't seen: why you can't sense me and who on the staff is helping Lysander. We suspect Isobel, but have no proof. Listen for Thauglor. When you hear him, unleash Balor.
>
> I love you,
> Mina

I stare at her words, the paper heavy in my hands, the ink slightly smudged where her pen lingered too long. My throat constricts as I pass the letter to Balor, watching his expression darken like the gathering storm clouds above us.

"This is fucking insane!" he hisses, his eyes flashing with barely contained rage. A vein pulses prominently at his temple as he thrusts the note towards Klauth. The paper crinkling in his white-knuckled grip.

"Our mate has a plan," Klauth says, his voice measured but tight with strain as he motions across the bay to the ruins of his former home.

The broken stones rise like jagged teeth against the horizon, dark and forbidding. "I just hope it doesn't backfire on her. Ziggy, please get us over there, just in case we need to move quickly."

Ziggy nods, his face grim. The sound of waves crashing against the rocks below intensifies as we approach the ruins, the stone path slick and treacherous beneath our feet. Each thunderous collision sends tremors through the ground, as if the sea itself tries to breach the ancient barriers that separate it from the crypts below.

The setting sun casts its last rays through the broken arches of the ruins, painting everything in a bloody glow that makes the shadows seem alive and writhing. In a matter of moments, we find ourselves standing before the gaping maw of the tunnel entrance. The damp, musty smell of the earth fills my nostrils, mingled with the metallic scent of minerals seeping through the stone walls and something else —something older and more primal that raises the hairs on the back of my neck. Droplets of water fall rhythmically from the ceiling, each one striking the ground with a soft, hollow sound that echoes through the darkness, like the ghostly footsteps of those long buried beneath our feet.

"If she's in the catacombs, it will take some doing to dig down to where she is," Klauth says, his breath forming small clouds in the cold air. The tunnel before us seems to swallow all light, an abyss of darkness stretching endlessly downward.

"I can find her," Balor declares, his voice rough with determination. The muscles in his jaw work beneath his skin as he stares into the darkness, shoulders tense and coiled with pent-up energy.

"I know you can." I reach out, resting a hand on his shoulder, feeling the hard knots of tension beneath his jacket. His skin radiates an unnatural heat, fever-hot even through the thick fabric. Balor's gaze meets mine briefly, his eyes reflecting the dim light like a predator's, before dropping to the ground. A small muscle twitches beneath his left eye, betraying his barely contained fury.

"Klauth, can we send him down to watch from the shadows, just in case she needs him sooner?" I glance at Klauth, my hand still on Balor's shoulder, feeling the slight tremor running through him. My mouth tastes bitter with anxiety, heart hammering against my ribs so hard I wonder if the others can hear it.

"Do it," Klauth commands, his voice echoing off the stone walls. "Balor, get down there and do whatever is needed to keep Mina safe until Thauglor can get to you."

It's as if a fire has been lit beneath Balor. He shifts immediately, his form melting and transforming before our eyes. His skin ripples and hardens, taking on the scaled pattern of his basilisk form. The sound of bones cracking and reforming fills the air as his face contorts, jaws extending to reveal rows of razor-sharp teeth. Within seconds, the man is gone, replaced by the massive serpentine form of his basilisk. The creature slithers into the dark opening of the cavern leading to the catacombs, scales scraping softly against stone as he disappears into the shadows. The rhythmic sound of his powerful body moving deeper into the darkness fades, until all I can hear is the steady drip of water and my own ragged breathing.

I watch as he vanishes completely into the darkness, a knot of unease tightening in the pit of my stomach. The air feels colder suddenly, raising goosebumps along my arms beneath my sleeves.

"What's that look for?" Abraxis asks, moving closer, his boots scraping against the rocky ground. His brow furrows with concern, deep lines etching themselves around his mouth. The scent of his cologne—sandalwood and something sharper, more primal—wafts toward me as he leans in.

"I feel like we should be doing more," I confess, kicking at the loose rocks at my feet. They skitter across the stone floor, the sound echoing off the walls like tiny gunshots. My fingers flex and curl at my sides, nails digging half-moons into my palms. "Standing here while she's in danger is torture."

Abraxis sighs, his gaze fixed on the tunnel that swallowed Balor. His breath mingles with mine in the cold air. "Trust me, we would be if it weren't for Lysander being a basilisk in a small containment area. The odds of being turned to stone are very high in this situation."

I nod, understanding the danger, but it does little to quell the restless energy thrumming through my body. The taste of fear is metallic on my tongue, my mouth dry despite the dampness of our surroundings. The weight of Mina's absence feels like a physical thing, a hollowness beneath my ribs that aches with each breath.

All I can do is hope that Mina's plan succeeds and that we'll be reunited with her soon. The alternative is too painful to consider. I press my palm against the cold stone wall, feeling its ancient strength, and send a silent prayer to whatever god might be listening: *Bring her back to us.* Outside, the last sliver of sun disappears beyond the horizon, plunging the world into twilight. The waves crescendo against the cliffs in a deafening roar, as if announcing the coming of night. Standing here, with tons of earth and stone between us and the crypts below, I can't shake the feeling that we're merely scratching the surface of something vast and malevolent—a darkness that has waited patiently for centuries, and now stirs at the presence of Mina in its domain.

Lysander's words hit me like a sledgehammer, the impact stealing my breath more effectively than a physical blow. The cold realization spreads through my veins like ice water—the male I killed was his son. The taste of bile rises in my throat, acidic and bitter. "What happened to having dragon-kin?" My voice sounds hollow even to my own ears, bouncing off the stone walls around us.

"Lies. Dragon kin are produced when the pair are not mates." He hisses, the sound sharp and grating in the enclosed space, and his serpentine tongue flickers out, tasting the air near me. I can feel the slight disturbance in the air it creates unnervingly close to my skin. "You should go into heat again sooner than later. Such perfect timing." His words repulse me to the point I shiver, goosebumps rising along my arms despite the damp heat of the cavern.

"I'll never give you hatchlings." I turn my head away from him, the muscles in my neck protesting the movement, and catch the momentary glow of red eyes in the darkness, like burning coals nestled in shadow. The scale on the back of my neck warms slightly, a pleasant heat against my otherwise chilled skin, and my breath catches in my throat, heart skipping a beat. Balor is here. The faint, familiar scent of him—earth and smoke and something uniquely his—reaches me even through the stale cavern air, so subtle I might have imagined it.

"See, that's where you're wrong. You have three choices. Provide me heirs, bind your soul to a vessel and become a dracolich, or simply die a slow, horrible death in my coils." He lunges forward, the air displacing with a whoosh, and grips my jaw, his fingers digging painfully into my skin, forcing me to face him. His breath washes over me, hot and smelling of rotting meat and something chemical I can't identify. "You already have one basilisk in the nest. Why not add a different subspecies?"

"Subspecies?" Out of habit, I make my scales rise over my ribs and up my throat just in case, feeling them shift and overlap beneath my skin with a sensation like thousands of tiny razors sliding into place. The sound they make is imperceptible to human ears, but to me, it's a soft, comforting rasp, like chain mail settling. Slowly, they spread down and over my soft stomach to protect my intestines, the weight of them reassuring.

"Balor isn't the only type of basilisk out there. Mine is admittedly smaller, but no less deadly." His eyes are more of a red-orange when they shift to his basilisk's, the pupils narrowing to vertical slits as they focus on me with predatory intensity. The air between us seems to thicken, becoming harder to breathe.

Reaching deep within myself, I am just starting to feel my dragoness again, a warm, familiar presence unfurling in my core, and the faint echoes of my bonds to my mates. Each connection feels distinct—one a cool, steady pulse, another a gentle warmth, a third a rhythmic thrum. I find the one that seems like it's burning, a connection that sears through my consciousness like a brand, and push as much energy towards it as I can, the effort making my temples throb. *'Come to me...'* I call down that bond, hoping beyond hope it's Thauglor's. "I'm too young to bear offspring safely." I fight for control of my head, trying to pull away from him, the bones in my jaw creaking under his grip.

"Another myth. As soon as the first heat hits, a female is breedable. You simply need to lay your eggs as your dragon to survive." Lysander says, his voice taking on a lecturing tone that makes my skin crawl. His fingers tighten on my face, leaving bruises I can already feel forming.

Fuck, he knows... My heart sinks, the heavy weight of dread settling in my stomach like a stone. I stare into his eyes as coldly as possible. I try to mask the fear I know he can probably smell on me, sour and sharp. "I would rather die than breed with you." I growl at him, the sound rumbling deep in my chest, and spit in his face. The glob of saliva lands on his cheek, sliding down slowly. Flat palm, I hit his chest as hard as I can, the impact jarring up my arm. What I wouldn't give to have my talons right now, to feel them slice through his flesh. What the hell did he give me to keep me from shifting? My skin itches with the need to transform, to tear him apart scale by scale.

"Fucking bitch." He backhands me across my face, the crack of his palm against my cheek echoing in the cavern. Pain explodes across my face, bright and hot, as I go sprawling. The ground is rough beneath me, scraping my palms and knees as I land, the taste of copper flooding my mouth where my teeth cut the inside of my cheek. When I look up, blinking away stars, I see Balor watching from the shadows, his six eyes glowing with barely contained rage. I shake my head slightly, telling him no. *Not yet. Wait for the right moment.*

Lysander rips me up off the ground by my hair, each individual strand feeling like it might tear from my scalp. Pain lances across my head, bringing tears to my eyes that I refuse to let fall. "I guess you choose death. Your father will be so disappointed." Manic laughter escapes his lips, high and unhinged, and I feel a shiver move down my scales along my spine, the sensation both foreign and familiar. I believe he's finally lost it. "He told me you would choose me over death." The laughter continues as his eyes flicker between human and serpentine, never quite settling on one form. The surrounding air seems to waver, as if reality itself is struggling to contain him. Lysander has finally become unhinged, and I'm in the hands of a madman. The realization is more terrifying than any physical threat.

Before I can say anything, Lysander's form contorts, bones cracking and reshaping with wet, sickening pops as he shifts to his basilisk. His serpentine form isn't as long as Balor's, and his scales are large plates versus heavily armored scales, gleaming dully in the dim light. His basilisk only has two eyes instead of six, but they burn with malevolent intelligence as they fix on me. He coils around me slowly, the scales rough against my skin through my clothing, starting to crush. The pressure builds gradually, pushing the air from my lungs in small, desperate gasps.

An enraged roar echoes down the tunnel, the sound so powerful I feel it vibrate in my chest cavity. I smile, my split lip stinging with the movement. I call back as loud as I can, a primal sound of defiance and recognition, before Lysander tightens his coils around me. Gasping, I wiggle, fighting for breath, the edges of my vision darkening. I manage to get myself into a position lined up with one of his larger scale plates that allows me to catch my breath a little. The small pocket of space is a momentary reprieve. The sounds of something clawing at the earth echoes through the chamber as dirt falls from the ceiling, raining down on us like fine brown snow, filling my nose with the scent of loam and minerals.

I turn my head slowly in the direction where I last saw Balor, each movement an agony of careful precision, and mouth **NOW** to him, my lips forming the word with deliberate clarity. Before I can blink, his basilisk launches out of the darkness, a blur of coiled muscle and gleaming scales striking Lysander just below his head. The impact sends vibrations through Lysander's body and into mine, his surprise manifesting as a high-pitched hiss that hurts my ears. Lysander uncoils a little bit, though still not enough for me to get free, his muscles rippling beneath his scales in confusion.

Balor coils up again, his massive form gathering potential energy like a spring, and strikes at Lysander. The sound of scale tearing from scale a horrific screech that sets my teeth on edge. The scent of reptilian blood fills the air, coppery and alien. I can almost shift my hands now, feeling the familiar burn as my talons begin to push through my fingertips. The sensation is both painful and welcome. My talons almost extend fully, the sharp points catching the dim light. Once they can, I'll be able to cut my way free, the thought filling me with savage anticipation.

Balor's basilisk keeps striking at Lysander's smaller basilisk, the impact of scale against scale echoing through the cavernous space like thunder. His massive body moves with deadly precision until Lysander's coils loosen enough that I can crawl free. My skin is scraped raw where the rough scales had pressed against me. Panting, I move off to the side to catch my breath, my lungs burning with each desperate inhale of the damp, musty air. The stone floor is cold beneath my palms and knees, gritty with dirt and age-old dust that clings to my sweat-slicked skin.

Something has shifted inside me—I can feel my mates again, each connection distinct and vibrant. The bond with Abraxis pulses cool and steady like a mountain stream, while Ziggy's flutters with anxious energy. Whatever Lysander gave me is almost completely out of my system, the drug's haze lifting from my mind like morning fog burning away. Klauth's tether burns bright, a searing presence in my consciousness, and I feel a surge of power through it, hot and insistent. He's trying to force my shift to save us, his desperation a tangible force through our connection. The next surge burns through me, even more powerful, and it's not from Klauth but from Thauglor. He roars again. The sound is so powerful it rattles my teeth and vibrates through my bones. More dirt falls down into the catacombs, pattering on the stone floor like rain.

The first glimpse of his white maw peeks through the dirt above us, massive teeth gleaming like polished ivory in the dim light. My chest constricts, heart hammering against my ribs. "Balor!" I yell at the top of my lungs, my voice raw and cracking, just as my shift overtakes me. The transformation ripples through me—bones cracking and reforming, skin stretching to accommodate my larger form as my dragoness emerges. The pain is exquisite and familiar, a burning rush that consumes me from within before subsiding to a dull throb. I barely fit down here in the confined space, my wings pressed uncomfortably against my sides, scales scraping against the ancient stone.

I crawl to the area with the highest ceiling, talons gouging deep furrows into the floor, and it's still not enough—I can't stand up. My head brushes the ceiling, sending more dirt and small rocks showering down. The air is thick with dust, making my nostrils flare as I struggle not to sneeze. Balor strikes Lysander again, the wet sound of tearing flesh accompanying the ripping of a sizable chunk of scales off the smaller basilisk. Blood spatters across the floor, dark and viscous, filling the air with its metallic tang before Balor slithers quickly towards me, his body a sinuous blur of motion. I lift a wing; the membrane stretching tight, and he darts under quickly. I feel him shift back to his human form beneath the protective canopy of my wing, his body heat radiating against my side as I pull my wing tight to my body.

The loudest roar I can muster escapes my maw, the sound reverberating through the chamber and making small pebbles dance across the floor. I crawl backwards towards where Thauglor's maw is breaking through the ceiling, my tail sweeping behind me, knocking against sarcophagi and sending them crashing to the ground. The sound of crumbling stone grows louder as huge black talons reach down and rip upward, taking a massive chunk of earth with them. The scent of freshly turned soil fills the chamber, rich and loamy, mingling with the sharp scent of male dragon musk.

Lysander's basilisk is wounded but not badly enough that it's stopped trying to fight. He slithers slowly towards us, his movements jerky and uncoordinated. Balor's strikes must have damaged muscles. Blood trails behind him, a dark, glistening path that marks his progress across the stone floor. By the time he's halfway to us, Thauglor has his entire face in the catacombs, the massive white scales around his maw gleaming with an iridescent sheen in the dim light. His eyelids are shut tight, leathery folds sealed against the dirt and debris. I feel his presence tickling the back of my head, a light pressure that seems to ask permission.

Relaxing, I let him see through my eyes, our connection strengthening until I can feel his rage burning alongside mine. His mouth opens like a blackened abyss, rows of dagger-like teeth catching what little light there is. His long, sinuous forked tongue curls out, tasting the air, sensing the location of his prey. A pop and a hiss can be heard, like the sound of pressure being released, before a torrent of green gaseous acid escapes his lips. The air immediately fills with an acrid smell that burns my nostrils and makes my eyes water. Within seconds, Lysander is bathed in the acid, and I watch in horrified fascination as his flesh melts slowly off of his bones. The sound is worst of all—a bubbling, hissing sizzle accompanied by a high-pitched keening that I realize is Lysander's death cry.

I lay there in awe, feeling Balor's rapid heartbeat against my side through my scales, seeing the full magnitude of what a great wyrm black dragon can do. His acid hits and rolls off of my scales harmlessly, the droplets beading up and sliding away like water off oiled leather. I dare not move until Lysander is reduced to a pile of molten goop and bones on the ground. The stench of dissolved flesh and acid filling the chamber with an unbearable stench. The last of him—a segment of spine collapses with a wet splash into the bubbling puddle that was once a living being. All that's left is his skull, empty eye sockets staring into the abyss.

As I crawl through the acid on the floor, the caustic liquid making small popping sounds beneath my weight. Thankfully, it cannot penetrate my thick scales. I make my way to the hole that Thauglor made. The edges are rough and uneven, dirt still crumbling down in small cascades. When I can, I rise up onto my hind legs, muscles straining with effort, and start climbing up the tunnel he dug. My talons find purchase in the soft earth, pulling me upward toward freedom. The scent of salt water and dragon musk fills the air as I near the surface, growing stronger with each foot I climb. The clean, open smell of the ocean breeze mingles with Thauglor's distinctive scent—like thunderstorms and ancient forests. Freedom has never smelt so good. The promise of open sky and unfettered flight makes my heart soar even before my body can follow.

Thauglor growls deep, the sound so low it's almost subsonic, more felt than heard, vibrating through the ground beneath my talons. His eyes track Balor's movements, pupils narrowing to dangerous slits. I move to block his line of sight and growl low in response. The sound rumbling up from my chest like distant thunder. I raise my scales and frill, each plate sliding into place with a soft rasp that sends shivers down my spine. Fanning my wings out wide, the membranes stretching taut with a sound like leather being pulled. I use them to shield my other mates. The air around us crackles with tension, hot and electric.

I can feel the moment the lightning starts arching over my scales and up my frill to my horns. The energy raising the fine scales along my frill, making every nerve ending tingle with power. No one, not even another mate, will threaten what's mine. Baring my teeth, I roar at Thauglor, the sound tearing from my throat with enough force to shake the leaves from nearby trees. Lightning strikes the soil at his feet with a deafening crack, the acrid smell of scorched earth rising instantly. Thauglor leaps back, his massive form surprisingly agile, tail whipping behind him and sending rocks scattering.

"Oh, shit..." Ziggy says from somewhere behind me, his voice high with tension. The scent of his fear reaches me, sharp and pungent, mixing with the charged air.

Klauth chooses now to shift back, bones cracking and reforming with wet sounds. He stands between us, his bare chest gleaming with sweat in the sunlight. "Settle, he doesn't mean any harm. He has no solid bond with you, and another male threatens him." His voice is calm but firm, a steadying presence in the chaos.

Growling again, I snap at the air, clacking my jaws in threat. The sound is like stone striking stone, echoing across the clearing. *'He needs to shift back before I will,'* I toss at Klauth mentally, still staring Thauglor down. I have Abraxis and the rest of my mates behind me, their scents mingling with mine. After being bathed in acid in order to dispose of Lysander, I'm a little pissy, my scales still tingling from the exposure.

Thauglor lunges forward, his jaws open wide, revealing rows of gleaming teeth. I lower my head, letting my long spiral horns embed in the roof of his mouth with a sickening crunch. He reels back, shaking his head, blood dripping out of his mouth and spattering the ground like crimson rain. The metallic scent fills the air, sharp and primal. I growl again and clack my jaws once more, the sound decisive and threatening. I may not be as big as the two great wyrm mates in this nest, but I will not chance my other mates getting hurt. I don't raise my head to appear dominant, but I hold my ground, protecting what's mine. My tail lashes behind me, sending dirt and small rocks flying.

The standoff lasts for what feels like hours, tension thick enough to cut with a talon. The only sounds are our breathing—mine controlled and steady. Thauglor's is heavier and more labored—and the occasional shift of weight, claws scraping against stone. Finally, Thauglor relents and shifts back, his massive form contracting with a series of pops and creaks.

My first thought is that he's handsome. Thick shoulders, just as broad as Abraxis's and Vaughn's, tapering to a narrow waist. His skin is a deep bronze, stretched over defined muscle. His hair is as black as the void, similar to Ziggy's displacer beast form, falling in thick waves to his shoulders. It's his eyes that catch me off guard. They are as blue as the ocean on a summer day, flecked with gold around the pupils. They seem to hold centuries of knowledge, ancient and knowing.

He takes a knee before my dragoness and rests his forearms over the raised knee, his muscles flexing with the movement. He spreads his wings wide, showing off their span and strength, the leathery membranes catching the light in iridescent shimmers. "Mate, will you please honor me by allowing me to see your human side?" He lowers his head and closes his eyes, exposing the vulnerable nape of his neck, a gesture of submission that speaks volumes.

I glance over at Klauth, who seems to be in a state of shock, his usual composure replaced by wide-eyed wonder. Slowly, I turn my head to look at Abraxis, and he nods, the slight movement carrying his trust and approval. I shift back to my human form, the transformation rippling through me in waves of hot and cold sensation. My bones contract, scales receding beneath my skin with a feeling like thousands of tiny pinpricks. I roll my shoulders, working out the tension, and let out a long breath. My leathers thankfully are fully intact, the smell of my sweat rising from them. I move to stand before Thauglor, my boots silent against the grass-covered earth.

His huge obsidian wings are spread wide in submission. He wants to be inspected, the veins visible beneath the thin membrane catching the sunlight. Slowly I circle him, looking every inch of him over, noting the scars that tell stories of ancient battles, the way his muscles shift beneath his skin with each breath. Here is a powerful ancient at my feet because he comes from a time when females were revered and honored. The realization sends a shiver of power through me, heady and intoxicating.

When I am done looking at him, I drop to my knees before him, the soft earth cool against my skin. His eyes are still closed, thick lashes casting shadows on his high cheekbones. I scoot closer, the leather of my pants creaking slightly, and press the bridge of my nose under his jaw. The contact sends a jolt through me, his skin warm and smooth against mine. I breathe in his scent, memorizing it—the scent just before it rains and something darker, more primal. Thauglor gasps, the sound sharp in the quiet. I feel his body shudder from the contact, a tremor that passes from him to me. I withdraw slowly and tilt my head to the side, exposing my neck in a gesture of trust. "Look at me, mate," I whisper, the words barely audible even to my sensitive ears.

His eyes pop open, the blue startling in its intensity, and he just stares at me. I can see my reflection in them, small and fierce. His mouth works, trying to form words several times and failing, his throat working with each attempt. I glance over at Klauth and offer him my hand to have him help me up, the movement deliberate and unhurried.

Thauglor is on his feet in seconds, moving with a speed that belies his size, scooping me up in his arms and crushing me to him. The sudden movement forces the air from my lungs in a surprised gasp. His body is hard against mine, radiating heat like a furnace.

"My mate," he breathes, the words reverent and filled with wonder. He buries his face in my long hair and breathes in deeply, his chest expanding against mine. I wrap my arms around him and rest my head against his, holding him tightly. His heartbeat thunders against my chest, matching the rhythm of my own. In this moment, despite all the danger we've faced, I feel strangely at peace, complete in a way I hadn't realized I was missing.

I REMAIN in Thauglor's embrace for a lot longer than expected. His heartbeat a steady rhythm against my chest, his skin radiating heat that seeps through my leathers and warms me to the bone. The scent of him—petrichor and ancient stone, with undertones of something primal and untamed—fills my lungs with each breath. I mouth to Ziggy to take everyone except Klauth home, his sharp eyes catching my silent command from across the clearing. Thauglor doesn't need to know that Abraxis may never fly again. That wound is still too fresh, too raw to expose to a new mate.

"We need to fly to my nest," I whisper near his ear, my lips brushing against the sensitive skin there. I feel him shiver in response, his arms tightening around me momentarily.

Reluctantly, he lowers me down his body until my feet hit the ground, the friction between us sending sparks of electricity dancing across my skin. The earth feels cool and solid beneath my boots after the warmth of his embrace.

"I need to mark you, mate," Thauglor rumbles as he kisses my jaw, his voice vibrating through me like distant thunder. His lips are surprisingly soft against my skin. A gentle contrast to the power I can feel coiled within him, ready to strike.

I roll my head to the side, baring the left side of my throat to him, the skin there tingling in anticipation. My pulse quickens, fluttering visibly beneath the surface. My eyes lock on Klauth as I wait for Thauglor to mark me, seeking reassurance from my established mate. The air between us feels charged, heavy with unspoken promises.

"You bear many bites, mate," Thauglor rumbles as he kisses my throat where he intends to bite me, his breath hot against my skin. His finger traces the scars left by my other mates, each touch sending a shiver down my spine.

"Our mate has built herself a powerful nest. Offensively and defensively, it's extremely well thought out," Klauth says as he moves closer, his footsteps barely audible on the soft earth. The familiar scent of him —smoke and cinnamon—mingles with Thauglor's, creating a heady mixture that makes my head swim. Klauth's hand threads up and into my hair until he can grab one of my horns. The sensitive base sends a jolt of pleasure through my body at his touch. A deep purr escapes my lips as I stare into his crimson-flecked amber eyes, the gold, and red dancing like flames in the fading light.

"I can taste her power for one so young. We are lucky," Thauglor murmurs, his voice laced with reverence and hunger. Without further warning, he sinks his teeth into my throat, and I feel his strength bleeding into me, hot and electric. My body arches in his arms as his teeth dig into my flesh, the sharp pain giving way to waves of pleasure that radiate outward from the point of contact. Every moment he holds onto me, the more his power flows into me, filling every space within me. It feels as if every synapse is firing faster than a lightning strike, my skin buzzing with energy. When he releases me, I'm breathless, trying to find my footing. My head swims from the feeling of being remade, colors more vibrant, sounds sharper, scents richer than before.

"You need to bite me as well, mate," Thauglor says, his voice low, oozing of sex and bad decisions. The timbre of it slides over my skin like dark silk, a tangible caress. If there was a type that my mother would have warned me to steer clear of, it definitely would be Thauglor. His blue eyes have darkened to the color of a storm-tossed ocean, pupils dilated with desire.

"I do..." I sound breathy, almost attention-starved, my voice unrecognizable to my own ears. His fingers thread through my hair, replacing Klauth's grip on me, the slight tug sending shivers of anticipation down my spine. He directs me to the left side of his throat, the bronze skin there smooth and unmarked, pulsing with the rhythm of his heart.

I bite him without hesitation, my teeth breaking through his skin with a satisfying give. My heart thunders in my chest, the sound filling my ears as his ichor fills my mouth, bursting on my tongue with the mixed flavor of iron and copper, with undertones of something ancient and powerful. I swallow down every gulp until every cell in my body feels supercharged, my limbs tingling with newfound strength. Carefully, I withdraw my teeth and lick the wound clean. The taste of him lingering on my tongue before pulling away. A thin string of saliva and blood connects us briefly before breaking, a crimson testament to our new bond.

Before he can say anything, I dart off and shift seamlessly into my dragon form, bones cracking and reforming, skin stretching and hardening into scales with a sensation like thousands of tiny needles pricking from within. My emerald and silver scales reflect the waning light of the setting sun. The wind rushes past as I launch myself into the air, each powerful beat of my wings carrying me higher, closer to home. The loud sound of massive ancient wings beating behind me fills the air, the rhythmic whoosh creating currents I can feel buffeting my tail.

I glance over my shoulder and see Klauth and Thauglor flying side by side, their massive forms blocking out portions of the sky. Klauth's scales gleam like fresh-spilled blood in the sunset, while Thauglor's absorb the light, seeming to create a void in the sky. These two are going to be trouble, I just know it. The way they move in tandem, anticipating each other's movements without communication, speaks of their long history. They've fought together, shared a border between their territories. They have a history that I bet the books got wrong, just like everything else they warned us about.

Soon enough, my two great wyrm mates flank me, their wingspans dwarfing mine, creating protective shadows on either side. Klauth with his scales the color of fresh-spilled blood, radiating heat like a forge. Thauglor, whose scales could make the blackest night jealous, carrying the scent of storms and ancient forests. The air between us vibrates with power, three apex predators soaring through the darkening sky. I have two war machines in my nest, and I have never felt safer. The thought brings a rumble of satisfaction from deep within my chest, echoing across the open air as we fly toward home. The last rays of sunlight catching on our scales in a final blaze of glory before night claims the sky.

"Other than Callan having to redo the date night calendar again, nothing. We all knew this was coming." Balor shrugs as he crosses one ankle over the other, his boots gleaming under the warm lights of our living room. His nonchalance grates against my raw nerves.

Ziggy approaches with quiet footsteps, the cold glass of a beer bottle pressed into my palm. The condensation trickles between my fingers as I finally give voice to the fears that have been clawing at my insides. "Easy for you to say. My father is about to lose our ancestral lands, and I may be flightless."

"Mina went head to head with a great wyrm that is unbonded. She stood her ground protecting all of us," Ziggy says confidently, his eyes reflecting absolute faith. "She will not let anything happen to any of us."

Shaking my head, I knock back the beer, the bitter liquid burning a path down my throat as I finish half of it in one shot. The carbonation bubbles against my tongue, a sharp contrast to the heaviness settling in my chest. "You can still phase everywhere. If I can't fly..." The words stick in my throat, and I sigh heavily, staring down at the bottle in my hand, watching the amber liquid swirl inside.

"Who cares!" Mina's voice cuts through the room like a thunderclap. I look up to see her striding into the living room, the floorboards vibrating slightly beneath her purposeful steps. Both ancients follow in her wake, their imposing presence filling the space with a palpable tension that raises the hair on the back of my neck. "Do you think you were chosen as my mate because of your wings? Flightless or not, you are a powerful male, Abraxis."

Mina closes the distance between us, the scent of lightning and rain clinging to her skin as she grips my leathers. Her fingers are warm through the material, her grip firm enough that I can feel the strength coiled in her slender hands. "Anyone that challenges you—I already have a game plan for that, right, Balor?" She smiles, looking over her shoulder at the man in question, her eyes flashing with that dangerous glint I've come to both fear and adore.

"Anyone of dragon blood within a nest can fight in another's place," Balor explains, his voice rumbling with pride. "I can turn my opponent to stone without so much as shifting." He winks at Mina before grabbing two more beers for the ancients, the caps hissing as he pops them off. "It seems being mated to Mina has made my scales harder, my toxin stronger, and my ability more deadly."

"Descendant..." Thauglor's voice echoes in the living room, the bass tones reverberating in my chest as he draws my attention to him. The ancient's scent is primal—earth and acid and something older than time itself.

"Yes?" I lower my head out of respect for him, fighting the instinct to bare my throat completely.

"Mina shared with me what happened. What you did to ensure our mate and future progeny were safe." He steps closer, his footfalls heavy against the floor. I watch Mina tensing, her body coiling like a spring as she sizes him up. Her protective stance warms something deep within me.

I rest a hand on her shoulder, feeling the heat of her skin through the thin fabric of her shirt, and ease her out of the way. Her reluctance is evident in the tight muscles beneath my palm.

"You were willing to die so that our mate would live," Thauglor continues, his ancient eyes boring into mine with an intensity that makes it difficult to breathe. "You have honored our noble bloodline, descendant. My wings and talons are yours. Any that challenge you, challenge me." He extends his hand toward me, the skin weathered and marked with centuries of battles.

I take it swiftly and shake it, feeling the calluses against my palm, the incredible strength held carefully in check. "I appreciate that," I manage, my voice steadier than I expected. He reaches out and pats my shoulder, the weight of his hand like an anchor, before taking a seat on the couch that groans beneath him.

"You stinky boy need a bath," Mina pinches her nose playfully, staring at Thauglor. The playful gesture is at odds with the power dynamics swirling in the room.

Klauth full-on belly laughs, the sound rich and warm, filling the corners of the room at the look of confusion crossing Thauglor's face. "Better do as she says. She can partially wield her lightning in her human form."

"I do not stink," Thauglor tilts his head at the angle we all know pisses Mina off, the tendons in his neck standing out prominently.

A low growl escapes her lips as she stares at him, the sound raising goosebumps along my arms. Klauth leans in and whispers something in Thauglor's ear, his breath causing the ancient's hair to stir slightly, and immediately, Thauglor adjusts his posture. "Would you be so kind as to show me where this bath is you speak of?" He stands and bows deeply to Mina, and I damn near forget to breathe, the oxygen catching in my lungs at this unprecedented display.

"Right this way." Mina wiggles her fingers at Thauglor, her nails catching the light. He closes the distance and takes her hand, allowing her to lead him off. Their footsteps fade down the hallway, accompanied by the soft murmur of voices.

As soon as they are out of earshot, Klauth rounds on me, the sudden movement causing me to tense instinctively. "She survived his acid." He arches an eyebrow, his expression intense enough that I can almost feel the heat of his gaze.

"Okay? It's a known fact she can withstand acid." I glance over at Balor and Callan as he enters the room.

"Your acid, yes. A green dragon's, absolutely." Klauth's voice drops lower, compelling me to lean in despite myself. "A great wyrm's acid is more concentrated. Mina said her scales tingled a little. That was it. Her scales should have melted or been burnt. Yet there's not a single scratch on her." He raises an eyebrow like I'm supposed to understand what he's getting at, the implications hanging heavy in the air between us.

"Do you think it's because of being fully bonded to you, or her plans to have a clutch next year?" Balor asks before he finishes his beer off, the empty bottle clinking as he sets it down on the wooden coffee table.

"Both. Her dragoness is gearing up for war." Klauth's words send a chill down my spine despite the warmth of the room. "Once she bonds Thauglor, I don't know how indestructible she'll be."

Ziggy passes out fresh beers to us, the tops hissing as they're twisted off, releasing the hoppy aroma into the air. The condensation from my bottle seeps into my palm as I take it.

Mina comes walking back out, her bare feet silent against the floor, and heads straight to the fridge. Her thin cotton dress moving on a phantom breeze. The door opens with a soft suction sound, and cool air billows out as she pulls out a bottle of wine. The dark glass gleams under the kitchen lights. Shifting a finger to a talon—the transformation so smooth it's barely noticeable. She pulls the cork out with a satisfying pop and pours two glasses. The rich, burgundy liquid cascades into the crystal with a gentle gurgle.

She looks up at us and tilts her head, her hair falling across her cheek in a way that makes my fingers itch to brush it back. "What? I don't like beer." She shrugs her shoulders, the movement fluid and graceful.

"Who's the second glass for?" I sip at my beer as I move to sit on the stool, the cold metal pressing against the back of my thighs through my pants.

"Thauglor. I asked if he wants beer or wine. He said wine." Smiling broadly, Mina purrs, the sound vibrating in the air between us, sending a jolt of awareness through my body. "I finally have one of you to drink wine with. Well, besides Lee." With both glasses in one hand and the bottle in the other, Mina leaves us all behind speechless. The gentle sway of her hips as she walks away draws my gaze like a magnet.

"He hasn't eaten in over a thousand years, and she's giving him wine," I say with a laugh that feels rough in my throat.

Balor coughs, having inhaled his beer, the liquid spraying slightly as he struggles to breathe. "She's gonna get him drunk."

All eyes turn to Klauth, and I watch as the blood drains from his face, leaving him pale as bone. "Shit." The word comes out as a strangled whisper before he takes off running down the hallway after them, his footsteps thundering against the floor.

If she makes Thauglor submit to her, all hell is going to break loose at her next cycle. The thought settles in my gut like a stone as I take another long drink of my beer, the carbonation burning all the way down.

I DON'T EVEN WANT to know what's happening in there. My eyes follow Klauth's retreating form as he sprints down the hallway towards the main bathroom, the thundering of his heavy footfalls echoing against the stone walls. Shaking my head, I turn to go outside, the cool metal of the door handle a welcome relief against my palm. The hinges creak as I push it open, and a gust of crisp mountain air rushes in, carrying with it the scent of pine and distant rain.

Being up here in our private nest has its advantages. I stand at the edge of our terrace, the rough stone railing pressing against my forearms as I lean forward. My eyes scan the sprawling landscape below, now Mina's territory. The vastness of it makes my chest tighten with a strange mixture of pride and apprehension. I watch Warwick's people working on the lower courtyard, their movements like busy ants from this height, the clang of metal and distant shouts drifting up on the breeze.

Mina never wanted any of this, and yet she's taking to it like a duck to water. The thought tugs at the corner of my mouth, almost forming a smile. My sister and nephew live downstairs in the lower quarters, with a new hatchling on the way. I can almost smell the fresh paint from here—they've been preparing the nursery for weeks. Three new young couples have come to join the flight from my mother's people. Their scents are still unfamiliar enough that I can pick them out from the others when the wind shifts. Our legion grows by the day, and I don't think Mina realizes the magnitude of what's happening.

Several other species of dragons have petitioned to join us, each offering different forms of tribute. The thought of their gifts— gleaming metals, rare artifacts, and pledges of allegiance—sits heavy in my mind. My musings are interrupted as I catch movement out of the corner of my eye. I watch my father's dragon form gliding in from the west, his massive wings casting a shadow over the courtyard as he circles several times before landing. The ground trembles slightly beneath my feet as his weight settles on the stone.

"How are you, son?" His human form shimmers into existence before me, bringing with it the familiar scent of sandalwood and smoke that has always meant safety to me. He closes the distance between us, and we hug briefly, his arms strong and sure around my shoulders, careful to avoid my injured wing.

"As well as can be expected." I step back and spread my wings, the muscles protesting slightly but holding firm. For the first time since the incident, I can spread both equally, the injured muscles no longer pulling awkwardly to one side. The sun warms the thin skin between the bones, and I relish the sensation I feared I'd never feel again.

"That looks much better." He motions to my wings, his eyes crinkling at the corners, as he examines them with a critical gaze.

"Mina spends hours each day stretching my wings and rubbing the salve on the muscles." The memory of her fingers, gentle yet insistent, working the healing ointment into my damaged tissues makes my skin tingle. "I hear her when she thinks I'm distracted. I hear her cry." A huffed out sigh escapes my lips, the sound hollow even to my own ears. "Sometimes I think it hurts her more than it does me." I stare at the earth below my feet as I kick several stones, watching them tumble over the edge and disappear from sight. The soft patter of their landing is lost in the distance.

"When are you going to try to fly?" My dad walks with me to the edge of the cliff, the leather of his boots scraping against the stone. The drop before us is dizzying, a sheer plummet that would have once exhilarated rather than terrified me.

"This week. Klauth and I are going to go out alone. That way, if I fall, Mina doesn't have to see it." My eyes drift over the lands below us, the forests and fields stretching to the horizon, painted in hues of green and gold by the afternoon sun. The vastness that once represented freedom now looms as a challenge I'm not sure I can overcome.

"Where are you going to try?" Dad tilts his head, watching me, the wind ruffling his silver-streaked hair.

"Over the ocean, so if I fall, the water may be more forgiving than land." Shrugging my shoulders, I tilt my head back, drawing in a deep breath. The taste of salt is faint but present, a reminder of the crashing waves that await. My stomach clenches at the thought of plummeting into those depths, but I keep my expression neutral.

"Are you sure Klauth will save you?" Dad asks as he rests a hand on my shoulder, his palm warm and heavy through my leather vest.

"If he doesn't, Mina will kill him." I arch a brow and smile at my dad, the expression feeling forced on my face. The thought of Mina's rage is almost amusing—her lightning crackling around her, her eyes glowing with fury. The image is both terrifying and oddly comforting.

"That's true." Dad nods and looks back towards the entrance to our den, the massive wooden doors carved with ancient symbols that seem to shift in the changing light. "Where's Mina?"

Smirking, I look at my father, noting the way his expression softens at the mention of her name—everyone falls under her spell, eventually. "Trying to get Thauglor drunk. Don't worry, Klauth is in there to make sure she doesn't." I laugh, the sound genuine this time, bubbling up from my chest as I think about how she's going to react to him ruining her plans. I can already hear her indignant huffs, see the dangerous flash in her eyes that makes even the ancients pause. The thought warms me more than the sun on my wings.

"Are you going to join me, mate?" He flexes his wings, the movement sending a gentle wave across the water's surface. My eyes lock on the powerful muscles that span from his neck to his shoulders, taut and defined like carved bronze.

"Enjoy the bath for a bit. I'm not the one that's been imprisoned for a thousand years. We have forever to get to know each other." I climb onto the cushioned chair and cross my legs under me, the soft velvet upholstery warm against my skin as I settle in to watch him. The rich aroma of the wine mingles with the steam and the subtle scent of cedar from the bath oils.

The next thing we know, Klauth comes barreling into the main bathroom, the door banging against the wall as he enters. He skids to a stop on the slick floor, his breathing heavy and quick. We both turn and stare at him like he's a hydra that's sprouted an extra head. The sudden tension in the room is thick enough to cut with a talon.

"Are you okay, old friend?" Thauglor asks as he swims closer to us, the water lapping gently against the sides of the tub with his movement. His voice carries concern, deep and resonant in the steamy air.

"Yeah, I just thought…" Klauth's eyes dart from me to the wine, then back over to Thauglor, his normally composed features twisted with worry. A bead of sweat trickles down his temple, whether from his rush to get here or from the humid air. I can't tell.

"Thought what?" I smile like the cat that swallowed the canary, feeling the curve of my lips and the heat rising to my cheeks. I know exactly why he's in here. He thinks I am going to get Thauglor drunk, then make him submit. It's a forbidden ancient tradition among our kind that would shift the power dynamics significantly.

Klauth looks absolutely flustered as I lean forward and grab my glass of wine, the cool crystal a stark contrast to my warm fingers. I sip at it innocently, the rich flavor blooming on my tongue—notes of blackberry and oak with a hint of vanilla.

"You know exactly what I was thinking." He waggles a finger at me. His brow furrows deeply, creating lines across his forehead that betray his age despite his otherwise youthful appearance.

I sit the glass down before I stand up. The chair creaking softly beneath me, and walk slowly towards him, exaggerating the way my hips sway. The soft fabric of my clothing whispers against my skin with each deliberate step. His eyes are locked on every movement, his pupils dilating slightly in the dim light.

"You were thinking," I step into his space, close enough to feel the heat radiating from his body, and walk my fingers up his chest, feeling the rapid beat of his heart through the thin material of his shirt. "I was going to get Thauglor drunk." I reach up and kiss the underside of his jaw, my lips tracing a path all the way to his ear, breathing in his scent of smoke and cloves. "Then get him to submit to me." I bite his earlobe gently and smile against his skin, feeling the slight roughness of stubble against my lips.

Slowly I turn and press my back against his front, feeling the solid warmth of him behind me. Reaching back, I grab his hands, the skin rough and calloused from centuries of battles. I lock eyes with Thauglor across the room and run Klauth's hands over the curves of my hips and up to my chest. I throw my head back, exposing the vulnerable length of my throat, the ultimate gesture of trust among our kind.

"It's so much more fun to surrender and just feel everything," I whisper, my voice husky and low. The tension between the three of us crackles like lightning before a storm. Each of us is acutely aware of the ancient power dynamics at play.

"You're playing a dangerous game, mate," Thauglor rumbles as he steps out of the water. The sound reverberates through the tiled room, deep and commanding. My eyes trace the path the water droplets take down his chest and between his defined muscles. Each droplet catching the amber light like liquid gold. The surrounding air seems to shimmer with heat, steam rising from his bronze skin in the cool bathroom air.

"Not dangerous." I tilt my head, exposing his mate mark to him, feeling the stretch in my neck muscles and the coolness of the air against the sensitive skin there. "I know what I want and what we need." I cross my arms behind my back, then press them back into Klauth's stomach, feeling the firmness beneath my touch. He inhales sharply, the sudden rush of air audible in the quiet room.

"Are you sure about that, mate? It's been forever since I've felt the touch of a female," Thauglor purrs dangerously low as he lowers his lips to my throat.

Waves of heat roll off Thauglor's body as he moves closer, the temperature in the room seeming to rise with each step he takes. His hands caress my shoulders, his touch gentle yet possessive, leaving trails of warmth that spread across my skin like wildfire. The connection between us pulses with ancient energy, a bond that transcends the physical.

My inner dragoness stirs, restless and powerful, urging me to take control. But I resist, curious to see what happens when two ancient dragons align. The tension in the room is palpable, hanging in the steamy air like an unspoken promise.

Unexpectedly, Klauth turns me when Thauglor steps back. It's now that I know Thauglor sees the scales that span the width of my shoulders, up my neck and down my spine to my hips, where they fan out again. The scales shimmer in the dim light, iridescent and otherworldly against my human form. His lips press against my scales, and it sends a jolt of energy straight through me, like lightning dancing across my skin.

"You honor us, mate." His lips caress the width of scales on my right shoulder, his voice filled with reverence and awe. The vibration of his words against my scales creates a sensation unlike anything I've ever felt.

Before I can respond, Thauglor suddenly lifts me in a swift motion and leaps into the tub. I squeal in surprise before we hit the water. The sound echoing off the marble walls. When I surface, I'm laughing, water streaming down my face and hair plastered to my skin. I spin in his arms, feeling weightless in the warm water.

A second splash announces Klauth's entrance, and he appears at my back, his presence solid and comforting. The water ripples around us, creating gentle waves that lap against the sides of the tub.

Did I die?

Or am I having one hell of a sex dream?

The connection between the three of us intensifies, an ancient bond forming. The water seems to amplify every sensation, every touch magnified, as if the very elements are celebrating our union. My breath comes faster, my heart racing with the significance of this moment.

"Tell me now that you don't want this," Thauglor says, his eyes capturing mine, gold flecks dancing in sapphire depths like stars in a night sky. He wiggles his length, teasing me right where I need him most.

"I want it," I whisper, my voice barely audible over the gentle lapping of the water. The words seem to hang in the steamy air, a commitment that goes beyond the physical, touching something primal and eternal.

"Shhh... Don't rush," Thauglor says against my lips as Klauth steadies me with firm hands on my waist. "This bond has waited centuries. We have time." Thauglor says against my lips as Klauth takes control of my hips and presses me down onto his best friend's length.

I gasp, feeling how thick Thauglor is. He has the same bumps on his length that Klauth did when he knotted me. My core flutters and pulses, knowing exactly what that means for me. Intense pleasure, feeling him everywhere all at once and being stuck together until he releases me. When I'm halfway down his length, he slams up into me, burying himself to the hilt. I cry out and arch back towards Klauth. He kisses me deeply, holding me as Thauglor rolls his hips agonizingly slow.

The ancient connection strengthens, feeling the power of it coursing through my veins like liquid fire. My entire being pulses with energy, responding to the ancient call of my mates. This is more than physical desire—it's the union of souls meant to be joined.

I arch back towards Klauth, seeking his strength as the intensity of the moment overwhelms me. He kisses me deeply, grounding me as the power of our three-way bond reaches its peak. The water around us seems to vibrate with energy, responding to the ancient ritual of mates connecting for the first time.

Klauth's hands cup my breasts, rolling my nipples between his fingers until I cry out. My core pulses hard, trying to milk Thauglor's length for all its worth. He pulls me away from Klauth and encases me in his wings, slamming up hard into me with each thrust. He grunts into the curve of my neck with each thrust. A deep growl builds in his chest as I feel his length changing within me. The bumps raise hitting spots I thought only Klauth could hit. Then there's the fullness of his flair that locks him fully in place. I cry out just as he roars his release, throwing his head back. His voice echoes in the bathroom, rattling things off of shelves and sending them crashing to the floor.

I can hear the bathroom door slam open, the heavy wood colliding with the marble wall with a thunderous crack that echoes off the tiled surfaces. The sound of multiple footsteps fills the room, shoes squeaking against the wet floor and voices raised in surprise. Steam swirls in the disturbed air, momentarily obscuring the intruders.

"Nothing to see here," Klauth says behind me somewhere, his voice tight with irritation. The water ripples and sloshes against Thauglor's wings as Klauth wades through the pool to usher everyone out.

"Mina, I'm leaving food," Balor calls out, his deep voice resonating through the humid air. I hear the heavy ceramic tray hit the marble table close to the side of the pool we're on, the dishes clinking softly against each other. The rich aroma of freshly cooked meat and herbs wafts over, making my stomach clench with unexpected hunger.

All I can do is stare into Thauglor's gold-flecked sapphire eyes. They glow faintly in the darkness created by his wings, which curve around us like a living canopy, sheltering us from prying eyes. Beads of water cling to his long lashes, catching the dim light filtering through the steam. My fingertips trace his high cheekbones, feeling the warmth of his skin and the barely perceptible texture of ancient scars so faint they're invisible to the eye.

I stare at one of the most beautiful men I have ever seen. His skin is damn near flawless, a beautiful dark bronze that gleams with moisture in the low light. My fingers dig into his thick, wavy hair, slightly coarse against my palm, as I pull him to me for a kiss. His lips are surprisingly soft against mine, tasting faintly of the wine I drank earlier, mingled with something uniquely him—wild and ancient, like storm clouds and earth.

It's different with Thauglor, something about him is magnetic. The scent of him—acid and ancient forests—fills my lungs with each breath. My dragoness wants to be curled up under his wing, safe from the world that constantly demands more from me. I've never craved the idea of being kept safe, of making myself small. The concept of not having to be the strong one all the time is foreign, yet strangely enticing. It settles in my chest like a warm stone, heavy but comforting.

Thauglor has that quiet dominance, the kind that simply is. He doesn't need to be loud or aggressive. Each subtle shift of his muscles, each controlled breath, radiates power. His presence alone screams dominant male—*don't fuck with me*. Even the water seems to yield to him, parting around his form as if acknowledging his authority.

The bathroom door closes with a soft click as the last intruder leaves, and I feel rather than hear Thauglor's low chuckle against my lips. The vibration travels through my body, settling low in my abdomen.

Deep down, I know he's exactly what my nest needed.

What I needed.

The realization crashes over me like a wave, undeniable and all-consuming. His arms tighten around me, as if sensing my thoughts, solid and secure. For once, I allow myself to surrender to the sensation of being protected rather than being the protector.

"It is truly amazing to witness," I almost whisper, not wanting to disturb the tranquility of the scene before me. My voice, unused to such gentle tones after centuries of silence, sounds rough even to my own ears.

"Klauth has reclaimed his empire. She is this continent's Queen." Abraxis says softly as he pulls the sheet up Mina's body to mid-back, the silk whispering against her skin. His movements are tender, practiced, speaking of countless nights spent watching over her. The subtle scent of her fills my nostrils—lightning and rain and something uniquely female that makes my ancient heart quicken its pace.

"She is more than a queen. Those scales alone say when she hits maturity, she will be able to raze the continent alone." A sigh escapes my lips as I watch her sleep. Her face peaceful in repose, absent of the fierce determination I've already come to associate with her. The weight of this realization settles heavy in my gut. "Is there something you need, descendant?"

"Just needed to see her." His tone softens, and I can see the hold our mate has on her nest. The bond between them is almost tangible, a vibration in the air that speaks of battles fought together and sacrifices made.

"It's understandable." I motion for him to leave the room, and I follow behind, my larger frame casting long shadows across the sleeping form of our mate. The wooden floorboards of the hallway creak subtly beneath my weight, a stark contrast to the silence of the carpeted bedroom.

The basilisk mate waits outside the door, his pupils vertically slitted in the dim light of the hallway. The air around him carries the faint tang of venom, a warning, and a promise wrapped into one scent.

"Balor or Ziggy are usually on guard duty for Mina." Abraxis mentions before the male in question enters the room and shifts. The sound of scales sliding against hardwood fills the air momentarily, followed by the soft thud of a heavy reptilian body settling into position. His heavily armored basilisk form coils around the bed facing the door, muscles tensing then relaxing as he adjusts his position. The subtle rasp of his scales against the wooden floor sends a shiver of recognition down my spine—the sound of a predator preparing to defend what's his.

"Does she truly need to be so heavily guarded?" I ask as we walk, the corridor stretching before us, lined with photographs and artifacts that speak of a life I've yet to fully understand. My fingertips brush against the wall, feeling the texture of the paint. Still strange after centuries imprisoned in darkness.

"She feels better not waking up alone. Mina scared is not a fun event to deal with." He says as we head to the living room, the scent of other dragons growing stronger with each step. My nostrils flare, categorizing each unique scent, mapping out the complex hierarchy of this unusual nest.

Everyone, including another descendant of mine, is waiting for us in the living room. The soft murmur of conversation dies as we enter, all eyes turning toward us. The atmosphere shifts instantly, becoming charged with anticipation. I see two more black dragon descendants, their eyes carrying the same gold flecks as mine. Two bronze dragons stand beside them, clearly the mates of the black dragons. Their skin gleaming like polished metal even in human form. A hatchling that is another descendant sits on the floor, his small fingers working through a puzzle with focused determination. Then there are the rest of Mina's mates, each with their own distinct scent and presence, forming a protective circle around the room.

"What is happening?" My eyes scan the room slowly, heat beginning to build in my chest as anger rises at having others in my mate's nest while she sleeps. The temperature seems to rise several degrees, my control slipping just enough to let my displeasure be known.

"Steady, old friend. Mina loves your descendant's family and allows them in the living room and dining room." Klauth says, motioning to the four newcomers. His hand on my shoulder is firm, grounding, the cool touch a contrast to the heat radiating from my skin.

"Before it is forced upon me, I wish to come and surrender my rights to the lands that were once yours." The older male black dragon says, stepping forward. His voice carries the weight of authority and ancient pride. I glance from him to the mate known as Abraxis, and he nods— it's his father. The family resemblance is striking, from the set of their shoulders to the particular way they hold their wings.

"I, Vox Havock, of the Blackhaven nest, surrender the lands back to their rightful owner, Thauglor Mrithun, my ancestor, and alpha." My descendant drops to his knees before me per tradition, the sound of his knees hitting the hardwood floor resonating through the quiet room. The air grows heavy with the significance of the moment. Centuries of dragon tradition condensed into this one act of submission. I rest a hand on his shoulder to allow him to stand again, feeling the powerful muscles beneath my palm tense, then relax at my touch.

"I accept." Tilting my head, I look at this proud male before me and breathe in deeply, catching the scent of his bloodline—my bloodline— mixed with centuries of life I missed while imprisoned. The familiar yet different scent stirs something primal in me, a recognition of kin that transcends time. "I would, however, want you to remain in control of the flight for now. Let them know that I have returned and that the lands are mine once more."

A collective exhale seems to sweep through the room, the tension draining away like water. The hatchling, unaware of the significance of what just transpired, laughs as he completes his puzzle. The bright sound cutting through the solemnity of the moment, reminding us all of the future we are building—a future that, after centuries of darkness, I am finally part of again.

I STAND on the edge of the cliff shoulder to shoulder with Klauth and my descendant, looking out over the world. The wind whips around us, cold and biting against my face, carrying the scent of pine and distant rain. Far below, the landscape stretches out like a living tapestry—forests of deep emerald, winding ribbons of silver rivers, and the distant smudge of the academy on the horizon. The vastness of it all, after centuries of imprisonment, still takes my breath away.

"There's one threat left," Abraxis says as he flexes his wings. The membranes stretch taut between the bones, catching the late afternoon sun in a translucent glow. I can hear the subtle creak of healing tissue, the faint pop of joints that haven't fully recovered.

"More than one. The professor Kai," Klauth says as he looks over at me, his eyes narrowed against the harsh sunlight. The tension in his jaw is visible, a muscle ticking beneath the skin.

"Mina returns to school tomorrow," Abraxis says as he runs his hands through his hair roughly, the dark strands standing up in spikes from the force of his frustration. His scent shifts subtly, anxiety threading through his natural musk.

"I have meetings all day," Klauth says as he turns to look at me. His leather jacket creaks softly with the movement, the material polished to a subtle sheen.

Nodding, I smirk, thinking about all the hell I can raise. The anticipation of it sends a pleasant warmth through my veins, a sensation I had almost forgotten during my long captivity. "I'll go. I wonder how shocked they will be with me walking the halls with her. Will Balor be with us?" Tilting my head, I look at the two of them, tasting the metallic tang of thunderclouds gathering on the horizon.

"Yeah. He won't leave her with her father still hunting her. And now with the threat of Kai, and who knows how many other teachers are involved," Abraxis says as he flexes his wings again. The sound of the membrane stretching is louder this time, followed by a barely suppressed wince he tries to hide.

I watch his eyes darting over the edge several times, flicking between the distant ground and the open sky. He wants to fly or at least glide. The desire is written in every line of his body, in the way he shifts his weight forward slightly, unconsciously preparing for flight.

"Let's go," I say, my voice carrying on the wind. I run and leap off the cliff, the momentary sensation of free fall sending a jolt of adrenaline through my system before I take flight, spreading my wings. The air catches beneath them with a satisfying whoosh, lifting me upward. The sudden shift from falling to soaring still thrills me, even after countless centuries. Turning, I hover, looking back at my wounded descendant. The downdraft from my wings stirs up dust and small pebbles on the cliff edge. "You know you want to do it. Take the leap and at least try to glide," I flap and hover in place, waiting for him to take a chance. My muscles work smoothly, powerful strokes keeping me aloft in the turbulent air.

Abraxis walks to the edge and then leaps over it, his body silhouetted briefly against the vast sky. He spreads his wings wide, the injured one extending just as far as the healthy one. He falters for several moments, dropping altitude in quick, heart-stopping lurches. My own muscles tense in sympathetic response, ready to dive if needed. Then he stabilizes, catching a thermal that lifts him gently. I fly closer to where he is, and we glide together on the rising air currents, the warm updrafts cushioning us from below. The sensation is euphoric—the perfect balance between control and surrender.

Within moments of us gliding, I hear the roar of Mina's dragon behind us. The sound reverberating through the valley and sending flocks of birds scattering from the trees below. Soon she's under us, her massive form casting a shadow over the ground as she offers us a place to land. Her scales gleam in the sunlight, a mesmerizing mosaic of emerald green and silver that shifts with each movement, reflecting the light like precious gems. Her frill is tight to her back, and I land next to it, feeling the solid strength of her body beneath my feet. I watch Abraxis land too, his touchdown less graceful but successful.

"I did it!" Abraxis smiles and jumps up and down several times, excited. His boots create dull thuds against Mina's scales, which she seems to barely notice. His face is flushed with triumph, eyes bright with accomplishment, and sweat beading along his hairline from the exertion and stress.

"Congrats, descendant." I pat him on his back and sit down to lean against Mina's frill. The ridged scales are warm from the sun, radiating heat against my back. She rumbles deeply to us, the vibration traveling through her body and into mine, a physical manifestation of her voice as she talks about school tomorrow.

The sound is soothing, primal, like distant thunder that promises rain rather than threatens destruction. Her breath smells of lightning and something metallic, washing over us in warm gusts as she speaks. She has plans for everything that is coming to pass. Her confidence evident in the steady rhythm of her enormous heart that I can feel pulsing beneath the armored exterior. Leaning back, I close my eyes briefly, savoring this moment of connection with my mate and descendant. After centuries alone in darkness, these simple moments of belonging feel like the greatest luxury imaginable.

"Why did you pause, mate?" Thauglor whispers before kissing the shell of my ear, his breath warm and carrying the faint scent of coffee from breakfast. The gentle brush of his lips sends a shiver down my spine that I struggle to suppress.

I can't tell him the real reason; he'll go on a rampage. The thought of his rage makes my stomach clench with anxiety. "I'm not a fan of this class. I already have mates. Taking a class on pheromones and mate selection is pointless." I roll my eyes and lean back against him, sighing as his thick arms wrap around me. The solid wall of his chest behind me feels like a fortress, his heartbeat slow and steady against my back.

"You need this class for graduation, so we must attend," he says softly, his voice a low rumble that vibrates through my body where we touch.

"I know." I sigh, the sound heavy with resignation, and shove the door open. The hinges squeak in protest, drawing the attention of the few students already seated. My gaze immediately finds Abraxis and Balor sitting in the back rows where I normally sit. The familiar scent of Abraxis's cologne—sandalwood and something uniquely him—wafts toward me, mingling with Balor's more earthy aroma. "What's happening?" My eyes jump between the two of them, taking in Abraxis's relaxed posture and Balor's tense alertness.

"Getting ahead of the bullshit. Kai will call you out on being with Thauglor and threaten to tell me about your indiscretions." Abraxis smiles, the expression not reaching his eyes, which remain cold and calculating. He shakes hands with Thauglor, the sound of their palms connecting sharp in the quiet classroom, before guiding me to sit between them. The wooden seat is hard and uncomfortable beneath me, a stark contrast to the plush furniture I've grown accustomed to at the nest.

Until now, I have never been concerned about sitting between my dragon mates. A pair of surly black dragons will not be a fun experience. Their combined body heat envelops me from both sides, almost stifling in the already warm room.

I settle in and feel Balor behind me, the back of my chair shifting slightly as he leans forward. "This is going to be a blast," he says, his breath tickling the back of my neck. I turn to face him, the movement causing my hair to brush against his chin.

"What do you mean?" Arching a brow, I watch Balor's grin turn sinister, his teeth startlingly white against his tanned skin.

"Klauth has plans." He laughs and leans back in the chair behind me, the wood creaking ominously under his weight.

My stomach drops and my heart rate skyrockets, the sudden rush of adrenaline making my fingertips tingle. What have my mates planned? They haven't let me in on? I realize with the force of a physical blow. I have three of my strongest, deadliest mates with me. Klauth is inbound if what I am sensing is correct, a distant pull in my chest that grows stronger with each passing minute.

I wrap an arm around Thauglor's, feeling the powerful muscles beneath his sleeve, and just stare down at the stage at the bottom of the lecture hall. The amphitheater-style room seems to stretch and contract in my vision as anxiety builds. Every minute feels like twenty, the ticking of the wall clock painfully slow, until the teachers' entrance finally opens with a soft swoosh against the carpeted floor.

A deep rumbling laugh escapes Thauglor's lips as they curve up slowly. The sound vibrates through his arm and into mine, raising goosebumps along my skin. Kai steps out onto the stage and places his book on the stand in the center. The heavy tome lands with a dull thud that echoes in the now-silent room. His tailored suit looks freshly pressed, but I notice a slight tremble in his hands as he adjusts his papers.

"The fourth marking period ends soon, and we are preparing for the final in two weeks." He doesn't bother looking up, his voice carrying clearly through the excellent acoustics of the hall. "Those that have mates will be expected to take the final just like everyone else." It's now that he looks up and sees I'm flanked by two black dragons with

Balor behind us. His face pales visibly, the blood draining away until his skin takes on an ashen hue. His scent changes instantly, fear souring the air between us even from this distance.

"Are you okay, professor? You look like you've seen a ghost?" Abraxis says before I can open my mouth, his tone deceptively casual but laced with an underlying threat. I don't bother looking over at my mate because I already know the look on his face. He wants to melt Kai in a pool of acid like Thauglor did to Lysander. The memory of that incident sends a chill down my spine despite the warmth of the room.

"Everything is fine, General. I wasn't expecting to see you today." Kai's eyes slide over to Thauglor's and then lower immediately, his submission almost palpable in the air between them. A bead of sweat trickles down his temple, catching the harsh overhead lights. The tension in the room is thick enough to cut with a talon. I find myself holding my breath, waiting for whatever is about to unfold.

Kai starts his lecture, his eyes glued to the tome before him. The fine scales along the back of my neck raise, a sensation like thousands of tiny needles pushing up beneath my skin. Something doesn't feel right. The air in the room suddenly feels too thick to breathe, carrying a subtle wrongness that makes my pulse quicken. Before I can say anything, Thauglor pulls me onto his lap and wraps his arms around me, his body a furnace against my back.

"Shh... All will be well..." He kisses my cheek, his lips warm and slightly rough against my skin. The familiar scent of him—earth and acid and something ancient—fills my nostrils, but it doesn't calm me at all. My muscles remain tense, coiled like springs beneath my skin.

The doors behind us open with a heavy creak that echoes through the now-silent lecture hall. It's then that Klauth steps in with several royal guards flanking him. Their boots striking the floor in perfect unison, creating a rhythmic sound feels like a war drum. Their polished armor catches the harsh fluorescent lights, throwing dazzling reflections across the walls. *When did he get personal guards?* I arch a brow, looking up at my mate, confusion twisting in my gut.

He extends his hand to me, the pale skin a stark contrast to the dark suit he wears. I take it, feeling the familiar calluses against my palm. When I stand, he places the diadem that Ziggy gave me on my head just in front of my horns. The metal is cool against my skin for just a moment before warming to my temperature. Its weight is slight but noticeable, a physical reminder of a position I never sought. He threads his fingers with mine, and we walk down the stairs to the front of the classroom, each step resonating through the silent room.

"By the order of me, and my authority as the King and sovereign ruler of the Aurelian Isles, I am placing you under arrest, Kai Martz." Klauth's voice fills the room, deep and commanding, vibrating through the floorboards beneath my feet. He moves his hand in a subtle gesture, and his guards move forward to take Kai into custody. The sound of their armor shifts with each movement like metal scales sliding against each other.

"What are the charges?" Kai yells as the guards restrain him, his normally composed voice cracking with panic. The acrid scent of his fear cuts through the air, sharp and unpleasant.

"You assisted in the abduction of a royal and assisted in the plotting of that royal's attempted murder." Klauth says, as he presses his lips to my temple. His breath is warm against my skin, carrying the faint scent of mint. That's when Kai goes pale, the blood draining from his face until his skin appears almost translucent under the harsh lights, his veins visible beneath the surface.

"It was all Lysander and Abaddon. They want to turn her into a dracol-ich. All I did was supply the phylactery." Kai says as his eyes lock with mine, almost pleading. Sweat beads on his forehead, catching the light as it trickles down his temple.

The smell of ozone rises around me, sharp and electric, like the air before a storm. I feel the sparks of lightning dancing in my hair, raising each strand until it floats around my head like a living halo. The tiny jolts of electricity tingle against my scalp, a sensation both foreign and exhilarating.

"Is that all?" I ask as I shift my hands, allowing my silver talons to gleam in the harsh lights. The transformation is painless, more like a glove being removed than a change in form. Interestingly enough, sparks of lightning jump effortlessly between my talons, creating tiny arcs of blue-white energy. I stare at the lightning, mesmerized by the dance of electricity, and then focus my gaze on Kai. The world narrows to just him and me, the periphery fading into insignificance.

"Hmm, interesting new development, mate, since you claimed Thauglor." Klauth says his friend's name, and Kai goes even paler, if that's possible, and starts hyperventilating. His chest heaves with each rapid, shallow breath, the sound wet and desperate.

"The black egg hatched?" He pants out between gasping breaths, his words barely audible over the rasp of his breathing.

I feel the way my lips turn up in a feral grin. The muscles pulling tight across my face in an expression that feels more predator than human. I tilt my head to the side, exposing Thauglor's mate mark on my neck. The air caresses the sensitive skin there, a reminder of the moment his teeth broke my flesh, claiming me as his.

"Yes, and he's my mate." My eyes drop to my talons, watching the lightning dance along their lengths. Each spark is a tiny sun, blindingly bright against the silver of my claws. "Seems like I've had a bit of an upgrade." To test the theory, I flick my wrist and send a bolt of lightning to hit the stand beside him. The wood explodes on impact with a deafening crack, splinters flying in all directions, and starts burning. The acrid smell of scorched wood fills the air, mixing with the ozone. *I can wield lightning without Iris now.* The realization sends a thrill of power through my veins, heady and intoxicating. "Oh, this is going to be fun," I purr, still staring at my talons and the way the light plays on the scales on my hands and forearms, the iridescent green, and silver catching and refracting the light like living jewels.

"Take him away. I may want to turn my young mate loose on him later." Klauth kisses my temple again, his lips lingering this time, just as Thauglor arrives at my side. He takes my taloned hand in his, the heat of his skin a stark contrast to the cool feel of my claws. He looks at the scales and the length of my talons, his expression one of fascination and pride.

"Our mate is powerful indeed. These talons look to be titanium in origin, not iron. They are too light in color and far too sharp to be an iron's talons." Thauglor says as he examines my hands, his touch gentle despite the strength I know resides in his fingers. His thumb traces the junction where scale meets skin, sending shivers up my arm.

"As far as I know, my mom was just an iron dragon." I shrug my shoulders, the movement causing my scales to shift and catch the light differently. It's not like I can ask her; my father murdered her. The thought brings a familiar ache to my chest, dull and persistent.

"Most iron dragons have titanium in them. The only difference is the percentage is what changes things." Klauth says as he rubs my hand, soothing me enough to get the talons and scales to retract. The transformation is like water flowing over stone, smooth and natural, leaving behind human skin that still tingles with residual energy.

"Her talons ripped through quarter-inch plate steel in the war simulation room." Balor supplies as he steps closer, the subtle scent of his musk reaching me even from several feet away, sharp and acidic.

Klauth and Thauglor turn to look at him, their movements so synchronized it's almost comical. "Show us," Thauglor says before Klauth has the chance to, his voice carrying an undertone of command that makes Balor straighten almost imperceptibly.

Balor winks at me, the gesture playful despite the tension in the room, and leads us out of the Arcanum Campus and over to Shadowcarve. The sudden transition from the climate-controlled building to the outside air raises goosebumps along my arms. The sun is bright overhead, warming my skin and making me squint until my eyes adjust. Secretly, I am hoping to spot Ziggy and get him to take me home. Unfortunately, as we cross the campus, the students that pass us notice the royal guards, Klauth, and then me. Their whispers follow us like a wave, growing louder and then fading as we move past. Next year will not be fun in the least bit.

We eventually cross the threshold for Shadowcarve, the temperature dropping several degrees as we enter the stone building. The familiar scent of old books and weapon oil fills my nostrils, a scent I've come to associate with training and pain and triumph. We head upstairs to the classrooms, our footsteps echoing against the stone floors and walls. Vaughn is in class with Callan, and I wave as we walk past the door, glimpsing their surprised faces through the narrow window.

Balor pulls keys out of his pocket to open up the simulation room for us, the metal jingling softly in the quiet hallway. The door opens with a hydraulic hiss, revealing the cavernous space beyond. Once inside, he flips on all the lights. The fluorescents flickering to life with an audible buzz. The station I clawed up stands out, the metal twisted and torn like paper. The edges gleaming raw and bright where my talons ripped through them.

Thauglor and Klauth walk over to examine it, their movements careful and measured as if approaching something dangerous. The torn metal looks even more dramatic under the bright lights, the damage more extensive than I remembered. Abraxis moves to stand behind me and pulls me back flush with his chest, his arms encircling my waist. His heartbeat is strong and steady against my back, grounding me in the moment.

"You are definitely part titanium dragon, Mina," Thauglor says softly, his voice barely above a whisper yet carrying perfectly in the quiet room. "An iron dragon's talons are not strong enough to rip through metal." I stare into Thauglor's gold-flecked sapphire eyes, losing myself momentarily in their ancient depths. The implications of what he's saying hits me like a boulder that was dropped off a cliff. The impact stealing the breath from my lungs.

My mom was part of two of the strongest dragon species known to exist. My strength and resilience comes from my mom. The same woman that rejected me because of the color of my scales. The irony is bitter on my tongue, a taste like ash and disappointment. I caress my bond with Ziggy, calling to him, the connection between us vibrating like a plucked string. Within seconds, he arrives with a displacement of air that stirs my hair, and I step away from my dragon mates and into his arms. His embrace differs from theirs—cooler, less imposing, but no less strong. Ziggy knows what to do when I'm like this. I need quiet and comfort and just to be held until I process everything that was just dumped on me.

Within seconds, we've gone to one of my favorite places in the world, my poison garden up in the branches of the ancient tree. The phasing is jarring, a momentary sensation of being everywhere and nowhere at once before solidifying. The familiar scent of my plants—some sweet, some acrid, all deadly in their own way—wraps around me like a comforting blanket. The filtered sunlight through the canopy above dapples the ground with patches of gold, and the soft rustling of leaves in the gentle breeze creates a soothing white noise that calms my racing thoughts.

among the deadly nightshade or perched up in the ancient willow tree that impossibly thrives in the center of her sanctuary.

When I enter the gardens, I feel like I've come home. The heavy wooden door creaks shut behind me, and immediately, my shoulders relax. Here, vines crawl up stone walls, and plants with leaves sharp enough to slice skin spread across the ground. This is one of the few places I shift and slither around without worrying about hurting anyone—one of the few places where my true form is an asset rather than a threat.

The minute the wrought-iron gate locks behind me with a satisfying click, I let my shift wash over me. My skin hardens, scales rippling across my body in waves of obsidian. My bones crack and elongate as my form stretches, my jaw unhinging to accommodate my fangs. Flicking my forked tongue against the humid air, I already know where Mina is—her scent, honey, and lavender with an undercurrent of fear, stands out among the poisonous flora.

Slowly, I coil around the tree and work my way up the trunk. My scales grip the rough edges of the bark as I move, muscles contracting in a fluid rhythm perfected over centuries. Once I hit the branches, it becomes easier to navigate through the maze of limbs and leaves. Mina sits perched with her back against the tree, her legs dangling over the side of a thick branch. Sunlight filtering through the glass ceiling catches in her copper hair, setting it ablaze.

"Oh no, I'm being hunted by the big bad basilisk," she giggles as she looks down at me, her golden eyes sparkling with a hint of their old mischief.

I shift back to my human form and perch on a branch about eight feet below her. The transformation is quicker this time, my body remembering its human shape with practiced ease. "If I was hunting you, you never would have seen me coming," I smile as I close the distance between us, moving from branch to branch with predatory grace.

"But I like seeing you come," Mina says with a smile and winks at me, her cheeks flushing with color.

"So you do remember how to flirt?" I climb up and sit on the branch across from her, close enough to touch but giving her space to breathe. "What's wrong, Mina? Talk to me." Reaching out, I take her hands in mine. Her fingers are icy despite the garden's warmth.

Her golden eyes search mine for what feels like forever, the seconds stretching between us like honey. "Lysander said that dragon kin are only produced when it's not true mates." She lowers her eyes and stares at our intertwined hands, her thumb tracing nervous circles against my skin.

"If he's telling the truth, that's good news." I raise Mina's hands to my lips and kiss her delicate knuckles, inhaling her scent. Even through her anxiety, the smell of her calls to something primal inside me.

"That would be nice." She sighs and scoots forward, pressing her forehead against my chest. Her heartbeat flutters like a trapped bird.

I carefully maneuver us so my back is against the tree trunk, and I can pull her flush against me. Her weight settles against my chest, familiar, and right. "Your sister sent a letter." I reach inside my leather jacket and offer the envelope to her.

Mina's hands shake as she holds it, her knuckles going white with pressure. Her scent drastically changes as fear and anxiety rocket through her, making her lithe frame tremble against mine. The sound of the paper tearing seems amplified in the quiet garden, like an explosion in the stillness. I watch as she slides the letter out and reads. Mara apologizes for everything that happened. She tells Mina about her mate and the clutch they have together.

"They hatch tonight?" Mina's bottom lip trembles as she looks up at me, her eyes shimmering with unshed tears. I can see the war waging in her eyes—go see her sister's progeny or remain here and ignore the event entirely.

"Basilisks can sense when eggs are going to hatch down to the hour. It's a gift of ours." I shrug, watching the range of emotions Mina cycles through—fear, longing, anger, hope—each one clear as day to my enhanced senses.

"Can we go? I mean, will they allow me in their den? Nest? Clutch? Pit? Whatever it's called?" She presses the bridge of her nose to the underside of my jaw, and I'm done for. The gentle pressure of her skin against mine sends electricity racing down my spine. I'd knit a sweater out of Lysander's intestines if she asked me to.

"We can, and your other mates are already aware. Ziggy can drop us close, and we can traverse the last bit alone." I offer and give her a gentle squeeze. I can feel the minute she reaches for Ziggy's bond and gives it a caress. Sometimes it's unnerving how in tune to Mina I am— how I can sense the subtle shifts in her energy when she connects with the others.

Ziggy phases into existence before us and almost tumbles off the branch, his form solidifying from mist to matter in an instant. I reach out and grab him before he can fall, my reflexes lightning-quick. "Whoa, that was close. Good catch, Balor," Ziggy smiles as he looks between us, his green eyes assessing our tangled position.

"I'd like to go see my sister," Mina's voice sounds so small, and it makes Ziggy and me pause. Seeing her sister's clutch may do good for both of us. Hopefully, they are fully shifted into either completely—not caught between worlds like the hybrid monsters that still haunt Mina's nightmares.

\#

The territory of my kind is a shadow of what it once was. The Shadow Mount looms before us, jagged and imposing against the night sky. Its obsidian peaks catch the moonlight, creating an eerie silver outline that both beckons and warns. The entrance to our subterranean world gapes like a wound in the mountainside—as dangerous as it is beautiful. The wind carries the scent of ancient stone and primal danger, stirring memories of a time when basilisks ruled these lands unchallenged.

Ziggy phases us within three hundred yards of the entrance, the air crackling with electricity as we materialize on solid ground. The sudden shift from nothingness to existence makes my stomach lurch, though I'm accustomed to his particular method of travel.

"I don't dare go any closer," he mutters, stepping side to side uneasily. His normally confident posture is tense, shoulders hunched as if expecting an attack. The scent of his fear—sharp and acrid—drifts between us.

"It's okay. Mina and I have it from here." I rest a reassuring hand on his shoulder and offer him a smile that I hope conveys more confidence than I feel. "Mina can fly us home later." The leather of my gloves creaks as I squeeze his shoulder gently.

Ziggy hugs and kisses Mina goodbye, his movements hurried and anxious before he disappears before my eyes, leaving behind only the faint scent of his musk.

Mina and I stand in our black fighting leathers, the material clinging to our bodies like a second skin. The supple leather moves with us, designed for both protection and effortless movement. Her hood rests atop her head, her mask hanging loosely against her throat. I can feel the unease radiating from her—a tangible thing that makes the air between us heavy and thick. I lean in and kiss her cheek, my lips brushing against skin as soft as silk yet cool to the touch.

"Come on, let's go meet the little ones when they get here." I take her hand, feeling her slender fingers intertwine with mine, and start walking toward the entrance. The jagged opening yawns before us, appearing like it has teeth with the way the stalactites and stalagmites hang—mineral fangs ready to snap shut on unwary travelers. The damp, mineral-rich air carries the unmistakable scent of my kind—earth, stone, and something venomous that burns the nostrils.

With every step closer, her hand tightens on mine until I feel her talons threatening to emerge. I know it's not fear that drives her reaction, but apprehension. The leather of our gloves creaks with the pressure of her grip. She hasn't seen her sister in almost two years, and now she's invited into her pit. This singular moment can make or break what's left of their relationship. The weight of it hangs in the air between us, unspoken but understood.

I help Mina past the opening, my boots crunching on loose pebbles. The temperature drops immediately, the cool subterranean air raising goosebumps on the exposed skin of my neck. I see her eyes glow golden in the darkness as she stares down the tunnel, adjusting to the dim light faster than any human could.

"It smells dangerous," she whispers, her voice echoing softly against the stone walls. She tilts her head again, breathing in deeply, her nostrils flaring. "There's a couple hundred basilisks down there." Her voice is steady as she assesses what we're about to walk into, but I can hear the slight acceleration of her heartbeat.

"That's correct. There are two dozen different pits with smaller pits attached to them." I pause for a moment, trying to explain how our group's work. My fingers trace idle patterns on the back of her hand as I search for the right words. "So there's a dominant female in a pit. Her daughters create pits off their mother's main living space. Sons are driven off to find their own female." I bite my bottom lip, the slight pain focusing my thoughts as I watch to see if my explanation makes sense to her.

"So it's similar to a flight. A dominant female assumes the largest nest, then others branch off of hers. Kind of like having Cora in the lower level." She tilts her head, looking at me with those intelligent eyes that miss nothing.

"Exactly like that." I pull Mina against my side, feeling the warmth of her body through our leather armor. The scent of her—honey, lavender, and something uniquely dragonic—mixes with the earthy smell of the cavern as we step into the main chamber where all the pits connect. Mina pauses, taking it all in. I watch as she scans the interior, her eyes widening slightly at the sight of hundreds of holes in the walls at varying heights. The cavern itself is massive, the ceiling disappearing into the darkness above us. Distant sounds of movement and hushed conversations echo throughout the space, creating an eerie symphony of basilisk life.

"In strength order," I motion to the holes, my voice low and respectful in this sacred space. "We keep the youngest or weakest of our kind up high." The logic is brutal but effective—the stronger you are, the closer to the ground your pit is.

Mina stares at the wall again, her gaze calculating. "Where's yours?" Her eyes transform into dragonic slits as she looks at me, the golden irises glowing brighter.

"Second from the bottom. There's only one pit below mine." Pride colors my voice despite my attempt at humility. I walk Mina over to what would be my space. There're dozens of offerings in the entryway —gleaming gems, polished bones, and other treasures carefully arranged on stone pedestals. The items catch the dim light of the phosphorescent fungi that grows along the walls, creating a subtle display of wealth and desire.

Mina looks at me puzzled, her head tilting in that endearing way that betrays her curiosity. "Offerings from single females trying to get me to choose them." The words taste bitter on my tongue, especially with Mina beside me.

Mina's eyes take on a dangerous edge, the gold darkening to amber before her talons extend with a soft *snick* sound. She climbs into the opening, the movement fluid and predatory. I watch as the scales rise and cover her throat, emerald with silver edges that catch the light as she pulls off her hood. The scrape of scale on stone sounds like nails on a chalkboard, sending shivers down my spine. Mina is marking my space as hers, claiming territory in the most primitive and undeniable way.

She leaps down with graceful precision, landing beside me without a sound. Immediately, she rubs the scales on her throat against my armor, scent marking me. The rasp of her scales against my leather creates a friction that generates both sound and heat. It's interesting to see Mina possessive of me—I kind of like it. The display makes something primal and possessive unfurl in my chest, a pleased rumble escaping my throat.

When she's done, she puts her hair back up in her hood and just stares at me, her eyes challenging me to object. I can smell her scent now mixed with mine—a declaration to any basilisk with a functioning nose that I am claimed.

"We need to climb up to your sister's pit." I point to the one halfway up the wall, and Mina nods and motions for me to lead the way. The damp stone glistens in the dim light, making the climb look more treacherous than it actually is.

Instead of shifting, I climb up the wall slow and steady until I reach the pit entrance. My fingers find natural handholds in the rock, muscles straining pleasantly with each upward pull. The sound of Mina's talons sinking into the stone as she climbs makes the hairs on the back of my neck stand on edge—a primal response to a predator at my back, even if that predator is my mate.

"Amara, Zeb, I brought Mina with me," I call into the pit, my voice reverberating against the stone walls. The air here smells different— like a mixture of basilisk and dragon, with underlying notes of nesting materials and fresh water.

"I'll be right there," Zeb calls back, his voice carrying the slight hiss common to our kind.

Soon he approaches the opening and stares down at Mina, his pupils constricting into thin lines as he takes a step back. Fear radiates from him in waves, his scent souring with it. "She's okay, she's my mate," I offer, seeing the fear in his eyes. His scales rise defensively along his neck, a subconscious reaction to perceived danger.

"Okay," he says, the word clipped and uncertain. He offers me his hand and pulls me up into the entrance per tradition, his grip stronger than necessary. "I'll let you gather your female. Meet me in the sitting room." Zeb turns and leaves quickly, the sound of his footsteps fading down the tunnel.

I pull Mina up and in, and I watch her sniffing the air, her nostrils flaring slightly. "There's more than my sister and her mate here." Mina draws in a deep breath, and I watch as her dragonic slits recede, returning to more human-looking eyes.

"His family is here, as well as the matriarch." I reach down and take Mina's hand, feeling the tension in her fingers as I lead her down the tunnel. The walls here are smoother, polished by generations of basilisks moving through the narrow passage. Small glowing crystals embedded in the ceiling provide gentle illumination, casting our shadows in strange, elongated forms against the walls. I stop us at the entry to the sitting area, the sound of multiple conversations growing louder.

"Only family is allowed here, Balor. You know the rules." The matriarch says as she stands, her ancient body moving with surprising grace. Her scales have lost their luster with age, turning from vibrant obsidian to a muted gray black, but her eyes remain sharp and calculating. The air in the room shifts, growing heavier with her authority.

"Mina is Amara's half-sister and was requested to be here to represent her side of her family." I pull Mina flush to my side, feeling the coiling tension in her body. Her muscles are tight, ready to spring into action at the slightest provocation. The scent of her changes subtly, taking on a metallic edge that warns of danger.

"Her sister is a green dragon. They are not welcome here." The matriarch says with a hiss, her forked tongue flicking out to taste the air. The other basilisks in the room shift uncomfortably, their bodies rustling against stone and fabric.

"Good thing I'm not a green dragon." Mina's voice cuts through the tension like a blade as she takes off her hood, letting her green and silver hair fall to her waist in a cascade that catches the light from the crystal lamps. The twin silver horns on her head that stretch back over a foot should have been enough proof of her heritage. She shifts her hands, allowing her silver talons to emerge as well as the mostly silver scales with an iridescent green sheen to them. The transformation is beautiful and terrifying all at once—skin giving way to armored plates that gleam with metallic brilliance.

The matriarch backs up two steps as Mina's presence fills the sitting room. The air is growing heavy with power. "Our mother was a titanium and iron dragon. My sire was indeed a green dragon. If you dare to feel my scales, you know I am my mother's daughter." Mina hisses back at the matriarch, the sound more serpentine than human.

I take the handle of my knife and hit Mina's scales. The metallic sound of metal hitting metal rings out, echoing in the chamber like a bell. Her scales are as hard as an iron dragon's, the proof undeniable to all present. The impact sends vibrations up my arm, and I suppress a wince at the unexpected intensity.

The other basilisks talk among themselves in hushed whispers, their voices creating a susurration like dry leaves in the wind. Amara emerges from a side tunnel, her movement fluid and graceful. Unlike the others, her scales bear a similar metallic quality to Mina's, though hers lean more toward bronze than silver. She dives into Mina's arms with enough force to make Mina step back to maintain balance.

The change in Mina is immediate—her scales recede as she snuggles her sister, the hard edges of her defenses softening in an instant. The scent of her emotions shifts from defensive to joyful, the air around her warming with it.

"You're the dominant female. Do you have a flight?" Amara asks with a smile as she peppers Mina's cheeks with kisses, each one making a soft sound against Mina's skin.

"I am. I have twelve families under my protection as of right now. Another eight want to join," Mina says, nuzzling her sister, their foreheads touching in a gesture of intimacy that makes my chest tighten with affection.

"She is your mate?" The matriarch directs the question to me, her ancient eyes narrowing suspiciously. Her voice carries the weight of centuries, dry and crackling like old parchment.

"She is." I stand up a little taller, proud of the female I get to call mine. My chest expands with the declaration, shoulders squaring as I meet the matriarch's gaze without flinching.

"We are losing too many males to the dragons. Our species will die out, eventually." She growls, the sound rumbling deep in her chest. Mina's head whips toward her, the movement so fast it disturbs the surrounding air.

"Evolution is about change." Mina says calmly as she pushes her sister behind her, the gesture protective and instinctual. "Dragons are doomed to die off because they favor a dragon bond above all others." She glances over at me and lowers her eyes for a moment. A gesture of respect in basilisk culture that doesn't go unnoticed by the others. "Your people, like mine, are suffering with infertility issues because of limited genetic diversity."

Mina flexes her hands as if ready to get into a fight, the soft sound of her talons extending, sending a ripple of tension through the room. "I am immune to your venom and your stone gaze because my bloodline is diverse. By the looks of the main pit, you are having more weaker-born basilisks than strong ones. It's from lack of diversity." Mina narrows her eyes at the matriarch, the golden color intensifying with her emotion.

I feel the shift in the matriarch before it happens—a subtle change in the air pressure, a faint scent of venom. Her eyes shift to her basilisk form, slitted and deadly, and she tries her stone gaze on Mina. The power of it ripples through the air like heat waves, making the very atmosphere distort. Mina thankfully covers her sister's eyes in time, her movement swift and precise.

Within seconds, Mina's eyes glow golden as they shift to her dragon's, the light from them illuminating her face from within. She stares back, unflinching in the face of an attack that would turn most creatures to stone. "You can't hurt me." A deep growl escapes Mina's lips as her dragon's dominance floods the room, the sound vibrating in my chest cavity.

The other basilisks hit the ground as Mina's presence makes the room feel dangerous, the weight of her power pressing down on them like a physical force. The sound of bodies hitting stone echoes through the chamber, followed by the rasp of scales against the floor as they prostrate themselves. I'm the only basilisk left standing, and I tilt my head, looking at her with undisguised admiration.

Mina winks then touches the scale on the back of her neck—my scale —the one we exchanged during our bonding. The scale exchange is what's protecting me from her dominance display. The connection between us hums with energy, a tangible link that keeps me anchored against the storm of her power.

"My love, release them. I'm sure they've learned their lesson." I kiss Mina's cheek, tasting the salt on her skin. She turns and presses the bridge of her nose under my jaw, a submissive gesture that contradicts the display of power she just unleashed. Her warm breath against my throat sends a shiver of pleasure down my spine. Slowly she exhales and settles down almost immediately, the pressure in the room dissipating like fog under the morning sun.

"As you wish, my love," Mina says loud enough for everyone to hear her, the declaration of submission to me specifically designed to save face for the other basilisks. Her voice has returned to its normal register, the growl gone as if it never existed.

"Our eggs should be hatching any minute now," Amara says as she moves to stand before us. Her excitement is palpable, her scent sweet with anticipation.

"I can't wait," Mina says as she holds my hand, giving it a gentle squeeze that conveys her mix of emotions—excitement, nervousness, and a lingering trace of apprehension.

Amara leads us deeper into her pit, the tunnel narrowing before opening into a warm chamber filled with soft nesting materials and the pulsing heat of incubating eggs. The scent here is different—new life, warm stone, and the distinctive odor of hatching fluids beginning to seep from the eggs' tiny cracks.

Today could have ended very badly. Thankfully, Mina's temper is finally under control. I squeeze her hand in silent appreciation, feeling the weight of what we've accomplished. We've navigated dangerous territory, both literal and metaphorical, and come out stronger for it. As we approach the clutch of eggs, their surfaces beginning to show the first signs of hatching, I can't help but feel a surge of hope for the future—for us, for our kind, and for the evolution that Mina spoke of with such conviction.

stories told of anxious pacing and sleepless nights as my shell hardened and prepared to crack.

The first sound of a crack splits the silence like a thunderclap, making me sit up quickly. My spine straightens so fast I feel Balor flinch beneath me.

"Amara!" I yell for my sister as I move closer to the nest, my voice echoing against the stone walls. The soft nesting materials crunch beneath my knees as I crawl forward. I sniff at the eggs, the scent of new life and something distinctly reptilian filling my nostrils. The egg in the back moves and rolls onto its side with a soft scraping sound against the nesting material.

My dragoness coils and uncoils within me, restless and hungry for this experience. I feel her pushing against my consciousness, wanting this for herself. The sensation is like molten metal flowing beneath my skin, burning and insistent.

'*Mate, settle. You will have your own soon.*' Thauglor's voice echoes in my head, rich and deep like distant thunder. I can feel the minute he looks through my eyes, the bond between us warming as he shares this moment with me. A deep purr follows, the sound reverberating through our mental connection like a physical touch. '*When it's safe, we will give you as many clutches as you want.*' Thauglor's promise echoes in my mind, and I can't help the smile that spreads across my face, my lips pulling back to reveal teeth slightly sharper than human.

"What made you smile?" Balor asks as he comes to sit next to me, his movement fluid and predatory despite his bulk. The leather of his armor creaks softly as he settles beside me, his shoulder pressing against mine.

"Thauglor checked in with me. He said when we're all safe, I can have as many clutches as I want." Biting my bottom lip, I taste the copper of my blood as my fangs pierce the delicate skin. I stare at the furthest egg as it cracks almost all the way around. The sound reminds me of ice cracking when the temperature changes—sharp, crisp, and somehow both delicate and violent all at once.

"You have other plans though," he whispers as he nuzzles my cheek, his scales cool against my flushed skin. His breath smells like mint and something metallic, his voice low enough that only I can hear.

"I do. One clutch. A small one, maybe not the four eggs I envisioned." I whisper back as I press my cheek alongside his, our skin warming where we touch. My eyes never leave the eggs, watching them closely as if my gaze alone could protect them from harm. The narrow end of the shell falls away with a soft tinkling sound, and a black snout appears in the opening. My muscles tense, strung tight as bowstrings, not sure what's happening. The air feels too thick to breathe, time slowing to an agonizing crawl.

A small black serpent slithers out, its scales catching the light like polished onyx. Balor gasps beside me, his breath catching in his throat. "Your sister birthed a basilisk." The pride in his voice is unmistakable, a rare display of emotion from my usually stoic mate.

We watch the mini basilisk slither around the interior of the nest, its movements jerky but determined. Its body leaves small indentations in the nesting material as it explores its new world. Its head looks more dragonic than serpentine, with a slightly elongated snout and ridges where horns will eventually grow. Instead of having six eyes like a pure basilisk, it has only two—large, blood-red orbs that seem too knowing for a newborn.

The next egg starts moving, rocking back and forth with increasing urgency. The same tinkling sound can be heard, but louder this time, more insistent. This one almost explodes out of the egg, shell fragments flying in all directions. One piece hits my cheek, sharp enough to draw blood, but I barely notice.

The black and bronze hatchling stumbles out on four legs, flapping its wings frantically as it tries to balance itself. Its claws scratch against the stone beneath the nesting material, making a sound like nails on slate. My sister darts forward, moving faster than I've ever seen her move, and picks up the hatchling. She holds it to her chest, crooning softly to it. The sound is musical and soothing, a melody that seems instinctual rather than learned. Meanwhile, Zeb gently lifts the baby basilisk, its tiny body draping across his palm like liquid shadow.

The next two eggs crack at the same time, the synchronized sound creating an eerie harmony in the chamber. Two more baby basilisks come slithering out, their bodies glistening with birthing fluid that catches the light like diamonds. Zeb's face transforms with joy, his usual stern expression breaking into a smile that reveals his fangs. He's clearly overjoyed seeing that his mate birthed more of his species than her own. His happiness creates a palpable energy in the room, almost electric.

But when I look at my sister, I see it in her eyes—disappointment, deep and raw, darkening her golden irises to amber. Her shoulders slump ever so slightly. A movement so subtle that only someone who knows her well would notice. I lean over and kiss her cheek, tasting the salt from tears she refuses to shed, and hug her to me. Her body is rigid against mine, unyielding.

Zeb runs down the hallway with the three basilisk hatchlings, his footsteps fading into the distance. His excitement is a stark contrast to my sister's quiet resignation.

"May I?" I hold my hands out toward the remaining hatchling, the gesture reverent. Amara places the small creature in my palms, its weight surprisingly substantial for something so new to the world. It has the blood-red eyes of the basilisk, gleaming like rubies in its dark face. The hatchling squirms against my touch, its scales smooth and warm against my skin.

Rolling the hatchling over carefully, I see it's male. His tiny claws scratch lightly against my palms as he tries to right himself. "You have a beautiful son, Amara." I hold the little male and look him over closely, memorizing every detail. His scales are similar to Balor's—so black they seem to absorb light rather than reflect it. His wings are like my sister's, and how I remember my mother's to be—delicate membranes stretched over strong skeletal structures, tinted with bronze that catches the light when he moves. He has two little silver horns on the top of his head, but also spikes around his cheeks and under his jaw like a basilisk. The hybrid nature of him is beautiful and terrifying all at once.

I kiss my nephew on the top of his head, feeling the soft, warm scales against my lips, and hand him back to my sister. The scent of him— new life, basilisk, and something uniquely dragon—lingers on my skin.

"I should find Zeb and see the Matriarch with him." Amara's voice is flat, her words clipped. The sadness in her tone is unmistakable, hanging in the air between us like a physical barrier. There's nothing I can do about it, and the helplessness burns in my chest like acid.

"I'll come visit again. Or you can come visit us." I try to keep my voice light, but the strain shows through. "I'm redoing the old flight. The entire downstairs has been redone to the point it doesn't look the same anymore." I watch the way my sister's eye ticks at the mention of our old home, the slight muscle spasm betraying emotions she tries to hide. The reaction is immediate and visceral—a traumatic response she can't control. "I dug my nest high in the mountains if you're more comfortable there." I bite my bottom lip, the familiar gesture a tell of my anxiety as I watch her every move. She's still a shadow of who she could have been, her spirit dimmed by circumstances and history.

"I'll think about it," she offers before turning and leaving, her son cradled protectively against her chest. The finality in her tone says more than her words.

I bite my bottom lip harder, tasting blood again, and nod. The metallic flavor floods my mouth, oddly comforting in its familiarity. Not much has changed between us. We're never going to be close because of who my father is and what he did to our mother. The chasm between us feels wider than ever, a gulf too vast to bridge with mere words or intentions.

"Let's go home," I turn to look at Balor, my voice thick with emotions I refuse to name. His eyes—green with slitted pupils—search mine, understanding without words. He nods once, a sharp gesture of agreement.

He takes the lead, and I hold his hand, following behind him. His grip is firm and reassuring, anchoring me to the present when my mind wants to drift into painful pasts and uncertain futures. We make it to the sitting room, and the Matriarch is ecstatic, holding the three basilisk hatchlings against her ancient, scaled body. Her joy is a knife twisting in my gut. I want to burn her to ash for making my sister feel bad, for valuing blood purity over the miracle of new life in any form. The urge to unleash my lightning is so strong I can taste smoke at the back of my throat, feel heat building behind my sternum.

I don't say a word as Balor leads me out through the labyrinth, the stone walls seeming to close in with each step. The air gets fresher as we approach the exit, the heavy mineral scent of the pit giving way to cooler, cleaner air from outside. Once we hit fresh air, the night sky vast and star-filled above us, I drop to my knees and scream at the top of my lungs. The sound tears from my throat, raw and primal, echoing across the mountainside like the cry of a wounded animal.

The scales along my back and shoulders ripple as I let all the pain out. The sensation is like thousands of tiny needles pushing through my skin, each scale emerging with a pinprick of pain that builds to a symphony of agony. I can feel the dragons in the bond tense, their consciousness pressing against mine as they feel the pain I'm releasing. Through our connection, I share with them all that I saw and heard and felt. The images flow from me like a torrent—my sister's disappointment, the Matriarch's joy at the "purity" of the basilisk hatchlings. The gulf between my idealized version of what I thought reuniting with my sister would be like versus the harsh reality of what happened.

My head hangs low, hair falling forward to curtain my face as I try to quell the storm raging in my chest. The cool night air burns my lungs with each ragged breath. Balor's hand rests on my shoulder, his touch gentle but grounding. All the fight drains out of me at that simple contact, leaving me empty and exhausted.

Slowly I turn to look up at him, the movement requiring more effort than it should. His eyes search my face, taking in the tear tracks on my cheeks, the blood on my lip where I bit it, the scales that haven't fully receded at my temples. He nods, understanding without words. "Yeah, my people suck. They're backwards and broken and far worse than the dragons ever could be." His honesty is refreshing, a balm to my wounded spirit. He helps me to stand, his firm hands lifting me as if I weigh nothing, then hugs me to him. His body is solid against mine, a wall between me and the world's cruelties.

"Both species have issues if we're being honest." I kiss his cheek, then back away. The night air fills the space between us, chilling the warmth where our bodies touched. "Let's go home." My voice sounds stronger now, more resolved.

I walk far enough away that when I shift. The transformation begins as a burning in my core, spreading outward like wildfire beneath my skin. My dragoness surges to the surface, bones cracking and reforming, skin giving way to scales that catch the moonlight like hammered metal. Every fiber of my being wants to torch the pit, to reduce it to smoldering ruins. Fire builds in my chest, hot and insistent, begging for release.

I stare at the mountain entrance, breathing heavily as Balor climbs onto my back. His weight is familiar and comforting, settling just behind my shoulder blade. I feel the pull from my three dragon mates through our bond—concern, love, and quiet strength flowing to me across miles. Their presence in my mind is like a lighthouse guiding me home, and I cannot ignore it.

As soon as Balor is seated securely, I launch into the air. My wings unfurl with a sound like sails catching wind, powerful muscles propelling us skyward. The earth falls away beneath us; the pit becoming smaller with each powerful wingbeat. The night air is chilly against my scales, the stars above us like diamonds scattered across black velvet.

I take flight towards home, towards my mates, towards whatever future we can carve out in this world that seems determined to keep us apart. The mountains shrink below us, becoming just another dark shape against the horizon. With each mile that passes beneath my wings, the pain in my chest lessens, replaced by determination. I may have lost my sister again today, but I still have a family—one I've built rather than been born to. And sometimes, that's enough.

plants beneath our feet, releasing bursts of fragrance into the air—mint, nightshade, and something uniquely toxic that makes my nostrils burn.

Thauglor joins us, his massive frame blocking the dim light from the entrance as he steps through. The ground trembles slightly beneath his weight. Before any of us can speak, we feel Mina's emotions go erratic through our bond. The sensation is like being caught in a whirlpool. First, the craving of a clutch of her own, the longing so intense it makes my chest ache. Then, not long after, the feeling of things not right between her and her sister. The bond between us turns cold, like ice spreading through my veins.

I watch Thauglor's eyes glow, changing from their usual blue to a stormy sapphire that illuminates his face in the dim light. I hear his voice echo in my head, the sound both everywhere and nowhere at once. He soothes her, his mental voice a deep rumble that reminds me of distant thunder. But I know Mina's plan. She's going to have a clutch to lure her father out. The thought sends a chill down my spine despite the humid warmth of the garden.

Thauglor shakes his head and growls low, the sound vibrating in my chest cavity. "She wants a family. Why don't we just hunt her father down and torch him?" Thauglor huffs, and a bellow of acid escapes his lips, sizzling as it hits the grass. The acrid smell burns my nostrils and makes my eyes water. Abraxis is nodding along with Thauglor, his jaw set in determination, muscles tense beneath his skin.

I run my hand down my face, feeling the day's stubble scrape against my palm. I have two black dragons on my hands. One with a legendary temperament and his mini-me that's trying so hard to be big and bad like his ancestor. The thought would be amusing if the situation weren't so serious.

"Because we can't just keep going around killing people," I motion towards the skull. The bone yellowed from the acid but still intimidating. "He died because he stole our mate. I chased her father across half the continent because he was going to kill our mate." The memory of that pursuit burns hot in my mind—hours tracking through the wilderness, the scent of fear and hatred guiding me.

"Mina killed an entire flight of fire drakes because they had been making her life hell. And they kept trying to kill her," Abraxis adds, his voice carrying a note of pride. The leather of his vest creaks as he crosses his arms over his chest.

"She did?" Thauglor asks, turning to face Abraxis, his eyes widening with surprise and something that looks suspiciously like approval.

"She's killed ambush drakes. Her first one was before she could shift into her dragon," Abraxis adds, rocking back on his heels as he delivers this information.

"What do you mean 'before she could shift into her dragon'?" That catches my attention. My heart rate increases as my mind races through the implications. The room suddenly feels too small, the air too thin.

"Females can't shift into their dragons until their twenty-first birthday, males their seventeenth. Why?" Abraxis looks between Thauglor and me, confusion clouding his features. His scent changes subtly, taking on a sharper edge that betrays his unease.

"When did that start happening? We've always had access to our dragons," Thauglor asks, and it dawns on me like a lightning strike, illuminating darkness I didn't know existed.

"The anointing ceremony. There's something in that oil that locks their dragons away." My eyes jump from Abraxis to Thauglor, the realization bitter on my tongue. My hands clench into fists at my sides, nails digging half-moons into my palms.

"No hatchling of mine will ever have the oil touch them," Thauglor growls, and the walls shake. Small pebbles dislodge from the ceiling, pattering down around us like rain. The sound of his rage is primal and ancient, something that speaks to the predator in all of us.

"I agree, and I bet if we tell Mina our suspicions, she will agree." Stepping forward, I adjust a stick to change how open the basilisk skull is. The smooth bone is cool beneath my fingers, its teeth still razor-sharp.

"What will I agree with?" Mina's voice fills the room, her scent—honey, lavender, and something metallic that is uniquely her—reaching me before I fully register her presence. We all turn slowly to face her, guilty expressions no doubt clear on our faces. Before I can open my mouth, she shoves past me, her shoulder brushing against mine with enough force to make me step back.

She approaches the skull in her garden, her footsteps nearly silent on the grass. She growls at it for a minute straight. The sound rumbling deep in her chest like distant thunder. Her stance is wide, confrontational, as if the skull might rise and challenge her. Finally, she turns to look at us, her golden eyes glowing in the dim light. "It looks wonderful. But what will I agree with?"

"Mate…" Thauglor starts and moves forward to take Mina's hands in his. Her fingers look delicate against his massive palms, but I know the strength those slender hands possess. "We," he pulls a hand away and waves it at Abraxis and me, "believe the anointing oil blocks a dragon's ability to shift. Back before Klauth and I were captured, we could shift back and forth from the moment we hatched." Thauglor drops the bomb, and we wait. The silence that follows is heavy, pressing against my eardrums like a physical force.

Mina's eyes dart over to me, then back to Abraxis, then back to Thauglor. Each movement is quick and sharp, like a predator assessing threats. "I will rend the flesh from anyone that tries to anoint my child. They'll be scorched into a blackened splat on the floor." Her growls get deeper, vibrating the very air around us. The rage she's feeling is twisting her features, her canines lengthening visibly as she speaks.

The scales along her throat rise, catching the dim light like polished metal.

The angrier she gets, the more Thauglor is smiling, his expression one of fierce pride. She screams her rage; the sound echoing off the stone walls and making my ears ring. She spreads her fingers, making a cage with them. A ball of lightning forms between her hands, crackling and spitting blue-white sparks that illuminate her face from below, casting strange shadows that make her look otherworldly. The hair on my arms stands on end as the electrical charge fills the room, making us take a collective step back. The scent of ozone fills the air, sharp, and tangy.

"When did that start happening?" I thought it was a one-off freak occurrence when she wielded lightning the last time. My voice sounds strangled even to my own ears, tension constricting my throat.

"After taking Thauglor as my mate," Mina purrs, the sound a stark contrast to her previous rage. The lightning dissipates as quickly as it formed, leaving spots dancing in my vision. She dives into the male in question's arms, her movements fluid and graceful. She throws her head back, smiling up at him, exposing the elegant column of her throat in a gesture of trust that makes something primal stir within me.

"Oh, and my descendant is cleared for flying again," Thauglor says as he bends down to kiss Mina on her forehead. His lips linger there, a gesture of affection that seems at odds with his fearsome reputation.

"He is?" She squeals, the sound high and girlish compared to her earlier growls. She turns and dives into Abraxis's arms, her body moving with an eagerness that makes my chest tighten with a mixture of jealousy and affection. She immediately presses the bridge of her nose under his jaw, purring. The sound is soothing, vibrating through the air like a balm for frayed nerves. That is a welcomed sight. I wonder what changed.

"Come with me to stretch my wings?" he asks her as he kisses her temple, his breath disturbing the silver strands of her hair. Mina doesn't answer; instead, she grabs his hand and starts to drag him out of the garden. Her enthusiasm is palpable, crackling around her like a tangible force.

Something makes her stop, a hesitation that ripples through her body like a wave. She waits for Abraxis to lead her out, her head tilting slightly to expose her neck to him. This change in behavior has Thauglor written all over it—his influence on her is unmistakable. I exchange a glance with him as they leave, his sapphire eyes glowing with satisfaction in the dim light.

As their footsteps fade, I turn back to the basilisk skull, its empty eye sockets seeming to mock me. The garden feels emptier without Mina's presence, the air stiller, less charged. Thauglor moves to stand beside me, his massive frame blocking some of the chill that seeps in from the corridor.

"I'm guessing you've been working with our mate?"

I may as well ask the question that is eating at me. The words taste like copper on my tongue, a mixture of curiosity and jealousy that I'm reluctant to admit even to myself. We head into what is now my office in the upper nest, our footsteps echoing against the polished stone floor. The room smells of leather-bound books, aged parchment, and the lingering scent of Mina—honey and lavender and ozone.

"I have," Thauglor answers, his voice rumbling like distant thunder. He smirks, sapphire eyes glinting with satisfaction, and huffs a little as he moves to the minibar to pour himself a whiskey. The crystal decanter clinks against the glass as he pours the amber liquid, its rich, smoky aroma filling the space between us. "We talked at length the other night after we bonded."

He shakes his head; the gesture seeming almost wistful, then looks back at me. "Her father did some real damage." His voice drops lower, the words weighted with something dark and dangerous. "She takes control when she's afraid. So when she tries to take control, we need to assess what may make her uneasy. We have two choices at that point —either fix it or walk her through it." He says this calmly, as if discussing the weather rather than the psychological wounds of our shared mate.

"So it's a stress reaction. She wasn't allowed to be afraid, so instead of being afraid, she gets aggressive." I lean forward in my leather chair, the material creaking beneath me as Thauglor offers me two fingers of whiskey. The glass is cool against my palm, a stark contrast to the heat that seems to perpetually radiate from my skin these days.

"Basically, that's it in a nutshell." He shrugs like it's the simplest thing in the world, his massive shoulders rising and falling with the move-ment. The leather of his jacket stretches across his broad back, making a soft sound that's almost lost beneath our breathing. "Just to let you know, my great wyrm gift is to see memories of others. So Mina let me see hers. It's how I've been helping her."

Taking the seat before my desk, he reclines slightly, the chair groaning under his weight. The scent of him—ancient stone, smoke, and some-thing primal that speaks to the predator in me.

"Honestly, I'm not sure what mine is yet." I tilt my head, looking at him. The sapphire eyes that have seen millennia come and go. Then I turn to stare at my drink in my hand, watching the way the light catches in the amber liquid, creating patterns like tiny flames.

"Besides commanding presence? I'd rather have that gift than to snoop in people's memories." Thauglor rolls his eyes, the gesture surprisingly human from one so ancient. Then he pauses, his entire body going still in that way predators do before they strike. The air in the room seems to thicken, charged with sudden purpose. "I need to get to Blackhaven. I can read Kai's memories. Maybe I can find where that bastard of a father of Mina's is hiding."

Thauglor stands suddenly, the movement so swift that it disturbs the air, sending the scent of aged whiskey wafting toward me. His intention is obvious in every line of his body—he's ready to hunt. Before he can race out of the office, Ziggy manifests in the room with a subtle shift in air pressure that makes my ears pop. The scent of his musk announces his arrival before he's fully visible.

"Just the man we need," I say, setting my glass down with a soft clink against the polished wood of my desk. "I want you to take Thauglor to Blackhaven to interrogate Kai. I'll message Vox to let him know he's on his way."

Ziggy nods, his green eyes assessing the situation quickly. He extends a hand out to Thauglor. His slender fingers are a stark contrast to the ancient dragon's massive hand.

"Closing your eyes helps with the nausea," he advises, his voice light but carrying undertones of wariness. He takes Thauglor's hand, and before Thauglor can speak, they are gone. The air rushes to fill the void where they stood, creating a soft whoosh that stirs the papers on my desk.

We're one step closer to finding out where Abaddon is hiding. The whiskey burns pleasantly as I take a long swallow, warmth spreading through my chest. The other issue is figuring out what teachers are working against my young mate. I tap my fingers against the desk, the sound rhythmic and soothing as I think through the possibilities. The last piece of the puzzle is settling Thauglor in as the new headmaster, whether or not he wants it.

mountain home. Granted, it's not as fast as it used to be, but at least the skies weren't robbed from him. The relief I felt seeing him airborne again was so intense it brought tears to my eyes, the salt of them burning hot against my cheeks.

The warmth of my impending heat is starting to burn through me again. It begins deep in my core, spreading outward like wildfire beneath my skin. That ache that can't be quenched—the kind that makes my scales ripple across my skin unbidden, that makes my blood feel too hot for my veins. I know what that means. My heat is almost upon me, and I can't let it happen. Not with three drakes in the nest, and they still aren't settled. The tension between them is palpable, filling the air with the scent of dominance and challenge.

They need more time.

Ziggy returns from Blackhaven with the tonic I requested, appearing in my chamber with that distinctive shift in air pressure that makes my sensitive ears pop. The scent of the potions reaches me before he fully materializes—bitter herbs, roots, and something metallic that makes my nostrils burn.

"Are you sure, Mina?" he asks as he holds three vials out to me. The glass is cool against my overheated skin as I take them, the liquid inside a deep purple that catches the light from the crystal lamps.

"I'm going to start with two of them. If I need the third to put me under, then give it to me." My voice sounds strained even to my own ears, roughened by the heat building in my throat. I hand the third one back to him, and we head towards the planning room where most of my other mates are all gathered. The stone corridor feels endless, each step requiring more concentration than it should as the heat pulses through my body in waves.

Their raised voices echo down the hallway, and I shake my head, the movement sending a cascade of copper hair across my shoulders. "This is exactly why I'll sleep through this heat." We stop in front of the door, listening to the arguing. Even through the thick wood, I can smell them—earth and stone from Balor, ancient smoke from Thauglor, mountain air from Abraxis, and that distinctive scent that is uniquely Klauth, like wild fires and pine.

When the bickering settles down, I push the door open to find Abraxis, Klauth, Thauglor, and Balor on opposite sides of the table. Between them is the diorama of the Aurelian Isles, meticulously crafted with tiny trees and mountains. The air in the room is thick with tension and the mingled scents of my mates—a heady combination that makes my dragoness stir restlessly beneath my skin.

"Sorry to interrupt." I pause, feeling a wave of heat wash over me so intense it makes my vision blur at the edges. My skin feels too tight, too hot, as if my very bones are trying to expand beyond their confines. I have eight virile mates. Three powerful dominant drakes that my dragoness craves with an intensity that terrifies me. Their scents intensify as my dragoness recognizes them, becoming almost unbearably enticing.

When my mates try to approach, I hold my hand up, stopping them in their tracks. The effort it takes not to leap into their arms is monumental, every muscle in my body trembling with restraint. "My heat is upon me," I pant out, trying to keep my thoughts straight as another wave of burning need washes through me. "I want to sleep through it." A rumbling purr escapes my lips as I catch everyone's scents better. My senses heightening with each passing moment.

"Mina, no..." Klauth almost begs me, his crimson flecked amber eyes darkening with desire and concern. His voice sends shivers down my spine, making the scales along my back rise in response. "We handled it last time. Everything was okay." He steps closer, and I step backward, my back pressing against the cool wood of the door. The contrast between it and my overheated skin is startling.

"There are three dominant drakes in the nest now. You three need to work on your issues before someone accidentally gets hurt or hurts me." I pant, trying not to breathe in through my nose. Each inhale brings their scents deeper into my lungs, making my control slip further away. My talons extend fully, digging into the palms of my hands, the pain a welcome anchor to reality.

"Ziggy discovered a hidden chamber off of the hot springs. It's big enough to hold a great wyrm." I lower my head, trying not to sway on my feet. This heat is so much worse than the last few. It feels like molten metal flowing through my veins, each heartbeat sending a fresh wave of burning need throughout my body. The room spins slightly, the faces of my mates blurring together.

"I plan to phase Mina and Thauglor into the chamber and then sedate her," Ziggy says as he moves closer to support me as I sway on my feet. His arm around my waist is both comforting and not enough—not what my dragoness craves. I want him too. "At night, either Klauth or Abraxis will switch out with him. Since no one knows Thauglor has hatched, we can hide his existence for a while longer."

"That's a solid plan. Good thinking, Ziggy." Balor says as he looks at the way I'm hanging on Ziggy. His black scales have risen along his jawline, a response to the pheromones I'm undoubtedly releasing into the air. "If you need me to switch out, I don't have classes to teach the last week of school."

"Having you in the chamber with us would be helpful," Thauglor says and extends his hand to Balor. The gesture is one of truce, surprising in its sincerity. Through my haze, I feel a spark of hope—perhaps they can work together after all.

"Ziggy, I need to go. I can't resist much longer." I breathe in deeply, my lungs filling with the intoxicating scents of my dominant mates. The room tilts again, and I grip Ziggy's arm tighter, my talons almost piercing the fabric of his shirt. I look at all of my mates, memorizing their faces through the haze of my heat. "I love you. See you soon." My voice breaks on the last word, emotion, and need, making it difficult to speak. I nod at Ziggy, and he phases us into the hidden chamber.

THE WORLD DISSOLVES AROUND ME, replaced by the sensation of being everywhere and nowhere at once. When reality solidifies again, I'm standing in a massive cavern, the walls glowing with embedded crystals that cast a soft blue light across the space. The light pulses gently, almost like a heartbeat, illuminating the rough stone surfaces and casting long shadows across the floor. The air is heavy with moisture from nearby hot springs, steam rising in delicate tendrils that dance in the dim light. Droplets of condensation form on my overheated skin, offering momentary relief from the burning fever of my heat.

The cavern smells of mineral-rich water, ancient stone, and something earthy and primal that speaks to my dragonic nature. Each breath I take fills my lungs with the moist, warm air, making it feel as though I'm breathing through cloth. My sensitive hearing picks up the subtle dripping of water somewhere deep in the cavern. The sound echoing off the stone walls in a soothing rhythm.

Ziggy helps me to a nest of furs and blankets that's been prepared in the center of the chamber. The furs are luxuriously soft against my fingertips, a stark contrast to the rough stone floor beneath them. They carry the mingled scents of my mates—earth and smoke, pine, and sky —a comforting mixture that makes my dragonic side purr despite the pain. My legs give out as I reach it, muscles trembling with exhaustion and need, and I collapse onto the soft surface. Every nerve ending in my body screams for relief, my skin feeling too tight, too hot, as if I might burst into flames at any moment.

The scent of the sedative is sharp and medicinal as Ziggy uncorks the first vial, holding it to my lips. The glass is cool against my burning mouth, a small mercy during this torment. The liquid inside is a deep, rich purple that catches the crystal light, swirling hypnotically.

"Drink," he urges, his green eyes filled with concern. His voice seems to come from far away, muffled by the roaring of blood in my ears. "Thauglor will be here soon."

The liquid burns down my throat, bitter, and metallic, like drinking liquid iron mixed with the most pungent herbs. I swallow convulsively, fighting the urge to gag as it coats my tongue with its astringent flavor. I close my eyes, feeling it spread through my system like frost creeping across glass, dulling the edges of my heat but not extinguishing it. My heartbeat slows, the frantic pace easing to something more sustainable.

Ziggy leaves for a moment, the air shifting with his departure. I feel the atmosphere displace again, molecules rearranging themselves as he returns, this time bringing Thauglor and Balor back with him. Their scents hit me immediately—Thauglor's ancient smoke and something primordial like the earth before time began, and Balor's scent of stone, earth, and a hint of venom that makes my nostrils burn pleasantly. I have three of my eight mates with me, their presence both a comfort and a torment as my body craves what I'm denying it.

Balor moves close, his hair catching the blue light as he kneels beside me. The fur beneath him compresses with his weight, tilting me slightly toward him. He offers me the second vial. The glass clinking softly against his rings. "Drink, Mina. One isn't enough with as strong as you've become." I see the sadness in his crimson eyes, the emotion darkening them to the color of dried blood. He hates doing this to me, even though it's my request. His hand trembles slightly as he holds the vial, betraying his reluctance.

The second vial burns, but not as bad as the first. The liquid slides down my throat more easily, my body already numbed by the first dose. It tastes of bitter roots and something almost sweet beneath the medicinal flavor. Thauglor chooses now to shift, his massive form changing with a sound like mountains moving. Bones crack and reform, skin gives way to scales with a sound like leather stretching. He lays down, his enormous body making the ground beneath us tremble. His scales, black as midnight, reflect the blue crystal light, creating patterns across the cavern walls like stars.

He extends a taloned hand, each claw longer than my body, gleaming wickedly in the dim light. The scales of his palm are smoother than those of his back, designed for handling precious things. Ziggy lays a soft fur-lined lambskin in his hand, the white wool stark against the obsidian scales.

A yawn escapes my lips as my vision swims, the world blurring at the edges like watercolors in the rain. My limbs feel leaden, my eyelids impossibly heavy. Balor scoops me up, his arms strong and secure around me. The scent of him—earth after the rain, stone warmed by the sun—envelops me as he cradles me against his chest. His heart beats steadily beneath my ear, a counterpoint to my slowing pulse.

He lays me in Thauglor's dragon's taloned hand. The scales are surprisingly warm against my skin, radiating heat that matches my own fevered temperature. My body feels heavy, as if being pulled under by invisible weights. But I'm still awake, clinging to consciousness like a drowning person to driftwood.

My vision swims again, colors blending and shifting, and I swear I see Abraxis in front of me. His features seem to float, disconnected in my drug-hazed perception, but his scent—mountain air and something uniquely him—confirms his presence. "Sleep, Mina. We'll all take turns watching over you." Abraxis kisses my forehead, his lips cool against my burning skin. He smiles against my skin, the gesture intimate, and tender. "I have it on good authority that Thauglor will either torch or eat any that dare disturb you."

I turn my head, feeling as if my world is tilting on its axis. The movement sends a cascade of silver and emerald hair across my face, the strands sticky with sweat. Through the curtain of my hair, I see the white face of Thauglor's great wyrm black dragon looking down at me. His eyes are like molten sapphires in his alabaster face, ancient and knowing. Pupils contracted to slits in the dim light. Steam rises from his nostrils with each breath, adding to the misty atmosphere of the cavern.

He rumbles softly to me. The sound vibrating through his talons and into my body. It's a tune a drake sings to its mate to soothe her, a melody as old as dragon kind itself. The notes are too low for human ears to fully appreciate, but my dragonic side hears them perfectly. I feel the echo of it in my bones, reverberating through my marrow like the deepest bass, calming the raging fire of my heat.

The fight drains out of me with each note of his song, my muscles relaxing one by one until I feel boneless in his gentle grip. My eyelids flutter, growing heavier with each passing second. The crystals on the ceiling blur into a sea of blue stars as my vision darkens at the edges. The last thing I'm aware of is the combined scents of my mates, the warmth of Thauglor's scales beneath me, and the soothing rumble of his song carrying me into oblivion. I drift off to sleep, safe knowing that I am protected, cherished, and, above all, loved.

THE CONCLUSION:

Queen of the Cursed Egg

Glossary

Glossary of species of the Aurelian Isles:

Green Dragon: Green dragons were most notable for the large, waving crest or fin that started at the dragon's nose and ran the entire length of the dragon's body. They also had exceptionally long, slender forked tongues. Green dragons' scales did not fully harden, granting them greater flexibility than other chromatic dragons. They also had particularly long legs and elongated necks. Green Dragons are known for being poison masters and assassins. Most famous nest is Risedale where the Shadowblades are trained by Abaddon Bladesong, head of the Shadowblades. Breath Weapon: Acid

Red Dragon: They were supremely confident of their own abilities and were prone to making snap decisions without any forethought. The largest and most powerful of the chromatic dragons. Red dragons were physically distinguished by their enormous size and wingspan, which was the widest of all dragons, both in absolute size and relative to body length. Most Famous nest was the Marzana nest where King Klauth Ragnar reigned from until his capture. Breath Weapon: Fire

Black Dragon: Black dragons appeared abnormally slender in comparison to other chromatic dragons—wiry, but not gaunt. Physically, they were most distinguished by their horns, which protruded from the sides of their heads and wrapped around, projecting forward. A large frill adorned the upper part of the neck. Most Famous nest was Blackhaven where Thauglor Mithrun lived until his capture. <u>Breath Weapon: Acid</u>

Blue Dragon: Also known as storm dragons, were a breed of chromatic true dragon. Their breath weapon was a line of lightning or a large electrical discharge. Blue dragons were physically distinguished by the single large horn protruding from their heads and by their ears, which were rather large and frilled. Semi-hard scales. The neck was short and broad. The tail was thick and flat. No Famous Nests associated with this species. <u>Breath Weapon: Lightning</u>.

Bronze Dragon: While most of its body was a reflective bronze color, the wings were often tipped with green. The dragon had four large horns on each side of their heads, three protruding from each cheek and one from the top of their head, pointing back towards the tail. A large frill ran down the upper part of its neck. <u>Breath Weapon: Cone of repulsion energy</u>

Iron Dragon: were intelligent and deadly dragons. They were the most powerful of the ferrous dragons. They had broad, almost shovel-shaped heads with multiple thick, backwards-pointing horns, and large plates that resembled shark fins ran down their spine. They possessed the hardest scales of any dragon to exist. <u>Breath Weapon: a cloud of sleep gas, and cone of lightning</u>.

Fairie Dragon: Faerie dragons were extremely small in comparison to their large metallic or chromatic dragon cousins—about the size of a cat. Each had an iridescent coat of scales that reflected all colors of the rainbow, predominantly reflecting one particular color which changed with age. They had a long, prehensile tail and platinum-colored, butterfly-like wings. <u>Breath Weapon: Unknown</u>

Gem Dragon: were friendly, curious dragons. They enjoyed conversing with other creatures but sometimes came into conflict with other dragons due to shared preferences in habitats. They were the smallest of the gem dragons and had translucent, crystalline scales. <u>Breath Weapon:</u> a blinding cone of white light.

Phoenix: Are enormous birds with brightly colored feathers ranging from orange to red and violet, and blue-violet beaks and claws. Their talons had the consistency of diamonds. Their eyes were a glowing ruby color. A phoenix's body was naturally bright and shed its own light. Phoenix bodies were almost immaterial, composed of flame taking solid shape.

Greater Basilisk: A phenomenally lethal creature, direct eye contact with a Basilisk would result in instantaneous death, but an indirect look would merely render the victim Petrified. Highly venomous. True serpent basilisk with six eyes and can grow to be over 40ft long. Scales are harder than most armor, only a titanium dragon's talons can cut the hide.

Lesser_Basilisk: Similar to a greater Basilisk but can only get to be about twenty foot long and softer scales. Can only petrify its victims. No venom to speak of.

Green Hag: Like all hags, the strength behind a green hag's frail physique was not to be underestimated, for not only were they resistant to magic but their calloused flesh made them resistant to physical attacks and their hardiness extended to their flesh-rending claws. A green hag's touch could sap strength with even the slightest brush.

Manticore: were true monsters. They were giant beasts with the bodies of lions, the wings of a dragon, the head of a man, and a tail that ended in a mass of deadly spikes. The coloration of these various body parts was similar to that of their base creature. The mouth of a manticore was full of rows and rows of razor-sharp teeth, similar to that of a great white shark. It used these teeth to feed upon any creature the manticore could catch, be it animal or human. Tail holds a paralytic venom.

Gargoyle: appeared to be winged statues of demon-like humanoids. These creatures could stand motionless for long periods of time, which added to the façade of their statue-like appearance. Nearly indestructible, able to roam about in the daytime with a daylight charm. Without the charm they are forced to become nocturnal.

Nightmare: their warhorse-like exterior was revealed to be entirely superficial. They had huge heads, fangs like vipers, and malevolent dark eyes often illuminated by red-hot flames, and they sprouted orange fire when their nostrils flared. Wreathed in fire, their manes were wild and their tails unkempt. The titular power of nightmares was their ability to appear in dreams or cause nightmares.

Gryphon: A griffon had the body of a lion with the head and wings of an eagle. The forelimbs of the gryphon were often like those of an eagle, ending in sharp talons, but this was not always the case. Just as lions and eagles had varying physical characteristics based on where in the world they are found.

Fire Drake: Fire drakes resembled lithe, 12-foot-long dragons with fiery yellow eyes and scales that ranged in color from blood red to bright vermilion.

Ambush_Drake: These creatures had elongated jaws and muscular builds, though their wings were quite stunted for their size. These wings were only used, when necessary, the ambush drake instead preferring to get around on its four legs.

Sphynx: a race of intelligent, immortal magical beasts. It was said that they once held a vast kingdom given to them by the gods in an effort to teach mortals the way of truth. The sphinxes had their own methods, however, by teaching mortals to think for themselves with riddles and parables.

Gorgon: Greater medusae were quite rare, being born at only one in ten births. Like their more common kin, they had heads of living snakes and bodies covered in fine scales, but instead of a woman's lower body, they had snake tails.

Displacer Beast: are large cat-like creatures, sometimes described as panther- or puma-like with six legs and a pair of tentacles 5 feet long sprouting from their shoulders. The tentacles ended in pads with sharp horny edges, brownish yellow in color. They were covered in a pelt of blue-black fur. Displacer beasts were generally strong creatures, and their tentacle barbs were hard enough to punch through pure steel armor. Able to phase over long distances in an extremely short period of time.

Watch Spiders: breed of huge spiders that were raised and trained to obey a master. Watch spiders were fast, both when running and climbing webs or walls. They could leap up to 30 feet. A single strand of their silk was strong enough to support their weight plus one additional medium-sized creature. If allowed to spin a web, they could know the location of any creature that touched their web. Some were bred to have a paralyzing venom, the paralytic effect had an onset time of one to two minutes and then full-body paralysis set in for twenty minutes to over an hour. The victim could see and hear, but not move or speak and would eventually die.

Asperii: also known as wind steeds, were magical horses that possessed keen minds and telepathic powers and the ability to fly. Asperii appeared as normal horses, averaging around 8 feet (2.4 meters) tall. They had hides that were dun, gray, or white and long manes that were most often light gray, silver, or white. Asperii were sentient creatures, being more intelligent than most humans. They were usually very gentle, except when it came to their enemies.

Terms and Items mentioned:

Nest: A central gathering consisting of a female and however many males she has taken as mates.

Flight: Only found with dragons. It's where other nests join the nesting area of a dominant dragoness for protection.

Den: Living space of solitary male dragons or some fur bearing creatures.

Pride: Usually found with Displacer Beasts.

Herd: Found with horse-like creatures or those of cloven hoof.

Clutch: A group of eggs or a gathering of gargoyles

The Accords: Rules for dragon kind were amended as time went on.

Right_of_Inheritance: When an elder of an area / comes to reclaim what is rightfully theirs.

Right of Succession: When the strength of an elder / parent is questioned the most powerful progeny of the drake may challenge or hunt their sire. It further says that they may name another to find or hunt down their target.

Cursed_Eggs: Dragons bound by mages in eggs until certain criteria are met.

Also By Serenity Rayne

Contemporary Pen Name - Anita Ruffino

Stolen - The Nightshade Chronicles

Dragonis Academy:

Trials of the Cursed Eggs

Guardian of the Cursed Egg

Klauth

Progeny of the Cursed Egg

Queen of the Cursed Egg

Shifters:

Claimed by the Alpha Pack

Embraced By the Alpha Pack

Coveted by the Alpha Pack

Finding Forever with the Alpha Pack

Children of the Moon: New Moon Rising

Children of the Moon - Waxing Crescent

Children of the Moon - Full Moon

Her Elemental Mates

The Aurora Marelup Saga

Ascend

Hunt

Fight

Attack

Welcome Home

The Aurora Marelup Omnibus 5 year special edition

The Aurora Marelup Holiday Edition

About the Author

Serenity Rayne is a multifaceted author bringing you heroines that either grow over time or are powerhouses right out of the gate. She is known for writing paranormal reverse harem romances that immerse you in her characters' worlds.

What sets Serenity apart is her ability to weave romance that engages every sense. Readers taste the copper of a mate bite on their tongues and feel the electric charge when fated mates first touch. Her intimate scenes crackle with otherworldly energy, whether it's the heat of dragon shifters, the intoxicating pull of fated bonds, or the wild freedom found in werewolf pack dynamics.

Serenity's heroines don't just fall in love—they ignite, transform, and claim their power alongside the captivating supernatural beings who are drawn to their fire. Whether her protagonist is a hesitant newcomer to the paranormal world or a seasoned supernatural force to be reckoned with, she always emerges stronger, more powerful, and thoroughly loved.

Serenity has stepped into the world of romantasy as well as the academy scene, bringing you her newest bestselling series, The Dragonis Academy, where danger is as expected as the sunrise. Dive into her worlds and be captivated from page one.

Facebook: Serenity Rayne

Readers Group

Twitter: Author Serenity Rayne

Instagram: Author Serenity Rayne

Goodreads: Serenity Rayne

BookBub: Serenity Rayne

Amazon: Serenity Rayne

WebStore - https://serenityrayneromance.com/

Newsletter: https://mailchi.mp/serenityrayneromance/serenitys-journal

Signed Books and Merch

www.SerenityRayneRomance.com

This is the only place to get official Serenity Rayne Merchandise as well as book swag and signed books.

www.ingramcontent.com/pod-product-compliance
Lightning Source LLC
Chambersburg PA
CBHW070827020826

48982CB00015B/783